Praise for
7 Days & 7 Nights

"This debut romantic comedy puts a clever spin on an age-old formula.... The novel's real strength is the witty clash of the two gender-battling shows and the glimpse it offers of the wacky world of radio."
—*Publishers Weekly*

"Wax's first romantic comedy is a witty, battle-of-the-sexes tale and a perfect summertime read."
—*Library Journal*

"Delightful! Don't miss this sexy, snappy, fun read."
—Haywood Smith, author of *Queen Bee of Mimosa Branch* and *The Red Hat Club*

"What a fun read! This story is a clever romantic comedy, in every sense of the word.... 7 DAYS & 7 NIGHTS is a fast-paced story that will have readers wanting more. It's the perfect summer book!"
—*Hawthorne Press Tribune/Lawndale Tribune*

"Entertaining, lively, and engaging, this is an excellent summer read." —*Booklist*

Also by Wendy Wax

---

7 Days & 7 Nights

Leave It to
CLEAVAGE

Wendy Wax

Bantam Books

LEAVE IT TO CLEAVAGE
A Bantam Book / August 2004

Published by
Bantam Dell
A division of Random House, Inc.
New York, New York

Bantam Books and the rooster colophon are registered
trademarks of Random House, Inc.

ISBN 0-553-58614-9

Manufactured in the United States of America
Published simultaneously in Canada

OPM   10   9   8   7   6   5   4   3   2   1

For John,

who likes to remind me that

"the first fifty years are the hardest."

Leave It to
CLEAVAGE

Miranda Smith was looking for a stamp when she discovered just how good her husband looked in ladies' lingerie.

It was 5:30 P.M. on the coldest January 8 on record, and the Truro Post Office was already closed. But for Miranda—who was now conducting a room-by-room search—the stamp was no longer postage, but a symbol of every New Year's resolution she'd ever made. And failed to keep.

One week into the new year she'd already given up on becoming a better daughter and reading her way through the classics. She wasn't going to wimp out on the only resolution she still had a chance of keeping.

Somewhere in this five-bedroom, four-bath, six-thousand-square-foot home—which she'd just tossed like a petty thief looking for loot—there had to be enough postage to get her credit card payment in on time.

Miranda stood in the foyer outside Tom's study, debating her next move.

With less than twenty minutes to get ready for dinner at her parents', she *should* be heading upstairs to shower and change, not preparing to strip-search another room.

It was just a stamp, she told herself as she turned toward the stairs; paying an occasional late fee was not cause for shame.

Placing a hand on the banister, she took the first step. On the next step she decided next year's resolutions would include buying stamps regularly, which would definitely enhance her chances of eliminating late fees in the future. Or maybe she'd just pay the whole damn lot of them on-line.

As if she'd be making resolutions next year when she'd folded so easily this year.

The thought stopped her in mid-step, turned her around, and propelled her back down the stairs, determined to find a stamp or die in the attempt.

Marching through the foyer and into the study, Miranda snapped on the overhead light and crossed to Tom's desk. Finding the desk drawer slightly ajar, she pulled on the knob, gritting her teeth in frustration when it didn't budge.

Beyond impatience, Miranda wrapped both hands

around the knob and yanked with all her might. The drawer sprang free and sent a packet of photos, which must have been holding up the works, spilling across the floor.

Miranda crouched down to gather them up. She duck-walked across the floor, cramming the photos back into the envelope, muttering to herself, and trying to figure out where else she might find postage in the next thirty seconds.

Until she actually *looked* at the photo in her hand. The one of her husband, the former linebacker, in a red satin bustier and matching bikini panties.

Her first clear thought was that there had to be some mistake. As president of Ballantyne Bras, her husband was expected to supervise the design, production, and sales of a comprehensive line of women's undergarments.

He was not supposed to wear them.

And yet here he was in a black lace teddy. And a fuchsia merry widow—with some woman's hand on his rear end.

Miranda squinted at the hand, trying to recognize it, but other than its French manicure and obvious familiarity with her husband's derriere, it could have belonged to anyone.

The next photo revealed Tom in a cream-colored thong that looked as if it had been custom made for him. Her head began to pound as she realized it probably had.

Unable to tear her gaze from the sight of Tom's

rugged torso sheathed in such feminine trappings, Miranda gathered up the rest of the photos and pulled herself up into the chair.

She thought of all the times she'd seen her husband smile and wink and say "Hi, I'm Tom Smith, and I'm in ladies' underwear," and never imagined he was telling the truth.

Or that he looked as good in it as she did.

Drawing in one shaky breath and letting out another, she dragged her gaze from the photos to stare out the study window. Porch lights twinkled from the house across the cul-de-sac, and she could see snowflakes beginning to fall in the arc of a street lamp, though it was hard to fully appreciate the winter landscape with her brain so full of the vision of Tom decked out in Ballantyne's biggest sellers.

Her thoughts moved slowly, and she felt strangely detached, as if someone had swabbed her with Novocain. There was no sharp stinging pain, no specific point of impact, only a spreading ache of hurt and disbelief. And the sixty-four-million-dollar question: How could she not have known?

In this town where her family's business had been the largest employer for more than a hundred years, someone should have known... and blabbed. And yet until a moment ago, she would have sworn her husband's only interest in ladies' underwear was manufacturing it.

The images ricocheted through her brain, bouncing

off each other, raising more questions she couldn't answer.

Who had taken the pictures? Who did the female hand belong to? And how could a man who'd spent much of his waking life in a jockstrap and cleats look so good in a pale pink corset with tiny rosebuds down the front?

Miranda laid the pictures out on the desk. This was her husband. The man she'd met her first miraculous year of business school at Emory University. The man her family had deemed perfect for her ... and whom she'd married fifteen years ago in the biggest wedding Truro had ever seen. The man she'd been trying to have children with for most of those fifteen years. The man who'd turned out to be somewhat ... less ... than she'd expected, but with whom she'd fully intended to grow old.

Icy tendrils of fear and dread wrapped themselves around her as she realized that no matter what happened next, her life would never be the same. If her husband wasn't who she thought he was, then who did that make her?

She fanned the photos out as a card player might, forcing herself to look at them again. Lifting the last one to the light, she studied the disembodied woman's hand resting so possessively on her husband's bare buttock, and a hot flash of anger melted some of the ice.

Another woman had fondled her husband's naked buns while he was dressed in women's lingerie.

Her stomach clenched, and she asked herself again

how this could have happened. It was normal for married people to fall into their individual routines, normal for the excitement to dissipate after so many years together. It was not normal to miss something as big as this.

Had there been a "Gee, honey, I hope you don't mind but I really get off on dressing up in women's underclothes—which is really convenient since I run your family's brassiere and lingerie business—and I especially like to do this with other women's hands on my butt"?

Had she smiled over the morning paper and her to-do list for the Ladies' Guild and Miss Rhododendron Prep program and said, "That's nice, Tom. Can you pass the preserves?"

She sat, still numb, staring out the window trying to see . . . something. Trying to imagine what in the world she was supposed to do now.

For a wild, wonderful moment she contemplated pretending she'd never found the pictures. She peered at the photos more closely, but couldn't find a date. Maybe Tom didn't even dress up like this anymore. Maybe it had grown old for him, like the white-water rafting and the iron man triathlons. Who knew how long those pictures had been stuck in the drawer?

Experimentally, she picked up the photos and dropped them in the wastebasket. Then she turned her back on the trash can and leaned against the desk with studied nonchalance. Okay, so her husband liked to dress up in women's underwear. And he'd never mentioned this to her. And he did it with other women. Okay. Things could be worse. Things could always be worse.

Right.

Miranda bent over to retrieve the packet of photos, which now had strips of shredded paper from the wastebasket clinging to it. She knew, without thinking, what her mother would say. "Make him give up Miss Manicure, Miranda. And do your best to forgive and forget."

Sure. Then they could get matching underwear made—they owned the company, after all—and, and, well, she wasn't sure exactly what you did once you were dressed up that way with your husband, but maybe it would be fun. Just because she didn't dress up didn't mean she didn't have an adventurous spirit.

Maybe her mother had a point. Maybe she could just show Tom the pictures and ask who took them. Then she could ask him to explain why he liked to do that. And why he'd never mentioned it. And who the hell the woman with the manicure was.

Right.

Miranda set the packet of photos in front of her. Idly, as she tried to follow that scenario through to its logical conclusion, she peeled the strips of shredded paper off the packet and began to shuffle them around the desktop. Words began to leap out at her. Words that pushed the images she'd just confronted right out of her mind. Words like "Ballantyne" and "receivables," and the truly alarming "auditors to investigate."

With trembling fingers, Miranda retrieved more shredded pieces from the wastebasket and began to fit them together. They appeared to be part of a letter from Ballantyne's primary lender, and though there were some gaps, the end result was every bit as life-altering as the photos.

Not only did her husband like to dress up in women's underwear, he had put Ballantyne—the company that had been passed down by the women in her family for generations—in a precarious position with its bank.

She couldn't seem to get any air into her lungs, and despite the snow outside, little beads of sweat popped out on her forehead.

The phone on the desk in front of her rang, and she jumped. Heart racing, she attempted to think lofty, composed, queenlike thoughts, as she'd been taught before her first beauty pageant. She pictured the crown on her head and imagined Bert Parks asking her the inevitable question about world peace, but she couldn't seem to catch her breath. Oh, God, what if it was Tom?

Wary, she picked up the phone and brought it to her ear.

"Miranda, I thought you were coming for dinner," Joan Ballantyne Richards Harper said without preamble.

Miranda unclenched at the sound of her mother's voice, which was not her normal reaction at all.

"You're supposed to be here at six-thirty, but your

father tells me he saw Tom headed up toward the lake house about an hour and a half ago."

"The lake house?" She'd winterized the lake house just after Thanksgiving and hadn't been up there since. Tom hadn't mentioned being up there, either. Apparently there were a lot of things her husband hadn't mentioned. "But it's snowing." Through the window Miranda could see the flakes falling faster. What would Tom be doing at the lake house now?

"Rosalee already has dinner in the oven. I hope you're not going to be late."

"Well, um, actually, I don't think we're going to be able to make it at all."

"Miranda, that's not accepta—"

"I'm, uh, not feeling well." She paused. It was the truth. "And Tom's got something going on." Another truth. "I've got to run. I'm sorry. I'll talk to you later."

Her mother's stunned silence rang in her ears as she put down the phone, but for once her mother's reaction was immaterial.

She absolutely could not sit here another second; would not sit here waiting for Tom to come home with some half-baked story about where he'd been and what he'd been doing.

Running on pure adrenaline, Miranda pulled on her coat and grabbed up her keys. Snow splattered against her windshield as she raced through Truro to the mountain road that would take her up to Ballantyne Bald. Winding upward, she tried to plan what she would do and say when she confronted Tom, but she was too agitated to form a coherent thought, let alone a plan.

When she turned off the paved road onto the gravel one that twisted the final two miles up to the lake, she saw headlights coming at her and was forced to hug the hard rock of the mountainside as the other car sped past. Through a layer of tears she peered out at the passing car, but the only thing she could see for sure was that it wasn't Tom's white Mercedes.

His car wasn't parked in the clearing between her and her grandmother's houses, and she didn't see it down at the edge of the lake where he often left it. The damp cold sliced through her wool coat as she parked in front of the house then trudged around to the back. His car wasn't there, either, but when she stepped up on the back porch, Miranda could see the glow of a light in the rear bedroom. Pulling the lake house key out of her pocket, she fit it in the lock, took a deep breath, and threw open the door.

Shit. Pumped for naked limbs and stammered apologies, what she got was an empty house and a strange sense of disappointment.

In the master suite the bedside lamp glowed and the coverlet had been pulled back, but the sheets appeared fresh and unrumpled. In the nightstand drawer, she found a half-empty box of condoms, something she and Tom hadn't used since she'd started trying to get pregnant, and Tom's Dopp Kit sat open on the bathroom counter. The damp sink with its glob of shaving cream told her he'd shaved.

Her husband had been here and it looked like he'd been expecting someone, but if they'd had sex, they hadn't bothered with the bed. And if he'd been planning on a quickie before dinner at her parents, where was he now?

Miranda thought about the car she'd passed on the way up, but other than confirming it wasn't Tom's, she'd been too preoccupied and had too little time to examine it further. Nothing that had happened tonight made sense, and as she went through the house pulling open drawers and looking inside cupboards, she began to feel more and more like Goldilocks outing the three bears. Or Alice in Wonderland stumbling through some X-rated looking glass.

When there was nowhere else to look, she shoved the handcuffs, the blindfold, the oscillating penis, and the crotchless panties she'd found into the garbage. Then, brushing the tears off her cheeks, she drove back down the mountain with one thought in mind: throwing Tom Smith out on his satin-covered behind.

chapter 2

Tom's butt wasn't at home when she got there. Nor did it come home later.

At midnight she stopped priming for confrontation and climbed the stairs to their bedroom where, for the third time that night, she began to open drawers. Though she was now braced to find satin or lace, she found neither. She didn't find anything in white cotton either, because Tom's drawers were completely empty. In the walk-in closet she found more of the same. Or was that none of the same?

Numb now, she turned and walked back into the bedroom, stopping at the king-size bed she'd shared with Tom Smith for the last fifteen years.

There, propped on her pillow, sat a small square envelope. Miranda sank onto the edge of the bed, picked up the envelope, and pried it open with clumsy fingers.

In a firm hand, with well-formed curves and nicely dotted i's, Tom had written,

> Dear Miranda,
>   By now you've probably figured out that I'm not coming back. We had a good run, but there's no need to look for me. I don't plan to be found. I'm sorry about Ballantyne. Sorry about a lot of things. Have a nice life.
>
>   Tom

Miranda balled up the note and threw it at the dresser mirror as the pressure built behind her eyelids.

Her husband liked to dress up like Madonna and had affairs with other women. Her husband had left her without giving her the chance to throw him out first. This absolutely could not be happening to her.

The tears went into free fall and Miranda didn't bother to wipe them away. Her husband wore black lace and red satin and he didn't love her anymore.

The tears slid down her cheeks and took the last of her makeup with them; she tasted their hot saltiness as they plopped into the corners of her mouth.

She lost track of how long she cried, but when she finally looked into the mirror, a pitiful woman stared back. Miranda sat up straighter and squared her shoulders, but the woman still had tears streaming down her face. Searching for something to cling to, Miranda grabbed onto the pageant instruction her mother had been drilling into her since her fifth birthday, and which she now—more gently—passed on to others.

Okay, then. Sometimes you didn't win the crown. Sometimes, though she didn't have prior personal experience with this, you didn't even make the final five. You could still put on the smile, and you could still walk the walk. If there was anything she knew how to do, it was that.

She'd get right on it just as soon as the woman in the mirror stopped crying.

As it turned out, the woman in the mirror possessed an inexhaustible supply of tears. She cried for hours at a time, eating up the entire weekend with body-wracking sobs that trickled down to wimpy little sniffles, then built back up again.

The future was too bleak to contemplate, and the past, at least in hindsight, didn't look all that attractive, either. Unsure what else to do, Miranda picked up the phone, forced the quiver from her voice, and used a fictional flu to cancel everything. Then she pulled the covers up over her head and hid from the world while the emptiness washed over her.

Her grandmother Richards was the first to breach Miranda's beachhead of fictional germs and very real misery.

A week after Tom's decampment, Gran appeared in Miranda's bedroom holding an artfully arranged tray that bore a heavenly-smelling bowl of soup and a plate of saltines. A glass of water with its requisite slice of lemon sat next to a folded linen napkin. A single rose stood in one of Miranda's cut-glass bud vases.

At seventy-five, Cynthia Ballantyne Richards was no longer as tall as she had once been, but her loss of height did not detract from her regal bearing. Her short white hair was as artfully arranged as the tray, and she wore one of her bridge-at-the-club uniforms— a red wool pantsuit with an Hermès scarf tucked into the neckline.

Her grandmother had always been the most astounding mixture of genteel sophistication and backwoods outspokenness, what Miranda secretly thought of as Granny Clampett after boarding school and a European tour.

Without asking, she sat down on the side of the bed and settled the tray across Miranda's lap.

Miranda had never been so glad—or so horrified— to see anyone in her life. Tom's taste in underwear and his empty closet loomed between them. She had never successfully lied to her grandmother, and they both knew it.

"Do you know what day this is?" her grandmother asked.

"No." The aroma of her grandmother's chicken vegetable soup wafted up from the tray, and Miranda breathed it in.

"Do you care?"

"No, not really."

Her grandmother reached over, unfolded the napkin, and tucked it into Miranda's pajama top. Then she picked up the spoon and placed it in Miranda's hand.

"This, too, shall pass."

Miranda tore her gaze from the soup, which was making her mouth water, to stare up into her grandmother's eyes. A fine line of wrinkles radiated outward from their corners, and somehow, without Miranda's noticing, her grandmother's skin had become paperthin.

"Yes, well . . ."

"Where's Tom?"

Miranda froze, the spoon midway to the beckoning soup. But it was all too raw, too humiliating to share with her family. "He's, um, out." *Out of the house. Out of my life.* "Out of town."

Something flickered in her grandmother's eyes and for a long moment they stared at each other, weighing the silence, waiting for the other to speak. Miranda had the oddest sense that her grandmother knew . . . something.

Please, God, she thought, *please don't let it be the cross-dressing part.*

She braced herself for the third degree, though that was more her mother's style than Gran's, and breathed a huge sigh of relief when her grandmother let the subject pass.

"The Lord does not give us burdens without equipping us to carry them."

She definitely knew something. Something that she didn't want to say and which Miranda definitely didn't want to hear. Stalling, Miranda dipped her spoon into the soup and brought it to her lips.

"Mmmm, Gran, nobody makes chicken vegetable like you do."

One of her grandmother's silver eyebrows rose. "I am not vain about my cooking."

"No, no, of course not." Miranda took another spoonful and almost sighed at the warmth and perfection of it. "Though you easily could be."

Like she had as a child, Miranda dipped a saltine in the soup and ate most of it in one bite.

"Lord, you're half starved."

"Mmmph." Miranda swallowed. "I haven't had much of an appetite." Nor could she remember when she had last eaten.

"Yes, I can imagine." Her grandmother speared her with a look but didn't ask what she'd been eating or when Tom would be back, for which Miranda was deeply grateful.

"You know, sometimes disaster and opportunity are just opposite sides of a single coin. It's only when we're tested that we find the motivation to become more than we have been."

Miranda reached the bottom of the bowl and the end of the saltines. If anyone but her grandmother had been sitting there, she would have lifted the bowl to her lips to drain the last drop.

"You're sounding awfully prophetic, Gran." She raised her own eyebrow in direct imitation. "But you make a mean bowl of chicken vegetable."

Her eyelids were heavy and her stomach felt pleasantly full for the first time in a week. The hurt and horror of Tom's betrayal was still there, and she had no more idea how to handle things today than she had a week ago, but her Gran was here. She wasn't completely alone.

Her eyelids fluttered open as her grandmother stood and lifted the tray off Miranda's lap, leaving the rose on her nightstand.

"I think there are things you'll tell me when you're ready, Miranda. In the meantime, all I ask is that you remember who you are and where your responsibilities lie."

"Wow, Gran." Miranda yawned and stretched, comforted by her grandmother's presence and the warmth of the soup now filling her belly. "I'm going to have to nominate you for Town Oracle." She yawned again. "Maybe Ballantyne should sponsor a Mystical Wise Woman Pageant."

Her grandmother bent over and kissed the top of her head, and for a brief moment Miranda was a little girl again, and all was right with her world.

"Get some sleep, Miranda. It'll help you mend. I'll lock up on my way out."

For the first time since Tom's departure, Miranda slept for more than a few minutes at a time. She slept for eleven hours, deeply and completely and without a single dream about Tom—or what his absence would do to her life.

She woke at 7 A.M. and flicked on the television set. She lay there for a while half listening to the news, letting her mind wander, until the tragic story of a small-town manufacturer grabbed her attention.

It was widgets, not bras, and the town was called Henryville, not Truro. But the company had been clipping right along for several generations, until the family member running it absconded with a large chunk of the employee pension fund.

Miranda's eyes flew open, and she sat straight up in bed as she realized it wasn't just her and their marriage that Tom had pummeled so mercilessly. She didn't know what sorts of red flags he'd waved at Fidelity National, but he'd left Ballantyne, her family's single most important asset, leaderless. If anything happened to the company it wasn't just her family who would suffer; its three hundred employees would be out of work.

Miranda threw the covers off, sat up, and swung her legs over the side of the bed.

Without jobs, and no other sizable employer around to provide new ones, they and their families would be wiped out.

And so would Truro.

Oh, God.

Her legs were weak from lack of use, but Miranda

made it to the dresser, where she pulled out underclothes and stared in dismay at her reflection in the mirror.

The thick dark hair that normally hung down her back stuck straight out in an impressive Medusa imitation, and her face was so pale that the freckles across the bridge of her nose stood out like chocolate chips on an underdone cookie. Her green eyes looked as dull as the algae that sometimes filled the pond out back, and she had a bad feeling that she'd lost weight—not a plus when you were almost six feet tall and already skinny as a rail.

Miranda tried a smile. Her lips quivered and made her look like a dog that had just spotted the rolled-up newspaper in its master's hand—but at least she wasn't crying anymore. At this point, a day without tears was way up there next to winning the swimsuit competition and making the top ten. Funny how low your expectations could drop.

In the master bath she flicked on the small TV and confirmed that it was Monday morning, which meant she'd spent two more days feeling sorry for herself than it had taken God to create the universe.

Careful not to confront herself in the mirror again, Miranda stripped off her pajamas and stepped under a pulsing stream of hot water. Cradled in the steamy warmth, Miranda drew air into her lungs and turned her face up to the stream of water, wishing she could stay in this warm wonderful place forever.

For a few bracing moments she stood naked and alone in her steamy cocoon. Then she forced herself to open the glass door, reach for a towel, and step back into the real world.

It was time to get down to the plant and hunt for clues to where Tom had gone, and find out how bad things really were at Ballantyne.

chapter 3

Miranda drove through the front gate of Ballantyne Bras' corporate headquarters, wincing as she always did as she passed under the archway that read BALLANTYNE BRAS . . . SUPPORTING TRURO FOR OVER A HUNDRED YEARS.

She ignored the security guard's surprise—he couldn't be any more startled to see her than she was to be here at eight-thirty on a Monday morning—and parked her BMW in Tom's spot.

In the lobby she stopped briefly at the front desk. "Good morning, Leeta."

The receptionist choked on her doughnut. "Sorry, Mrs. Smith." Leeta patted her throat while Miranda waited for her to swallow and catch her breath. "With Mr. Smith away on business, I wasn't expecting . . ."

Miranda's mind leaped at the tidbit of information. They knew Tom was gone and they thought he was coming back. Evidently they hadn't gotten their kiss-off notes yet. "It's okay, Leeta." Miranda pulled her gaze from the receptionist's closely cropped fingernails to meet the middle-aged woman's gaze, wishing she could come out and ask exactly where Leeta thought Tom was. "Tom, um, asked me to pick up a few things from his office."

"Do you want me to . . ."

"No, it's okay. I'll show myself in."

Miranda sailed down the corridor and through Tom's office door. Closing it behind her, she leaned back against the hard wood surface, surveying her husband's domain while she stilled her heartbeat and got her breathing under control.

She wasn't sure what she was afraid of. She was a Ballantyne, and the current, if abandoned, wife of the president and CEO; it was unlikely anyone would demand an explanation for her presence. It was equally unlikely that Tom had circulated a memo announcing his intention to desert her. All she needed was a clue or two, something that would help her figure out where Tom had gone and why.

The knot in her stomach loosened slightly as she sank into a chair behind the mahogany partners desk that had once belonged to her grandfather. In its glossy reflection she could still see herself and Tom, fresh from business school at Emory, newly married and ready to carve out their niches within the company.

She'd intended to be the first woman of her family since Great-grandmother Rachael to take a hands-on role in the business. She'd thought she would sit behind this desk one day—or at least share it with Tom. She blinked back tears as she thought of all the other things she'd thought that had turned out to be wrong.

She'd had her first miscarriage that year. And her second the year after that. Everyone was very careful of her feelings, but her role as the bearer of the future heir was clear, and it never occurred to her to stop trying. She'd been waiting a lifetime to be the kind of mother she'd wanted hers to be.

Two years later she was on progesterone and off her feet for long periods of time—not exactly conducive to the running of a thriving corporation.

Before she knew it, she'd been relegated to family spokesperson—a role for which her years as a beauty pageant contestant had amply prepared her. And Tom, who refused to even discuss adoption, became the chosen one, learning the business from her father, earning his praise, and apparently developing a very personal affinity for the fruits of his labor.

Her father. Miranda reached for the phone, already imagining the relief she would feel at the sound of his voice. She could lay her troubles at his feet just as she had as a child, and then . . .

Her hand froze. She wasn't a child any longer; at

thirty-eight she was long past the age when she could go running to her daddy.

"Okay, then," she said aloud as she began her search. "You've tossed two houses, you should be able to finish this place in ten minutes, tops."

Unfortunately, Tom's laptop wasn't there, and none of the files stacked neatly on his desk were labeled "All the Bad Stuff I Did" or "This Is Where I'm Hiding." She worked her way through the desk drawers, hoping to stumble onto something important, hoping it would turn out to be like shopping, and she'd know what she was looking for when she found it.

What she found was a box of paper clips, six dog-eared business cards, a roll of stamps—God, she hated irony—and an ancient Ballantyne catalogue. She found absolutely nothing of interest—no photos, no ladies' underwear, in Tom's or anyone else's size—and nothing that could remotely be construed as a clue to where Tom had gone. Or what he'd done to Ballantyne.

Leaning back in the chair, she drummed anxious fingers on the desktop and tried to figure out her next step. An attempt to buzz Tom's assistant, Carly, produced no response.

"Leeta?" she said into the intercom, "where's Carly?"

"Carly took a personal day today, Mrs. Smith. Her little girl is sick. And with Mr. Smith out of the country..."

Okay, here was another sliver of potentially useful information; at this point she'd take anything she could get. "You know, Leeta," Miranda said, "I seem to have left Tom's contact number at home, and I have a question about some of the things he wanted me to pick up for him. Do you have a phone number handy?"

She waited hopefully.

"He didn't leave one this trip. He said he was going to be on the move until it was time to come back."

Miranda clamped a hand over her mouth to stop herself from asking "when" and "from where."

"Can you spell the name of the city he's in for me? I don't know why I'm having so much trouble getting it right."

There was a long silence, and then Leeta complied. "Sure, Mrs. Smith. That's H...O...N...G"—she paused to let the first four letters sink in—"K...O...N...G."

There was another protracted silence.

"Right, then," Miranda said brightly. "Um, thanks."

Okay, so Leeta thought she was a moron, but she now knew that Tom had made his absence appear work-related, which meant Carly might have booked his flight and made his hotel reservation. Even if he weren't still in Hong Kong, at least she'd have a trail to follow.

Miranda thought about Tom moving on to a new life, not coming back. A much-too-familiar lump formed in her throat, and her eyes welled up. Shoving away the hurt, she forced herself to think. In order to go anywhere beyond Hong Kong and stay there, Tom would need money. Lots of it.

Miranda's stomach dropped as she realized that the

company wasn't the only monetary source Tom might have tapped.

With a sudden sense of urgency, Miranda picked up the phone and punched in the main number of the local bank where they kept their personal accounts.

Her heart raced as she followed the prompts to put in their joint account numbers, first for the household checking and then their savings and money market accounts. She barely breathed while the computerized voice spelled out the bad news with all the emotion of a tin can. But it hardly mattered, because she had enough emotion for all of them.

She called back again, hoping she had misheard, but the tin voice refused to change its story. It was gone. All of it. Except for a balance of two thousand dollars and seventy-five cents in her household checking account, which now constituted her entire net worth.

Tears formed and her lower lip quivered. Stretching an arm out on the cool mahogany, Miranda laid her head down on her arm and squeezed her eyes shut in a futile effort to halt their flow.

When the knock sounded on the door, Miranda scrubbed at her eyes with the back of her hand and sat up in her chair. "Yes?"

The door opened and Ballantyne's head bookkeeper stepped into the room. Helen St. James was a few inches shorter than Miranda and a couple of years older. She was what Gran would call a handsome woman—not beautiful, but nice enough to look at—

with shoulder-length auburn hair and classically even features that Miranda was having a hard time focusing on.

Closing the office door behind her, the bookkeeper crossed to the desk. "I've been trying to reach Mr. Smith for almost a week now."

Miranda bit back the "Join the club" that sprang to her lips.

"It's very important that I speak to ... Mr. Smith ... right away."

Miranda noted the strange emphasis on the word "Mr." and dropped her gaze from the other woman's face to the hands clamped at her sides. Helen St. James's manicure was both French and impeccable, and she had an amoeba-shaped birthmark on the back of her wrist. Were these the hands that had rested so familiarly on her husband's butt?

"If you speak to him, will you ask him to call me?"

Sure she would. Right after she had him hauled off to jail for emptying all their bank accounts and scaring her to death.

"He needs to know that ..." The bookkeeper cleared her throat and started again. "He needs to know that I'm having a little trouble reconciling the numbers."

"Yes, yes, I'll be sure to ..." Miranda stopped as the bookkeeper's words sank in. With great effort she dragged her gaze from the French manicure up to the bookkeeper's face. She didn't like what she saw there at all.

"Fidelity National called," Helen St. James said.

"They want to move up our audit. Something's not right with the receivables."

The house was cold and univiting, the afternoon sun too weak to offer any warmth. Miranda walked through the downstairs, hiking up the thermostat, turning on lights, trying to chase away the chill in the too-empty house.

Upstairs her unmade bed beckoned. She could curl up and hide there, maybe turn on the soaps and watch fictional people suffer for a while—anything would be better than this crushing quiet and emptiness. She felt like a compass without its North point, whirling around aimless and lost. She'd never considered herself dependent on Tom, but she was beginning to realize how much she'd been defined by him. If she wasn't Mrs. Tom Smith, who was she? And what was she supposed to do now?

Her husband had taken off and left her behind. Alone. Unwanted. Unnecessary to whatever new life he was planning to live. An image of Tom on a white sandy beach materialized. Palm trees swayed in the breeze and a big blue ocean shimmered in the background. He had a great big pirate's chest full of money, and a naked woman was rubbing coconut oil on his naked buttocks. With her perfectly manicured fingers.

Miranda located the magnifying glass in the kitchen junk drawer and carried it into Tom's study. Opening the packet of photos, she pulled out the hand-on-butt shot and forced herself to study it through the glass.

Magnified, the blond hairs on Tom's rear became . . . magnified . . . as did the intricate weave of the fuchsia lace, but the woman's hands must have been moving when the picture was taken—Miranda definitely didn't want to think about that—because they were slightly blurred and the angle wasn't right to expose the back of the woman's wrist. If it had an amoeba-shaped birth-mark, she couldn't make it out.

But if they were Helen St. James's hands, what would that prove? Wouldn't he have taken the woman and her hands with him?

Miranda's mind swam with questions for which she had no answers. Over and over she asked herself: If Tom was so unhappy, why hadn't he said something? Why sneak away rather than ask for a divorce? And how could there have been so many things about him she hadn't known?

What she wanted to do was sic the police on him, or at least tell her family so her father could beat Tom to a bloody pulp while Gran tucked her back into bed with a bowl of soup and a beautifully laid tray. But it was all too humiliating. And she couldn't bear to be-come fodder for the Truro gossip mill until she knew where Tom was and what action she could take. And, of course, there was Ballantyne. Given how easily Tom had jettisoned her, who knew what he had done to the company.

Desperate to *do* something, Miranda hauled out her

laptop, set it up on the kitchen table, and logged on to AOL. Holding her breath while she keyed in Tom's password, she sighed with relief when she was able to pull up his mail. Only to discover there was nothing there worth finding.

No mail had been sent from Tom's account since the day before he'd left, and the incoming mail, which consisted primarily of Helen St. James's progressively more panicked pleas for his attention, had tapered off to almost nothing as he'd apparently failed to respond—at least from this account.

Scrolling down she found unread ads for Viagra, a penis enlarger, and discounted antidepressants. A brief tour of his Favorite Places revealed porn sites and other men in women's underwear—none of whom looked half as good in them as her husband did.

Logging off, she dialed Tom's older brother Brad in Richmond, hoping Tom's only living relative might be able to provide a clue.

"Oh, hey, Randa," he said. "How's Tom?"

No help there. "He's away," she said, once again sticking as close as possible to the truth. "I wondered if you'd heard from him lately."

"We talked on New Year's Day like we always do, and he said he was going to be out of the country. Been meaning to call and see if he was back."

But Miranda knew that call would probably have taken place on Easter; the Smith boys were not much for chitchatting in between major holidays.

Tears pricked her eyelids as Miranda contemplated

all the information she'd managed to gather: Tom had initiated no E-mail activity or contact with his only living relative. And he had a hairy butt. If this represented the extent of her sleuthing abilities, Nancy Drew had nothing to worry about.

The damned tears welled up again until she could barely see through the sheen of them. She was no Nancy Drew, and her husband needed ladies' underwear and other women. But he didn't need or want her. The tears slid down her cheeks and plopped onto the keyboard. She wasn't even good at being Miranda Smith.

And what was she doing about it? She was sitting at her kitchen table in her horribly empty house blubbering like a child. Again. How pathetic was that?

The tears kept coming and the dull ache that had begun in the center of her chest spread outward. She tried to whip up fresh anger at Tom, but deep down inside she knew that somehow she had failed.

Stumbling upstairs, she searched for something—anything—positive to cling to. In the end she was forced to settle for feeling lucky Truro didn't have a tattoo parlor. Because then she'd feel compelled to have an L for loser tattooed on her forehead.

chapter 4

Chief of Police Blake Summers cruised the main business district of Truro, which took about ten minutes. It was colder than any mid-January he could remember—it had barely hit the teens yesterday—and not too many folks were rushing to work any earlier than they had to. The snow was undoubtedly piled high up at Ballantyne Bald, and most of the narrow mountain roads outside of town were bound to be impassable.

Calls today would be weather-related and require tow trucks and Truro's lone snowplow rather than guns and bullets. Not that there was a hell of a lot of what qualified as real crime in Truro even when it was warm. He'd seen a lot more action on the force in Atlanta, but he didn't regret coming home. There was a certain symmetry to the town bad boy coming back as its chief of police, even if he'd had to leave a wife behind to do it.

Blake stashed the cruiser in the lot behind City Hall and walked down Main Street to the Dogwood Café. Here he knew everyone, and found satisfaction in that fact as he waved his hellos to the morning crowd and took his usual seat at the counter. He smiled his thanks when Jewel Whitman set a steaming mug of coffee in front of him.

Fifteen minutes later he'd read *The Atlanta Journal-Constitution* from front to back, demolished the He-Man Breakfast Special, and drunk enough cups of coffee to enable him to float to his office.

"Jewel, if you pour me one more cup of coffee or put one more morsel of food on my plate, I'm going to have to arrest you." Blake put a hand over the top of his cup and gave the waitress a look that had once made an armed felon throw down his gun.

The waitress patted her beehive hairdo and flashed him a smile. "You sure you don't want some more grits? I could fry you up another egg or two."

"Jewel, you're killing me, here."

"Well, I know you're not getting enough real food with no woman there to do for you."

"Do I look underfed to you?" Blake unfolded his six-foot-two-inch frame from the stool and patted his trim stomach before reaching into his pocket for his wallet. "The women in this town seem to think being male eradicates the cooking chromosome. Grandpa and Andie and I have been on our own for almost three years now. I think it's time to scratch us off the Meals-on-Wheels list."

"Joke all you like," Jewel said. "But two crotchety males trying to raise a teenage girl? Why, you've turned that cute little thing into the biggest jock in six counties."

Blake grinned and pulled a couple of bills out of his wallet and laid them on the counter. "Don't you worry about us; we're doing just fine. And I'll lay you odds that little jock of mine will be heading to Duke on a full athletic scholarship in two years' time." Sport had been his salvation, and he intended to make sure his daughter reaped its benefits as well.

"Be that as it may . . ."

"We're used to doing things ourselves. It gives a person backbone and determination."

"Not to mention ring-around-the-collar."

"Possibly." Blake stuck his wallet back in his pocket. "But we're fine, Jewel. Really. If it'll make you feel better, you can give me an extra piece of bacon tomorrow."

The dry cleaner and the hardware store were open by the time Blake made his way back up Main Street. Diane Lowell was turning on lights in the Blue Willow Antique Mall and Sandwich Emporium. At the end of Main, Blake stamped his feet on the mat outside the Truro Police Department and stepped through the door into the luxurious warmth of the brand-new building. Unlike the original hundred-and-fifty-year-old structure, which had been moved to a final resting place just outside of town, this one had shiny linoleum floors and smooth plaster walls. It also had new desks and an even newer computer, but its most impressive feature—at least in light of recent temperatures—was the central heating and cooling.

Blake stepped into the toasty warmth of the reception area, hung his coat on the hall tree, and stopped at the front desk for messages.

Anne Farnsworthy's fingers flew over her keyboard at top speed, and she had a phone cradled between her shoulder and ear. When she noticed him, she stopped typing long enough to hand him a pile of message slips, then finished up on the phone.

"Morning, Anne. What do we have so far?"

"Well, Tyler Poole's pickup got stuck in a snowdrift, and I sent Jim out to help him. Got a couple more of those strange hang-up calls—evidently somebody only wants to talk to you—and Andie's math teacher called. She left her homework at home again, but I called your grandfather and asked him to run it on over. Ed's going to be a little late getting in. Other than that it's been real quiet."

She looked him up and down. "Did you have breakfast? I brought in some sweet rolls in case you didn't have time to—"

Blake groaned. "How in the world did I get appointed chief when the female population of Truro believes I can't feed or clothe myself? How helpless do I look?"

"Those are trick questions, right?"

"Absolutely."

In Blake's experience, which was vast, watching a man and child get dumped by their respective wife and mother did one of two things to a woman. It either turned her on or heightened her maternal instincts. And it almost always sent her scurrying to the stove.

The phone rang and Anne picked up on the second ring. "Truro Police Department," she said. "Uh, wait, hold on. He just walked in."

She clamped a hand over the mouthpiece and motioned to Blake. "It's her," she said quietly, "the one who keeps calling and asking for you, but won't leave a message. She's calling from a pay phone."

"I'll take it in my office." Blake moved quickly through the reception area and closed his office door behind him. A second after he picked up the phone, the call was put through.

"Chief Summers."

"I want to report foul play." It was a woman's voice, muffled and distant sounding, but definitely a female.

"Who is this?"

"It doesn't matter who I am. What matters is that Tom Smith is missing and nobody's doing anything about it."

"Mrs. Smith?" He tried to picture the elegant Miranda Smith huddled in a phone booth placing an anonymous phone call to the chief of police.

The woman's laugh was muffled, but he could tell how lacking in humor it was.

"Hardly. But then maybe she hasn't noticed he's gone. The Ladies' Guild can be *soooo* time-consuming." Though her voice remained unidentifiable, the sarcasm came through loud and clear.

"And what makes you think something's happened to Tom Smith?"

"Because he's disappeared. And I know he would have contacted me if he were able to."

"If you want me to investigate, you're going to have to give me more than that."

There was silence on the other end, but he could hear the woman's breathing.

"If you don't identify yourself or give me something concrete, there's not much I can do."

"Wouldn't want to upset the Ballantynes, would we, Chief? Sort of like taking a stab at the Royal Family."

He ignored the jibe. "It *is* up to the family to file a missing persons report. Don't you think a woman would file a report if her husband were missing? What possible reason would she have for keeping such a thing to herself?"

"Now those are real good questions, Chief. And if I were you, that's exactly what I'd be asking Miranda Smith."

Then there was a click, and a moment later he was listening to a dial tone.

Miranda stayed in bed for two days. She crawled under the covers after her unsuccessful Nancy Drew imitation and just couldn't make herself get out. She watched a *Brady Bunch* marathon, a documentary on sheepdogs and the herding instinct, the movie *Titanic*, followed by a special on the real-life tragedy, and back-to-back episodes of *Sesame Street* before she finally turned off the television and simply lay there listening to the phone ring. Around midnight of the second night she forced herself downstairs to play back the messages.

"Miranda." Her mother's voice rang out in the silence. "You cannot continue to hibernate in this way. I want you out of that house and over here for dinner tomorrow night at six. No excuses." She could hear Gran's voice in the background. "Your Gran is threatening an intervention. Don't make us come over there and drag you out."

The rest of the messages were from Ballantyne. "Uh, Mrs. Smith..." Leeta's tone was tentative and laced with worry. "Mr. Smith didn't come in yesterday like we expected and we, uh, have a few questions. Can you ask him to call the office?"

The next voice belonged to Tom's assistant, Carly. "Um, Mrs. Smith? We're not sure what's happening, but we really need to talk with Mr. Smith. There's a problem in production and we've had some orders returned. Will you ask him to call in?"

The last voice was Helen St. James's and it held an odd mixture of panic and anger. "It's imperative that I speak to Mr. Smith. Fidelity National is ready to set a date for the audit." There was a pause. "I'm not sure how to proceed. They want to come in next week."

The early morning sky was steel gray and the promise of snow hung heavy in the air as Miranda drove through a just-waking Truro to Ballantyne.

Even as she passed under the archway and parked in the employee lot, she wasn't sure why she had come or what she hoped to accomplish. All she knew was the ship seemed to be foundering and there was no one at the helm. And although she was too ashamed to call her father, she couldn't just lie in bed while the ship went down.

She greeted Leeta in the lobby and walked toward Tom's office, analyzing possible outcomes. Best-case scenario, Carly Tarleton would provide some clues to Tom's whereabouts so she could hunt him down like the dog he was and make him fix whatever was wrong. Worst-case scenario, the crew would realize they'd hit an iceberg and their captain had not only deserted the ship but taken the only lifeboat.

She really shouldn't have watched that *Titanic* special.

In Tom's office, she closed the door behind her and took her place at his desk. *Do not panic*, she instructed herself as she placed her laptop on the mahogany surface and booted up. Only her self didn't seem to be listening.

At 9 A.M. muffled voices rose out in the hallway and

phones began to ring. It was clearly time to *do* something, but the best she could manage was to swivel around in the desk chair and stare out the window at the distant peak where her family's lake houses perched.

She was still staring out the window when a sharp knock sounded on the office door. Before she could spin around, the door opened.

"Thank goodness you're back." Quick footsteps tapped across the office floor and approached the desk. "I brought my diploma in, Mr. Smith, just like we talked about. And Myrna really liked my new drawings. I know you must be tired from your trip. Did you get held up in—"

Miranda swiveled around to face her husband's assistant.

"Oh!" The young woman's blue eyes widened in surprise, and her mouth snapped shut.

Embarrassment suffused the apple-cheeked face and the hands that held the document in its cheap black frame fell to her sides, but not before Miranda took in the stubby, unpolished fingernails. These hands, at least, had not been photographed on her husband's butt.

"Good morning, Carly."

The young woman swallowed and wiped her free hand on her navy skirt. The diploma still dangled from the other. "I'm sorry, Mrs. Smith. I was expecting..."

"Yes, I know. But Mr. Smith won't be in today." She didn't add the "or ever" that flew to her tongue. "What do you have there?"

"My college diploma. It took me a while, but I did it."
The blonde raised her chin, along with the document
that bore the name of a small commuter college two
towns away.

Carly Tarleton was somewhere in her mid-twenties,
and to Miranda's knowledge was the first of the
Tarleton clan to earn a degree of any kind. Several of
them had barely made it out of grade school; a few of
the men were languishing in prison. The women had a
reputation for reproducing, with and without benefit
of marriage. If Miranda remembered correctly, Carly
had a young daughter and no evidence of a husband.

"Earning a college degree is a great accomplish-
ment. Congratulations."

"Thank you." Carly looked around the room. "So
when will Mr. Smith be back?"

"I'm not sure. He's still in China." She swallowed. "I
think he's moved out of Hong Kong, gone farther, um,
inland."

Carly's gaze swung back, interested. "Do you think
he's found any new suppliers?"

Miranda felt a flash of annoyance that this young
woman with her illegitimate child and poorly framed
diploma knew more about what her husband might or
might not do than she did.

"I, uh, don't know." But she thought it unlikely, unless they were supplying G-strings in Big & Tall Men's
sizes.

Miranda studied the chunky blonde with the earnest blue eyes. "Did you book Tom's flight and accommodations for this trip?"

"Yes." Carly studied her back. "He was booked from Atlanta to San Francisco and then on to Hong Kong. With a return two nights ago."

Miranda looked down at her own fingernails for a moment. "Was anyone traveling with him?"

Miranda could hear her heart beat in the silence. She forced herself to look up into the appraising blue eyes.

"Not that I know of," Carly said. Then she hesitated. "But he could have dealt directly with the airline."

"Who do we book through?"

"The Delta ticket office in Claymore."

"Will you get them on the line for me, Carly? And please tell Helen St. James I want to see the latest financial statements along with all our receivables and pertinent client files immediately."

Surprise washed over Carly's face. She opened her mouth then closed it. With a nod, she turned and left the office, closing the door softly behind her.

Two minutes later Miranda was talking to the agent who had booked Tom's flights.

"I booked him through San Francisco just like I always do," the woman said.

"Yes, yes, and I know he was very happy with the flight." Miranda coughed. "Um, did you book just the one ticket?"

"I'm sorry?"

"Was he traveling alone?" Miranda was prepared to

describe the woman's manicure if necessary, but she never got the opportunity.

"Who is this?"

"This is Miranda Smith. His wife."

What followed was a really dead silence, which Miranda hastened to fill.

"What if you just tell me whether you sold the seat next to him to anyone else."

The woman did silence better than anyone Miranda had ever encountered. If keeping quiet were an Olympic sport, this woman would be taking home the gold.

"Right, then." Miranda chose another tack. "Can you tell me if the seat next to him was occupied at all?"

"No."

"How about telling me whether he actually *used* his ticket to Hong Kong."

"Can't."

This was getting really annoying.

"Is there anyone at the airline who can?"

"No."

"How *can* I get information about the seating arrangements?"

"You can't."

"Because . . ." Miranda prompted.

"Because the passenger manifest is not a public document."

"Because . . . ?"

"Look, Mrs. Smith." The agent abandoned the monosyllables with a vengeance. "The only person in this universe who can answer these questions for you is your husband. I suggest you ask him."

Miranda flushed and put down the phone. Then because she was apparently a glutton for punishment, she dialed American Express's customer service number and gave the answering agent Tom's credit card number. The woman's "We're here to help" tone lasted about five seconds.

"Are you reporting the credit card stolen or not, ma'am?"

Miranda rubbed her forehead. "Well, I don't actually know that it's been stolen. I'm just trying to understand why there's no activity on it."

There was a silence and then, "Could it be because no one is using it?" The words themselves were inoffensive. The tone was not.

And of course the customer service agent was right. Anyone with half a brain knew that credit cards left their own breadcrumb trail. Tom had watched all the same *Rockford Files* reruns she had. She was wasting her time trying to find him on her own.

"I don't suppose you can tell me whether another account has been opened under the name of Thomas J. Smith?"

"No, I certainly cannot."

Miranda hung up the phone and began to gather her things. She'd been wrong to come here. Wrong to try to keep Tom's desertion to herself. Stupid to think she could track him down. She couldn't pay her bills on time or get a simple answer out of a customer service agent. Her own husband didn't think she was worth hanging around for; what made her think she could keep a leaky old ship from sinking?

Much better to go home, lick her wounds, maybe cry herself another little river. If she left now, she could ask Gran to bring over some soup and be tucked into bed in time for her favorite soaps. And then she'd call her daddy.

Clutching her laptop to her chest, she slung her purse over her shoulder, and stood. There was a commotion at the office door and she looked up to see Carly sprinting toward her with Helen St. James on her heels.

"Mrs. Smith, she won't—"

The bookkeeper stepped around Carly and squared off in front of Miranda. "I don't know what's going on here, but you have no right to—"

Miranda studied the bookkeeper. She watched the French manicure flash before her eyes, thought about the number and tone of the E-mails Helen St. James had sent to Tom, considered the woman's proprietary attitude. She'd just taken a ton of attitude from two different customer service agents. She was in no mood to take any from a woman who might have been sleeping with her husband and, for all she knew, had a hand in damaging the business.

"I don't have the right to what?" Miranda asked Helen St. James. "Ask for figures from bookkeeping? Try to determine why Fidelity National is worried about our receivables?"

She heard Carly gasp and turned to Tom's assistant. "That doesn't leave this room."

Carly nodded, her eyes wide.

She'd wasted their last encounter assessing the bookkeeper's manicure, but she'd come here today to try to figure out what was going on; she was not going to let *this* woman stand in her way.

"Tom Smith is the president of this company. You are only—" Helen began.

"His *wife*." Miranda straightened her shoulders and concentrated on projecting, just as she taught her girls in the Miss Rhododendron Prep class to do when answering those stressful onstage questions during pageants. She spoke slowly and clearly, maintaining eye contact with Helen St. James, intent on communicating absolute certainty, hoping neither Helen nor Carly could hear the knocking of her knees.

"This company belongs to the Ballantyne family. And I am a Ballantyne. Tom," she paused for a moment, surprised by how strange his name was starting to feel on her lips, "is not here." She swallowed but didn't look away. "And he may not be here for a while."

She saw the bookkeeper blanch and heard Carly gasp again and imagined their reaction if she just went ahead and blurted out the truth. *She'd* undoubtedly feel better for a good five seconds or so, right up until the moment when they realized she was all that was standing between them and joblessness and the panic began to spread.

"I just had an, um, E-mail from Tom a few minutes

ago. He's leaving for," she wracked her brain for the name of the town she'd looked up at dawn, the one about five hours farther inland, "Guandong, and he's asked me to keep an eye on things until he gets back."

"But I e-mailed him and heard nothing. I . . ."

Miranda raised an eyebrow at the bookkeeper just as she had learned to do at committee meetings when someone questioned her opinion. Or with beauty pageant contestants who weren't paying attention to their coach.

"Tom has always spoken very highly of you, Helen." She used the woman's first name intentionally. "And we would not like to lose you. But I need to see our latest financial statements and a breakdown of the payables and receivables, as well as our cash balances, immediately. If you don't have them on this desk in the next thirty minutes, I'll have to hire someone who will."

Then she and her laptop swept past the two dumbfounded women, rounded a corner, and marched straight into the ladies' room. Where they spent the next thirty minutes gathering up the courage to go back to work.

chapter 5

Leaving the toilet was tough. Facing the files Helen St. James had left on the desk was even tougher. But as she worked through the financial statements, Miranda began to feel a faint glimmer of hope. After years of shrinking profits, these statements showed steady growth over the last six months, most of it due to an unprecedented number of new accounts.

Here, on paper, things looked very good. When all those new receivables came due over the next weeks, Ballantyne Bras would be in its best cash position in years. They'd be solvent, liquid, fluid, all those wonderful water-based terms that meant they could focus on growing the business instead of struggling to tread water.

So why, she asked herself, had Tom bailed out? Why, right before Ballantyne was about to reap the rewards of his efforts, had he grabbed a life preserver and jumped ship? If it was only her he'd wanted to leave, he could have asked for a divorce. The key had to be in these receivables.

Staring out the window, Miranda thought about the shreds of the letter she'd found the night Tom disappeared, and the bank's concern about the number of new receivables. There *were* a lot of them, and they'd all been opened by Tom. Then she thought about the terms they'd been given.

Most customers got thirty to sixty days to pay for their goods, but Tom had given the new customers a hundred and twenty days. Four months.

The hair on the back of Miranda's neck prickled.

"Carly," she said into the intercom, "will you bring me a copy of the orders and contact phone numbers on all the receivables due over the next two weeks, please?"

Miranda had to remind herself to breathe as she waited for the information she'd requested. With shaking fingers she dialed the phone number of the first company. Her mouth was dry and she wasn't sure how she was going to talk around the lump of fear in her throat.

On the fourth ring the phone was answered. Miranda was just letting out a sigh of relief when she heard, "Joey's Pizza. The special today is ..."

Miranda hung up, waited a full sixty seconds, and then hit the redial button.

"Joey's Piz—"

Miranda slammed down the phone. She looked up at Carly, who was standing expectantly in the doorway. "Did you need anything else?" she asked the assistant.

"Is everything all right?"

"Yes. Yes, of course," Miranda lied. "Um, that'll be all."

Carly put a hand on the doorknob.

"And will you close the door behind you?"

She waited until Carly left the office, waited a few more seconds for the door to click shut, then waited another mind-numbing thirty seconds for the assistant to move away from the door.

Miranda wanted to go home, put on her flannel pajamas, and get back in bed. A really stiff drink would be good, too.

She picked up the phone and dialed the second company on the list.

"Thank you for calling the Asheville Biltmore. How may I direct your call?"

Miranda put the phone down quietly. She then dialed a Laundromat in Winston-Salem, a bowling alley in Macon, and a state prison in north Florida.

Of the ten new accounts, all of which had allegedly placed and presumably been shipped orders over the last six months, not one was real.

These nonexistent customers owed Ballantyne more than three million dollars—money the company needed to pay suppliers, create new inventory, and pay down their line of credit at Fidelity National.

Miranda's head was throbbing full force now, and she sincerely wished she and her laptop had never come out of the bathroom.

Where had the goods gone? Had Tom intentionally created the fictitious customers so that he could sell the ordered goods to finance his new life? Or had he just been trying to make Ballantyne look better on paper and then fled when faced with an audit that would reveal the truth?

She dug in her purse for a Tylenol as she considered both possibilities. As his wife, the distinction was important. As the person left holding the bag, Tom's motivations couldn't have mattered less.

Not having the money or the goods was bad enough. Creating fictitious accounts and receivables was worse.

Not to mention completely illegal.

That afternoon Miranda tried to outswim her panic and fear in the country club swimming pool. It was mercifully empty and she swam full-out, kicking with all her strength, reaching with her arms, pulling with her cupped hands. She tried to make her mind as empty as the pool itself, tried to ditch the worst-case scenarios that kept playing out in her head, but she wasn't having a whole lot of success.

Normally the embryonic silence of the water buoyed

and comforted her; swimming smoothed out her thoughts and produced a sense of well-being she found in no other place. But today her mind churned even faster than her feet and arms. Messages she didn't want to hear echoed in her brain, crashing through the quiet and demanding her attention.

We're broke, we're doomed, breathe. We're broke, we're doomed, breathe.

She did a racing turn, pushed off the wall, and sliced through the water, and the message changed to: *It's fraud, it's over, breathe. It's fraud, it's over, breathe.*

You're all they've got, gasp.

Up and down and back and forth she swam until her arms began to tire and her brain finally began to numb. The messages continued, but they didn't echo quite so loudly. Her strokes slowed and her kick became a more steady flutter. She hadn't found peace or any kind of answer, but she thought she might be able to pry herself out of the pool soon before all of her body parts were completely and irreversibly shriveled.

Edith and Lois Turley delivered lunch to the police chief's office. Blake had brought a small Caesar salad and half a rare roast beef sandwich from home, but when the elderly sisters showed up on the stroke of noon with a picnic basket stuffed with fried chicken, biscuits, and potato salad, he'd had no choice but to let them spread the feast out on the desk in front of him.

It took him twenty minutes to put away enough

food to satisfy the sharp-eyed duo, and another ten to ease them—and the apple pie they seemed to think he had room for—out the door. Then he put on his coat and hat and went looking for Miranda Smith.

He tracked her down at the Truro Country Club, where Nancy Bell, the alarmingly perky receptionist, informed him Mrs. Smith was swimming laps. He followed the signs through the tastefully decorated lobby to the soaring glass wall of windows that enclosed the indoor pool. Entering through the men's locker room, he walked toward the pool in his winter-weight uniform and hard-soled shoes.

Wet heat, all the steamier after the frigid air outside, assaulted him. The floor was slick with water, the room echoed with sound, and the damp, overheated air carried the scent of expensive eau de chlorine. Within seconds, his clothes were limp and perspiration was trickling down his back.

Trying not to breathe in the heat or the chlorine, he scanned the Olympic pool for Miranda Smith.

She swam in the last lane, her slim arms flashing in and out of the water in a practiced crawl, her breathing synched to her stroke, the flutter of her feet steady and sure. She was the lone occupant of the pool.

At the deep end wall, she made a smooth underwater flip turn, and as she resurfaced he got a brief flash of dark hair and goggles before she resumed her stroke. He hunkered down in front of her lane and waited for her to reach him, not quite sure how he was going to play the whole thing.

Her right hand landed on the wall first, and her other came to join it. For a brief moment he thought she meant to keep on swimming, but then she stopped and stood, removing her goggles and running a hand over the top of her head in an automatic smoothing gesture.

The water eddied around her waist, hiding what lay beneath, but the black one-piece was molded to her body like a second skin, and droplets of water clung to her chest and arms.

He brought his gaze up and had to bite back a smile at the raccoonlike imprint the goggles had left around her green eyes.

"Hello, Miranda."

"Chief."

They regarded each other for a moment, neither speaking. She didn't make a move to get out of the pool, but just stood there looking up at him, waiting for him to say something. They'd known each other since birth, though that knowledge had been tempered by the social divide between them. He'd been the son of a real estate agent who died before Floridians discovered Truro's quaint charm, and a dissatisfied Miss Rhododendron who'd deserted her husband and eight-year-old son when her life didn't live up to her expectations.

Miranda Smith had been a Miss Rhododendron, too, plus a whole lot of Miss Something-or-Others he hadn't bothered to keep track of. From what he could tell, she'd lived the life his mother had aspired to.

"How are you?" he asked.

"Fine." She flashed the beauty pageant smile a fraction of a second late. "And you?"

"Good, good." He made a point of staring her right in the eye, despite the natural inclination to drop his gaze lower. As he studied her he realized that her individual features were not particularly beautiful, but the sum of those parts was hard to look away from. "And Tom? How's Tom?" he asked.

If he hadn't been watching so closely he might have missed the hesitation. She swallowed and cocked her head in his direction. Then she pulled out her beauty contestant smile again.

"Why, he's fine, Chief. Thank you for asking." She finished her Scarlett O'Hara impression with another flash of white teeth. Any minute she was going to bat her eyelashes at him.

"I haven't seen him around for a while," Blake replied.

"No?"

"Nope."

She fidgeted slightly. Nothing major, just enough to tell him she was uncomfortable with the turn the conversation had taken.

"That's because he's out of town."

"Oh? Where is he?"

She didn't look away, but he could have sworn he could feel her mind racing.

"He's out of the country right now. In China."

"China, huh? Business or pleasure?"

She blushed, which he found interesting. And then she batted her eyelashes.

"Business, of course. He's attempting to develop new suppliers."

"And when are you expecting him back?"

She laughed, a hollow sound that sent his law enforcement antennae quivering.

"Why, I do believe you're interrogating me, Chief Summers. And here I thought you were just passing by." She aimed her gaze at the uniform shirt now clinging to his chest.

Her tone intimated this was nothing more than a casual chat, but he sensed the tension in her body. And she kept making eye contact with him, which felt distinctly odd.

When he didn't respond, she pulled herself halfway out of the water and twisted to sit on the edge of the pool, her long legs dangling.

"Why the sudden interest in my husband?"

He didn't hesitate, eager to see how she reacted to the truth. "Because somebody called my office claiming your husband had met with foul play."

He studied her carefully as her whole body went still. He waited for the outrage, the fear, some sort of admission of . . . something. But she just threw back her head and laughed.

"I imagine the foulest thing Tom's met with so far is a lack of cheeseburgers, and poor potty facilities." She brought her knees up and pushed upward to a standing position, and he did the same, trying not to watch the droplets of water slide down her body. "But I promise I'll let him know people are worried about him the next time he calls."

She was very damp and dewy, and her legs pretty much demanded a second look. But her smile was too bright and her shoulders too stiff. And she didn't even ask him who the caller was. For some reason he didn't yet know, she was lying to him.

She glanced up at the clock and reached over for the towel hanging on the wall. "I'm out of time, Chief, and I really need to shower and change. Is it all right if I go now?"

He nodded and tried not to watch too closely as she swept past him on the way to the locker room.

Something definitely wasn't right. Every instinct he had—both personal and professional—told him so. But it wasn't the way Miranda Smith looked in a bathing suit.

Miranda stayed in the locker room until she was sure Chief Summers was gone. Her whole body shook from the effort of trying to act normal under his sharp-eyed regard. God, she hoped she'd been convincing.

She sat in the sauna and thought about who might have reported Tom missing. Then she thought about the fact that she had lied to the chief of police. Surely that wasn't an arrestable offense?

Her hands continued to shake as she showered and dressed. What if he started investigating? What if he found out the CEO of Ballantyne was guilty of fraud? What would happen to them all then?

She dried her hair and clubbed it back in a French braid, too preoccupied to bother trying to smooth it.

Why had she told Helen and Carly she was filling in for Tom? Why hadn't she just told the truth and let the chips fall where they may?

Her personal finances were nonexistent; her husband had come close to bankrupting the company and then apparently committed fraud to hide what he'd done. And no one at Ballantyne was likely to be reassured to know a Miss Rhododendron was stepping forward to save the day.

Slipping on her coat, Miranda took her car from the valet and drove slowly toward her parents' house trying to analyze her options. Things had changed. This was no longer a straying husband and the need to steer the ship until a new captain was named. This was a failing company and bank fraud and a chief of police sniffing around. She was in so far over her head, they were all likely to drown.

As she pulled into her parents' driveway she made her decision. As much as she'd like to do the right thing, and as embarrassing as it would be to tell her parents the truth, her father was the logical choice to put the company back on solid footing. She'd hand the mess over to him, and then she'd find a divorce attorney in Atlanta who could tell her how to proceed. No one who knew her would expect her to handle this disaster by herself. Why, it was ridiculous, really.

At the front door, she told herself she should feel relieved. But she felt like a failure.

"Hello, darling. Where's Tom?" her mother asked as she opened the door and ushered Miranda inside.

Miranda averted her eyes, hoping it would seem like less of a lie later if she didn't make eye contact now. "He, uh, he's in China. On business."

"Goodness." She took hold of Miranda's hand and pulled her toward the stairs. "Your father's in the living room." Her mother's eyes clouded momentarily then cleared. "But I want to show you something first."

"Mother, I . . ." All Miranda could think about was laying down her burden. Now, during cocktails, would be the perfect time.

But her mother drew Miranda up the stairs to her childhood bedroom, where stepping through the door was like stepping into a time warp. The theme was early pageant, and the walls were papered with pageant programs and photos of Miranda in evening gowns, in swimsuits, in the front line during opening production numbers. Above the canopied double bed, lined up in precise rows on specially built shelves, were her crowns, neatly ensconced in Plexiglas cases. Little Miss Truro and Little Miss Sunflower ultimately led to Miss Hayfield County, Miss Sweet Potato, Miss Vine-Ripe Tomato; there were lots of fruits and vegetables over which she'd ruled.

Under a spotlight set off by itself was her Rhododendron crown, which her mother moved to now.

"Mother, you really should do this room over. I'm almost forty. It's time to move on." What she really wanted to move on to was the subject of Ballantyne. "Let's go downstairs and . . ."

Her mother reached into the display cube and removed the Rhododendron crown. "I've been thinking about the Guild Ball, Miranda."

This was not news. Joan Ballantyne Richards Harper spent a great deal of time thinking about the Guild Ball. She'd chaired the yearly hospital fundraiser too many times to count, and now had unlimited opinions about how Miranda should handle this year's event.

It was the last thing on Miranda's mind at the moment. She'd canceled several meetings since Tom had left, but vowed now that once she handed Ballantyne over to her father, she'd get things back on track.

"Mother," Miranda said, "let's go downstairs. I could really use a drink, and there's something I'd like to run by Dad."

Her mother's brow furrowed at the mention of her father, and she caressed the tiara's centermost rhododendron as if looking for comfort. "I think," her mother paused as if for a drum roll, "you should reintroduce the tradition of crowning the chairwoman. It would add such drama. And it's such a shame to leave this beautiful crown unused."

Miranda groaned. "Mother, there is no way—"

"And we'll get a crown for Tom too. He looks so marvelous in a tux."

He doesn't look too bad in black lace, either, Miranda thought, as she inched toward the bedroom door. And come to think of it, *he'd* probably enjoy the crown.

"You know, Tom's been traveling a lot," Miranda said. "I'm not even sure he'll be here for—"

"You tell Tom you won't accept any excuses," her mother insisted. "A chairwoman never attends the ball without her husband." She hesitated. "Except that year Adrian Wright accidentally ran hers over with her Suburban."

Miranda just nodded while she pictured a Tom Smith pancake. Who knew what Adrian Wright's husband had been up to before she mowed him down? "Can we go downstairs now?" she asked. "I actually wanted to talk to Daddy about some things at Ballantyne. There's a serious problem with—"

"Oh, no, sweetheart," her mother said. "You can't do that." She replaced the crown and slowly turned to face Miranda. Real concern showed on her face. "I wasn't going to say anything, but your father saw the doctor today. He's been having minor chest pains and his blood pressure is out of control. Dr. Chainey put him on a diet and medication. And he's talking about an angioplasty."

Her mother's eyes filled with tears, a shocking sight in its own right. "He's been instructed to avoid stress at all costs," she said. "He's not to think about anything more taxing than his golf game."

Miranda wasn't sure how she made it through the meal. It was like traveling through a desert dying of thirst and actually reaching an oasis full of fresh water only to be told you weren't allowed to drink.

Her father was right there. He called her "Button" just like he always did, and he kicked up a real ruckus about not being allowed his usual martini or Rosalee's buttermilk-fried chicken. Heart-healthy baked chicken was clearly not the same.

But Miranda could see the fear in his eyes. And she noticed that although he ranted for form's sake, he ate and drank what he was served—a sobering confirmation that he knew this was for real.

Miranda pushed the food around on her plate and made polite conversation, trying not to be afraid for her father and trying to put the best possible spin on his chances for avoiding the very real specters of angioplasty and bypass surgery.

Her mother was right, her father's health had to be protected at all costs. There would be no laying down of anything at her father's wonderful feet. The burden of saving Truro was going to stay on her own inadequate shoulders.

Saturday morning's *Truro Gazette* carried the usual amalgamation of small-town life. Births and deaths, the latter outweighing the former; the latest shenanigans of Truro's greediest developer, who was "turning their lovely mountain haven into a magnet for Florida retirees and worse"; what was served at the St. Paul Baptist Church's annual potluck supper; and assorted

community happenings. But the column everyone—
Miranda included—turned to first on Saturdays was
Clara Bartlett's "Truro Tattles."

Miranda and her family had appeared in the column for as long as she could remember. Normally
Clara contented herself with glowing accounts of the
Ballantyne family's pet charities and Miranda's public
appearances on the company's behalf, but this week's
column was something shy of fawning.

Miranda's heart sank as she sat at her kitchen table
and read:

WHO'S MANNING THE BRA FACTORY?

This reporter can't help but wonder what Ballantyne's President and CEO was thinking when he
took off for the Orient for such a long period of
time.

We realize the company has been manufacturing the same sorts of unmentionables for over a
hundred years, but can it really operate on automatic pilot?

Shouldn't *somebody* be running the show?

chapter 7

On Sunday morning Blake sat between his grandfather and his daughter at the Truro First Methodist Church and pretended to listen to the minister. His grandfather was still as stone, and Blake was fairly certain he was asleep with his eyes open, a skill the old man had perfected recently and which occasionally scared Blake half to death.

His daughter Andie wasn't anywhere near as accomplished, and Blake had lost track of the number of times her eyes had fluttered all the way shut before she jerked back awake at the sound of the church organ or a responsorial reading.

Blake's particular skill was feigning interest while his mind wandered where it would. When he was

Andie's age, he'd passed the time replaying football games in his mind. At thirteen he'd begun picturing the female members of the choir naked, until that awful day when he'd accidentally mentally unwrapped the minister's two-hundred-pound wife and sworn off the exercise for life.

Today his brain teased at the puzzle of Miranda Smith and the absent Tom, and he knew his brain wasn't alone. Clara Bartlett's column had accomplished its mission: Folks were busy wondering and whispering, and a whole lot of eyes were trained on the Ballantyne family pew.

When it was time for the final hymn, Blake stood with the rest of the crowd, clapped a hand around his daughter's shoulders, and added his voice to a robust rendition of "How Great Thou Art." A few minutes later Andie had made herself scarce, and he and his grandfather stood out in the cold, shaking Reverend Simmons's hand.

"Great sermon, Reverend," Gus Summers said, as if he'd actually stayed awake to listen to it.

"Thank you, Gus. Blake." The pastor smiled and moved on to greet the rest of his flock.

Blake and Gus lingered on the lawn, making conversation as the crowd thinned out. Out of the corner of his eye Blake kept track of Miranda Smith, watching her move through the thinning crowd in her grandmother's wake. They made an arresting picture, the smaller white-haired woman with the tall dark-haired one behind her, both of them with their chins tilted at the same proud angle. With a nod to his grandfather he moved to intercept them. Gus fell into step beside him, smoothing a hand over his tie as they walked.

"Augustus." Cynthia Richard's voice rang out bright and clear as they approached. "You're looking well."

Blake watched his grandfather preen under the woman's regard and saw him steal a quick glance his way to see if he'd noticed.

"You're holdin' up pretty well yourself," Gus replied.

"Why . . . thank you," Miranda's grandmother said. "I baked brownies last night and thought you all might like some. I've got them in the car."

"Thank you, ma'am." Blake smiled at the older woman, then at Miranda, who looked like she'd prefer to be almost anywhere but there. He peered over her shoulder and then pretended to visually search her handbag. "What, no food? And here I thought we were walking around with signs on our backs that read, 'Feed Me.' "

Miranda raised an eyebrow. "I don't know, Chief," she said coolly. "My grandmother taught me not to feed wild animals. It can make them dependent and unable to fend for themselves." She paused. "And it's dangerous to let them associate you with food."

Gus guffawed and Miranda smiled with mock regret. "Did you forget to put nuts away for the winter?"

Blake laughed as Miranda Smith's green eyes lightened and he couldn't help wondering what kinds of things she was hiding behind them. Was it something as simple as marital discord? Or something more complex, as his anonymous caller had suggested? The questions, like the woman, intrigued him.

"I imagine we'll survive," Blake replied. "And I'm glad you don't feel guilty about not feeding the . . . animals." He leaned closer to Miranda and caught himself wondering why Tom Smith would go off and leave this woman alone for any length of time. He lowered his voice. "If there's anything you *do* feel guilty about at any time, you be sure and let me know."

"You bet, Chief." Her tone said *NOT*. "You'll definitely be the first."

He held her gaze, once again trying to plumb her depths. He'd been fascinated by puzzles since childhood; that fascination was one of the things that had ultimately drawn him into police work. He prided himself on not giving up until he found and fit all the available pieces together.

Miranda Smith's puzzle presented all kinds of interesting possibilities. He looked into her eyes once again and smiled. He could hardly wait to get started.

Up on the church playground, Andie Summers wiped at a grass stain on her navy wool blazer, then leaned back against the sturdy trunk of the old oak to stare up through the naked branches.

She was so focused on the winter sky above her that the tap on her shoulder almost sent her hurtling out of her skin.

"Who are you hiding from?" Jake Hanson's freckles

dotted the prominent bridge of his nose. He had dark hair that brushed the top of his shoulders and more than a couple of inches on her, which forced her to look up into his face as she barked her surprise.

"Jake the Rake" was Truro High School's starting center. Even Andie had to admit he moved like a dream on the court, and she could definitely understand why the girls in her homeroom pretended to swoon when they said his name.

Andie had never been this close to him before, and had never felt the impact of the warm brown eyes focused entirely on her. She had the feeling he could see all the way inside her. He had a basketball in his hands.

Slowly, as if her heart wasn't pounding and the blood wasn't whooshing in her ears, Andie pushed off from the tree and took a step away from him.

"I'm not hiding," she said. "I'm just checking out the view."

Together they peered down at the parking lot, which was rapidly emptying. Her dad and great-grandfather were standing there watching the Ballantyne women get in their car. In a minute they'd be looking for her.

"Yeah, best parking-lot view in town." Jake's gaze swung back to her face. "I saw you in the game against Franklin."

His voice was deeper than most of the other boys', and he had what looked like peach fuzz on his cheeks. Andie flushed. They'd lost the Franklin game by a good ten points.

He smiled and spun the basketball around on his

fingertip. "You all were looking pretty good right up until that last quarter."

"Yeah." Andie remembered her shot bouncing off the rim and into the hands of Franklin's center and felt her face fall.

He spun the ball again, then let it plop into his hands. "It happens."

Andie bristled. "Not to me."

He shrugged and spun the ball again. For a minute she thought he was going to ask her to shoot some hoops with him, but then a female voice floated up to them on the wind.

"Jake?"

They turned to see Mary Louise Atkins come up over the rise. She was a good four inches shorter than Andie, with a figure full of curves that had been poured into a pale pink skirt-and-sweater set under a gray wool coat. Her dark hair stirred lightly in the breeze, and her lipstick was the exact same shade as her sweater.

Mary Louise pretended to be out of breath as she came to stand next to Jake, even though Andie knew she did the mile in under seven minutes and worked out with a vengeance. Her eyes skimmed quickly over Andie before dismissing her.

"Hey, Jake, what are you doing way up here?"

Her affected southern purr made Andie want to hurl, and she automatically rolled her eyes. For a wild moment she thought Jake had rolled his too, but when she looked again he was smiling down at Mary Louise.

"Just talking basketball, ML. Nothing you'd be interested in."

He gave Andie a friendly nod and slipped an arm around the other girl. Then they turned and walked down the hill, the girl chattering and shooting adoring looks at Jake, the top of her head barely reaching his shoulder.

Andie watched until they disappeared from sight. Then she just stood there next to the tree, feeling tall and awkward and envious until, with a snort of disgust, she too, headed down to the parking lot. All the way down she wondered whether Jake Hanson even knew she was a girl.

Miranda spent Sunday afternoon in Tom's study filling a yellow pad with notes and ideas on everything from new stalls in the Ballantyne ladies' room—when you and your laptop spent long periods of time in one, you couldn't help noticing its deficiencies—to developing a new product line. But her notes, like her thoughts, were an unsatisfactory jumble of images and fragments.

The house was too quiet. She could feel it pressing in on her as she stared out the study window. *Alone*, it seemed to say to her. *You're all alone.*

"Tell me something I don't know," she answered back.

In the Dempseys' yard next door the birdbath was frozen. In the bare branches of the tree beside it, a squirrel hung by its tail and feasted on the cylindrical birdfeeder, totally focused on its mission.

She'd won countless beauty pageants by focusing that strongly on one event at a time: Win the interview, move on to the swimsuit, then focus on the evening gown. Nail the stage question and let the points add up. That was the way to salvage things at Ballantyne.

Miranda skimmed down her notes until she reached the word "receivables." If Fidelity National discovered the fake receivables on their own—and if she'd found them there was no way a team of accountants wouldn't—she'd never get the chance to put the company back on a firmer financial footing. Because there would be no company.

There was also the chance they wouldn't stop with just putting Ballantyne out of business. Even large financial institutions took the concept of fraud very personally. Fidelity National might not consider the matter finished until *somebody* went to jail.

Okay. Miranda wrote the words "Stall audit" in big black letters and added three exclamation points. If she could put together the resources to guarantee the line of credit, this might actually be possible. She made a note to schedule a meeting with the bank.

Number two? She thought for a second and wrote "Find Tom" in big block letters and tried to push aside the ache that accompanied it. At night when she lay in bed wondering when he had stopped loving her and why, she was afraid to explore what, if anything, she still felt for him. He had taken such complete control in leaving that her feelings seemed . . . moot and too often contradictory.

One minute she never wanted to see him again; the next she wanted the face-to-face confrontation she'd been denied. But most of all, she craved an ending to this limbo he'd left her in. After her appointment with the bank, she'd meet the attorney she'd been referred to and find out what her options were. Maybe then she could move on.

Number three was a little easier and a lot more enjoyable: dinner with Gran.

Shoving the legal pad aside, Miranda called her grandmother to let her know she was coming, then placed their usual order at Ling Pow's. She didn't intend to spill all the sordid details, but she did need a sounding board. And she also needed assets to pledge.

Gran's cottage was a cozy guest house on the grounds of the home she'd grown up in. After her husband's death, Gran had passed the big house down to Miranda's parents, along with the running of Ballantyne, and thrown herself into the renovation of the once derelict cottage. The two-bedroom home sat on the far side of a small orchard and allowed her to set up housekeeping at what she had declared the perfect distance from her daughter: far enough away to maintain her independence and close enough to impose her will . . . at will.

Some of Miranda's happiest childhood memories had been made in this cottage, where her grandmother's unconditional love and approval had been a welcome relief from her mother's more demanding form of affection. When Miranda turned sixteen, she'd been given her own key, and in the years that followed, Gran and her home had provided an important demilitarized zone in the escalating war between Miranda and her mother.

Late each spring Gran decamped for her house near the summit of Ballantyne Bald, where the higher elevation kept the small lake cold year-round and no airconditioning was required even on the hottest summer days. Her wedding gift to Miranda had been the adjoining lakefront acreage on which Miranda's small retreat—and Tom's love nest—now sat.

But Gran spent winters in the lovely stone cottage with its blazing fireplace and old mullioned windows. It was a place for kicking off one's shoes and curling up for a good read or whispered confidences. Miranda had learned to navigate the waters of small-town life from this life raft. Tonight she planned to ask for an oar without revealing where she intended to paddle the family canoe.

While Gran stoked the fire, Miranda deposited the "to go" cartons onto the farm table in the great room, then went back to the kitchen for plates and chopsticks.

They took seats across from each other at the scarred wooden table, and for a few moments the only sounds were the crackle of the fire and the rustle of cardboard as they served themselves.

Miranda began to relax as they chatted idly. Being with Gran was so much easier than fielding her mother's fitful attempts at communication, which swung between snippets of unsolicited advice and not-so-silent bouts of parental disapproval.

Miranda did not look forward to the day Joan Ballantyne Harper discovered her daughter had been dumped. And she sincerely hoped there were no pageants for almost-middle-aged women without husbands, for her mother to try to push her into.

She looked up and caught her grandmother eyeing her.

"So what do you hear from Tom?" Gran asked.

"Not, uh, much." *Make that nothing.* As always the *whys* of it stalked her. *Why* hadn't Tom shared the problems at Ballantyne and allowed her to help? *Why* hadn't he loved her enough to stay and face the consequences of his actions? *Why* had he needed lingerie and other women?

"He's gone inland to find new suppliers." God, she hated lying to her Gran.

"Tom certainly has an eye for satin and lace," Gran said almost conversationally.

Miranda froze as the silence stretched out between them; she actually had to clamp her mouth shut to keep from dumping the truth in her grandmother's lap.

"Well, perhaps in this case no news is good news," Gran finally said. "Tell me what you've been doing at Ballantyne."

"There are a few things that Tom has," Miranda cleared her throat and looked away, searching for words that would prevent an outright lie, "left me to take care of."

"And do you want to talk about those things?" Her grandmother, too, seemed to be choosing her words with care.

"Not exactly." Once again Miranda longed to lay down her load and go on about her life . . . or what was left of it. But she was the one who'd chosen a man who'd trashed the family business and then run off. With her father unavailable, it was her responsibility to try to clean up the mess. "But I do need to ask you for something, Gran. And I need to ask it on our old terms—no questions asked."

"You mean like when you took your mother's Volvo and transported that sow and her piglets in it? Or the time you faked a fever so you wouldn't have to participate in the seed-spitting competition at the Miss Watermelon pageant?"

"I thought older people were supposed to get feeble and forget things," Miranda said. "Do you remember every single thing I asked you to keep to yourself?"

"Just the highlights, darling. Your exploits have always helped keep me young, though I must say your life hasn't been anywhere near as entertaining since you married Tom."

No, nothing about her marriage to Tom felt very entertaining at the moment. She tried to dredge up an image of him posing for a Ballantyne catalogue, but the image just made her want to cry.

Miranda reached out a hand and placed it over her grandmother's. "I may have to pledge some personal assets to guarantee something at the bank, and I was hoping you'd sign the house on Hilton Head over to me. It's supposed to be mine on my fortieth birthday, but it would help to have it in my name right now."

"If it's money you need, Miranda, all you have to do is ask."

"I don't want your money, Gran. I just need to look a little better on paper right now." At least she intended to back up her claims with *real* assets rather than fake receivables.

"Well, of course, Miranda. That house is yours, and it makes no difference to me when you take possession of it."

"And you won't say anything to Mom or Dad."

"My lips are sealed." Her grandmother moved her chopsticks toward the remaining piece of pork and smiled as she lifted it to her mouth. "You wouldn't believe the secrets I can keep."

Blake took a beer from the refrigerator and went into the family room, where he sank down into the perfectly worn leather recliner. Gus and Andie were in their rooms, and the only noise was the muffled thump of the bass from Andie's stereo on the other side of the house.

In the relative quiet, Blake eased all the way back in the recliner, toed off his boots, and considered the existing pieces in Miranda Smith's puzzle.

To date he had one anonymous phone caller, lots of gossip, and Miranda Smith's sudden interest in her family's brassiere company—plenty of small things that didn't add up, but nothing big enough to sink his teeth into.

Of course the Truro grapevine was busy producing all kinds of theories about the state of the Smiths' marriage. At the Dogwood Café, odds were being laid on how long Tom Smith would stay away and how much his wife might or might not want him back. No one except his anonymous caller actually considered Tom Smith missing.

A troubled marriage wasn't really a matter for the law. But Blake could do some discreet poking around. He could have a little chat with the bank and the airlines; maybe get in touch with his buddy who handled investigations for Visa and MasterCard. Just a little nosing around to get a feel for the situation. If, in fact, there *was* a situation at all.

Of course, his best potential source of information was Miranda Smith herself. He raised the beer to his lips as he pictured the long legs and the clear green eyes. Then he replayed their encounters at the pool and at church, and the odd look in her eyes when she'd talked about Tom.

Something was going on, that much was clear. And

he was just the man to figure out what it was. All he really had to do was put himself in her path, let her know he was watching, and see what happened. He'd be just like that proverbial penny and just keep showing up.

chapter 8

The day of her meeting with Fidelity National, Miranda got up at dawn and drove to Atlanta for a 10:00 A.M. hair appointment. She'd prepared for the meeting as best she could; now she needed a new look to go with the corporate image she intended to present. It was critical that she be taken seriously.

By ten-thirty the floor around Miranda's chair was littered with strands of long dark hair. *Her* long dark hair. Just lying there. No longer attached to her head. She forced her gaze up from the dark piles covering the salon floor to the mirror in front of her. Antonio had pulled out a razor and was wielding it with abandon, transforming her long, heavy locks into a short, businesslike hairstyle—the kind favored by news anchors and corporate VPs—the style she'd asked for and which she now sincerely regretted.

Her gaze stayed fixed on the stranger in the mirror while Antonio spritzed something all over what remained of her hair, poofed up the top layer with his fingers, and whipped the cape off with a flourish.

"Ees really something, no?"

What it was was short. Very short. Miranda swallowed. "It's really, really…something all right." She swallowed again and told herself that grown women didn't cry over their hair—at least not in public.

She leaned in toward the mirror and tilted her head from side to side, but her hair was still short. With a last longing glance at the hair she was leaving behind, Miranda followed the stylist to the front desk. Without the familiar weight of hair on her shoulders, she felt naked and exposed. The air tickled her neck and tears pooled in her eyes.

"Ees very stylish. Very now," Antonio enthused.

She nodded, her voice little more than a whisper. "And very, very short."

"Jes, exactly." He smiled, pleased, before heading off to greet his next client.

Determined to keep her greater goal in mind, Miranda paid for the haircut and drove to Phipps Plaza in Buckhead, where she made her way to the designer department of Saks.

"I need a suit," she told the silver-haired saleswoman. "Something corporate but feminine. And I'll need shoes and a bag to go with it. And I wondered if someone at the Lancôme counter could freshen me up?"

An hour and a half later she was seated in the reception area of the Atlanta office of Fidelity National in a black Armani power suit over a winter white silk blouse. A new Coach bag sat on the floor at her feet next to the matching shoes.

Any minute now she would have to walk into John Anderson's office and start lying. If she was very lucky and he believed her tall tales, she would then go back to Truro and find a way to make those tales come true.

Miranda reached up to flip her hair over her shoulder in an automatic gesture she'd been making since childhood, but encountered nothing but shoulder. She was still adjusting to her lack of locks when an assistant arrived to escort her to John Anderson's office.

"John," she said, extending her hand for a brief, but firm, handshake as the banker came out from behind his desk to greet her. "Thank you for fitting me in today."

"Glad to do it." He led her to a seating alcove in the large corner office and motioned her to a chair.

Miranda sank down smoothly, folded her hands in her lap, and continued to maintain eye contact, something John Anderson wasn't managing so well.

"I was surprised to hear from you rather than your husband." He raised his gaze from her legs. "What can I do for you?"

Careful not to fidget, Miranda tilted her head and gave her version of the truth. "Tom is in China establishing suppliers for a new line we're considering producing. We felt it made more sense for him to stay until everything's set up satisfactorily, rather than waste time and money flying back and forth."

As she spoke, she modulated her voice and controlled the speed of her delivery, being careful not to speak so fast as to appear nervous, or so slow as to appear uncertain.

"Very sensible."

She smiled. "He's asked me to keep things running while he's away. You know, my husband and I met at Emory while we were working on our MBAs."

"I didn't realize..."

"Many of the decisions made at Ballantyne since my father retired have been made jointly by Tom and me."

She didn't mention that those decisions had been about wallcoverings and carpet. After all, she'd had better grades than Tom all the way through college, and her MBA carried just as much weight.

"I'm here because there's a problem with some of our receivables."

The banker looked surprised. "Yes, I sent a letter to your husband a couple of weeks ago stating our concerns."

"I know." She smiled again and managed not to mention where and in what condition she'd found the letter. She reached up to toss her hair, but, of course, it was no longer tossable.

"When I noticed the auditors were due next week, I decided to take a look at the receivables myself." She smiled yet again and moved to the crux of the visit. "I called all the accounts to verify the amounts and the dating." She paused and allowed concern to show on her face. "I'm afraid quite a few of them are having difficulty paying for the goods they received."

Once again he looked surprised by her admission. Walking into a lender and admitting to bad receivables was highly irregular. But not quite as irregular—or dangerous—as the bank discovering those receivables had never actually existed.

"I've contacted all of them to work out repayment plans," she continued. "But I don't want our line of credit jeopardized." She paused but kept her gaze locked with his. "I've come prepared to pledge personal assets to secure it."

Surprise flashed over the banker's features again. Miranda smiled and mentally crossed her fingers. For a moment she was back on a pageant stage waiting to hear the emcee call her name for the final five. When she thought she might pass out from holding her breath, the banker's face cleared and he smiled back at her.

"Actually," he said. "You've just made my life easier." He lowered his voice to a confidential tone. "One of our largest borrowers is experiencing a severe financial crisis, and I need to send a full team of auditors to deal with it. Perhaps now that we've clarified your position, I can postpone your audit until their situation is resolved."

Miranda smiled and uncrossed, happy to see someone else receiving the bank's full attention.

"Why don't I get the paperwork started on the pledging of those assets?" Anderson asked. "Then I'll be in touch again when we're ready to reschedule."

"Yes." Miranda stood and smiled again, barely managing to restrain her relief. "That would be fine."

She wanted to pump a fist into the air and do a victory dance on John Anderson's desk. Instead, she extended her hand in parting and made a graceful exit, being especially careful not to kick up her heels on the way out the door.

Miranda's euphoria was brief and didn't survive her meeting with Dana Houseman, Attorney-at-Law.

Somewhere in her mid-fifties, Ms. Houseman wore a conservative gray suit and sensible black shoes. Her makeup was minimal and she had a calm, understated manner. But her brown eyes gleamed with intelligence and her voice rang with authority as she gave Miranda a quick education on the way the world worked.

"I'll need ten thousand now and another ten thousand if we go to trial. And I'd like to put Harrison Maples on—he's our best PI—to track down your husband. That'll probably take another five thousand to start. The total will depend on whether your husband actually left the country or not. And how seriously he's hiding."

The attorney jotted notes on her legal pad and sat

forward in her desk chair. "The law *does* provide means to obtain a divorce whether your husband is ever seen again or not, but what we really want is to find him, serve him with papers, and haul his rear end into court so that we can watch him try to explain his actions to a judge."

Miranda definitely wanted to see Tom suffer, but she didn't necessarily want him surfacing until she'd gotten things under control at Ballantyne. What if she were in the middle of turning things around and he just showed up?

Dana Houseman speared her with a look that made her glad they were on the same side. "You need to understand that as long as he's running around out there he can show up and lay claim to half your business. Or do more damage to it. Or incur debt that you could be held responsible for. And if, as you've indicated, he's committed fraud in your company's name, you want to make sure he's the one who's punished for it."

Miranda looked over at Dana Houseman and sensed the attorney was just warming up.

"And *that's* assuming he's alive, Mrs. Smith. If he isn't, you could be looking at a whole other can of worms..."

"Yes, well." Miranda swallowed. "I can see why finding him would be a good idea." She smiled, but could feel the lack of wattage. The thought of actually seeing and speaking to Tom again felt completely alien and unimaginable. She'd been picturing him sunning on some Caribbean beach, but he could in fact be anywhere. Or nowhere.

Standing, Miranda slung her purse over her shoulder and leaned over to shake hands with the attorney. "I'll have a check out to you as soon as possible," she promised.

Just as soon as she figured out where to find the money.

In the rental car on the way back to Truro, Miranda compiled a mental list of things she needed to accomplish. All she had to do was convince the department heads she was working under Tom's auspices, come up with a scathingly brilliant plan for saving Ballantyne before Fidelity National showed up to do their audit, and find a ton of money to pay her new attorney and PI while appearing as normal as possible.

At this point it was the *normal* that was going to be the biggest challenge. Normal would require her to conduct Guild Ball committee meetings and her Rhododendron Prep group at the high school as if she didn't have a care in the world.

Normal.

It had a nice ring to it. If only she could remember how it felt.

Andie Summers slung a sweaty towel over her shoulder and wiped her face with one end. She'd shot something like a hundred free throws and spent another forty-five minutes working on her layup in preparation for Saturday's game against Claymore, and she was soaked through.

Tossing the towel out of the way, she dribbled down the court, automatically moving in at an angle to the basket to take her shot. The court was the one place she knew exactly what she was about; the rest of the time she felt like she was on a really bumpy rollercoaster and couldn't get off.

Her dad and great-grandpa meant well, but neither of them was exactly qualified to teach her how to deal with all the confusing things she was feeling. If she tried to explain it, her father would get that panicky look on his face and hand her some kind of booklet like the one titled *Now That You're A Woman* that he'd whipped out when she started her period. Her great-grandfather would make her tea and tell her not to worry. Both of them made complete fools of themselves whenever they were confronted with evidence that she was a girl.

Which was why she'd decided to take matters into her own hands.

A glance at the clock on the gym wall informed her she was too late for the shower she'd planned on. Hurrying now, she dropped the basketball into the rack and practically ran to the classroom where the first meeting of the Rhododendron Prep class was being held.

Twenty other girls were already seated and chattering

away when she arrived. They looked at her with a mixture of curiosity and pity, like she was some sort of alien life-form that had mysteriously landed in their midst.

Andie's insides twisted up, but she gave them the same shrug she'd been perfecting on her father, so they wouldn't know their laughter hurt. They, of course, were dressed in tight skirts and tighter sweaters, or low-slung jeans and cropped jackets. And of course they were mostly small and curvy, not tall and rangy like her.

Andie slid into a vacant desk at the back of the classroom, where she automatically slouched down as far as she could and studied the woman in front of the podium from underneath her lashes.

Truro was a small place, and Andie, like everyone else in the room, knew exactly who Miranda Smith was and what her family represented. Andie had seen her nodding regally at church on Sundays and when she passed by on the street—had even seen her talking to her own dad last Sunday—but Andie'd never come this close to actual conversation before.

Mrs. Smith was tall and lean and looked like she might have a steel rod surgically implanted in her spinal column. Her arms were long and well muscled, and though she was just wearing some kind of black pants and black turtleneck, even Andie, who didn't spend much time thinking about clothes, could tell they were NOT from the women's section at Wal-Mart or JCPenney.

Her green eyes seemed to be taking everything in and filing it away for future reference, but the thing that had everybody whispering was her hair, which *used* to be long and straight and now was short and kind of spiky looking.

"Good afternoon, everyone," she said. "I'm Miranda Smith, Miss Rhododendron of 1983. I'm also a part-time pageant coach, and my family's company, Ballantyne Bras, sponsors a contestant in the Miss Rhododendron pageant every year. This class is designed to teach pageant competition. At the end of the eight weeks, one of you will be chosen to represent Ballantyne in this year's pageant."

Uh-oh. Andie pulled out the mutilated course description and reread the things that had brought her here; Comportment, Beauty Tips, and Being Uniquely You looked pretty good, but pageant competition? Her dad thought she was taking extra basketball practice, and that's the way she planned to keep it.

"How many of you have already been in a pageant?" Mrs. Smith asked.

Half the girls raised their hands.

"All right." She smiled at them—a blinding flash of white teeth. "How many of you have *been* to a pageant?"

Three quarters of the room responded positively. Andie slouched down further in her seat.

"How many of you have watched Miss America on television and imagined yourself doing that final walk with the crown on your head?"

There were embarrassed giggles.

"It's okay. You can be honest."

Every hand in the room except Andie's shot up in the air. Andie did her best to disappear, which wasn't easy when you were five ten and a half in a room full of Lilliputians.

"We're going to cover a lot of ground over the next two months. Next week I'm going to sit down with each of you to help you develop a signature style—that special something that will set you apart. In preparation for that I want each of you to spend fifteen minutes in front of a full-length mirror."

There were giggles, and Andie guessed that for some of them this would be a decrease in mirror time. It didn't exactly sound like Christmas and the Easter Bunny to her.

"During that time you are to make a list of your physical assets and liabilities. Try to be honest."

Andie groaned and Mrs. Smith's attention swung her way. "I take it you're not looking forward to the assignment?"

"No, ma'am," Andie replied.

"You know, pageant competition doesn't differ all that much from athletics, Miss Summers. All you need is good raw material and the will to win."

Andie blushed.

"You do like to win, don't you, Miss Summers?"

Andie nodded slowly.

Miranda Smith nodded back and smiled, which took the sting out of her next words. "Of course, showering helps, too. Please make sure you've taken one before you show up next time."

There were some titters from the other girls, which Mrs. Smith squelched with one eyebrow. Andie sank back in her seat as Mrs. Smith ended the session. She stayed there while the other girls filed out.

When it was just she and Andie Summers, Miranda walked to the back of the room and slid into the adjacent desk. "Yes?"

"Do you think we could sort of skip ahead a little bit?" the girl asked. "I already know my liabilities and I, uh, was hoping to get to the fixing-them part as soon as possible." She leaned toward Miranda. "I don't know if you noticed, but I'm a little behind the rest of the pack."

Miranda studied the girl, intrigued. "Why don't you go ahead and list those liabilities for me," Miranda said. "Just so we're clear."

"Okay," Andie said. "I'm *too* tall, *too* thin, and *too* flat."

Miranda kept silent.

"There are other smaller things, but I think that pretty much covers the high points." She was trying for flip, but the anguish in her eyes was clear.

Miranda smiled. "You do realize that those things you just listed as negatives are things other girls would pretty much kill for?"

"Right." Andie's tone communicated her disbelief, but interest sparked in her blue eyes.

"You're tall," Miranda pointed out, "just like all those poor, underpaid supermodels."

She let Andie take that one in for a moment.

"And do you know why they have to be tall?" she asked.

Andie shook her head.

"Because clothes look better on tall people. They hang better, move better, show better."

The scowl left Andie's face.

"There is no such thing as too tall, unless you hang your head or," Miranda gave the girl another pointed look, "slouch down in your chair and act like you've committed some crime."

Miranda let the words hang between them before continuing. "Too thin? As long as you're not emaciated to the point of ill health, which is clearly not the case, there is no such thing. You're just not displaying your build to good advantage. Do you think Vendela and Kate Moss are sitting at home whining that they're too tall and too thin?"

Andie shook her head and sat up a little straighter in her chair.

"And as far as your bust goes, well, other than the obvious ribbing I get, given my family's business—one small liability does not a disaster make." They both glanced down at Miranda's less-than-formidable chest. "Luckily, you now have a contact in the bra business!"

Miranda grinned. "To recap . . . you've got brains, you've got tall and thin, you've got great athletic ability, and you've got tons of drive." She studied Andie closely, noting the high cheekbones, the vibrant blue eyes, and the naturally full lips, none of which the girl played up in any way. Her blond hair was thick and had potential, but it just hung there, contributing nothing.

She winced slightly as she imagined Blake Summers escorting his daughter to Stuart at the Truro Barber Shop and telling him to "take a little off the sides."

Miranda put a finger under Andie's chin and turned her face from side to side. She had the kind of angles a camera would love and her skin was creamy and free of blemishes.

She took out a piece of paper and started to make a list. "I want you to take this to Lupina at the Lancôme counter at Parisian in Claymore and tell her I sent you. She'll teach you how to apply the makeup you buy. There's a beauty supply store in the mall that will have the rest of the things you'll need."

She folded the piece of paper and placed it in the girl's hand. "I promise you nature has given you everything you need already, Andrea. The rest is just cosmetics."

Blake skipped his usual He-Man Breakfast at the Dogwood in favor of a large cup of coffee to go. He also started his morning patrol a little earlier than usual and extended it to include the beautifully manicured neighborhood of Chimney Crossings, which lay a good bit north of Truro's main business district, and which happened to be the neighborhood in which Tom and Miranda Smith lived.

It wasn't a completely conscious decision, and he wasn't sure exactly what he hoped to accomplish, but he figured the cul-de-sac in front of the Smiths' house was as good a place as any to watch the sun come up.

The neighborhood was nestled in a valley that had once belonged to a now wealthy farmer and commanded an uninterrupted view of the foothills that led up into the Blue Ridge Mountains. The Smiths' house was built in a plantation style, with tall white columns and a fan-shaped window above heavily carved double doors. Oversize wooden rockers lined a front porch that stretched the width of the house.

In Blake's humble opinion, the place called out for a family—or two. It was way too big for a couple; he could hardly imagine what it must feel like rattling around in the place alone.

Taking a sip of coffee, he let his eyes wander up to the second floor and passed a few pleasant minutes contemplating which room might be the master bedroom, and a few more picturing Miranda asleep in it.

He was still enjoying his little reverie when the garage door flew up and Miranda's bright red BMW began to back down the driveway. Before he'd gotten his coffee into the cup holder, she'd zoomed all the way down the drive and into the cul-de-sac. Two seconds later she was pulling into position beside him and lowering her passenger window.

Feeling slightly silly, he lowered his own window and raised his cup of coffee in silent greeting.

"Good morning," she said brightly while her garage door slammed shut. "Were you looking for me?"

"No," he replied easily. "Just, uh, patrolling the neighborhood." He holstered his coffee and offered his best "I'm here to serve and protect" smile.

"I didn't realize you did Chimney Crossings in the morning."

"Well, I like to mix things up a bit. It's not a good idea to be *too* predictable." He looked her in the eye. "People start thinking they can get away with things."

She was dressed and made up and had a briefcase on the seat next to her. When she blushed and lifted a hand to her neck, he realized it wasn't just her attire that looked different. "You cut your hair."

"Yes." She removed her hand from her neck and placed it on the wheel.

"And you're off to . . ."

"Ballantyne," she said. "Tom, um, asked me to take care of some things while he's away."

"Oh."

They studied each other for a long moment and he thought he sensed her inner squirm, but he had to admit she looked pretty damn calm on the outside. And remarkably businesslike, too.

"So, if you don't need anything, I guess I'll be off, then," she said, and put her car into gear.

"Yeah, me too," he replied, doing the same. "You go on ahead, I'll bring up the rear."

They played a very sedate version of follow-the-leader back through Chimney Crossings and out onto the two-lane road that wound back to Truro, him sipping his coffee and trailing behind her while she drove with exaggerated care, pretending she didn't mind having a policeman on her tail. There'd been no real exchange of information, but he'd let her know he had his eye on her, and he thought he'd done a pretty good job of maintaining control of the situation.

He was congratulating himself on his strategy when his cell phone rang. Surprised at the readout on the caller ID, he was trying to decide whether she'd actually called Anne Farnsworthy for his number, as he brought the phone up to his ear.

"Listen, Chief," Miranda said. "I wasn't sure if you were planning on following me all the way in to work, but I need to go a little faster—we're going two miles under the speed limit and it's costing me time."

"No problem." He added a little pressure to his own gas pedal when she increased her speed.

"Oh, and just so you know, I'm planning to drop a letter in the drive-through mailbox up at the post office, and then I thought I'd pick up something to go at the Dogwood, if you need a potty break or anything."

"Got it." He smiled and saw an answering flash of white teeth in her rearview mirror.

"Do you want me to get you something while I'm in there?" she asked way too sweetly.

"Uh, no, I think I'm fine, thanks."

"Okay." She laughed lightly in his ear. "Just thought

I'd check. I'm sure this stakeout business can be really draining."

He was still smiling over that one when she came out of the Dogwood, knocked on his window, and presented him with two glazed doughnuts and a fresh cup of coffee.

They parted ways in front of the gates of Ballantyne and he tipped a doughnut to her as he drove off. It was the most enjoyable bit of surveillance he'd done in a long time.

That night Miranda called the long-delayed Guild Ball committee meeting to order with a loud rap of the gavel on her mother's Country French kitchen table. The table, which was new and coordinated perfectly with the rest of her mother's recently redecorated kitchen, was covered with linen napkins in every conceivable shade of beige.

"You're joking, right?" Miranda stared at the napkin samples strewn across the oak table. "You didn't really just spend an entire week deciding between taupe and ecru?"

Angela Johnson bit a Botox-inflated lip. "Do you think I rushed things? There was another very nice cream-colored linen that could . . ."

Miranda bit her own lip. It had been an incredibly long day and she still had to come up with an idea that would halt Ballantyne's downward spiral. It was all very well to try to appear "normal," but who really cared what color the napkins were?

"Angela," she said. "This is not a matter of life and death. It's a napkin. For wiping one's mouth."

"But your mother is always saying it's the little things that make the event large." Angela's big brown eyes filled with tears. "And I heard you spent almost a month selecting those lavender tablecloths last year."

"You're not going to cry again, are you?" Miranda groaned. She had a company and a town to save and she didn't want to talk about napkins anymore.

Angela's permanently eyelined lids blinked furiously.

Feeling like she'd just kicked a puppy, Miranda turned her attention to the woman on her right. "Okay, why don't we move on to the entertainment report and come back to the napkins later?"

Angela sniffed her agreement. The entertainment chairperson, Vivien Mooney, perked up and cleared her throat. "At the last meeting we voted to ask Daniel Hawthorne's Band of Renown for a tape." Vivien paused. "Unfortunately, I don't have one to play you yet."

"Because..." Miranda prompted.

"Because Daniel Hawthorne sent me a recording from the Blumfeld bar mitzvah in Atlanta."

Miranda felt her eyes widen.

"Thirty whole minutes of 'Hava Nagilla.' "

There was a moment of silence while they all pictured the members of the Truro Ladies' Guild and their tuxedo-clad husbands circling the Masons' Hall in an unskilled attempt at Middle Eastern folk dancing.

"Right, then..." Miranda turned to the next committee chair. "Gloria, where are we with the menu?"

"Originally we were going to do a surf and turf. But then I polled some of the girls at the club, and Margaret suggested going French. Then Charles brought up the idea of going Italian." She frowned. "Maybe we should go back to the surf and turf and add a side dish of linguini."

"But if you do anything too saucy I'll have to look at darker napkins." Angela's voice trembled.

"I don't see how anyone could dance with all that heavy food in their stomachs, anyway," Vivien said.

Miranda considered pointing out that if they hired Daniel Hawthorne they could work off the heavier food doing the hora. But the members of the Ladies' Guild were not known for their senses of humor. "Look, ladies, all we need is entertainment, a menu, and some decorations. This is the Guild Ball, not consensus-building at the UN. How much time do we really need to spend on these details?"

The gasp was collective. Angela began to cry, while six sets of eyes stared her down across the table. Miranda fingered the wisps of hair on her neck.

Rebecca Wyndham reached out and put an arm around Angela, who now had tears running down her recently sculpted cheekbones. "What in the world has come over you, Miranda?" she asked. "These *insignificant* details used to mean something to you, too. But all of a sudden you've got an attitude the size of Montana." She cocked her head, and Miranda could tell she was about to let her *really* have it. "And I cannot figure out what you were thinking when you did that to your hair."

Ouch. Miranda ran a hand through the short part of her business "do" and told herself not to get defensive. Not long ago she'd been one of these women. Like them, she'd spent her days volunteering, playing tennis, and lunching at the club, with a few light PR duties for Ballantyne thrown in to make her feel like she was "doing something." If her life had left her a little less than satisfied, she hadn't been dissatisfied enough to do anything about it.

It wasn't their fault her life had changed so completely. Nor was it their fault that she could barely think of anything anymore but finding a way to save Ballantyne and Truro.

Miranda took a moment to really look at the other women at the table. For the most part, they were intelligent and well-intentioned. They gave their time and energy to their families and their causes. If their lives demanded no more of them than that, who was she to criticize?

There'd be time enough for being cut off from everyone once the news of her dumping and duping hit the Truro grapevine. Why should she alienate everyone now?

As she studied them, two of the women adjusted a bra strap and another did that subtle squirm that said her brassiere was cutting into her in some way. Miranda perked up and keyed into the women in the room, not as members of her committee but as bra wearers and buyers.

When had anyone at Ballantyne last asked their customers what they wanted in a bra? Women's wants and needs were constantly evolving. They expected different things from their lives than they had ten years ago; surely the same could be said for their bras. Truro was filled with women who wore Ballantyne bras out of a sense of loyalty and obligation. But when was the last time someone asked them how they felt about those bras?

Miranda stopped fingering her hair. "I'm sorry. You're right. I was way out of line. I've just been under a lot of pressure lately."

There were murmurings of forgiveness, but Miranda wasn't really listening. She had just figured out how to kill several birds with one simple stone. "We need to sample some dishes so that we can make a decision about the menu. And we need to choose the wines that will go with the meal. Most of the other decisions will evolve out of that. Vivien," she said to the entertainment chair, "why don't you try that group over in Franklin that played at Elaine Knight's anniversary party? And I can give you the number for the booking agent out of Nashville we used one year.

"I'll speak with Henri at Mais Oui Catering to try to solidify some of Rebecca's thoughts. Then we can all meet at my house at the end of the week to sample the wines, taste the menu suggestions, and listen to whatever demos Vivien comes up with."

"You don't have to do all that, Miranda," Rebecca said.

"No, I'd like to. It'll be fun."

"What can we bring?" Vivien asked.

"I'll arrange everything. I'm just going to ask one thing in return."

"Name it," said Rebecca, while the others nodded enthusiastically.

"Everybody who comes Friday night has to come prepared for a frank discussion about their bras."

chapter 9

Miranda stood outside the Ballantyne conference room in her new Armani suit. Placing her hand on the doorknob, she paused a moment to let her stomach settle. Once again she reached up with her free hand to flip her hair behind her shoulder, and once again, came up with air.

It was time to walk through the door, take her seat at the conference table, and lie to the department heads assembled inside. Before she could chicken out, she drew in a deep breath and entered the room.

Coming to a stop behind the empty seat at the head of the table, Miranda smiled at the group and made eye contact with each of them individually, just as she had been taught to do when walking into a pageant interview.

Panic swirled in her stomach, but Miranda knew she had only a matter of seconds to take command of the room. Several of those present waited expectantly. Others, like Helen St. James, were clearly waiting for her to fall on her face. All of them were staring at her hair.

Carly Tarleton sat at the far end of the table with her notepad in front of her. Her nod of acknowledgment was subtle, but reminded Miranda that she wasn't completely alone.

With her smile firmly in place, Miranda took her seat. She wanted her hair back so that she could flip it over her shoulder, would even have settled for running her tongue over her dry lips. Instead, she maintained eye contact and continued to smile, knowing full well that what she said now and how she said it was critically important.

"Tom is still in China and won't be back for a while," she began.

People murmured.

"I've been consulting with him regularly. In fact, he keeps sending me directives via E-mail." She flashed them a smile and lifted "Exhibit A"—the stack of E-mails she'd sent herself using his account.

Carly looked up from her note-taking, clearly surprised. Myrna, the head designer, and Todd Holmes, who led the manufacturing division, looked reassured, as Miranda had intended.

Encouraged, Miranda kept her voice steady and her tone matter-of-fact, as if running a department head meeting was something she did every day. "We've decided that I'm going to fill in for Tom while he's gone."

There was a stunned silence, which Miranda ignored. "And we're not going to just mark time waiting for him to get back."

"Why is he still in China?" Myrna asked.

"He's adding to our supplier base," Miranda replied.

"Are you sure he's not looking to go offshore?" Todd Holmes asked, referring to the trend to move manufacturing to other countries where labor was cheap.

"As long as there is a Ballantyne, manufacturing will take place in Truro," Miranda said.

"Who are *you* to promise that?" Helen St. James questioned.

The room went still again.

"At the moment, I'm the acting president of Ballantyne."

"And what qualifies you to lead this company?" the woman demanded.

The others looked shocked, but it was clear to Miranda the question needed to be addressed.

"My name qualifies me for this position," she said firmly. "I grew up in this business. It's in my blood." She paused to let that sink in. "And my MBA won't hurt, either."

Everyone in the room, except for the head bookkeeper, looked satisfied.

"We intend to take this company in new, more

profitable directions," Miranda continued. "To do that we need everyone pulling together."

Miranda looked at each department head in turn, but let her gaze linger on Helen St. James. "Anyone who can't handle that idea, or working with me in Tom's absence, should start sending out résumés."

Miranda waited for the other woman to look away first. The bookkeeper's hands, with their beautiful French manicure, were clenched on the table. Those nails, coupled with her hostility and her frantic E-mails to Tom, made Helen a top contender for the woman who'd posed with her hand on Tom's ass. But while she might have had an affair with Tom, she had seemed genuinely shocked that so many of the new receivables were fraudulent. Surely if she'd been Tom's accomplice, she wouldn't have stayed to take the fall.

"Ballantyne Bras is at a crossroads," Miranda concluded. "We can no longer afford to go head to head with the 'big boys.' We need to find a new niche, a new path to follow. I'd like you to make time this week to brainstorm ideas for a more profitable direction. The only stipulation is that manufacturing remain in Truro."

There was excited chatter as she ended the meeting. Only Helen St. James remained sullen and unenthusiastic. Knowing she had to neutralize the woman's negativity, Miranda motioned Helen to wait while the conference room emptied out. When it was just the two of them, Miranda faced the other woman. "You were in a position to know about the bad receivables. It's hard to believe you didn't."

Fear and anger showed on the other woman's face. Miranda looked into Helen's eyes and tried to imagine what she and Tom had been to each other.

"I didn't think to question them. They were Tom's accounts, and I . . ."

"Seem to have trusted the wrong person." Miranda let the statement sink in. She was tempted to add "Welcome to the club," but resisted. She needed to proceed with caution. If she acknowledged that Helen had been personally involved with Tom, she'd feel compelled to fire her and while that would be really satisfying, it wouldn't necessarily be in Ballantyne's best interests.

"But you're in luck," Miranda continued. "Because I don't particularly want someone new digging through the books right now." Miranda delivered the whopping understatement with a straight face. "Assets have been pledged to cover those receivables, and if you think you can keep the situation to yourself, you can stay."

"Why, you can't fire me anyway. Tom'll . . ."

"What, rush back to save your job?" She shook her head gently. "I don't think so." Miranda didn't elaborate, intentionally letting Helen think she'd made things up with Tom.

"And if I don't keep quiet?" the woman asked.

"Then I'll have no choice but to take the books to the authorities and tell them what I *think* may have happened."

It was a lie of course, but she'd told so many, what was one more? "My only concern right now is Ballantyne," Miranda said. "I'm not going to let anything or anyone jeopardize this company again. I won't be taking my eyes off you for a minute."

They stared at each other until Helen St. James finally nodded and looked away. Miranda held her breath as she watched the other woman go. As the old adage said, it was good to keep your friends close... and your enemies even closer.

It was almost six o'clock when Carly popped her head in to the office doorway. "Do you need anything else?" She already had her jacket on and her purse over her shoulder, but she'd brought a pad and pen.

Miranda motioned her in and waited while she took a seat on the other side of the desk. "I'd like to do a tour of the whole facility sometime next week. And I'd like some time built in to talk with key employees along the way."

Carly nodded and started making notes.

"Then I want to talk with Human Resources about employee benefits and incentives."

Carly's pen paused as she shot Miranda a questioning look.

"I also need the phone number for the research group and repping firms we use out of New York. And I'd like a written report from Bookkeeping on how new accounts are currently set up along with the shipping

addresses for these accounts." Miranda slid the list of
fictitious businesses across the desk. "If Helen gives
you too much grief, refer her to me."

"Thanks, Boss . . ." Carly stopped and they eyed each
other for a moment. Then the assistant bent her head
and scribbled something on her pad.

Miranda looked over the list she'd made once more.
"Am I missing anything?"

"No, you're being very thorough. More thorough
than I would ever have imagined." Carly tapped her
pen nervously. "In fact, this doesn't really look like the
to-do list of a person who is just filling in for a couple
of weeks."

Miranda met the younger woman's gaze. She was intelligent and efficient. Against great odds she'd earned
a college degree and appeared to be a dedicated
mother. She was also ambitious, and she knew the day-
to-day workings of the company in a way Miranda
didn't.

In order to pull off the resurrection of Ballantyne,
Miranda would need at least one ally; someone to help
run interference; someone she could trust to be on her
side. The idea of sharing the truth was so appealing it
made her head spin. She opened her mouth, already
anticipating the relief she'd feel when the burden was
no longer hers alone, and realized she couldn't take the
risk.

If word got out before she knew what direction to
take the company in or how to get it there, there could
be a panic from which Ballantyne might never recover.

Miranda licked her lips and swallowed back her confession. Then she looked down at her watch in a gesture of dismissal no one could misinterpret. "I'm just trying to take care of some things Tom's been too preoccupied to deal with," Miranda said, being very careful not to mention that it was dressing up in lingerie and stealing money that had distracted her husband from his job. "And I've invited members of the Ladies' Guild to my home Friday night to serve as a, um, a kind of focus group. I'd like you to be there to take notes."

"Sure." Carly stood and turned to leave. As she whirled around, her things got tangled up in her purse strap and flew out of her arms. A sketch pad bounced off the top of the desk and landed on the floor, its pages exposed. They both bent to pick it up at the same time.

Carly flushed as they each grabbed a corner and pulled. The top pages came free and scattered across the floor.

Miranda looked at the drawings that covered the sheets of paper. Surprised, she looked up at the other woman. "Where did you get these?"

The assistant swallowed. "I drew them."

"What are they?"

"Bras."

"Yes, I can see that," Miranda responded dryly. "But why are you drawing pictures of them?"

"Because I want to be a designer." Carly raised her chin a notch as if expecting laughter, but Miranda could barely take her eyes off the drawings.

"I've been studying in my free time with Myrna. And I'm also learning CAD—you know, computer-aided design. But I do better sketching by hand like Myrna does."

"And these are?" Miranda asked.

Carly stepped closer. "Drawings of a bra I designed for myself." She blushed again. "I'm petite but busty. Off-the-rack stuff doesn't work that well for me."

Miranda took the pad and flipped through the rest of the sketches. "What about this?"

"Well, Anna in marketing saw what I'd designed for myself and asked if I could design something for her. She wanted a different kind of cup and she likes the padded satin strap instead of the normal elastic strap."

"Have you had any of this costed out?" Miranda asked.

"No, but Myrna said it shouldn't be too expensive. I mean we already have all the pieces, you know? I'm just combining them in different ways."

Miranda handed the drawings back to Carly. She and the women in her family had always had custom bras. It was one of the perks of being in the business. But she'd never really stopped and thought about how other women got the right style and fit.

Miranda picked up her purse and a stack of folders from the desk and walked out of the office with Carly while the seed of an idea took root in her brain.

On her way home, Miranda stopped at Ling Pow's to pick up her takeout order. The restaurant was mobbed, and after squeezing through the front door, she began to maneuver her way toward the cash register. There she waited next to the fish tank, her gaze drawn to one unhealthy-looking fellow who seemed to be floating on his side, until Ling Pow himself beckoned her forward.

"Ah, Missy Smith. So sorry. I don't see your ticket here."

Miranda's stomach gave a growl of protest. She was tired and hungry and in no mood for crowds. "How long will it take if you start it now?"

"Want please, such good customer, but kitchen way behind. I go check."

Miranda stepped out of line and back into the empty spot near the fish tank. Her friend had rolled over onto his back and seemed to be staring up at the ceiling. Every once in a while his tail fin moved, but the other fish were giving him a pretty wide berth.

Unable to stand the look in the fish's eye, Miranda glanced up over the tank into the main dining room, where all twenty tables were occupied. Her gaze skidded to a stop when it collided with Blake Summers's.

She would have turned and run if she'd had any hope of getting out of there without looking like she was turning and running. She'd already backed up against the fish tank as tightly as she could without joining her walleyed friend.

Before she could think, she heard Ling Pow's voice beside her. "I put in usual order," he said. "Let me find place to sit. You eat now."

"No, I want to—"

"She can join us."

Miranda whipped her head around at the sound of Blake Summers's voice.

"No, I..." Their game of vehicular follow-the-leader was still fresh in her mind. She definitely didn't want to have a meal under his sharp-eyed scrutiny.

"Good. Good. You go sit. I get food." Ling Pow turned and headed back to the kitchen.

"It's okay," Blake assured her. "We almost never bite."

She suspected that was exactly what they were going to tell the floater in the fish tank right before they reached in with the net. Nonetheless, she followed Blake to the table where he pulled out her chair and Gus greeted her warmly. After a polite hello Andie buried her face in her menu.

"I almost didn't recognize you without your hair," Gus said.

Miranda ran a hand down the bare neck she was still getting used to. "Yes, well, it's still me." She smiled at Andie who, if she wasn't mistaken, was trying to become invisible. "Hair doesn't make the woman any more than clothes make the man." *Though apparently lingerie sometimes did.*

"Why the haircut?" Blake asked.

"I'm going through a sort of... corporate phase."

She kept her tone purposely flip, the carefree housewife trying on business for a lark. It wouldn't do to sound too desperate around Blake Summers; but she hadn't meant to sound quite so inane, either. There was something about the man that made her want to babble.

Blake shot Gus a look. Andie had turned her attention to a pamphlet of Chinese proverbs that Ling Pow left on each table. The girl was still a novice in the art of makeup application, but the mascara made her blue eyes pop, and the pale pink lipstick and blusher added a nice glow to her skin. Miranda would have liked to bring up the prep class so she could avoid the subject of her absent husband and ailing company, but Andie was acting as if they'd never met.

"Tom's in China right now visiting small manufacturing towns," Miranda volunteered unnecessarily. "It could take a while."

She was saved from further babbling by Ling Pow's arrival with their food.

"Always like see big smile on best customer," he said before bowing his way back from their table.

"So just how often do you eat here?" Blake asked, his tone still casual.

Miranda ate her soup as she considered the question. "Oh, I don't know, two or three times a week, I guess, if you include takeout. It depends."

"On what?"

She finished another spoonful of soup. "On, uh, Tom's schedule." Strange how difficult it was becoming to think of him in the present tense.

It hit her then how seldom she and Tom had dined at home alone. At some point it had gotten hard to keep the conversation going, and they'd begun eating out with others. Or popping into the club for a bite, where they'd be sure to run into someone they knew.

Then there were the nights Tom had worked unexpectedly through dinner. She looked up to find Blake studying her.

"Have you spoken to Tom lately?" he asked quietly.

Ling Pow arrived with her main dish, and Miranda busied herself passing back her empty soup bowl and taking a sip of freshly poured tea. When she finished, Blake was still waiting for her answer, his blue-eyed gaze fixed on her face.

"Actually, I speak to him regularly," she lied baldly. "When he's in some of the less-developed areas communication is more difficult."

"I see." Blake took a sip of his tea but kept his gaze locked with hers.

Miranda slipped her chopsticks out of their paper holder and imagined Blake Summers's reaction if she were to tell him her husband had left her and wasn't coming back. Maybe she'd reveal that part now and save the fraud and impending bankruptcy part for dessert.

Then she could ask him whether he preferred briefs or boxers, on the grounds that she didn't want to be attracted to another man who might own prettier underwear than she did. *Attracted?*

He took a bite of what looked like chicken with cashew nuts, and Miranda watched the food slip between his lips. In between her own bites she watched him ply his chopsticks with ease, watched the food

travel up and into his mouth. Watched him...
hokay...she tore her gaze from his lips and searched
her brain for a topic that wouldn't lead to her abandonment, the state of Ballantyne, or what he might
look like without any underwear on at all.

"I'm so glad Andrea decided to take my Rhododendron Prep class."

Both men's heads popped up and Andie froze in
mid-chew.

"What did you say?" Blake asked.

"I said, I'm glad Andie's in my Rhododendron Prep
class." She looked at the three shocked faces and her
speech slowed. "I, uh, definitely think it will be a great
experience for her."

Blake did a double take worthy of a Looney Tunes
episode. "Are you talking about *my* Andie?"

Andie winced and swallowed as he pointed toward
her.

"*This* Andie?"

"That would be the one."

"You're telling me that *my* daughter, who leads the
NCAA in free throws, and who is going either to Duke
or Chapel Hill on a full athletic scholarship, is preparing to be in a...beauty pageant?"

He said "beauty pageant" in exactly the same way
one might say "lap dancing" or "drug smuggling."
Miranda bristled.

"She's not actually required to enter the pageant,
but my class will prepare her for it if she should choose
to, yes."

"We're not talking Future Serial Killers of America here." Miranda laid a hand on the girl's arm. "Andie's a lovely young woman. There's no reason in the world why she shouldn't learn how to present herself as one."

"It's no big deal, Dad." Andie's face was flushed with embarrassment. "I just wanted to learn some, you know, girl kind of stuff."

They were spared from hearing how he felt about girl stuff by the arrival of Ling Pow, who took the remains of their dinners and left the bill. Miranda and Blake both reached for it.

Blake's hand was warm against hers, and Miranda almost jumped at the unexpected contact. Blake reacted too, and they both said, "I'll take care of it."

Gus guffawed. "I got it." He plucked the slip of paper out of their frozen fingers. "But you two need to simmer down. Nobody's goin' anywhere 'til they open their fortune cookie."

He opened his first and read, " 'The road to forever is traveled one day at a time.' " Augustus nodded his head solemnly. "What's yours say, Andie?"

Andie squinted at the thin rectangle of white paper. " 'Your game of life will be long and exciting.' " The girl rolled her eyes.

The old man motioned to Miranda, and she ripped the cellophane off her cookie and broke it open. Heat stole up her neck and across her cheeks as she read, " 'One must throw out the old in order to embrace the new.' " Gee, maybe Tom had gotten this one and taken it to heart.

Without prompting, Blake pulled out his sliver of paper. With a slow smile he recited the words allegedly baked into his fortune cookie. " 'Things are seldom what they seem,' " he said, nailing Miranda with those outrageous blue eyes. " 'But given time and patience . . . you will divine the truth.' "

chapter 10

The bills were spread across the dining-room table. Miranda had hoped that stacking them by category would make the piles appear smaller, but the opposite was true. There were the household expenses, which she'd never looked at all at once before and never wanted to again. Plus the club and both cars; she was still making the payment on Tom's Mercedes for fear they might come to collect a car she wouldn't be able to produce. Not to mention the loan on Tom's fishing boat and the ongoing balances on their credit cards.

Tom's paycheck, which was automatically deposited into their household checking account, was just enough to meet their regular monthly expenses. But with everything else wiped out, there was no room for error, no shopping for anything other than necessities, and no way to pay for a divorce attorney or a private investigator.

Was it just a month ago that her biggest worry was finding a stamp to pay a bill on *time*?

As she rearranged the stacks of bills, she noticed that the massive mahogany table, like everything else in the house, bore a fine layer of dust. Afraid to let the efficient but gossipy Maria in the house to spread word of Tom's empty closet and dresser, Miranda had held the woman off, paying her not to come while the mess and dust grew thicker.

The matching china cabinet was equally dusty, its glass front so cloudy she could hardly see the collection of Limoges inside.

The Elizabethan dining suite had been carted to the new world by long-dead Smith ancestors. They were important family heirlooms, but she doubted Tom had given them so much as a passing thought on his way out of their life. He'd written them off just as he had her.

Stung, she went into the kitchen, came back with a dishrag, and began to wipe away the coating of dust. Then she found the Windex and cleaned the glass so she could see the china inside.

It was then that she remembered Grady Harris of Asheville's Très More Galleries salivating after this very dining suite. Why, he'd been begging her to sell it since the first time he'd seen it.

Quickly Miranda toted up the dining suite's worth

in her mind. Then she moved into Tom's study, where she eyed the old oak desk and the antique rifle cabinet with its carefully collected contents. There was a complete Victorian bedroom suite in the guest bedroom at the top of the stairs.

Miranda fought back the twinge of regret at the thought of parting with such prized possessions and focused on the sweet feeling of relief.

"Grady Harris," she said out loud as she went to hunt down his business card, "this is going to be your lucky day."

Andie finished basketball practice and left school for the short walk home. Lights glowed in the neatly tended houses she passed and smoke curled up from chimneys. Everything was brighter and cleaner here than in Atlanta, and though she'd complained bitterly at first about the slowness with which everything happened in Truro, she'd gotten kind of used to the more relaxed pace and quiet friendliness. Everybody knew your business, but they didn't rub your nose in it too much. Here she was the chief's daughter and Gus's great-grandchild. Her mother called it Hicksville and refused to set foot in it, but Andie kind of liked it here. Not that she planned to mention that to her dad any time soon.

At the corner of Dogwood and Digby she heard someone coming up behind her and turned to see Jake Hanson eating up the sidewalk between them.

"Hey, wait up," he shouted, and like an imbecile Andie looked all around her. She barely managed to resist pointing at her chest and saying, "Who, me?"

He smiled again when he reached her. "Where ya headed?"

"Home," she said, only her voice got caught in her throat and it came out sounding more like "om." "I mean, *home*. I'm going home."

He smiled but didn't laugh, and she liked the way his eyes twinkled without making fun.

"Want some company?" he asked.

"Okay." Shrugging, she turned, and Jake fell in beside her. For once she was the one who had to take longer strides to keep up.

While they walked down Cedar Avenue, Andie tried to figure out what was supposed to happen next. She considered trying to make chitchat like she'd seen Mary Louise and her friends do with boys, but her mouth was too dry.

"You have practice today?" he asked.

"Yeah." Okay, it was only one word, but at least she hadn't tripped over it. Andie licked her lips and concentrated on putting one foot in front of the other.

"We're playing the Bobcats next week."

She snuck a peek at him and her brain shouted at her to say something but it didn't tell her what. "I, uh," she cleared her throat, "I saw their shooting guard at the playoffs last year. He's got a great hook."

"Yeah, we came out ahead the last time we faced them, but it was close."

Okay, this wasn't so hard. This was basketball. She'd been talking sports with her dad since she was five. "How, um, how many points do you think they'll score against you?"

Jake flashed really white teeth at her and then, miracle of miracles, he started to talk. For the next ten blocks he covered their chances to win district, and what he thought of every adversary he'd ever faced. He never bragged, and he even laughed at his own mistakes, which Andie really liked. Without realizing it she began to relax, so that when he asked her opinion she was able to answer freely. Before she knew it, they were having a conversation.

Too soon they were on Main Street and approaching the police station. Normally, she stopped in to say hi and get a snack from Mrs. Farnsworthy, or a ride home with her father. Today he was standing out front talking to the mayor. His eyes narrowed as she and Jake approached. Then his mouth stopped moving. The mayor turned to see what he was staring at.

Andie's cheeks went hot and her toe caught on an uneven place in the sidewalk. Jake automatically reached out and grabbed her arm to steady her. Real shock registered on her father's face.

Andie didn't know what to do. After a quick moment of silent prayer, she fixed her father with a stare that said, "Don't embarrass me or I'll never speak to you again," and slowed just a little.

"Hi, Chief. Hi, Mayor." Jake's tone was as casual as you please, but Andie could hardly breathe. She kept her gaze on her father, telegraphing her single all-important message, praying that just this once he wouldn't feel the need to haul her over and put her through the third degree.

His lips parted as if to speak, and from behind Jake's back, Andie silently, but adamantly, shook him off. She wanted to yelp with relief when he pressed his lips back together and did nothing more than nod politely and raise a lone finger to the brim of his hat.

Andie kept walking. As they passed, she lifted one hand in a very small wave. "Hi, Mayor. See you at home, Dad."

She could feel her father's gaze on her back all the way to Morrison, but he didn't shout after her to come back or demand to know what she was doing walking with a boy. Andie vowed to put an extra dollar in the collection plate on Sunday now that she had proof there was a God.

On Friday evening Miranda made it home from her Rhododendron Prep group just before the caterer was due to arrive.

She raced around the house stashing things out of sight, wiping down countertops and laying a fire in the fireplace, then dashed upstairs to shower and change. By the time the committee members began arriving, her house looked like her house again. Her antiques, many of which were putting in their farewell performance before heading off to auction tomorrow, shone from a recent application of lemon oil. A fire flickered in the fireplace and a Norah Jones CD played softly from the sound system.

While a server passed samples of suggested hors d' oeuvres, Miranda moved from group to group, a bottle of wine in each hand. As she circulated, she encouraged everyone to try each of the appetizers, took note of their opinions, and pushed the wine at every opportunity. Getting this group to talk freely about their bras was going to require serious priming of the pump.

Soon the buzz of excited female conversation filled the room.

"Red or white, Angela?" Miranda asked.

"Goodness, I never can decide."

"Maybe the white, then. There'll be plenty of opportunity to try the red when we sample the entrees."

"Red? But what if somebody spills it. Maybe I *should* choose a darker napkin. What if . . ."

"Angela," Miranda said calmly, "I don't know if you're aware of this, but we don't have to return the napkins in the same condition we get them. It's okay if they get dirty."

With a relieved smile, Angela tossed back her glass of wine with a speed that spoke of more experience than Miranda would have suspected. Without comment, Miranda continued working the room. She filled glasses and made chitchat, subtly introducing her thoughts and suggestions to the committee heads. The decibel level rose with each bottle of wine consumed, and when the committee members began threatening to undress in order to compare plastic surgeons, Miranda knew it was time to sop up some of the alcohol with food.

"Okay, everyone," she said, "be sure to take at least a taste of everything so we can get a vote tonight."

In the dining room the ladies flirted with Henri, whose European good looks and accent had helped make his catering business the most popular in three counties, then took their plates into the great room.

Angela Johnson stood and raised her wineglass. "I want to propose a toast to Henri," she proclaimed, her normal reticence discarded several glassfuls ago.

The crowd cheered.

"So here's to Henri." She smiled gleefully. "His sausage is first rate."

Titters greeted this drunken observation.

"And there's nothing wrong with his prawns, either!" a voice from the back added.

Miranda swung her gaze around the room. Women lounged on every available flat surface, and every one of them was stuffed to the gills with fine wine and good food.

"How about a nice round of applause for Henri and the fabulous food he prepared?" Miranda said.

Henri gave a small bow and blew a kiss to the crowd. There was a heartfelt round of applause, a few woo-woo-woo's.

"Girls . . ." Miranda began.

"I want him to do something French." Angela's

finely rechiseled features were flushed with wine and unnatural exuberance.

"Yeah. Me, too!"

Henri's smile faltered.

"Right," Miranda cut in. "Why don't I recap our menu choices while Henri packs up?"

"Merci, mesdames." He offered them a final wave, but his eyes darted about. Miranda suspected he was looking for possible escape routes.

Angela popped up again. She swayed to her own rhythm as she offered up a personal cheer. "Oh, Henri, he's so fine. He's so fine he blows my mind. Oh, Henri!"

"Sit down, Angela. You're embarrassing yourself," Miranda whispered.

"They're completely inebriated," Carly observed.

"And we're drunk, too!" someone shouted.

Henri fled and the crowd sighed in unison as the kitchen door closed behind him.

Deciding she'd better get to the real purpose of this meeting before her focus group became completely un-focused, Miranda raised her voice so she could be heard above the din. "Ladies," she said, "there's more wine if anybody wants some. But the time has come to talk about bras."

chapter 11

The room fell silent. Then Rebecca Wyndham reached for the bottle of white wine. "We thought you were joking about the bra thing."

"Nope, no joke," Miranda replied easily.

"I mean, what could we possibly tell you? Your family is in the business."

Miranda took a sip of wine and thought about that. "True. But I'm not asking you how to manufacture the bra. That's my problem. I want to know what you think would make the bra you wear . . . better."

There were murmurs, but it was clear no one wanted to be the first to speak.

"Okay," Miranda said. "How many of you own at least one Ballantyne bra?"

All hands went up, and Miranda wondered if they were afraid she'd insist on proof.

"Okay, then, let's just think of this as a customer survey. All I want to know is what you'd like to see in a bra. If you could design your own, what would you include or get rid of?"

Miranda saw Carly open a notepad and set it on her lap. They were all pretty much looped, so she figured it would only be a matter of time before somebody found the courage to speak out. She sat quietly and waited.

Marjorie Kendall, who sat in a corner of the couch, glanced down at her chest, which was even flatter than Miranda's. "I'd pay big money for something that stimulated growth."

There was laughter, but Miranda was too relieved to have someone speak up to let anyone stop the flow. "Try being this flat and born into the bra business. I'm lucky my parents didn't try to give me back!"

This drew more laughter, which Miranda leaped on. "It's like being a Hemingway and not knowing how to read."

"You should try being on the other end of the spectrum," Vivien said as she took a swig of wine.

Miranda looked more carefully at the entertainment chair, who appeared to be somewhere around a 38 double D. "So you're looking for something that—"

"I'd kill for real support without underwire. And just because I'm big-breasted doesn't mean I want to wear something that looks like prison-matron issue."

"No kidding," Gloria said. "I have dreams about a

front closure that doesn't pop open when you accidentally squeeze your boobs together."

"Yeah." Vivien grinned. "Happened to me last Sunday when I bent over to get something out from under the next pew. You should have seen the reverend's face."

Everybody laughed, but they were laughing *with* each other. Miranda couldn't help smiling herself. Out of the corner of her eye she saw Angela reach for the button of her blouse. "Ang—" she began.

"Do you all want to see the pair Malcolm bought me for my birthday?"

"No, thanks, Angela." Miranda purposely broke off eye contact, afraid the other woman would take any scrap of attention as a sign of encouragement. She took a sip of wine and knew real relief when Sheila Taylor spoke.

"I just want a bra that'll keep my boobies from banging into my knees when I walk."

Laughter.

"I don't need them up around my neck," she continued. "I just want them off my lap when I'm at the dinner table."

More laughter. Miranda looked over and spotted Carly scribbling like mad.

Angela stood and reached for her buttons again. "Anybody want to see four thousand dollars' worth of perky?"

Miranda reached out and gently pushed her back down into her seat.

"Right, so let's recap, shall we?" Miranda began. "Everybody seems to want soft, comfortable, and supportive."

"And that's good-friend supportive," said Karen. "Not maniacal-mother supportive."

"I don't even need support anymore," Angela crowed. "I've got my own built right in." She took another gulp of wine while everyone watched, fascinated. "You should see these suckers!"

"And pretty," someone else chimed in, drawing attention away from the eager-to-undress Angela. "I want comfort that's pretty; not flowery, but nice. Nobody does those two things really well together."

"I want something that lifts *and* pushes me up."

"And I like lace, but it has to be lined so it doesn't scratch."

"Oh, yeah. And don't forget the matching panties."

"Nylon uppers with real cotton crotches."

"I like straps set in the middle."

"And I need elastic, the double-wide kind."

The suggestions came fast and furious, and no two suggestions were the same. The specifics they wanted were almost as endless as Angela's determination to bare her breasts.

Miranda tried to imagine how Ballantyne could possibly find a way to make everyone happy when everyone had a different set of requirements and fantasies. The only way to make each woman happy would be to build her a bra by hand.

Like the one Carly had designed for herself, and the totally different one she'd designed for Anna in shipping.

It was then that the lightbulb went on. She closed her eyes and visualized the individual components of the bras Ballantyne currently manufactured. Then she visualized each of those components made available like options on a car. So that a woman's bra was built just for her, like a custom vehicle.

Miranda didn't know yet how to make the idea work, or what kind of money it would take to do it. But in that one bright shining moment she saw its fullness and perfection. Just like Angela Johnson's new breasts when she reached up and pulled her blouse up over her head.

Miranda spent Saturday morning straightening and puttering and trying to remember the days when a napkin color really mattered and she and Tom had been...content?

As the coffee brewed, she dreamed of having her old life back. Well, maybe not her whole life—maybe just the part where she didn't have to sell off or pledge her possessions to appear solvent and she didn't have the fate of the family business and its three hundred employees hanging over her head. And Clara Bartlett wasn't taunting her with headlines like today's BEAUTY QUEEN CRACKS WHIP AT BALLANTYNE.

The morning paper lay on the kitchen table, but she was not yet ready to read the rest of Clara's latest dig.

Instead, she poured coffee into a gold-rimmed Limoges cup and filled a matching plate with an assortment of Henri's hors d'oeuvres, then carried them into the next room so that she could enjoy the Elizabethan dining suite for the last time.

She feasted her eyes on the freshly polished woods and intricate carvings as she ate her breakfast, knowing that in a matter of hours the suite, her china, the Victorian bedroom furniture in the guest room, and the best pieces from Tom's study would be history.

She fingered the filigree handle of the Limoges cup, letting her lips linger over its lightly scalloped rim. She'd miss the china and the furniture. In fact she already regretted their absence from her life. But they were just things, after all. Beautiful, expensive things whose sole purpose in life was to decorate and impress—which was exactly what *she'd* been doing until reality reared its ugly head.

By Saturday afternoon Blake knew that Tom Smith had emptied his and Miranda's bank accounts sometime during the first week of January, and that Smith hadn't used any of his credit cards since the afternoon of January 7. His anonymous caller, who placed her sporadic calls from various pay phones around town, claimed she'd been having an affair with Tom up until the day he left, and no one he'd questioned had spoken to the absent Smith, except his wife, who seemed to have replaced him at Ballantyne.

On the surface it looked like nothing more mysterious than a divorce coming down the pike. Except that Miranda kept insisting her husband was only away on business and he didn't know if that was her pride talking or some sort of hope that things might get patched up.

Once again he drove through Chimney Crossings with no real plan other than to shake Miranda's tree and see what fell out. But this time he bypassed the cul-de-sac and drove up to the top of the driveway.

Feeling good and in command, he whistled a little tune as he took the front steps to the porch two at a time and knocked smartly on the door. The whistle died on his lips when he got his first sight of his quarry in the faded gray sweats.

Apparently no one had told her that sweat clothes were supposed to cover a person's body and leave them looking lumpy and unformed. Hers rode low on her slim hips and clung to her long shapely thighs. Worse, the sweatshirt ended just below her breasts, which left her midsection exposed. The neckline had been chopped up, too, so that it hung off of one bare shoulder and left large areas of smooth creamy skin naked to the eye.

She said hello, but his own greeting went the way of his whistle.

"Did you need something?" She tugged at the sweatshirt and wrapped her arms around her bare midriff. Her skin goose-bumped.

"It's cold," he managed. "Can we talk inside?"

Not giving her the opportunity to refuse, he steeled his body against its automatic reaction to her and stepped into the foyer. When she moved to close the door behind him, he dragged his gaze up from the firmly rounded rear end and reminded himself of the number of cops who lost their jobs each year due to women and alcohol. Unfortunately, he was having a hard time thinking clearly—a problem he attributed to all the blood that had left his brain in its mad rush south.

Trying to marshal her thoughts, Miranda took her time with the door, closing it carefully, waiting for it to click shut, then turning the dead bolt for no good reason other than the time it would take. Then she realized her mistake; she'd given Blake Summers time to look around. The room to the left of the foyer was the...

"What happened to your dining room?" he asked.

Quietly she pulled the door of the office closed and moved to stand beside him in the archway, where they confronted her recently emptied dining room. Swallowing, she fingered what turned out to be her bare neck and sorted through potential explanations.

"I'm...redecorating," she said, finally. "All those antiques were just so...old." She winced. "I'm planning to go more contemporary. You know, simpler, cleaner..."

"Emptier."

"Yes." She looked up into the blue eyes and told herself to shut up. "I mean, it'll only be empty until the new furniture arrives. It's, um, much easier to paint this way."

The silence grew between them. His presence unnerved her, and she had a bad feeling it wasn't only because he was a cop and she had something to hide. She was completely and irrevocably aware of Blake Summers, her naked midriff, and her lack of underwear, pretty much in that order. She cleared her throat and tried to picture herself fully dressed. In body armor.

"Change can be very positive," she added. "Very... freeing... don't you think?"

"That would depend on whether you're the changer or the changee."

She blushed as she remembered his mother's desertion and his wife's more recent refusal to move to Truro.

"I'm surprised you have time to redecorate when you're so busy 'cracking the whip at Ballantyne.'"

Miranda blushed again at the reference to Clara Bartlett's column. "I don't imagine you came here to discuss my decorating or that busybody," she said, relieved not to hear the nervousness she felt in her voice. "What can I do for you?"

Blake Summers leaned back against the archway and folded his arms across his chest. He regarded her with eyes of a blue she had heard referred to as "Mediterranean," but she could have sworn he was stumped for an answer.

"I uh, I'd like you to come up with a reason to drop Andie from the Rhododendron Prep group."

"You would?"

"Yes." And then with increased certainty. "Yes, I would." He peered over her shoulder and she was glad she'd managed to close the office door before he could see that it was empty, too.

"Why?"

"Because my daughter is a serious athlete." He nodded his head, apparently pleased with his answer. "And I don't think it's good for her to be distracted by . . ." He waved his hand, clearly trying to come up with an appropriate word.

"Being a girl? Learning who she is? Making the most of her assets?" She smiled. "I hate to break it to you, Blake, but your daughter is absolutely *dying* to be a girl. If she hadn't found me and my Rhododendron Prep class, she would have found someone else."

He stepped further into the foyer and shot a look up the stairs.

"She's not herself anymore," he said.

"I doubt that . . ."

He stopped looking around and focused completely on her. "She charged two hundred and fifty dollars at a department store makeup counter—two hundred and fifty dollars from a girl who's never even worn Chapstick. And she's got a boy walking her home. A boy! As if she weren't capable of making it home under her own steam."

Miranda laughed as the irony of the situation hit her: Blake Summers, the hottest of the hot all through high school and college, the last boy any father had wanted to see anywhere near his daughter, could not bear the thought of his own daughter falling prey to a high school hottie.

"Blake, she's a fifteen-year-old girl. All of these things are completely normal."

"Not for Andie." He shook his head in total denial. "I want my daughter back; the jock one who doesn't need anything more than a ball in her hand."

Miranda almost felt sorry for him, would have felt sorry for him if he hadn't used his daughter as an excuse to come snooping around.

He was standing so close she could feel his body heat and smell the clean, woodsy scent of him. Her skin goose-bumped again, only it wasn't from the cold. She had a brief and very clear flash of how great he'd look naked, and shocked herself further with the realization that she no longer had a husband to whom such a thought might seem objectionable; she had no husband at all.

"I'm afraid I have to excuse myself now," she said firmly. Miranda smiled at his surprise as she reached around him to pull open the door. "But you tell Andie I said hi. And that I'm looking forward to seeing her in class next week."

She ushered him out the door before he could protest and stood there listening as he stomped down the steps and drove off. Then she sagged against the door frame and concentrated on pulling her thoughts and hormones back from the dangerous ground onto which they'd strayed.

She didn't believe Blake Summers was all that worried about Andie getting in touch with her feminine side; he'd been mostly bluster, without a whole lot of objections to stand on. This had been an exploratory mission, pure and simple, but she was in no mood to be explored. She'd just started getting things under way at Ballantyne; the last thing she needed was the chief of police sniffing around.

chapter 12

Monday sped by, and it was after five o'clock when Miranda buzzed for Carly. The assistant wore the same navy skirt she wore every other day and the same cream white sweater accessorized by inexpensive costume jewelry, but she looked just as unruffled as she had when she arrived that morning. Miranda knew the younger woman's take on the "focus group" would be worth hearing.

"Do you have your notes from Friday night?" Miranda asked.

"Yes. And I made some sketches, too."

"Good, do you have them with you?"

Carly opened her pad and pulled out a handful of sheets, which she passed across the desk.

Miranda leafed through them, looking at each drawing and the notes jotted beside it. She felt a tug of excitement. "What's this?"

Carly craned her neck to see. "That's a bra that includes the extra support Mrs. Mooney was asking for, you know, without the underwire. I had Joe in Engineering work out the specs." She hesitated. "I think we could make it work in a variety of fabrics."

"What are all these straps?"

"Well...it seemed like everybody wanted something different, so I started with all the possible components. These are the different cup styles, these are the straps, and this is a list of materials. I figured they could sort of be mixed and matched, depending."

"On?" Miranda held her breath.

"On the customer's needs?"

Miranda smiled at the assistant, relieved. Perhaps she wasn't as far out in left field as she'd begun to worry she was. Her excitement grew. Without intending to, she began nodding her head, spilling her ideas, and—God help her—looking for confirmation.

"That's what I want to do, Carly. I want to take Ballantyne from a little company, trying to keep up with the big boys, to a manufacturer of custom lingerie. The only part I haven't figured out is how to market them."

She saw Carly's surprise, but she couldn't seem to stop the flow of words. This woman had captured the essence of her idea on these torn-out pages so that it was no longer a vague and abstract thing. If Carly

Tarleton could draw it, surely she, Miranda, could make it happen.

Her words came out so quickly she was practically tripping over them. "We're going to design a whole boatload of options. We are going to revolutionize the bra-buying experience for our customers so that all any woman has to do is make her choices. This strap with that cup, with this closure—" She pointed to the drawings. "In one of twenty fabrics. And then... then we're going to custom-fit it to her body. And then we're going to sew it for her—by hand, right here in Truro."

"But—"

"Imagine it, Carly. Right now bras are necessary evils. Women wear them because they have to. They don't feel good and they don't always do the job they're supposed to. I'm going to change that."

The possibility hummed inside her. She could see it so clearly now, and for some reason she couldn't explain, she needed Carly to see it, too. "I'm going to make each Ballantyne bra the perfect combination of support, comfort, and fit for the woman who wears it. It will be the one item of underclothing a woman is prepared to pay top dollar for—because it will be and do exactly what she wants it to."

"You're going to do this?"

Miranda nodded.

"But what about the Board?" Carly paused, and Miranda knew what was coming next. "What about Mr. Smith? What's he going to say when he comes back and sees what you're doing?"

Miranda looked Carly Tarleton in the eye.

Carly looked back, and Miranda could almost see the questions forming in her mind. "Where is Mr. Smith and when is he coming back?" she asked.

Miranda swallowed.

"He isn't in China, is he?"

There was a silence while they stared at each other, taking each other's measure.

"He could be," Miranda said carefully. She paused, uncertain whether to continue, then plunged ahead. "Or he could be on the North Pole." She hesitated again. "Or in the next town." It wasn't exactly a conscious decision, but before she knew it she was spilling out the whole ugly truth. "I have absolutely no clue where he is . . . where he's been . . . or where he might be planning to go."

It sounded so bizarre she could hardly believe it herself. And yet she felt incredible relief at finally speaking the horrible truth out loud, and a paralyzing fear that she had spoken it to the wrong person. "He left for work on the morning of January eighth, and I haven't seen or heard from him since."

"But that was more than a month ago." Carly's voice was incredulous.

Miranda nodded again.

"Did he take anything with him?"

"All of his clothes and most of our money. He left me a note saying he wasn't coming back."

The blue eyes got even wider, wider than Miranda would have thought it was possible for eyes to get. And all she could think was, *Oh, God, don't let her panic. And please don't let her tell anyone.*

Barely breathing, Miranda waited for Carly Tarleton's reaction. She braced herself for horror, imagined she might see fear, hoped she wouldn't get pity.

But the younger woman's smile was lopsided and her tone wry as she said, "I guess this wouldn't be the time to talk about the promotion I was promised."

The air whooshed out of Miranda's lungs, and she knew her own smile was filled with relief. "If we don't take this idea and make it work, Carly, getting a promotion will be the least of your worries."

At home that night, Miranda wrote a check for fifteen thousand dollars and signed the retainer agreement Dana Houseman's office had sent. After slipping them in the return envelope, she booted up her laptop and logged onto Tom's AOL account so that "he" could inform his staff of his confidence in his wife's ability to lead Ballantyne Bras on its newly discovered path.

She fired off E-mails to Myrna Talbot in Design and Todd Holmes in Production, spending a good bit of time trying to imitate Tom's terser communication style. Briefer messages went to Human Resources and Shipping and Delivery. When her fingers stilled on the keyboard, she noticed the silence around her. As always when things got quiet, her mind worried at the question that wouldn't go away. Where was Tom? Was he living happily somewhere on the other side of the world with a new woman, new friends, new interests, and new lingerie? Was he really on a beach as she'd pictured him, or somewhere farther north where he'd light a fire and bundle up with someone else?

How strange that someone she'd loved could rip her and her world out of his so completely. Was she so unimportant, so unmemorable that Tom could waltz off without a backward glance?

She logged off the computer, checked to be sure she'd locked the front door, and wandered the darkened house.

In the bare dining room, memories of their first Thanksgiving and Christmas assailed her. She could see herself and Tom hosting those first holiday meals in their brand-new home, remembered that surprising sense of acting like grown-ups, when in fact they'd been excited children.

Moving into Tom's empty office, she relived her disastrous stamp search and all that she had discovered since. Tom's collection of antique rifles no longer filled the far wall, but her only regret about that was that she hadn't had a chance to use one on him before she sent them to auction.

The office was a large, well-lit space, and as she imagined it redone to suit her taste, another truth hit her. Even if Tom reappeared tomorrow, they could never go back. She had hired a divorce attorney and once Tom was found she'd be a divorcée. There was no reason to leave this, or any other room, as it was. She could redecorate the whole damn house in hot pink and lime green if she chose—assuming she could do so without money.

Snapping off the office light, Miranda went up the stairs and past the now empty guest room. Too tired to bother with the creams and moisturizing oils she'd applied so meticulously in her previous life, Miranda washed her face and brushed her teeth quickly before sliding into bed, which she was surprised to note no longer felt too big or too empty.

"'Til death do us part" had been replaced by "Until things get tough," and while she was debunking myths and fantasies, it appeared that real men not only ate quiche, some of them also wore women's undies.

Staring up into the dark, she focused on plotting out her immediate future. She needed to keep Tom's disappearance under wraps until she'd won Board authorization and had Ballantyne on the road to her vision of recovery. She felt the flutter of excitement the custom-bra idea produced, and she vowed anew to make it happen.

Once she had Ballantyne on its feet, she'd deal with Tom and whatever that entailed. She shuddered as she imagined her rejection and abandonment reduced to fodder for Clara Bartlett's column, but she really didn't have much choice. Tom Smith had stopped being her husband the day he left her, if not before. The only thing she wanted from him now was her freedom.

Carly was hanging up the phone the next morning when Miranda arrived at Ballantyne. She had a strange expression on her face and looked quickly over her shoulder, clearly afraid of being overheard.

Miranda looked over her shoulder, too, though she wasn't sure what she was checking for. Everything looked like it usually did at eight-thirty on a weekday morning except Carly, who appeared ready to vibrate right out of her skin.

"Are you all right?" Miranda asked.

"I don't know." Carly looked over her shoulder again and dropped her voice to a whisper. "Guess what?"

Miranda leaned in closer, matching her hushed tones. "What?"

"I heard from Mr. Smith today."

Miranda's gaze swung to the phone. "He called?" She tried to gather her thoughts, but her head was spinning. "And you hung up?"

"No, not the phone. I got an E-mail. He wrote that he finally got to an Internet café in," she looked down at the sheet of paper in her hand, "Shen..."

"...zen," Miranda finished.

"Oh." Carly looked at Miranda, confused. "Did you get one too?"

"No, but almost everyone else did." She gave Carly a meaningful look. "I believe yours read, 'My wife tells me you're indispensable. Thanks for—'"

"Oh!" Carly said as realization dawned. "You mean you..."

Miranda nodded. "I thought it would be good for morale if everyone knew Tom was behind me."

Carly looked impressed. "Gee, that's a nice touch. I

mean, I knew, and I still thought . . . Did you say everybody got one?"

"Miranda?" Helen St. James strode toward them, murder in her eye.

"Not exactly." Miranda winked at Carly.

The bookkeeper came to a stop in front of them, her attention focused squarely on Miranda. "I heard that Mr. Smith e-mailed, and I don't understand why I didn't get one. I want my E-mail account checked."

Carly backed toward her desk. Miranda headed to her office, Helen right behind her.

"You didn't get an E-mail?" She tried to look regretful. "I told him you were hoping to hear from him the last time he called."

The bookkeeper fell back a step.

Miranda was getting ready to dismiss the woman when the intercom buzzed.

"Yes, Carly?"

"Mr. Smith's on line two."

It was Miranda's turn to fall back a step. Helen's head jerked up as if she'd been slapped. Miranda knew the feeling.

"Um, okay," she said to Carly.

After a long moment the assistant buzzed back. "Mrs. Smith?"

"Um-hmm?"

"If you want to speak to him you need to pick up."

"Oh, right. Thanks." She lifted the receiver to her ear and sank down into the desk chair. Helen watched as if she were contemplating leaping over the desk and wrestling the phone out of Miranda's grasp. Given how hard Miranda's hands were sweating, she doubted she'd offer much of a challenge.

Miranda cleared her throat and spoke into the phone. "Hello?"

There was a delay during which she and Helen St. James studied each other warily.

"It's me." Carly's voice whispered. "I thought a phone call might kind of reinforce the E-mail thing. Does Helen look really freaked out?"

The bookkeeper was practically sitting on her hands.

"Yes. Definitely." Miranda sat back and crossed her legs. "So, um, where are you calling from?"

"The supply closet."

Miranda bit back a laugh. "I see."

"It's a mess in here. Somebody really should—"

"That's great." Miranda plastered a smile on her face. "I miss you too, sweetheart." She considered putting her feet up on the desk, but decided that would be overkill. "So, what did you think about the...um... sketches I e-mailed you?"

Helen St. James leaned forward in her chair while Carly waxed eloquent about the sketches.

"Really?" Miranda laughed gaily and snuck a look at Helen. "Yes, me, too, darling. But you need to put your mind back on business." She giggled.

Helen St. James frowned and sat back.

"Does she have that pursed-lip thing going, like she swallowed lemons?" Carly asked.

"Absolutely."

"Good. And by the way, those sketches were obviously drawn by someone with real design talent. I think we should give whoever that is the promotion they were promised and a big fat raise."

"Do you really think so?" Miranda asked sweetly.

"You know I do!"

"Well, I'll keep the idea in mind."

Miranda heard a knock and the rattle of a doorknob through the receiver.

"Uh-oh," Carly hissed. "Hold on!"

"All right." Miranda smothered her smile. "I love you, too."

Helen jumped to her feet and crossed to the desk. "But I need to speak to—"

Through the receiver Miranda heard the scrape of metal and Carly saying, "I think I can reach that with the ladder."

Then she heard Carly shriek, and there was a loud thud, followed by the sound of the phone clattering to the floor.

"Is everything all right there?" Miranda asked cautiously.

No response.

"Um... Tom?"

Muttering, the scrape of metal, and the sound of footsteps resounded in the background. The receiver clattered on the floor again and then got picked up.

"Hello?" Miranda said. "Tom?"

Carly came back on the line full voice. "Phew, I thought she'd never leave."

"Yes, dear, me too," Miranda cooed while the book-keeper's face turned a very deep red. "Helen's here and she wants to speak to you."

And then, because she was only human and every instinct she possessed told her Helen St. James had been having an affair with her husband and continued to do her best to thwart her at every turn, Miranda puckered her lips and made really sickening smooching noises into the phone.

"Yes, darling," she added in a distinct simper. "I'll tell her you'll speak to her another time. I know we'll talk again soon."

Without a word, the bookkeeper turned and left the office, closing the door none too gently behind her.

"Yeah," Carly said on the other end of the line. "I think we should definitely talk again. But next time I'm calling from somewhere I won't need to climb a ladder, and I plan to hold you to that raise."

Miranda laughed into the receiver, well pleased with their unplanned charade. "Whatever you say, sweet-ums. I can't tell you how much I enjoyed the call."

And then she hung up, reflecting that revenge, how-ever small and petty, could be very sweet indeed.

chapter 13

Telling himself it had nothing to do with the ever-present memory of Miranda Smith in those gray sweats, Blake kicked Operation Bad Penny into high gear. At every opportunity—and in a town the size of Truro the opportunities were plentiful—he simply made it his business to run into her.

He gave up his usual spot at the counter for a table next to hers at the Dogwood; had his already spotless cruiser washed so he could chat her up in the waiting room of the E-Z-Suds Car Wash, and got Gus and himself and Andie invited to Sunday dinner at Cynthia Richards's.

Today he'd trailed her to Truro's answer to Starbucks, Hyram's House of Coffee. With a spring in his step and a double latte in his hand, Blake walked over to Miranda's table.

She looked up from her coffee as he approached and the green eyes became hooded. And then combative. Who would have thought being annoying could be this much fun?

"Ah," she said, "if it isn't my new shadow."

"May I?" He nodded to the vacant seat.

"And if I say no?"

"Then I'll sit over there." He pointed to the next table, less than a foot away. "No harm done."

With a snort of resignation she motioned him to join her. "I don't know what you hope to achieve by tailing me around Truro like this. People are starting to talk." She nodded toward the group of ladies watching from a corner table.

"They were talking long before I arrived."

"Oh?"

"Oh, yeah." He whipped out his notepad. "Would you like to hear some of what they're saying?"

She blinked. "You've been taking *notes*?"

He smiled. "I take my responsibilities very seriously."

Miranda took a sip of her coffee. "Read away," she finally said. Her expression was unconcerned, but the set of her shoulders and grim line of her lips told him otherwise.

"Well," he said earnestly as Hyram poured Miranda another cup of coffee and then retreated, "there *are* opposing theories. For example, Jewel down at the

Dogwood thinks Tom's staying away as a kind of trial separation."

Her mouth dropped open.

"Because as Enid over at Chez Nous said, and I quote, 'No man goes off on a business trip for over a month if his marriage is healthy. No, sirree.' And of course Suzanne—she does nails there—pointed out that you could have gone with him, if you'd had a mind to."

"You went to the beauty salon and asked people's opinions? About *me?*" Her tone dripped disbelief.

"Well, it wasn't a formal survey or anything. I just went in for a trim and the subject happened to come up." He grinned. "What do you think?" He ran a hand through his newly layered hair. "I like it, but I'm not sure it was worth the extra ten bucks."

A tic appeared in her cheek. He flipped through the notepad again, wondering what it would take to make her lose control completely. "Yep," he said. "Most everybody's going with marital problems. Except Grace at the Piggly Wiggly. She's kind of hoping Tom went over to bring back one of those international orphans."

Miranda choked on her coffee and Blake waited until he was sure she didn't need a clap on the back. Or mouth-to-mouth resuscitation.

She looked as if smoke might come out of her ears at any moment, so he didn't mention that some folks thought Tom had been fooling around for some time. Or that he'd claimed it was Miranda's fault they didn't have children.

The more he heard about Tom Smith the less he liked him, which was the direct opposite of how he felt about Miranda. "Quite a few people thought you'd be better off if Tom didn't come back at all." He looked her in the eye. "And one or two of them pointed out you haven't exactly been going around town boo-hooing for him to come home."

"Why, of all the—"

"Of course, I've still got that anonymous caller who insists you've done Tom in and buried his body somewhere so you could take over Ballantyne." For some reason he didn't understand, he didn't add that the caller had also claimed to be having an affair with Tom.

"I wouldn't have to kill him to do that," she said. "The company's not called Ballantyne for nothing."

He studied the woman across from him; took in the narrowed eyes, the rigid jaw, the way she was practically squeezing her words through clenched teeth.

There was no question she was hiding something. But whether it was the demise of her marriage or something more he couldn't tell. He was getting plenty of reactions all right; unfortunately he was having them, too. Knowing and understanding what was going on was becoming more than a game to him, and his gut told him she needed help of some kind. If she ever stopped lying to him, he might be able to give it.

"So." He stared into the green eyes behind which all the secrets were hidden. "Would you like to take this opportunity to set the record straight?"

"Not really."

"You don't have anything to add?"

"Nope."

"There's nothing you want to tell me? Nothing you think I should know?" He leaned in real close, close enough to kiss her if he'd had a mind to, while the ladies whispered over their coffees.

"Will you *leave* if I tell you something?" she asked.

"Um-hmm."

"All right, then." Miranda leaned so close he could feel her warm breath on his cheek and see the hazel flecks in her green eyes.

"I'm not completely sure, but I think you may have a coffee stain right there on your lapel." She smiled. "And I don't know if it's intentional or not, but you're really starting to bug the hell out of me."

In a futile attempt to obliterate Blake Summers and his probing blue eyes from her mind, Miranda did a half-hour workout in the club pool. Then she showered and changed back into her business clothes—a feat that now took half the time it used to thanks to her wash-and-wear hairdo and recently lowered standards—and met her mother and grandmother in the club's main dining room.

"Why, you look . . . good," her mother said with surprise as they air kissed each other's cheek.

Her grandmother enfolded her in a hug and then held her at arm's length, opting, as always, to do her own assessment. "Your mother's right, Miranda. Tom's absence seems to be agreeing with you. And I love your hair this way."

"Mother," Joan Harper warned, "you know people are already gossiping. Not to mention that ill-mannered Clara Bartlett."

No one spoke as they were led to their table, and Miranda sincerely hoped she wasn't going to get another rehashing of Truro's take on the state of her life.

When they were seated, Miranda's mother completed her warning. "You tell Tom you expect him back for the ball. And don't overextend yourself at Ballantyne. Too much stress makes getting pregnant even harder."

"So does an absent husband," Gran pointed out drolly. "And she's right to look out for the family interests. It wouldn't do to forget what oils the wheels that make our world go round."

This was always the way of it, Miranda realized. Her mother cautioning and worrying about appearances, her grandmother urging her forward. It was only lately that she'd begun to notice how much her mother craved her own mother's approval and how seldom she got it. Perhaps she and her mother had more in common than she'd realized.

"How's Daddy?"

"Still grousing about all the lifestyle changes Doc Chainey has ordered, but at least he's taken them seriously. If we can bring his blood pressure down far enough and he doesn't have any more chest pains, we may be able to avoid the angioplasty."

"Oh, thank goodness." The worry about her father had been ever present, a sort of low-lying hum that never went away.

They ordered, and after the drinks were served, her mother said, "Tell me what's happening with the ball, darling. I'm so sorry I missed the last meeting. Has Angela chosen a napkin color? And what about poor Henri? I hear he's still recovering from the sampling."

Her mother's eyes lit with interest, and Miranda knew she was just warming to the topic.

"Everything's going fine, Mother, but there's something else we need to talk about," Miranda said smoothly. "I want to call a meeting of the Ballantyne Board of Directors, and I'm going to need your help."

"You're going to call a board meeting?" Her mother looked shocked.

"Um-hmm."

"But shouldn't that be Tom's responsibility?"

"Yes, but Tom's not here and he, um, asked me to take care of this for him."

"He wants you to conduct a board meeting while he's gone?"

"Yes."

"On his behalf?"

"That's right."

"And it can't wait until he comes back?"

"Definitely not." Because she'd probably be in a nursing home by then—a very cheap one, considering what they'd all have left if she allowed Ballantyne to go under.

Her grandmother had been unusually silent, and
Miranda turned to her now. "I'm going to need you
both behind me on this. I have an idea that I believe
can do great things for Ballantyne, but it's a pretty big
leap from where we are. And you know how conservative Dad and the other directors can be."

Her mother began to demur, but Gran silenced her
with a raised eyebrow. "We've got half an hour until
bridge, Miranda. Why don't you go ahead and fill
us in."

"Mother, I really don't think—" Joan began, but
once again Gran cut her off.

"Of course I'm behind you, Miranda. And if she's
smart, your mother will be, too," Gran said. "Now let's
hear your idea. Fortunately for you, 'unconventional'
is my middle name."

Miranda woke to the sound of pounding rain and
gusty winds that made getting out of bed decidedly unattractive. She lay huddled under the covers, listening
to the storm howl outside, wishing someone else
would get up and put on the coffee and retrieve the undoubtedly drenched newspaper.

If Tom were here she could nudge him awake and try
to sweet-talk him into doing all the things she didn't
want to do right now. She felt the stab of loneliness and
then pushed it ruthlessly aside.

Once she might have traded a kiss per cup of coffee,
and offered a little more incentive for the trek out into

the rain. But it had been a long time since it had occurred to her to try to tempt her husband with anything out of the ordinary, and even longer since their sex life had been much more than perfunctory. It was little wonder she hadn't figured out that lingerie was the answer—she hadn't even realized there was a question.

Miranda swung her legs over the side of the bed and stood. Despite the sweats and thick socks she'd slept in, the room felt cold, and the overcast sky provided almost no light. After a cursory stretch and yawn, she padded downstairs, turning on every light switch she passed until the house was ablaze. It was 8:15 A.M., and she had no place to be and nothing to do. The day stretched out into infinity and beyond.

After grinding beans and putting on a pot of coffee, Miranda pulled on an old yellow slicker and a battered pair of galoshes and raced out into the tempest to retrieve a soggy *Truro Gazette*.

She started with "Dear Abby" and segued into the engagement and wedding announcements. Over her second cup of coffee, she decided to brave "Truro Tattles," and immediately wished she hadn't. The headline screamed: WHERE IS GUILD QUEEN'S KING?

Miranda put down her coffee and read the two paragraphs that followed. Twice.

Guild-queen-turned-bra-tycoon Miranda Smith is looking very corporate these days as she pinch-hits for her absent husband who, she claims, is away on an extended business trip to remote sections of China. There the king is purported to be drumming up new suppliers and not, as previously rumored, looking to relocate manufacturing.

Ballantyne insiders say that the king stays in touch by phone and E-mail, but has not been seen for some six weeks—not even by his queen of hearts.

The phone rang and Miranda knew, without checking the caller ID, that it was her mother. The boring day she'd been dreading began to look increasingly attractive.

"Good morning," she answered. "Queen Miranda speaking."

"Oh, darling, I'm so angry with that Clara Bartlett and her infernal column."

"Well, at least she referred to me as royalty."

"Yes, Miranda, and now's the time to be even more regal than ever."

Miranda looked down at her soggy newspaper and gray sweat socks. "Whatever you say, Mom."

"But not until *after* I sue her for every penny she has. And force her to print a retraction. Why, I'll..."

Miranda tried not to enjoy having her mother on her side, but it was too novel an experience not to be savored. "Mother, calm down. I'm not sure if you noticed, but she didn't actually print anything that's untrue. Tom has been gone for six weeks and he is in China. If it were possible to sue for attitude and innuendo, tons of publications would be out of business. Let's just ignore her and hope she gets tired of this."

"Darling, I think that's a very poor strategy. I mean, Clara doesn't actually *have* a life of her own, as I believe I pointed out to her after her last column. She could write about you forever."

"Believe me, Mother, 'no comment' is the way to go here. And I know this will sound odd, but you might want to cut out those personal attacks. They don't seem to be helping."

"Harumph!" This was her mother's version of "Screw her" and "That bitch doesn't know who she's messing with."

"That's right, Mom. Take some nice deep breaths." *Or possibly Valium.* "And try to calm down. It's just a couple paragraphs of silliness. Probably everybody's papers are too soaked to read anyway."

Twenty phone calls later Miranda knew this was not the case. Tired of trying to sound unconcerned, she finally switched on the answering machine and took a cursory look at the caller ID as each call came in.

By noon, when her grandmother called, Miranda was ready to climb the walls and in serious need of a more level head than her own.

"Miranda dear, are you all right?"

"Harumph," she said, horrified to hear how much like her mother she sounded.

"That's what I was afraid of," Gran said. "The rain's

let up a little. I want you to get in your car and drive over here right now."

"I'm all right, Gran." Her assurance sounded puny even to her.

"I won't take no for an answer, Miranda. I've got a beef stew started and a fire going. Bring *Singin' in the Rain*, and *Top Hat*, and *Houseboat*. We'll spend our afternoon with Gene Kelly, Fred Astaire, and Cary Grant. What could be better than that?"

"All right, Gran. I'll throw on some clothes, but I might have to stop for some Chunky Monkey on the way."

"That's fine, dear. There's nothing wrong with a little medicinal ice cream. And remember, Ginger Rogers did everything Fred Astaire did. Only she did it backwards and in heels."

After church on Sunday, Miranda cut out Clara Bartlett's column and pinned it to the bulletin board in her kitchen, right next to the others. Seated at her kitchen table, where she could see Clara's columns for inspiration, Miranda pulled apart the Sunday *New York Times*, and pored over the business section. She was skimming through an article about "the new generation of entrepreneurs" when a familiar face caught her eye.

Miranda studied the picture of her former pageant competitor with interest. Selena Moore's blond hair was no longer "big," but had been cut in a sophisticated style that brushed her shoulders. Her makeup had undergone a similar transformation. She looked, Miranda decided, like what she'd become: the CEO and driving force behind a growing empire of high-end boutiques. Boutiques that catered to the very market Miranda wanted for Ballantyne.

She'd already decided that opening their own stores would make her undertaking too expensive and unwieldy; she simply couldn't learn retail fast enough to market the custom line herself.

But Selena was already reaching Ballantyne's target customer, and according to this article, she had plans to reach more.

Miranda stood and walked to the bulletin board. She pinned the article about Selena in the center, then stared at the grainy photo of Clara Bartlett that appeared with each column.

"Stand back, O ye of little faith," she said to the gossip columnist's photo. "I do believe I've found the way."

chapter 14

Over the next weeks Miranda focused all her energy on Ballantyne. She flew to New York to meet with the marketing-research firm whose figures supported the direction she planned, called on several new repping firms she'd heard good things about, and reestablished contact with Selena Moore. Her days in Truro were spent ironing out the details of the line she intended to create and attempting to duck the highly attractive and much too persistent Blake Summers.

In her spare moments she pulled together documents for Dana Houseman and filled out a twenty-page questionnaire that forced her to face just how long her marriage had been sliding downhill.

The hours she devoted to Ballantyne were long,

the decisions difficult, and the setbacks many, but there were moments of pure exhilaration, too. Like Miranda's first glimpse of head designer Myrna Talbot's final drawings and samples of the variety of bras that could be created from the custom components Carly had originally drawn, and the designer's memo indicating that their basic in-stock fabrics would be perfect for the new line. Both of these things paled in comparison to Engineering's news that a retooling of the plant would not be necessary.

With a determination she hadn't realized she possessed, Miranda maneuvered around the negatives and capitalized on the positives, being sure to make the absent Tom a party to her plans.

During meetings she spoke glowingly of his progress on his China mission, and then checked her nose for telltale signs of growth. Like the Pinocchio she was afraid of resembling, she told herself each lie was the last, but inevitably one untruth led to another. And another after that.

Two months into her secret takeover, only Helen St. James continued to question Miranda's authority. In return, Miranda made sure that Helen was the only one "Tom" never e-mailed or asked to speak to, even though his loving-to-the-point-of-nausea phone calls to Miranda almost always occurred in Helen's presence.

It was after one such virtuoso performance that Helen St. James, seated in the chair across from what

Miranda now thought of as "her" desk, looked up and said, "I'm surprised that you two can go so long without seeing each other. It must be tough to be apart for so long."

Miranda considered the other woman. "Yes," she said faintly, "it is."

The bookkeeper's gaze was pointed. "It's March fifth. He's been gone, what, almost eight weeks?"

"Why, yes, he has," Miranda chirped as if just realizing it for the first time.

"I'm surprised he hasn't come back to visit or to check on things. They do have airports in China, don't they?"

If she hadn't seen a picture of this woman with her hand on Tom's butt, Miranda would have been tempted to shout "touché." "Yes, of course they do," Miranda replied.

Helen St. James tried the eyebrow thing, but Miranda wasn't having it. "In fact, I'm planning a trip myself."

"To China?" The bookkeeper looked genuinely surprised.

"Well, uh, no, we were talking about meeting in . . ." Miranda squinted and tried to remember where the ticketing agent had told her Tom had flown through. "In, um, San Francisco. In fact, Carly is booking my flight right now."

Helen appeared stunned, which gave them something else—other than sex with Tom—in common.

Miranda cleared her throat and spoke into the intercom. "Carly, how are you coming on that flight for me?"

There was a dead silence.

"The one to meet up with Mr. Smith," Miranda prompted.

"Ohhhh," Carly replied slowly. "You mean the one to mjummmppppp@@@@?" The word was so garbled it could have been anything.

She was definitely going to have to give Carly that raise and promotion.

"I'm just waiting for confirmation from the airline," Carly said. There was another pause and then, "Let me make sure I have those dates right."

Oops. This was the problem with making stuff up as one went along. Picking up her Palm Pilot, Miranda pulled up her calendar, realizing she was now obligated to commit to a date. And then actually go somewhere.

"Let's see." Today was March 5; she'd penciled in the board meeting for the end of the month, and the Guild Ball was the second weekend in April. That didn't leave a lot of room for her "rendezvous" with Tom.

"That was the weekend of March 19," she said, playing it out in her head, "and I want to fly out of Atlanta so I can meet with Selena Moore at her Phipps Plaza store."

"Got it," Carly replied. "I'll buzz you when I have flight numbers."

"Thanks, Carly."

Miranda turned her attention back to Helen St.

James, who no longer looked quite so cocky. "Was there anything else, Helen?"

The woman stood, smoothing the skirt of her gray wool suit and tilting her chin at a proud angle. "No, I think that's quite enough, actually. I can see that you're busy. I'll have those projections you asked for ready in the morning."

Miranda watched her go, no longer feeling quite so cocky herself.

That night Miranda grabbed a bite at Ling Pow's and met her mother, her grandmother, and the rest of the Guild Ball committee at Angela Johnson's to discuss decorations. With nobody pushing wine, Angela's "new pair" stayed decorously covered, but her dithering over details was as annoying as ever.

"Okay," Miranda finally said. "All in favor of eggplant for the napkins, raise your hands."

Angela wrung hers instead. "I don't know," she said. "Eggplant is so . . . vegetablelike."

Miranda sighed. "Why don't we just call it purple, Ang, and move on? All in favor of—"

"But purple . . . I mean, it just doesn't seem . . . serious enough."

Miranda's grandmother fixed the other woman with a stare. "It's the color of royalty. It would be hard to get more serious than that."

"Right," said Miranda. "Everyone in favor say—"

"Is *this* eggplant?" Angela pointed to the band of color on her shirt.

Miranda's mother cupped a hand to one side of her mouth and hissed, "She's not going to take her shirt off again, is she? I heard she pulled it right off at the last meeting."

"No, of course not, Mother," Miranda said wearily. "All those in favor of—"

"That's what happens when you don't attend," Gran observed. "You miss all the good stuff."

Miranda turned to Angela Johnson. "You're not planning to remove any of your clothing tonight, are you?"

Angela shook her head.

"Good." Miranda turned to her mother. "Satisfied?"

"Yes, dear, I just—"

"Okay. All in favor of—"

"What are we voting on again?"

"Purple. The napkins are going to be purple. And I think we should do the tablecloths in the ecru with black as an accent," Miranda said.

"Oh." Angela perked up. "You never told me I could use more than one color."

Miranda sighed again and glanced at the clock above the stove as her mother said, "I'd like to present an idea for consideration."

Miranda bit back a groan.

"If we're going with royalty, let's have Miranda wear her rhododendron crown and bring back the velvet robes for the king and queen. The committee chair and her husband always used to be crowned queen and king."

"Oh, no, Mother," Miranda got out. "Let's not..."

But after a night of interminable dawdling, the committee suddenly snapped to life. United in their love of the royalty idea, the group, who up until now hadn't reached a single decision, made a slew of them. And every one of those decisions was going to leave Miranda sitting on a throne, her old rhododendron crown on her head. Without a king by her side.

"Look, I really don't think—" she began.

"Oh, Miranda," Vivien crowed. "It's so perfect. And we can use your Rhododendron girls as a kind of queen's court. They can invite escorts and do a processional in their evening gowns. It'll be fabulous!"

"No! I mean, let's not—"

"I'll get the thrones out of storage," the decoration chair offered. "And you know what else we could do?" She jumped up, excited. "We could turn the hall into a palace garden. The winter's been so horrible it'll be the perfect antidote. We'll fill it with flowers so that it feels like spring!"

"But the forecasts are all calling for it to stay cold through April." Miranda tried to remain calm, but her committee was gathering speed like a runaway train. "Flowers would cost a fortune, and it just doesn't—"

"Oooh, oooh, I know." Angela raised a hand and jumped up and down. Her new breasts didn't even bobble. "We can use tissue-paper flowers—a garden full of them. It's so retro it'll be cool."

Miranda tried to apply the brakes, but her committee had jumped the track. "You know why those things went out of fashion, don't you?"

But everyone was buzzing with excitement.

"Because they're so much work!"

"I can just see it now," Angela exulted. "Tissue-paper flowers in every color of the rainbow. Annuals and perennials. Why, we can make flower beds full!"

"That would take younger hands and shorter nails," Miranda countered, hiding her own still nimble and short-nailed hands behind her.

There was a brief respite from enthusiasm and then, "I know," the newly decisive Angela exclaimed. "We can get your girls to make them!"

Like Andy Rooney and Judy Garland screaming "Let's put on a play!" the committee zipped through the details, once again painting Miranda into a corner she couldn't find a way out of.

"And maybe they could make extra to sell at school!"

"That money could go to the children's hospital, too!"

"The school could give the girls credit for community service!"

"Oh, I can just see the garden now!"

"Do you think we should put AstroTurf down?"

Miranda blinked, and it was all decided. She was going to have to wear her Miss Rhododendron crown and a velvet robe and sit on a throne in a garden of tissue-paper flowers made by her students, without a king by her side.

Talk about your defining moments.

Later, over cake and coffee, Miranda pulled her mother aside. "I wish you hadn't pushed this whole royal court thing. I'm not even sure Tom will be back in time for the ball."

"Not back? Why, he'll have to be." Her smile was grim. "I'm sure Tom wouldn't want to see you so publicly humiliated."

Miranda considered explaining to her mother just how little her son-in-law cared about potential humiliation. Or what he probably would be wearing under his king's robes if he had, in fact, been planning to show up. Instead she helped herself to another cup of coffee and rejoined the ladies seated around Angela's kitchen table, all of whom stopped talking as soon as they noticed her approach. Miranda's stomach dropped.

Angela looked away as Miranda set her coffee cup down, and every one of Miranda's self-preservation instincts shouted "run," "duck," "hide." But she'd learned enough from dealing with Helen St. James and the staff at Ballantyne to know it was better to confront this unpleasantness head on. "Did I interrupt something?" she asked.

Angela flushed with embarrassment. She was having trouble meeting Miranda's eye. "We were just wondering when Tom was going to be back from his business trip."

The attention of every woman in the room was now focused on them.

Her grandmother left her place near the counter and stepped over to stand behind Miranda, a move that spoke volumes in the too-silent room. Her mother stayed put.

Miranda felt as if she and Gran were starring in Truro's version of the shoot-out at the OK Corral. She sincerely hoped they were going to be the Earps.

"He's in China, visiting the smaller villages to find new suppliers. Textiles are very big in the more remote areas right now."

"He's been gone for a long time."

"Are you, I mean, *when* are you expecting him back?" Sheila Taylor's face belied her concerned tone.

"When he's done," Miranda said.

"It's been two months," Karen added. "How in the world are you managing without him for so long? The nights have been so . . . cold."

"Kind of like this room at the moment," Gran commented dryly.

"I have an electric blanket," Miranda replied.

There were titters, but everyone had pretty much given up the pretense that they were doing anything other than listening.

"Actually," Miranda continued. "I'm planning to meet Tom in San Francisco in a couple of weeks." She was very careful to maintain eye contact with her committee members. "We decided he wouldn't come home until all his business was complete, but, you're right, it's been much too long."

She smiled as she added, "Why, he's been gone so long I'll have to take a picture along so I can recognize him."

chapter 15

Miranda called Friday's Rhododendron Prep session to order, determined to put the best possible spin on her upcoming humiliation. "I am happy to report that you have all been asked to participate in the Ladies' Guild Ball in April."

There were murmurs of surprise and pleasure.

"You're going to serve as 'attendants' to the queen; that would be *moi*." She pointed a finger to her chest and inclined her head in regal fashion. "Which will require wearing evening gowns and doing the same sort of walk you'd do on a pageant runway. On the arm of your escorts."

The girls simmered with excitement, or at least most

of them did. Andie Summers slumped down in her seat and folded her arms across her chest.

"We'll be getting out our high heels in just a moment to practice, but first I want to tell you about something else you can be a part of."

She explained the whole paper-flower business as succinctly as she could and then pulled her own heels out of her bag.

Mary Louise's hand shot up. "How many flowers are we each supposed to make?"

"Well..." Miranda hadn't really thought that one out. "We need a ton of them to create the feeling of a palace garden, so the more the better."

Thinking the subject covered, Miranda held one shoe aloft but had barely opened her mouth to speak when Mary Louise raised her hand again. "I'll make fifty," she said.

"Me, too," said one of Mary Louise's friends.

Across the room, Andie sat up straighter, her face suddenly intent.

"That's great, girls, but it's quite time-consuming, and—"

"Seventy-five," Andie Summers said.

"I'm sorry?" Miranda lowered the shoe.

"I said I'll make seventy-five." Andie's chin jutted out just like her father's.

Mary Louise's head whipped around. "Eighty!" the girl said, turning back to face Miranda. "I can make eighty flowers!"

"Eighty-five." Andie's voice rang out strong and clear.

ML's hand shot up. "Ninety."

"Ninety-five."

Once again a group of females was taking the bit in their teeth and racing toward a finish line Miranda had never intended. "This is not an auction," she said. "Or a competition."

"I don't know how someone who can't even get her makeup right is going to be able to make that many delicate tissue-paper flowers." Mary Louise sniffed. "I'll make one hundred, since it's for such a good cause and all." She tossed her hair. "Plus the ones *she* doesn't finish."

"Ha," Andie sneered back. "I'll have my hundred and then some. Just because I'm new to this whole stupid face-painting thing doesn't mean I can't fold up some dumb tissue paper."

"All right, then." Miranda turned from the two combatants. "Thank you both so much for your generous contributions." She cleared her throat. "Anyone else?"

The other girls volunteered for smaller, more reasonable amounts, which Miranda made note of. She was very glad she wouldn't be around when Andie and Mary Louise discovered just how much work they'd goaded each other into.

"I know the ladies of the guild will be very appreciative. Now then," she continued, raising a strappy black dress sandal aloft. "Shall we begin?"

Andie felt like a skyscraper in the pointy-toed heels she'd found at the Second Time Around Boutique. She was used to towering over everybody, but doing it with her center of gravity thrown so far off kilter was a whole other thing. She'd survived her solo walk and turn, but now they were lined up in a big circle like circus elephants following each other, and they were supposed to be doing it with the short, fluid, on-the-balls-of-their-feet steps Miranda Smith had promised would show their legs and bodies off to best advantage.

Andie held her breath and attempted the subtle sway Mrs. Smith had demonstrated, but the only thing swaying was *her* as she teetered along behind the other girls like a rogue elephant tied to the back of the herd.

"Eyes forward, chin up. Don't look down. Glide, ladies, glide."

Andie closed her eyes in frustration and quickly realized her mistake as the toe of one shoe dragged on the floor and made her wobble wildly. Her eyes flew open, and her arms shot forward grasping for something steady to cling to, which in this case turned out to be Earlene Johnson.

"Hey!" Earlene tripped, then righted herself before turning to glare up at Andie.

"Sorry, but . . ."

"Don't give up, girls," Mrs. Smith said. "Remember, we're walking and gliding. We are positively floating on air."

Drawing in a deep breath, Andie squared her shoulders, then took one small step, then another, all the while fighting the urge to look down and check what her feet were up to.

"Yes, that's it. Lift your feet, but don't march. Very good, ML. That's it, Susan. Much better, Andie. Glide, girls, glide."

Andie gritted her teeth. The shoes pinched her toes, yet somehow managed to slide up and down on her heel, and she felt taller than she'd ever felt in her life, and that was saying a lot.

The second time around she teetered and clutched a little less, but she still couldn't find anything resembling her normal sense of balance. Keeping her chin raised and her eyes forward meant she was looking over the tops of the other girls' heads. She had her eye on the clock on the far wall when the girl in front of her stopped.

"Ooof." Unprepared and unsure how to downshift in the heels, Andie slammed into Earlene, who banged into Susan, who crashed into Mary Louise.

They went down like dominoes, each knocking into the other, so that the next person hurtled forward with a shriek or a gasp. Andie watched it all as she teetered in place, her long arms windmilling as she frantically tried to regain her balance. In her effort to get out of the way she stepped back and felt one foot catch under the metal leg of a desk. With no one to grab onto she, too, started to go down.

Blake raced to the high school with his siren blaring. It took him only five minutes to get there, but he spent those minutes with the image of a bruised and bloody Andie stuck in his head.

His heart slowed a little when he reached the classroom and confirmed the lack of blood at the scene. Then he spotted Andie, her long jean-clad legs splayed out in front of her, her back propped up against a desk, with Miranda crouched beside her. And he was torn between anger and relief.

Andie's right hand had a plastic bag full of ice on it and lay limply in her lap. A passel of girls stood in a semicircle around her, and every one of them had on a pair of high-heeled shoes.

The girls skittered out of his way as he hunkered down next to Andie. "Where does it hurt?" he asked, more gruffly than he meant to.

She sniffled, and he could see in her eyes how much she hated that. "Everywhere. But it's kind of numb now, and I—" She looked up at him and swallowed. "I can't move my fingers."

"I called Donald Greenwell, the head of orthopedics at All Children's," Miranda said. "We need to take her up there right away for X rays. He thought it sounded like a possible wrist fracture."

He looked into Miranda's face. Now that the fear for Andie was fading he felt his anger build. Mad as he was, his daughter's hurt and embarrassment called out to him. He wanted to scoop her up in his arms and cradle her against his chest as he had when she was a child; or read her the riot act and ground her for life. He settled for fashioning a quick splint out of his nightstick and a stray scarf while Miranda dismissed the other girls.

"Dad, I'm sorry I—"

Blake helped Andie stand. "Let's just get you taken care of. Then I plan to give you some serious shit for blackening the Summers name this way. High heels!" He shook his head and snorted in disgust. "I knew you should have gotten a pair with training wheels."

Miranda grabbed her and Andie's coats from the rack. "We can take her in my car if you'd like. It shouldn't take more than twenty-five minutes to get to the hospital."

"That won't be necessary. I've got the cruiser here and I can make it in fifteen." He walked Andie toward the door.

"You can drive if you want to, but I'm coming." Miranda was already pulling on her coat and draping Andie's over the girl's shoulders.

Apparently considering the conversation over, Miranda helped Andie into the front seat, positioning the injured hand so that it wouldn't get jostled. Then she slid into the backseat and waited for Blake to give up and take his place behind the wheel.

They made the trip in one of the thickest silences Miranda had ever experienced. Blake kept his eyes on the road and his mouth set in a grim line as they sped toward the hospital. Midway, Andie laid her head on his shoulder and Miranda noticed how careful he was not to make any sudden movements. Occasionally he looked down at his daughter, and the look of pure love he shot her pierced Miranda to the core.

Together they walked Andie into All Children's, where Dr. Greenwell was waiting. He ushered them through a series of X rays, which revealed a buckle fracture of the right wrist and broken middle and index fingers on the same hand, and then took Andie away to be casted.

Once Andie and the doctor disappeared around the corner, Blake fixed Miranda with an accusing look. "She got hurt prancing around in high heels."

"No one was prancing," Miranda said. "We were practicing."

"Practicing, prancing, what's the difference?" he said. "I told you before, this whole—" She watched him search for a word that would sum up his feelings *"pageant thing*... is not for Andie. You take a girl who belongs in high-tops and stick her in high heels and something's bound to happen."

"It was an accident," she pointed out calmly, which seemed to piss him off even more. "She was just starting to find her balance when she had to stop suddenly. It wasn't as if—"

"She had any need to be tromping around in shoes high enough to give her a nosebleed."

Now Miranda was the one gritting her teeth.

They stood toe to toe, their faces only inches from

each other, and only pulled apart when Andie came toward them. Her cast was neon orange and reached from her fingertips to the middle of her forearm. Her face was almost as dark as her father's.

"The doctor said this won't come off until after the state championship." A lone tear squeezed out of her eye.

"Yeah," Blake observed, as he slung an arm around his daughter's shoulders. "You're definitely going to be sitting this one out."

His tone softened and he gave Andie a wink. "But I wouldn't be surprised if you make the record books anyway. You're bound to be the first forward in the entire Southeastern Conference to get injured falling off a pair of high heels."

Miranda followed them out to the car, trying to understand what she'd just witnessed. How could a man be so irritating and so endearing at the same time?

chapter 16

Andie lay on the living-room couch and felt sorry for herself. Mrs. Smith had dropped off get-well balloons and a batch of oatmeal cookies, but her father was pissed off at her, her coach was pissed off at her, and the only reason everybody else wasn't pissed off at her was that they were too busy laughing at her.

Her right hand was propped on a pillow beside her, and she held the TV remote awkwardly in her left hand. When her father walked in to check on her, she was spoiling for a fight.

"Hey, Andie. You need anything?"

She kept her gaze on the TV screen, where a frustrated Wile E. Coyote was plotting yet another doomed trap for the Roadrunner.

"Andie, I'm talking to you."

"No," she grunted, not appreciating his tone. He wasn't the one everybody was laughing at. And he wasn't the one who wouldn't be playing in the basketball championship—even though he sometimes acted like he was. "I mean, no, thank you," she ground out, adding as much insolence as she thought she could get away with, given her injury and all.

"Don't take that tone with me," he said. "I'm not the one who put myself out of commission with a pair of high heels." He actually had the nerve to smile at her. "Well, at least now you have a good excuse to get out of that Rhododendron business."

She turned her head to meet his gaze for the first time since he'd entered the room. "What do you mean?"

"Well, you were injured in that class. I doubt anyone will expect you to continue."

She turned her head away and stared, unseeing, at the television. "You don't think I'm pretty enough to be in a beauty pageant, do you?"

"This has nothing to do with being pretty. This has to do with wasting your time."

"You're not answering the question." She flicked off the TV and turned back to face him. "Do you or do you not think I'm pretty enough to enter the Miss Rhododendron Pageant?"

He looked like a *Survivor* contestant who knew he was about to get voted off. "Don't be ridiculous, Andie. Why would you want to do that?"

"You're still not answering. Are you afraid I'm going to embarrass you? That people will laugh at the idea of Andie Summers thinking she might have a chance at winning a beauty contest?"

Her father's look turned even more wary. "You're not seriously considering..."

"Really, Dad. What is your problem with all of this?"

He thought about his mother and the dissatisfaction winning a crown had bred. Then he thought about Miranda Smith, who'd held pretty much every small-town crown there was and ended up toting her tiara around Truro for most of her life. He wanted more than that for his daughter. "You have so much athletic and academic potential, Andie. I don't want to see you squandering it on something so...so...frivolous."

"Frivolous like...Mrs. Smith?"

"I didn't say that."

"But you think women should be more...serious." She waited a beat. "Like Mom."

"Well, that might not be the best example." He was totally backpedaling now.

Andie pictured the satisfaction on Mary Louise's face if she were to drop out. But Jake didn't see anything strange about the idea of her entering a pageant, and neither did Miranda Smith. She was a competitor, her father had seen to that. And she wasn't going to be competing in basketball this year. Why shouldn't she just shift arenas and show a few people—her father included—what she was made of? "I'm not quitting now," she said.

"What?"

"I'm not quitting. And there's something else."

"I have a bad feeling about this," her father said.

"Yeah, well, I promised to make a hundred tissue-paper flowers for the Guild Ball, and I'm not going to be able to make them with my hand in this cast."

"I'm sure, under the circumstances, Miranda will let you off the hook."

She pictured ML's face again, heard her taunt about Andie's botched makeup. She was going to have to learn how to do it better and find a ball gown, too, if she was going to win the right to be the Ballantyne Bras contestant in this year's Miss Rhododendron Pageant.

"You always taught me to take my commitments seriously, Dad, and I don't want to be off the hook." She added a quiver to her voice. "I just need some help." She looked up at her father and let some moisture accumulate in her eyes. She was tempted to bat her eyelashes at him, but decided to stick with the tried and true. "You're so good with your hands. I bet Mrs. Smith could teach you how to make those paper flowers in no time."

"Andie, that is totally out of the question."

She started to cry in earnest then, squeezing big fat tears out of her eyes as she delivered the appropriate sound effects. They streamed down her cheeks and slid down the front of her shirt. Looking up through tear-soaked lashes she added the coup de grâce. "Believe me, I wish I had somebody else to ask. I'd ask my mother to help. Only I don't really have one!"

Her father groaned and shook his head, but even as he muttered about ungrateful children and the ridiculousness of making things out of tissue paper, she knew that she had him.

Then he brightened and said something about "bad penny potential," which made no sense at all. But it didn't really matter. All Andie could think about was rubbing those flowers in Mary Louise's face.

Miranda wheeled her grocery cart toward the Piggly Wiggly checkout line.

Ridiculously pleased, she contemplated her haul, which was unsullied by so much as a single fruit or vegetable. She hadn't been this close to this much junk food since her high school graduation party.

At the register, Grace Krump looked her up and down as she scanned in the contents of Miranda's bulging grocery cart.

"You got enough salt and fat here to clog up a whole passel of arteries," she said. "Or satisfy any number of cravings." Her eyes sparked with interest. "Why, I ate a whole gallon of chocolate chip ice cream and two grilled cheese sandwiches at eight A.M. one morning when I was carrying my Bobbie."

She finished bagging the items and then leaned in closer. "Of course, in my day nobody thought anything of a pregnant woman having an occasional nip. In fact, I'd like to see them doctors go without for a whole nine months." She nodded to the beer and wine Miranda had thrown in at the last moment. "But you be careful with that alcohol, honey."

"But I'm not . . ."

Grace patted her on the shoulder, and her tone turned sympathetic. "I bet if'n you told Tom about the baby he'd come on home."

"But there's no . . ."

"You take my advice now, you hear? You don't want to be raisin' that little one all by yourself."

"But there's no . . ."

Grace turned to offer a cheery hello to her next customer, and Miranda pushed her booty to the car, knowing the rumors were probably already flying. Ah well, she thought, as she stowed the bags in the trunk, thinking she was finally pregnant was nothing compared to what they'd be thinking when they found out Tom wasn't coming back. She was not looking forward to the day that shit hit the Truro fan.

At home she unloaded her groceries, put the wine and beer in the fridge, then headed upstairs to freshen her makeup and change into jeans and a sweater.

She caught herself humming as she padded back downstairs. Stopping in mid-hum, Miranda took a long, hard look at herself in the full-length hall mirror.

The jeans she'd wiggled into were low slung and skin tight. The sweater was an off-the-shoulder cherry cashmere that exposed a striking expanse of skin. Worse, her cheeks were flushed, her eyes were bright, and the sense of excitement she felt was clearly reflected on her face. She did not look like a woman who was going to spend an evening making tissue-paper flowers. And she definitely didn't look like a woman who wished her husband were here to help her make them.

This, she reminded herself sternly, was not a date. This was a sort of mini Guild meeting; a service to mankind; a mission of mercy. She was helping a student fulfill a commitment. There would be some snacks and then the folding of tissue paper, a completely impersonal exercise that even a happily married woman might choose to engage in.

Right.

Miranda checked her lipstick one more time and tucked a stray lock of hair behind her ear before averting her gaze from the woman in the mirror—the one who was too smart to fall for a single word she was being fed.

chapter 17

The roads were icy and nearly empty Monday night as Blake and Andie headed toward Miranda's. Blake drove slowly and carefully and told himself it was the opportunity to look for clues to Tom Smith's absence and not the prospect of spending an evening with the man's wife that was causing this unwelcome sense of anticipation. Or maybe it was the burrito he'd wolfed down for dinner.

When Miranda opened the front door, the very real stab of pleasure was a good bit harder to deny.

"Come in. Here, let me take those." Miranda took their coats and hung them in a foyer closet as he and Andie adjusted to the warmth of the house. While his daughter looked around in openmouthed amazement, he took in the still-empty dining room that had not yet been repainted, and caught a glimpse of an equally empty room across from it. A quick peek upstairs to see what else was missing was definitely in order.

In the great room a fire blazed in a stacked stone fireplace and snacks had been set out on a low coffee table. He and Andie sank into the cushiony sofa Miranda directed them to, and Andie reached for a curl of puffed cheese as she studied the room.

"Wow," she murmured when Miranda left them to get the drinks. "This place looks like something in a magazine."

He didn't respond, but as Miranda reappeared, he had the same thought about the woman walking toward them. Long and lean, with high cheekbones, carelessly sophisticated dark hair and body-hugging clothing, she could have stepped off the cover of a fashion magazine or out of any man's fantasy. She moved with unconscious grace, and her clothing moved with her, the soft fuzzy sweater molded against her breasts and slipping off creamy shoulders. The hint of a belly button peeked out at him when she raised her arms to balance the tray of drinks.

Setting a beer in front of him, she flashed her thousand-watt smile, and he caught a glimpse of cleavage as she turned, still bent at the waist, to hand Andie her Sprite. He took a long pull on his beer.

"How's your hand, Andrea?" she asked.

"It doesn't hurt too much anymore. I just can't *do* anything with it."

"No laundry, no cooking, not much in the way of homework," Blake added.

Andie smiled. "If I weren't missing out on the championship game it would be the perfect injury." She caught his glare out of the corner of her eye and had the grace to blush.

In the silence that followed, Miranda reached under the coffee table and pulled out a load of supplies. Blake took another long pull on his beer and studied them as Andie peppered Miranda with questions about the Guild Ball.

It was just colored paper, wire, scissors and the like, nothing overtly threatening. He took another sip of the Corona, listening to Andie and Miranda's chatter with only half an ear, and relaxed slightly. Once he finished this beer, folding tissue paper probably wouldn't feel quite so . . . girlie. After all, there were pro football players who had admitted to both knitting and needlepoint, and no one had questioned *their* masculinity.

"I printed out an extra set of directions." Miranda slid a piece of computer paper printed on both sides toward him. "But it's not all that complicated. You just . . ."

She began to demonstrate as she talked, and Blake knew he should be paying attention. But her fingers were long and dexterous as they pulled the tissue paper from the pack, and he couldn't help imagining the feel of them moving over his body. He took another sip of beer as she picked up the scissors and began to cut shapes out of purple and turquoise tissue paper and he discovered he couldn't help imagining a lot of things. He was trying to rein in that imagination when she held up an intricate purple and turquoise tulip by its long wire stem and said, "As you can see, there isn't a whole lot to it."

Blake nodded, a general acknowledgment intended to imply "no sweat," but as she began the next flower, his focus shifted from her fingers to her lips. He watched them move without hearing a word they uttered, as he once again imagined the feel of them against his own. And on other parts of his body that were currently lobbying for action.

With a flourish, she held up a white and yellow concoction that looked real enough to plant in the dirt. And then she flashed him a look that said she knew just how little attention he'd been paying and how much she was looking forward to what would happen next.

He snorted to himself and reached for a sheet of the tissue paper she'd piled in front of him. Women might worry about printing out directions and mastering a given process; men liked to figure things out as they went along, relying on their inherently superior reasoning skills and aptitude for making things work. Besides, he thought, as he turned the paper from side to side trying to decide whether it mattered where he began, how hard could something she did so quickly be?

An hour later Blake wiped a trickle of sweat from his forehead and thought about asking for a third beer. Two mangled wads of tissue paper that bore absolutely no resemblance to flowers lay on the table in front of him.

Andie looked over at the lumps of paper and the pieces of limp wire and frowned. "Do you need some help, Dad?"

"No."

"But those don't actually look like . . . flowers."

Miranda contemplated the lumps he'd created. "I don't know," she said. "They could be hydrangeas from another dimension. Or mums on steroids."

"You weren't paying attention, were you?" His daughter's tone was accusing.

"Don't be silly." He held one of the alien plant forms up and tried to lasso it with a piece of wire. "I watched every move she made."

One of Miranda's eyebrows sketched upward, then she cleared her throat and changed the subject. "Have you given any thought to what kind of gown you'll wear for the Guild Ball, Andie? Or who you're going to ask to escort you?"

"Gown?" Blake said. "Escort?"

"No to the gown. I wish, to the escort," Andie said.

"Wait just a minute—" Blake began.

"I'd like to ask Jake Hanson, but he's been dating Mary Louise."

"Jake Hanson?" Blake got in. "Dating? Why, he's—"

"Hot." Andie's eyes glazed over and her lips tilted

upward in a smile that looked—Blake realized in horror—exactly the way her mother's had the first time he'd made love to her.

"*He* doesn't think there'd be anything weird about me being in the Miss Rhododendron Pageant."

"*In* the Miss Rhododendron Pageant?" Blake knew he had to have heard wrong. "You told me this was just a prep thing. No one said anything about—"

"Boys your age are usually even more confused than girls," Miranda informed Andie, as if Blake hadn't spoken. "They're not always sure what they're doing, but it's obvious he's interested."

"Oh, he's interested all right," Blake interjected. "And he knows exactly what he's doing. You," he jabbed a finger toward Andie, "are the flower. Jake Hanson is the bee. And the only thing on his mind is pollination."

"Dad!"

"Don't be silly, Blake," Miranda said. "Not every teenage boy is—"

"Oh, yes, every teenage boy *is*. It is the one driving force in their lives, the only thing they care about more than sports."

"Daaaddy."

Miranda narrowed her eyes.

He sat back in his chair and folded his arms across his chest. "Teenage boys begin buzzing for only one reason. And they don't think straight when their stingers are involved. Which is pretty much all the time."

"That is *so* much more than I wanted to hear," Andie said.

"Me, too," Miranda agreed.

There was a brief silence and then, "So what do you think, Mrs. Smith, should I ask him?"

"Absolutely not," Blake said. "Boys don't respect girls who call them or ask them out. It's not . . . lady-like."

Miranda and Andie blinked.

"You don't think your daughter should go after what she wants?"

"That's not what I said. I—"

"I've seen this girl play basketball, Blake. You didn't teach her to sit back and wait on the court."

"That's different. I . . ."

"No, it's not."

Blake rolled his eyes and gritted his teeth. Across the coffee table Miranda did the same.

"I'm guessing your father hasn't dated since the Stone Age," Miranda said as she rose and motioned Andie to do the same. "I can at least give you some tips on how a modern woman would handle this sort of situation."

She led Andie toward the kitchen. With one hand on the kitchen door, she turned back to Blake. "We're going to have a little girl talk," she said. "Maybe you'd like to reinvent fire or drag a Mastodon back to the cave while we're gone." She smiled sweetly. "Or you could just mangle a flower or two in that adorable Cro-Magnon way of yours."

Blake let them have their laugh, but as soon as the kitchen door swung shut behind them, he headed for the stairs. He'd poked his head in the empty office and done a quick visual of the rest of the downstairs during an earlier trip to the bathroom. Now he sprinted to the upper floor, hoping he'd have time to check it out before Miranda and Andie noticed he was gone.

Quietly, he opened the door at the top of the stairs and discovered yet another empty room. The indentations in the carpet indicated it had once been filled with heavy furniture; he assumed it had been a guest bedroom of sorts, but now it was as vacant as the dining room and office downstairs.

Walking through the room's Jack and Jill bathroom he came to another bedroom. This, too, was empty, but without the signs of recent furniture removal. It had mint green walls and bright white moldings and a Humpty Dumpty border that ran around the room just above the chair rail. Blake stood there for a long moment imagining the anticipation with which that border had probably been hung. He could still remember the joy of bringing Andie home from the hospital and the excitement with which they'd prepared her nursery. The abandoned air of the unfinished room saddened him and he closed its door gently behind him as he left it.

Down the hall Blake came to the master bedroom. Brushing by the king-size bed with only a few wayward thoughts, he began opening dresser drawers. Miranda's underthings were there, but almost half the drawers were empty and there was no sign of Tom or his possessions anywhere in the room.

By the time he stepped into the walk-in closet Blake knew Tom Smith wasn't planning to come back anytime soon. And he knew without question that Miranda knew it, too.

Given his proficiency with tissue paper, he could stretch the flower making out all week and broaden the investigation at the same time. He'd place calls to the airlines and to Interpol because of the Far East connection, first thing in the morning. Then he'd rattle Miranda's cage a little harder.

On Tuesday Miranda's mother insisted on lunch at the club. They met at a table in a far back corner, and Miranda's inquiries about her father were met with terse reassurances. But the worst sign of all was that Gran wasn't there, a clear indication her mother felt the need to divide and conquer.

There were no smiles or air kisses as Miranda took her seat. When her mother didn't even bother to put on her game face for the waitress, Miranda knew things were very grim indeed.

"What in the world is going on?" Joan Ballantyne Harper asked without preamble.

"I'm sorry?" Miranda countered.

"Have you lost your mind?"

"I beg your pardon?" Miranda winced as she realized both of her last questions had sounded like apologies.

"I understand that Tom is ... away." Her mother's eyes and voice got vague on that last word. "But as far as this town is concerned, you are still a married woman."

Miranda had no argument there. "And?"

"You should be acting like one."

The waitress brought their drinks. Her mother got her requested glass of Chardonnay. Miranda got a glass of ... milk?

"Sarah, I didn't order this," Miranda said. "I ordered a glass of wine."

"Yes, well, I wasn't sure if you knew about fetal alcohol syndrome. Milk is a much better choice for you right now."

"But I'm not ..." Miranda began, but Sarah was already on her way to another table.

"You see what I mean?" her mother hissed. "Tom has been gone for two months and yet the whole town thinks you're pregnant. You insist on going to work every day, and you entertain the chief of police in your home to all hours of the night. The *divorced* chief of police."

"Mother." Miranda set the glass of milk away from her. "I am not pregnant, and I was not *entertaining* the chief of police. Blake and his daughter came over for some ... discussion about Andie's commitment for the ball."

"Oh, really, Miranda," her mother scoffed, "next

thing you'll be telling me the three of you were making paper flowers."

Sarah came back to take their orders and really wanted the "mother to be" to have the liver and onions.

"Sarah," Miranda said as calmly as she could. "I am *not* pregnant. And if you bring me liver and onions I'm going to have to send it back."

"Oh."

The waitress looked so disappointed that Miranda didn't have the heart to return the milk.

When Sarah had gone, Miranda nibbled on a piece of cornbread and tried to turn the topic, but her mother wasn't finished. Miranda began to wish the waitress would return. An extra shot of calcium and unwanted prenatal advice would be preferable to the rant her mother was on.

"We have a reputation to maintain in this community, Miranda," she said. "It's bad enough that Tom's been gone for so long and you're actually *working* at the plant. You're giving those gossip mongers way too much ammunition."

"Mother," Miranda said, her calm disappearing as she realized that once again her mother's primary concern was for the opinion of others. "I am not fooling around. And as I've already told you, I am not, unfortunately, pregnant. But if I'm ever lucky enough to have a child, I hope to God I'll have more faith in her than you have ever had in me."

Her mother's lips tightened and her body stilled.

"I'm working at the plant because Tom isn't and, although you seem unwilling to accept this, Ballantyne can't actually run itself."

She looked into her mother's eyes and wished, for the trillionth time, that this woman would just once look at her and see her strengths instead of trying to fix her weaknesses.

"I'm not stupid, Miranda," her mother snapped. "But you must be careful, and you absolutely have to find a way to resolve all of this before the Guild Ball."

The Guild Ball. What was it with her mother and the damned Guild Ball?

Miranda felt the familiar weight of her mother's disappointment and disapproval, but for once it was nothing compared to her own. She was thirty-eight years old and still unable to please her mother. She was sick to death of trying.

Miranda balled up her napkin and dropped it on the table. "You and Daddy taught me to accept my responsibilities and make the most of the hand I was dealt. That's exactly what I'm trying to do. A little acceptance and support would go a long way."

Her entire body shook as she stood. "And if you can't manage that, I hope you'll show up at the board meeting and at least *pretend* you think I have a brain in my head."

With her mother's huff of surprise ringing in her ears, Miranda turned her back on the table, just as Sarah returned with their lunches. At least, she thought, as she strode out of the dining room, she wasn't going to have to finish her milk.

chapter 18

The week passed in a flurry of activity as Miranda worked out the details of her alleged upcoming trip to meet Tom and the Ballantyne board meeting that would follow.

Each day she tried to tamp down her anticipation over seeing Blake that night, and each evening she raced home humming with excitement to freshen up and await the Summerses' arrival.

With Andie as their audience and safety valve, they feinted and jabbed, sparring with each other over Andie and every other topic that presented itself. When Tom's name came up, she turned the conversation, and by Thursday the sexual tension was thick enough to cut with a knife. Unaffected by the physical distances they kept between them, it hovered and sim-mered in the air until Miranda was convinced only Andie's presence protected them from it . . . and them-selves.

More alarming than the physical attraction was how much she enjoyed being with him. He was smart and quick-witted and, when it came to his daughter, en-dearingly old-fashioned. It was clear that if he could wrap Andie up in cotton wool and protect her from the world, he would.

As she had all week, Miranda raced home on Friday already looking forward to the evening ahead. After downing a ham-and-cheese sandwich, she showered and changed. In jeans and a tight-fitting turtleneck, she practically skipped downstairs to answer the door-bell. Blake stood on the threshold when she pulled the door open. Alone. Miranda poked her head out into the cold and looked behind him for Andie.

"She was running a temperature. I was going to call and cancel, but . . ."

"Don't tell me. She cried."

Blake nodded. "I know better, but I always feel so guilty that I'm all she's got. If I hadn't insisted on com-ing back to Truro to look after Gus, she might still have a mother. Of sorts."

Miranda took his hand and pulled him inside. "She's lucky to have a father so moved by his daughter's tears—manufactured or not. When did you turn into such a softy?"

"I believe it happened in the delivery room, right

about the time they put her in my arms. Her face was all scrunched up, and she was bald as a billiard ball. And she was the most beautiful thing I'd ever seen."

She dropped his hand as her heart twisted. Would she ever look down into the squalling face of a child of her own? Would Tom still be here if they had been able to create a new life between them?

She and Blake stood in the foyer contemplating each other.

"I shouldn't have come."

She looked up into his eyes. "No, you probably shouldn't have."

Heat shimmered off him and enveloped her. Her limbs felt heavy, and her blood thickened and pooled in places it had no business pooling. "But you might as well give me your coat."

He shrugged out of the down-filled jacket, and she took it from him, turning to hang it in the foyer closet. Without further comment she led him into the great room, where they sank down on opposite ends of the couch, each clinging to a rolled arm as if the width of two cushions was enough to keep them away from each other.

She'd meant to offer wine but thought better of it. "Would you like a Coke?" She asked.

"No, I'm fine."

"Good."

More silence.

With clumsy fingers, Miranda picked up a sheet of tissue paper and began to mold it into shape. Several long heartbeats later, Blake followed her lead. For a while they worked in silence, with just the crackle of the fire and the crumple of tissue paper for background— a far cry from the steady stream of chatter Andie had generated.

Miranda's pageant training had always enabled her to talk to anyone. Starting and maintaining a conversation had become second nature to her, but all of the things she was afraid of saying to Blake kept her silent.

The air between them throbbed with their awareness of each other, and a part of her—the abandoned, humiliated part—wanted to tell him that she was no longer married in any real sense of the word. A simple "Tom wears lace and he's left me, and I'm planning to get a divorce as soon as I save Ballantyne and find his thong-wearing rear end" would certainly clear the way for all the things her body wanted his to do to hers right now.

But then she'd also have to admit that Ballantyne was in serious trouble, that she had no idea where Tom was, and that she'd been lying to everyone, including him, for the past two months. Whoever said the truth would set you free probably hadn't been lusting after their chief of police.

With a sigh, she finished the flower she was working on and dropped it in the waiting vase. "You're getting faster," she commented.

Blake looked up, surprised.

"Not necessarily better, but faster."

He held up the big red ball with the black leaves to

the light. "You don't think I have a future in tissue paper?"

"I wouldn't give up my day job," she said, trying for a flip tone. "But you've done a nice thing." She nodded toward the vases of tissue-paper flowers that dotted the room. "There aren't a lot of men who would risk this sort of humiliation for their child."

"That's parenthood for you. If it's not your heart, it's your ego. You're always risking something."

"What about Andie's mother? Where's she in all of this?"

He shook his head and settled back on the couch. "The kindest word I can come up with is 'absent.'" He smiled, but there was no humor in it. "Not physically absent. She didn't up and disappear like my mother did. We know where she lives, and if I work at it hard enough, Andie gets to visit with her in Atlanta once in a while. I'm taking her in next weekend, in fact. But Sandra refuses to set foot in this, I think her insult of choice is 'one-horse town,' and her daughter is pretty close to the bottom of a very long list of priorities."

Miranda's heart twisted for both Andie and Blake, and at the same time she wanted to rail at the injustice. Women who didn't want them had children every day while she, who wanted one so desperately, had been denied that privilege.

She invited him into the kitchen, and as she bustled around making coffee, she thought of all the times she'd wished her own mother would leave her alone or butt out of her life; perhaps it was time to appreciate the love and attention, however judgmental, she'd always received.

They drank coffee and ate big helpings of a chocolate cake Miranda had brought from the Dogwood. Their conversation turned to more casual things, as both of them pulled back from the sexual precipice they'd teetered on earlier, and when they went back to work on the flowers, Miranda was reminded all over again that Blake Summers was good company, surprisingly well read and interested in what was going on in the world beyond Truro.

The exciting bad boy of twenty years ago had turned into a man who appeared completely comfortable with his place in the world. And if he regretted choices he'd made along the way, he was making the best of them and not looking for a means of escape. Unlike Tom, he made her feel as if her company was more than enough to fill an evening. And she was willing to bet big money he didn't need to parade around in women's underwear or cheat on his wife to keep things interesting.

"I can't believe it's already eleven." Blake looked down at his watch and stood, giving her a crooked smile. "What's our total?"

She looked down at the pad in front of her, then stood and moved toward him. "We have eighty-five. Only fifteen flowers to go."

They were standing much too close to each other. If she wasn't careful, they'd be close enough to . . .

"Maybe I should take the supplies with me and

finish up at home. I'm sure I can browbeat Gus into doing a few."

She felt a brief stab of disappointment, when what
she should have been feeling was relief. "If all else fails,
you can get Andie to shed some motivational tears.
And I can extend her deadline a few extra days. We
won't decorate the hall until just before the ball."

It was time for him to leave, but neither of them
moved. She could feel the warmth of his breath on her
hair and then on her cheek. Reluctantly, she leaned
down and gathered a pile of tissue paper and wire and
tucked them into a shopping bag, which she held out
to him. He took it but still didn't move. If she didn't do
something soon he was going to kiss her. And then
where would she be?

She took a giant step backward and tilted her chin
in the air. Then she was walking with him to the foyer
and pulling his coat out of the closet. It hurt to watch
him shrug it on.

"Thanks for all the help," he finally said. "Are you
okay with turning the flowers in, or do you want me to
come back and—"

"No, I'll do it." Normally she would have reached
past him to open the front door, but she was afraid to
get that close.

When she was perilously near breaking down and
wrapping her arms around him and planting her lips
on his, he reached for the knob and pulled open the
front door, letting in a blast of unspringlike air.

"So, I guess I'll see you around," he said, not moving.

"Yes." She stared up at him as the cold reached in and found them. "Tell Andie I hope she feels better."

"Will do." He stared down into her eyes for another long moment, and then he was gone.

Miranda stood in the open doorway watching him get in his car and back down the driveway. And then she waited some more for the cool night air to bring her body temperature down.

Saturday morning's "Truro Tattles" headline read QUEEN PREGNANT! WHERE'S KING? and spiraled downward from there. Miranda spent most of the weekend alternately trying to keep herself from threatening to drop-kick Clara Bartlett into orbit and mooning after Blake Summers, and neither activity put her in a particularly sunny frame of mind.

When she woke Monday to an impossibly beautiful sky, a glowing sun, and temperatures hovering in the low sixties, Miranda was totally pissed off.

When you had cramps, a business and town you had to save, a gossip columnist who was out to get you and now believed you were pregnant, a mother who was barely talking to you, plus strong and totally inappropriate feelings for the chief of police—which made you completely and unfulfillably horny—the Universe owed you dark and dreary.

Backing the car out of the drive, Miranda roared

toward town trying to ignore the sparkle of sun on the ice now melting off tree branches and the thin trickle of water slipping down the hard rock face of the mountain. The air was crisp, and the sky so blue and clear that she could see a lone hawk circling above Ballantyne Bald. Spring was practically here, and she felt like a Grinch looking for a Christmas to steal.

How could her world look so clean and shiny when the weight of it hung so heavily on her shoulders? And how could she be lusting after Blake Summers when that world could come crashing down at any minute?

In town, she screeched to a halt in front of the Dogwood and raced in to pick up a cup of coffee and two chocolate doughnuts, which looked like the closest thing to sexual satisfaction she was likely to get.

The place fell silent, and twenty-some pairs of eyes bored into her back as she took the bag from Jewel. When she turned slowly to face them, those eyes dropped to her stomach.

"I am NOT pregnant, and my personal life does NOT belong in the *Truro Gazette*."

No one blinked, and nobody spoke.

"Fine," she said. "Have a nice day." Dropping a five on the counter, Miranda squared her shoulders, stomped out the door, and roared through town in her BMW, hoping someone would be stupid enough to try to give her a ticket.

By the time she reached Ballantyne, her angst and sexual frustration had reached epic proportions. Helen St. James pulled into the parking lot right behind her, and as they crossed toward the building, Miranda waited for the bookkeeper to say something—anything—she could take exception to. The woman remained infuriatingly quiet.

Outside the front entrance Miranda rounded on her. "Don't mess with me today, Helen."

"Okay."

"I am in such a shitty mood that I don't even want to talk to me."

She gave Helen the eyebrow, but the other woman just smiled. "I know the feeling."

Oh, great, just what she needed, something else in common with her husband's girlfriend! She added the other eyebrow and the woman stepped back.

Good thinking. Miranda entered the lobby alone.

At the reception desk Leeta shot her a big grin and stole a peek at her stomach. "Mornin', Mrs. Smith. Beautiful day, isn't it?"

Miranda gritted her teeth and forced the corners of her mouth up in what she hoped would pass for a smile. If she didn't shake this mood soon she was going to rip someone's head off.

She checked her stride as she passed Carly's empty desk. Finding her own office door open, she called out as she entered. "Carly, I need you to—"

"My mommy's not here."

The little-girl voice stopped Miranda cold. She and the pint-size person sitting in her chair stared each other in the eye.

"That would make you Lindsey," Miranda observed.

"Uh-huh. My mommy wented to make coffee for the boss." The child smiled Carly's smile and twirled a single blond curl around a chubby finger.

"Well, now, I guess that would be me, since that's my desk you're sitting at." She gave the child the eyebrow, but it apparently didn't work on small, blond-haired children. "Are you planning to do my work for me today?"

"Sure." She held up a crayon. "What kind of picture do you need?"

"Lindsey?" Carly's horrified voice reached them from the outer office.

"In here," Miranda called.

Her assistant rushed in, coffee in hand, and came to a halt in front of Miranda's desk. "I'm so sorry, Mrs. Smith. I didn't have anyone to leave her with." She leveled a look at her daughter. "And she knows this room is completely off limits."

She hurried around the desk and lifted her daughter out of Miranda's chair. "I was thinking there might be a call from Mr. Smith later this morning when Helen comes in for the scheduled meeting."

"Sure." Miranda nodded numbly. Might as well torture someone else. It was no fun feeling this crummy all by herself.

"I'll take care of it," Carly replied. "And, uh, I was wondering if you'd like me to set up a lunch or something with your mother. We haven't heard from her for a while."

Leave it to Carly to notice the cold shoulder Joan Harper had turned Miranda's way.

"No," Miranda said, "that won't be necessary." There was no point in sitting down with her mother if she wasn't going to back down or explain completely, neither of which she could picture doing right now. "I'll talk to her when I get back in town. But I would like you to schedule an appointment for me with Dana Houseman while I'm in Atlanta."

"Okay." Carly's look of sympathy made her feel even more alone. As Miranda watched, she turned a serious parent face back to the child in her arms. "Tell Mrs. Smith you're sorry, Lindsey," she admonished as they moved toward the door.

Miranda looked from mother to daughter and back again as the child made her apology. Same smile, same eyes, same curly blond hair. She felt a prickling behind her eyelids. Her grandmother and mother had daughters. Blake Summers had a daughter. Even unmarried Carly Tarleton had a daughter. Everybody, it seemed, had a daughter but her.

"It's all right." Miranda grabbed a tissue off her desk and blew her nose to camouflage the sob that was trying to escape. "Maybe we should put her to work on our advertising campaign. I understand she has her crayons with her."

Carly smiled in relief and hurried the child out of the office, pulling the door closed behind her. Miranda waited a beat to be sure they were gone. And then she sat down in the still-warm chair and burst into tears.

chapter 19

It took Andie four days to work up the nerve to ask Jake Hanson to the Guild Ball. She wanted to be the kind of woman Miranda Smith had described—bold, sure of what she wanted, determined to succeed—but when she looked deep inside to see what she was made of, she discovered that she was built a lot like a Tootsie Pop—hard and shiny on the outside, soft and chewy on the inside.

Today, she'd decided, the wimpiness was going to end. Which was why she was standing in front of Jake's locker watching him and ML walk toward her. Jake's eyes got a really cool kind of twinkle in them when he spotted her, which was the only thing that kept her from abandoning her position. Mary Louise's eyes narrowed, and she wrapped herself more tightly around Jake, but Andie intended to see this through even if she had to conk ML on the head and stuff her in an empty locker to do it.

"How are those paper flowers coming?" The other girl's tone was snide. "Must be kind of rough with your hand out of commission and all."

"I'm managing."

"Too bad about missing the game," Jake said. "That would flat out drive me crazy."

"Yeah, you can say that again," Andie said.

Conversation stopped as Jake opened his locker. Mary Louise stepped even closer to him, then reached past him to pull a half-opened gift box off the top shelf.

"Here, Jake," she said, shooting a triumphant look at Andie. "Why don't you put on some of the cologne that I bought you?"

Jake looked distinctly uncomfortable, but before he could respond, Mary Louise lifted the bottle up and sprayed some behind Jake's ear. Then she sneezed.

Andie sucked the stuff into her lungs. It was heavy and musky, and totally obliterated that wonderful Jake smell. She coughed lightly.

Mary Louise's eyes watered as she doubled over from the force of another sneeze. "Ah-choo!"

Andie couldn't help noticing how bad ML's face looked.

"Oh, God, how can I be allergic to Libido by Donati?" Mary Louise wailed. "The saleslady told me it was her number one seller." She sneezed again as tears ran down her cheeks.

Andie and Jake exchanged looks.

"Gosh, Mary Louise," Andie said innocently. "Are those hives?"

The other girl shrieked. "Oh, my God, I'm starting to swell."

"Do you want me to take you to the clinic?" Jake asked. "You should probably take an antihistamine."

"No!" She shrieked again. "Don't look at me!"

Andie was trying not to enjoy herself. "Wow," she exclaimed. "Look at the size of those welts."

Mary Louise's fingers flew to her face, and she shrieked again. "Don't look! I've got to get home!" And she raced down the hall away from them, already whipping her cell phone out of her purse. The last thing they heard was a sneeze and a wail.

"Guess she should have smelled that stuff before she bought it for you," Andie observed.

"Yeah." She could tell he was fighting back a smile just like she was. She liked that he was too nice to crack up over it.

The bell rang and Andie knew it was now or never.

"So, um, I was wondering." She brought her books to her chest and paused to gather strength. "Did Mary Louise already ask you to be her escort to the Guild Ball?"

"Yeah."

Andie's shoulders drooped. "Okay." She knew she

should get to class. She'd lost track of how long ago the bell had rung.

Jake reached out and placed a hand on her arm. His fingers were warm, and his eyes were . . . God, she really liked his eyes.

"I was kind of hoping you'd ask me first," he said. "But when you didn't . . ." He shrugged. "Well, I figured maybe you'd asked somebody else."

Andie shook her head and tried not to sigh with disappointment when his hand dropped to his side. "Just slow," she said. *And chicken,* she thought, as she walked beside him to the office to pick up a tardy slip.

But Mrs. Smith was right. If she'd dragged her feet this way on a basketball court, she'd have had a permanent spot on the bench.

"Have a good trip," Carly called out as Miranda stopped at her desk on the way out of the office on Friday afternoon. "Tell Mr. Smith I said hey."

Miranda stopped in her tracks and looked around. She and Carly were completely alone.

"Sorry," her assistant said. "I got a little carried away."

Miranda sighed. The week had been long and brutal, and the only thing it had going for it was that it was almost over.

"I'll call you on Monday after I meet with Selena. You can reach me on my cell phone if you need anything before then."

"Got it, Boss!" Carly saluted smartly. "Maybe when you get back we can talk about that promotion..."

Too tired to raise an eyebrow, Miranda exited the building and crossed the parking lot. She'd cancelled her Rhododendron group in order to make her alleged flight out of Hartsfield-Jackson Airport in Atlanta, and now it was time to leave for her imaginary weekend with Tom.

In hindsight, the whole charade felt slightly ridiculous and unnecessarily expensive. She'd spent twelve hundred dollars on an airline ticket to a place she had no intention of going, and an arm and a leg on a suite at the Ritz-Carlton that she'd be inhabiting alone. Spending a weekend holed up at the Ritz in Atlanta wasn't going to solve any problems, but the further south she traveled the lighter her heart grew. A couple days outside the fishbowl could do great things for the fish.

Beginning to look forward to her weekend away, Miranda zigzagged down the mountainside, passing through Dillard and Mountain City on her way to Highway 985. She was approaching the on ramp when the BMW began to lose power. One minute she was moving along at a good clip, the next the car was decelerating, and putting her foot on the gas pedal had no impact whatsoever. Unsure what else to do, she steered the car onto the shoulder of the two-lane highway and rode the brake lightly until the car sputtered to a stop.

"Damn." Resisting the urge to beat her head against the steering wheel, Miranda put the car in park, clambered out, and used all of her pent-up frustration and anxiety to kick the front tire. When this failed to make her feel better, she took aim at the front bumper—another meaningless gesture that did nothing but dent in the toe of her shoe.

"Shit!" Fresh out of things to kick and unable to come up with anything more profound to shout, she popped open the hood, stomped back around to the passenger door, and leaned in to grab her purse from the front seat. It took a little longer to figure out whom to call.

By the time Blake made it back to the house to pick up Andie for the drive to her mother's in Atlanta, he was doing a slow burn. The day hadn't been all that great to start with, but it had taken a serious nosedive when the rest of the answers to his inquiries about Tom Smith had begun to trickle in.

He didn't know why he was so upset to receive confirmation that Tom Smith had never used the airline ticket to Hong Kong that Ballantyne had bought for him, or checked into, or been seen at, the Hong Kong hotel where he'd been booked, but the more he found out, the more confused and irritated he became.

There was nothing like wanting to sleep with a woman to make a man abandon all semblance of objectivity.

"Get a move on, Andie," he barked. "We're going to hit major traffic as it is." He wanted to drop his daughter and get to the airport in time to find out where Miranda was really going.

He and Andie made sporadic and unsuccessful attempts at conversation as they passed through Truro, their gazes locked on the road and the small towns that flew by.

They were almost to the Interstate when the traffic slowed unexpectedly. Blake spotted a tow truck backing into position and recognized Gabe Holcomb from Gabe's Gas 'n' Such in Truro at the controls. The car it was grappling was a bright red BMW.

"Hey, look, Dad. That's Mrs. Smith's car."

Blake pulled off the road and drove slowly up the shoulder toward the tow truck and its shiny prize. Miranda stood out of the way, shivering in her leather jacket, tapping the tip of one strangely dented shoe on the pavement. He and Andie got out of the car and walked toward her. Miranda greeted Andie warmly; he got a nod.

"What happened?" Blake asked.

"Not sure," Gabe replied. "I think it might be a leak in the transmission. I'm going to tow it in and look at it in the morning."

Blake glanced at Miranda. She had a dust-covered leather carry-on sitting at her feet and didn't look at all glad to see him.

"You okay?" he asked.

"Yes." She shifted her weight. "Just late."

"What time is your flight?" he asked as if he didn't know.

"An hour and a half from now." She shifted her weight again.

"We're going to Atlanta," Andie piped in. "We can give you a ride."

Miranda's look of panic was brief, but unmistakable.

Blake watched her face, willing her to say yes. Driving her to the airport would be a lot easier than trying to pick up her trail once he got there. "I have to drop Andie first, but I can run you on down to Hartsfield-Jackson after that. You can call the airline from the car and try to get on a later flight."

She didn't meet his gaze. "I really hate to put you out."

"It's no trouble." He picked up her bag and carried it to the Jeep. Andie slid into the backseat, but Miranda still stood where they'd found her. The tow truck's flashing light sent slivers of brightness streaking across her face. "Look," he said, walking back to her, "you can stand here on the side of the road and wait for a better offer. Or you can catch a ride back to Truro with Gabe and just forget about the whole trip. Hell, you'll barely have two days in San Francisco by the time you get there." He shrugged and began to wave Gabe over.

"No, wait." She swallowed. "I don't want to disappoint Tom."

"No, of course not." He paused. "Given how he's been away working so hard and all."

Her head jerked up. Without another word she went and conferred with Gabe, then stalked around his car, climbed into the front passenger seat, and slammed the door. Hard.

He spent the drive to Atlanta biting back the questions he wanted to hurl at her, but he couldn't help noticing that she didn't seem at all anxious about getting to the airport, and she hadn't bothered to get her cell phone out to call and make arrangements.

The number of things that didn't add up just kept adding up.

A few minutes after leaving Andie at her mother's, he and Miranda were on 85 speeding south toward the airport. Her face in the occasional spill of streetlight appeared pinched, and her gaze remained fixed on traffic. Her hands were clamped in her lap.

"Don't you think you should call and see about getting on another flight?" he asked.

She turned toward him for the first time. "No, I think I'll just wait until I get to the airport. It'll probably be easier to explain what happened in person."

"Are you going to call Tom?"

"Hmm?" She looked as if this had never occurred to her. "No, he, uh"—she looked down at her watch—"is probably in the air right now." She looked back out the windshield. "I'll call and leave a message at the hotel once I have a new arrival time."

They lapsed back into silence. He could feel the energy rolling off her and knew deep in his bones that she was as aware of him as he was of her. Part of him wanted to pull over and kiss her and tell her everything would be okay. The other part wanted to grill her mercilessly until he understood what in the hell was going on. Before he could figure out which approach to take, the signs for Hartsfield-Jackson Airport began to appear. A few minutes later they were pulling to a stop in front of the Delta check-in. They stood now beside the car with her carry-on wedged between them.

"Will you be all right?" he asked.

"Sure." Her gaze strayed toward the terminal and then scanned the traffic, settling on a taxi that whizzed by.

"Maybe I should wait and make sure you get on another flight."

"No!"

He cocked his head and studied her more closely.

"I mean, thank you, but I'll be fine."

"You're sure?"

"Absolutely. I'll be on the next plane out."

She went up on her toes and brushed her lips across his cheek, which created its own little burst of electricity, then stepped back quickly. "Thanks for the ride." Her gaze flitted over the traffic, the other passengers, everything but him. She didn't look toward the terminal, either. "I appreciate it."

"You're welcome," he said. "Have a good flight."

"Thanks," she said. "I'll do that." And then she picked up her bag and walked toward the terminal.

He watched her until she disappeared from view and then, because he was in the business of following up on hunches, and because the kiss she'd given him was not the kiss of a woman happily getting on a plane to visit her husband, he got in his car, drove it around to Arrivals, and pulled in to the curb just beyond the line of waiting taxis. When an airport cop came over to check him out, he flashed his own badge and settled in to wait.

Less than fifteen minutes later, Miranda came out of baggage claim and hailed a cab. He turned his head to hide his face as her taxi flew by, then he slid into the flow of traffic a few cars behind to follow her.

He could hardly wait to see where they were headed.

chapter 20

The bath in the suite of the Ritz-Carlton was glorious, the champagne from the minibar heavenly. Miranda continued to soak in the tub long after the water had cooled. Her body felt languid, and her brain, the one that had been racing at top speed for the last two months, had slowed to a comfortable jog. Best of all, no one from Truro could see her or judge her. No one could ask her to solve even the smallest problem. Or write an article about her. For this brief moment in time she was in complete control of her world, even if that world was about 730 square feet and located in Buckhead.

She climbed out of the tub with real regret, then wrapped herself in the terry-cloth robe the hotel had so thoughtfully provided. The feel of its bulky softness sliding against her naked skin made her tingle. Blake Summers popped into her head unsummoned, and she tingled some more.

Ho-kay. Padding barefoot across the bathroom's marble floor, she entered the bedroom and crossed to look out the marvelous bay window. Traffic inched along Peachtree toward Lenox Mall and Phipps Plaza, where Selena Moore's flagship store was located.

If she'd had any more antiques to sell, she could be shopping right now. Or being fussed over at any one of the day spas within a stone's throw of the hotel. But she'd shot her wad on this weekend escape—which, based on her bank balance, should have taken place in a Motel 6.

Searching for a distraction that didn't require dressing and going out, Miranda zeroed in on the room service menu. She pushed the extravagance factor from her mind and focused on the potential comfort factor. Food was good; large quantities of it even better. Making her selections used up a good ten minutes, but after placing her order she was back in bed staring inward. Her fears and responsibilities stared back.

"Oh, no, you don't." Closing her eyes, she pushed them away and searched for something more attractive to think about. Like Blake Summers. Naked. And knocking on the hotel room door.

Miranda groaned. The suite was spacious, but not large enough to allow her to outrun her fears or her feelings. She was alone in a beautiful suite designed for two, while her husband, who was probably wearing prettier underwear than she would have been if she were wearing any, was somewhere else and had no plans to return.

All of her hopes for Ballantyne hinged on Monday's meeting with Selena Moore and her ability to convince the Ballantyne board that Custom Cleavage—as she now thought of her idea—was the only way to save a business they didn't even know was foundering. Equally bad, she had become fodder for the Truro rumor mill, and people thought she was pregnant, even though she wasn't and probably never would be.

The first tear took her by surprise. It was hot and salty and took its time meandering down her cheek. The second came a lot faster. And it totally pissed her off. She swiped at it with the back of her hand and ordered herself to cease and desist. She was not going to be that woman in the mirror again; her crying days were over.

A knock sounded at the door, and she offered up a prayer of thanks for the interruption. Pulling the robe tighter, she went to the door and looked through the peephole.

A waiter, looking nervous, stood behind a rolling cart piled high with domed silver platters. She opened the door and discovered that a girl had to be careful what she wished for.

Blake Summers stepped, unsmiling, up behind the waiter. "Lucy," he said, taking in the robe and the cart full of food. "You got some serious 'splainin' to do."

Blake flashed his badge and the waiter hightailed it toward the elevator. Taking control of the cart, Blake pushed it into the room and closed the door behind them.

"Where," he asked, "is Tom?"

Too stunned to pretend, Miranda looked him directly in the eye and told the truth. "I wish I knew."

This little revelation rocked him back on his heels. "Then who did you come here to meet?"

"No one."

His features etched with disbelief, Blake swept through the suite, doing what looked like a very thorough check for potential felons.

Miranda followed along. "Aren't you going to look under the bed?"

He turned to face her. "Is there someone under there?"

"No."

"Then I'll skip it."

They regarded each other warily. They were alone and they both knew it. She was naked under the robe, and she suspected they both knew that, too.

His eyes became less hawklike and she could practically see his mind rearranging the facts as he knew them, trying to fit the pieces together in a way that made sense. As if that were remotely possible.

Miranda couldn't decide whether to laugh or cry or jump his bones. She contemplated doing all three, though not necessarily in that order.

"So if Tom isn't here, where is he?"

"Beats me."

"You're telling me you really don't know where your husband is."

She considered lying, but it was a lot harder to bluff without clothes on. Besides, she wasn't sure what the point was anymore. And she didn't think she had the strength. She really, really wanted to feel Blake's arms around her. A promise that everything was going to be okay would be nice, too.

She nodded her head and her eyes welled up. God, she was tired of crying.

He took a step toward her but stopped a good foot away and his voice turned coolly professional. "When did you last see him?"

"January eighth."

"Talk to him?"

"January eighth."

She could see that she'd surprised him again. She and Carly must have been pretty convincing after all.

He glanced around the suite again, and she had the sense that he still expected someone to jump out from behind the drapes or something. He was wearing khakis and a black T-shirt that pulled tight across his chest, but he didn't need a uniform to look like a cop. "And this is?"

"Camouflage . . . R and R . . ." She shrugged, and before she could stop it, another tear slid down her cheek. "I'm not sure anymore."

"Damn it, Miranda. You should have told me." His

tone turned wry. "It's not like I didn't give you every opportunity."

She sniffed and her eyes welled up again. "I couldn't." Lifting a sleeve, she swiped at her nose with the terry-cloth.

"But why all the secrecy? If your husband left you, why the charade?"

"Because Ballantyne is in trouble, and I was afraid everybody would panic if they realized he was gone and the only thing standing between them and bankruptcy was"—she sniffed—"*me.*"

She sniffed again, and he reached over and grabbed a tissue out of the box on the desk and shoved it at her.

"I can nail a pageant interview in five seconds flat, but I don't exactly have a track record of wowing them in the boardroom."

She watched his internal struggle through tear-filled eyes. He paced the room, still disbelieving, still trying to work it out. When he walked past her to sit on the sofa, she followed and sank into the corner next to him.

"Jesus, Miranda. Don't you have any idea where he is?"

"No." Another sniff. "He left a note saying he wasn't coming back."

"I'm assuming you've tried to find him."

"Yes, but I have a news flash for you. The reason the wife is always the last to know is because nobody wants to tell her anything. Not the airlines, not the hotels, not the credit card companies. I've been making car payments for a Mercedes I can't even find." She wadded the tissue into a ball and pressed it to her nose.

He went to the desk, rummaged in the drawer, and came back with a notepad and pen. When he sat down his gaze dropped to the bare triangle of skin where her robe came together, and she thought she heard a small groan. She didn't know if he'd ever questioned a semi-naked woman in a hotel room before, but it was clear he intended to try.

"I've retained a divorce attorney and a PI, but I can't afford any more spotlights in the 'Truro Tattles' until I convince the board that I have a plan to save the company."

She crossed one leg over the other, and both their gazes jerked downward.

Blake pulled his gaze back to the pad of paper. He scribbled something on it, then asked, "Do you *have* a plan?"

"I think so. I have a meeting here on Monday that I'm hoping will clinch it. Wednesday I get my chance to convince the board. But I need to put that plan into effect before everybody realizes how far into the toilet Tom put us."

She didn't think this was the time to bring up the word "fraud." And as much as she wanted to be honest with Blake, she didn't think this was the time to initiate a full police investigation. Or mention that she now knew Tom had shipped himself the goods intended for the fictitious accounts and pocketed the money. And really, when you came right down to it, what would exposing Tom's love of lingerie or the affair he'd apparently been having achieve?

She watched Blake make notes on his pad and told herself she wasn't actually lying to him; she was just withholding certain details until the time was right.

He made another note and then looked up to meet her eye. "Do you have *any* clues at all?"

She could see just how hard he was working at staying focused and wished she could admire him for it. But she'd told him everything she felt she could, and her body's tingling was turning into a pretty persuasive clamoring. "It's hard to pump people for information when you're pretending you don't need any."

He wrote something else, and she leaned forward to try to make it out. Her robe fell open and the room grew unnaturally quiet. And hot. In fact, she felt warm all over.

Blake's eyes moved to her lips. And stayed there.

"You're not going to kiss me, are you?" she finally asked.

"God, I hope not."

"Yeah, me too." She licked her lips. "Because that would be a really bad idea until I figure out how to find and divorce Tom. And then there's Ballantyne. I'm really preoccupied with trying to save it." Her voice trailed off.

"I can see how busy you are with that." His eyes roamed downward to the place where the robe's lapels had once met.

"Getting involved with you would really complicate things," she said.

The sash of her robe loosened and the robe fell completely open. She swallowed. "And you definitely don't get the pageant thing. Or your daughter for that matter."

He was no longer even trying to meet her eye. His gaze on her body felt like a caress.

She looked down, too. Her nipples were hard and straining toward his touch, and she was afraid to open her mouth because a whimper might escape. She was hollow deep in her belly, and she wanted him. If a voice of reason was going to be raised, it wasn't going to be hers.

He took a finger and drew it slowly down between her breasts. "This is such a bad idea," he said. "It's stupid, ill advised, and completely unprofessional."

And then he kissed her. Good God, the man could kiss.

Before she could stop herself she was climbing into his lap, wrapping her legs around his waist and looping her arms around his neck so that he could carry her into the bedroom. Her heart was pounding so hard she could hardly hear, and when his lips moved to her breast she gasped and may have stopped breathing altogether. Which made conversation especially difficult.

Fortunately there wasn't a whole lot that needed to be said at the moment; at least nothing that couldn't be communicated with a moan or a sigh.

There'd be time enough for finding the right words

in the morning. Right now Miranda was having a perfectly lovely tête-à-tête with Blake's tongue.

Blake woke first. It might have had something to do with the warm breasts pressed against his chest or the round buttock beneath his hand.

Miranda burrowed closer in her sleep, and his body responded. Short strands of dark hair stuck out in a million directions, and her skin was warm and smelled of their lovemaking. He absolutely could not believe he had done anything this stupid.

Her eyes opened. They were a cloudy green and full of questions for which he had no answers.

"Good morning," he said as conversationally as he could, given their nakedness and the size of his erection.

"Mmmm, good morning." Burying her face in the crook of his neck, Miranda pressed herself more tightly against him. He groaned as her hand moved down to find him.

Unable to resist, he rolled onto his back and pulled her on top of him. She was already wet, and as he began to move slowly inside her, he tried not to think about how perfectly they fit. Or whether giving in to his desire for her a second time automatically made him twice as stupid.

The next time he awoke, sunlight was streaming in through the window, and the scent of coffee filled the room. He opened one eye and saw her sitting in a club chair with her feet tucked under her, a china cup raised to her lips. She was wearing the white terry-cloth number and a smile.

"Good morning again." He yawned and stretched, then kicked the sheet out of his way.

Her eyes dropped to his lap for a moment, then found his face. "He awakes."

"He does." He rubbed a hand against the stubble that covered his jaw.

"There's a razor in the bathroom, and plenty of hot water. After all," she looked up, and her smile was lop-sided, "it's the Ritz."

He stood and leaned over to drop a kiss on the top of her head. Ten minutes later he was showered and shaved and fully dressed, though he'd been forced to go commando. Sitting on the sofa in the living room of the suite—where everything had begun the night before—he reminded himself again just how many cops lost their jobs every year because of alcohol and women, but it was a little bit late for reminders.

Blake located the pen and picked up the notepad, quickly flipping past his sketch of the fully aroused bumblebee. "Let's go back over what happened on January eighth and immediately afterward," he said. "It's been over two months, which makes his trail pretty cold. But maybe you can give me somewhere to start."

He listened carefully as Miranda told him the little she claimed she knew. But she was nervous and had trouble meeting his eye, and she still didn't mention that Tom had emptied their accounts or offer any specifics of what exactly her husband might have done to Ballantyne.

He was amazed at how many balls this woman had managed to keep in the air, and he wanted to help her for more reasons than he could count. But he had a very bad feeling about all the things she was leaving out. He was definitely going to have to keep his hands to himself until he found Tom Smith and hauled him back to Truro.

chapter 21

Miranda simmered with anticipation as she walked into Selena Moore's flagship store on Monday morning. The boutique was as sleek and sophisticated as the clothes it showcased. With four locations in Atlanta, seventeen others in high-end malls throughout the Southeast, and plans to expand nationwide, the company was the perfect star to which to hitch Ballantyne's wagon.

"Hello, Selena." Miranda offered her hand to her former pageant competitor. "Thanks for fitting me in." She followed the willowy blonde to a back office and took a seat on the opposite side of a very expensive-looking glass desk. As high school girls and then college students, they'd taken turns beating each other in pageants across the Southeast, and while their friendship had been tempered by a decade of competition, their respect for each other had never wavered.

They chatted for a few minutes about other girls they'd known in their pageant days, and as she sized the other woman up now, Miranda almost licked her lips in anticipation. It would take some delicate maneuvering to convince Selena that exclusive representation of Ballantyne's custom business was a plum to be snatched. Looking too eager would be a mistake; appearing too standoffish would be equally fatal. Carefully, Miranda steered the conversation around to business.

"I saw the piece in the *New York Times*," Miranda began. "I loved the whole 'Former Miss Dogwood Builds Retail Empire' thing."

Selena smoothed a hand over her already impeccable chignon. "Yes. That article did great things for our initial stock offering." She smiled with satisfaction. "I absolutely adore the shock on their Wall Street faces when they realize I have a brain. They think anyone who ever set foot on a pageant stage is dumb as a post. They stroll into meetings smirking and walk out trying to figure out what hit them. There's nothing quite so satisfying as a mystified man."

Miranda laughed. "If there's anyone who can keep them baffled, it's you." She paused, and her tone turned more serious. "I have a lot of respect for what you've accomplished, Selena." She paused again. "And I think there may be a way we can help each other."

Selena's features communicated polite interest, nothing more, as she waited for Miranda to continue.

"I'm in the process of reinventing a family company that's been around for over a hundred years." She made eye contact and leaned forward as casually as she could. "I'm looking for the right chain of upscale boutiques to help me introduce our new product line to our target market."

They studied each other carefully.

Selena's smile was noncommittal. "I'm assuming this is where I would come in?"

"Possibly." Miranda opened her briefcase and pulled out her samples. Each component had been done in a basic beige satin that wouldn't detract from the piece itself. She had three kinds of cups, straps and closures of every variety, and three types of underwire. Then she pulled out five different bras, each a different compilation of the individual components. She laid them out on Selena's desk and explained her concept as succinctly as possible.

"Are you looking for an investment from me?" Selena remained cool, but her body language was just a shade too casual.

"No, just a corner of each store, committed sales help, and an agreed-upon amount for co-op advertising."

Selena leaned forward in her seat. "Totally custom is perfect for our clientele," she admitted cautiously, "but what about taking true measurements? That would be critical."

Miranda knew she had her as soon as the other woman began to focus on the details, but she was careful to keep her mental happy dance to herself.

"You're right. According to industry statistics, one out of five women is wearing the wrong size."

"So how do you plan to handle that?" Selena sat back and crossed her arms.

"I'm going to provide fitters for every store. In the beginning, our fitters will do all the measuring and ordering, but they'll be training store staff at the same time. When we think the store people are ready, we'll give them a complete written manual and we'll staff a help line around the clock for any salesperson or customer with a question or problem. Total service, total fit, and total comfort is what we plan to deliver."

"Well..."

Miranda could see Selena's mental calculator tabulating the pros and cons. It took every shred of self-control she possessed to keep her tone casual. "Oh, come on, Selena," she said. "Admit it. You haven't had an opportunity this good since Janice Finch broke out in chicken pox right before the Miss Black-Eyed Pea Pageant."

Still Selena hesitated, but Miranda had her fish on the line, and she wasn't leaving until she'd reeled it in.

"Ballantyne has been passed down by the women in my family for five generations," Miranda said. "It's mine now, and I intend to give other women what they want and need—even if they don't know what that is yet. And I intend to stand behind every bra we sell."

She watched Selena carefully, looking for some sign that the woman was going to cave. Finally the other woman tugged on her right earlobe in a signal of capitulation Miranda remembered well, then leaned across her desk to finger a demiunderwire with an extra-wide elastic strap.

"I'll commit to a trial period for our Atlanta stores. But we're going to have to spend some time hammering out the terms of a broader joint venture. And I need more information on price point and terms of delivery. And how we'll share the profits." The other woman looked her in the eye. "Shall I have my attorney call yours?"

"Yes." Miranda offered her hand and stood. When you'd gotten what you wanted, it was always best to get up and get out before the other party could reconsider. "Anytime after Wednesday is good."

They walked to the front of the store together chatting easily. As they parted company Miranda managed to hold back the whoop of triumph she wanted to send echoing through the mall.

Looking for a socially acceptable release, she turned and followed her homing instincts toward Saks Fifth Avenue. Vibrating with excitement and relief, she browsed store windows and thought about what would come next. When Blake Summers popped uninvited into her mind she pushed him back out. His daughter was allowed to remain.

It was in the window of a store called Timeless that she spotted the ball gown. It was clean-lined and elegant and would be absolutely perfect for Andie. She would have loved to put it on hold and bring the girl back to see it, but there was a good chance her mother had already helped her choose something, or that Blake might not like the idea of Miranda being the one to introduce his daughter to the fine art of shopping.

Still, the dress begged to be bought. So Miranda hurried in, spent a highly enjoyable twenty minutes picking out accessories to go with it, and left with the entire ensemble tucked under her arm.

There was nothing like a little shopping to cleanse a woman's soul.

And nothing like a meeting with your divorce attorney to muck it back up again.

"I wish I had more to report," Dana Houseman said later after they'd gone over the marital history Miranda had completed. "But so far we have no strong leads as to your husband's whereabouts."

"But I thought you said we could proceed even without Tom."

"We can, but we can't go to court until we find him and have him served, or prove to the court that we've made a diligent effort to find him and have published notice."

"And how long do you think that will take?"

Her attorney shook her head. "That I don't know. But I do know that Harrison Maples is one of the best

PIs in Atlanta. And right now finding your husband is his top priority."

On the day of the Ballantyne board meeting, Miranda woke before the alarm. Clad in her flannel pajamas, she stood in front of the mirror and ran through her presentation to the Board from start to finish, anticipating the exact way she'd use her visuals and how she'd place her samples, and coming up with an appropriate counterpoint to every objection they could possibly make. Using all the visualization techniques she'd learned as a pageant contestant, she pictured herself convincing the Board and driving toward her winning outcome.

When she could put it off no longer, she took a quick shower and dressed, choosing the Armani suit and, for luck, the strand of perfectly matched pearls her grandmother had given her on her eighteenth birthday.

Too nervous to eat, she poured a cup of coffee into a travel mug and drove to the office. Carly was already at her desk when she arrived.

"Are you as wired as I am, Boss?"

"Who, me?" She put a hand to her chest. "Why, I just live to be thrown in front of an audience where I get to tap dance without music while balancing the fate of the free world on my shoulders."

Carly smiled.

"If I pass out or anything, just drag me under the conference table and take over, okay?"

"Okay."

"Does Helen have the projections?"

"Yep."

"She's just there for window dressing, Carly. If she starts anything, I want you to put knockout drops in her coffee."

"A pleasure, but why wait until she acts up?"

Miranda laughed, and some of the tension seeped out of her.

"So about that promotion . . ." Carly began.

"If we win board approval today, *you* are Ballantyne's new assistant designer. Myrna will be kissing my feet. Maybe Lindsey can take over your old job; she's not afraid of anybody."

"Well, she *is* really good with a crayon." Carly reached over and smoothed the collar of Miranda's suit jacket. "You'll knock 'em dead. They won't know what hit them. You'll—"

"Enough," Miranda interrupted. "Let's just pray my mother shows up." She handed Carly the box of samples and picked up the presentation folders she'd prepared for each board member. "The charts and graphs are already in the conference room, but I'd like to go up now and run through everything one more time. The best defense is a strong offense."

By 9:00 A.M. the stage was set, and Miranda stood, her lips turned up in a professional smile, her mouth dry as the Sahara, ready to greet the arriving members of the board. Her father was the first to walk through the door.

"Hello, Button." Her father kissed her on the cheek and patted her on the shoulder.

"Hi, Daddy." She kissed him back and tried not to wince at his use of her old nickname. "You're looking great," she said, relieved to see that it was true. She hoped that would still be the case when the meeting was over.

Longtime Ballantyne family attorney Reuben Blainsford arrived next. Miranda shook his hand and passed him on to Carly for seating. Reuben's father had been legal advisor to her own great-grandfather, and he was as fiscally conservative as they came. He'd be most swayed by the numbers and projections, and Miranda was counting on the fact that her plan would require no real retooling or investment to help make up his mind.

Hartley Mellish, Claymore's self-proclaimed Chicken King, was next through the door. Having recently sold his chicken-processing plant to Tyson, he understood the necessity of taking risks to earn big rewards. He pumped her hand and then gave her father a hearty clap on the back before taking his seat next to Reuben. Miranda knew better than to count her Chicken King before he hatched, but she fully expected Hartley to see things her way.

Her grandmother and mother arrived together, and her father's look of surprise told her he had not been expecting either of them. While Gran occasionally sat in on meetings and received board communication on a regular basis, her mother had been content to leave the business in her husband's hands—a practice Miranda had also followed until recently. Miranda sent her mother a peacemaking smile and realized just how precarious things were when her mother didn't return it.

Helen St. James entered with less fanfare and took the open seat between Carly and Gran. After waiting a few moments for everyone to settle in, Miranda called the meeting to order. While a vote of unanimous support would be wonderful, all she really needed were three of the five. Her mother was the wild card, and although Miranda wanted to take her appearance as a good sign, she wasn't sure what her mother would do once she understood what was being proposed.

It would take all of Miranda's skills of persuasion to convince this group to follow her lead, especially without giving away the full extent of Tom's treachery.

When she had their attention, Miranda began to speak. She called on every scrap of public-speaking experience, gleaned primarily in pageant interviews and on pageant stages, to present her vision for Ballantyne. She spoke for thirty-five minutes, with Carly doing a corporate Vanna White by her side.

"As we've demonstrated," Miranda concluded, "there will be virtually no capital outlay for retooling or fabrics. Selena Moore Boutiques, which are already located in twenty-one of the most upscale malls in the Southeast, has committed to carrying our new custom line in their four Atlanta stores with plans to be a part of their chain nationwide. All we have to supply are the fitter/trainers and, of course, the end product."

She paused. "As you can see from the financials, our bottom line is grim right now. In order to compete in today's marketplace we have to either take production offshore, which we are committed NOT to do, or radically change our niche in the marketplace. By shifting our focus to hand-sewn custom pieces and redeploying our labor force in new ways, we can build a better, more solvent company."

She'd decided not to mention the fake receivables, in the belief that pledging her own assets had alleviated the risk of prosecution. She glanced over at Reuben Blainsford before continuing. "The figures speak for themselves. Our line of credit will see us through the next six months, and because I believe so strongly in the company and what I want it to become, I've pledged personal assets to guarantee that line of credit."

Her heart hammered in her chest, and her palms were sweaty, but she kept her gaze level and her hand steady as she paused to take a drink of water. She studied each director, trying to get a sense of which way they would vote, but after her impassioned plea, the only clear yes she saw was Gran. Had her effort not to trash Tom prevented her from making them understand the precariousness of the company's situation? It appeared she was about to find out.

"Before we call for a vote, are there any questions?" Miranda asked.

"Where's Tom?" Hartley Mellish's question sent Miranda's heart plummeting to her knees. It was imperative, at least in her mind, that they look forward and not back.

"Tom has been away for the last several months. The losses we've sustained were a direct result of his leadership. I am the acting president of the company and will remain so unless the board sees fit to remove me. My résumé is in the presentation folder. As most of you know, I have an MBA from Emory, which I am at last putting to use." She smiled ruefully. "And connections to an important retail chain that could be our salvation."

"But where's Mr. Smith?" Helen St. James got her question in before either Gran or Carly could cut her off.

"It doesn't matter where he is. He's not coming back." She looked the other woman in the eye without flinching. "I think he's done enough damage already, don't you?"

Helen's lips pressed into a tight line, but not before Miranda saw the hurt in her eyes.

"I know," Miranda said softly, surprised by the pity she felt. "We all expected more of him."

"So Tom is not in China looking for suppliers?" Her father's voice was laced with disappointment and disbelief. His were the hardest eyes to meet.

Miranda shook her head. "No."

"So you've been lying all along," he said quietly. It wasn't a question.

Miranda felt his disapproval keenly. "I've tried to act in the best interests of this company. Ballantyne suffered huge losses under Tom's leadership, and he left rather than own up to them. I lied to prevent a panic, while I attempted to come up with a viable solution." She raised her chin. "And I think I've done that."

"I can't believe he just dumped all this on you." Her father shook his head sadly, and Miranda saw his reluctance to accept the truth about the son-in-law he'd treated like a son.

"Someone I know once taught me to play the hand I was dealt," she said, offering him a small smile. "That's what I've tried to do."

Gran stood. "I've heard enough. I move that we accept Miranda's proposal and put the weight of the Board behind her effort to reinvent Ballantyne." She looked around the table. "Do I hear a second?"

There was a long silence while they studied Miranda. It took everything she had not to fidget.

"I'm sorry." Reuben shook his shaggy head. "I appreciate your efforts, Miranda, but I'd have to see more numbers to be sure."

The Chicken King gave her a smile. "I think Miranda's done a bang-up job. And if you all aren't able to see it, I'd be glad to recommend her to the folks at Tyson. I second Cynthia's motion. And I vote in favor."

Miranda nodded her thanks, but she was having a hard time breathing. She needed one more vote in order to proceed, and one of her parents was going to have to give it. Her mother and father studied each other across the table. Try though she might, Miranda couldn't remember her mother even attending a board meeting before; she'd certainly never taken exception to any business decision her father had ever made.

Miranda's hands fisted at her sides. Years of frivolous living flashed before her eyes, and she wished she could take them back. Why hadn't she taken herself more seriously? If it all fell down around her ears right now, she'd have no one to blame but herself. She drew a shaky breath and silently promised God all kinds of things if only he'd step in and make this turn out okay.

Her father opened his mouth. "I have to say . . ." he began.

Miranda closed her eyes. And promised God she'd never ask for anything else—not even a child.

"I'mgoingtovotemystockmyself." Her mother's words came out in a rush, running together so that it took a moment to understand them.

Miranda's eyes flew open.

Her father's head shot up. "What did you say?"

Her mother rose slowly then turned to face the man to whom she'd been married for almost forty years. "I said," she swallowed, "I'm going to vote my stock myself."

Shock registered on her father's face. Hope blossomed in Miranda's heart.

"But you've never—" he began

"No, I haven't," Joan Ballantyne Harper said sadly. "I've always let others play my cards." A small smile appeared on her lips. "But I think our daughter has taken some really poor cards and turned them into a remarkable hand. And I think it's time for me to ante up, too." Her smile grew as she walked around the table and came to stand behind Miranda and her own mother. "I want to put my vote behind Miranda. I believe she's exactly what Ballantyne needs."

Miranda let out a ragged breath and managed not to yelp with happiness. Evidently, even in Truro, Georgia, the occasional miracle still happened.

Of course, she'd be even more ecstatic if the first person she wanted to tell wasn't Blake Summers.

chapter 22

Blake found Andie sitting on the bleachers in the school gym. She wasn't exactly crying, but the expression on her face told him she might start any moment. Her cast rested on her right knee, and her gaze was fixed on the far hoop as if she were meditating, or maybe offering up a prayer.

"Your cast'll be off soon."

"Yeah," she said without enthusiasm, as Blake climbed the risers and slid in beside her. They stared at the empty court for a few moments in silence, and then Andie said, "I can't believe I didn't get to play in the championship game."

"They would have had an easier time of it with you, but they managed to squeak by. The scouts'll be back."

They both contemplated that one for a moment.

"You know," she finally said, "the fact that I kind of like the whole pageant thing and boys and all doesn't mean I don't want to play basketball."

He sighed, but managed to remain silent.

"And just because Jake's a guy, it doesn't mean he's always thinking about his . . . stinger."

"Yes, it does."

She rolled her eyes, but scooted a little closer. "Why doesn't my mom want to be with me?"

Blake ran a hand through his hair and searched for the right words. How did you explain the unexplainable to a fifteen-year-old girl? He'd rather go back over the whole birds and bees thing. "I always hoped she'd explain things to you herself, but I'm not even sure she understands why her work always comes first." He slipped an arm around Andie's shoulders and was reminded, yet again, that she was no longer a little girl. "She grew up poor and neglected and got shuttled from relative to relative. She once told me that the only thing that kept her going was her determination to succeed; to prove they were all wrong not to want her."

He thought about his own disappointment when he'd realized his wife just didn't have room inside for anything else. "But no matter how well she does, it's never enough. And so she works harder and longer." He shook his head. "It hurts. I know it does. But she does love you. She just has no earthly idea how to show it."

Andie blinked back tears. Like she had as a child, she laid her head on his shoulder.

"You know, my mother left us when I was eight." Blake thought about his beautiful mother and her prized Rhododendron crown; it was one of the few things she'd taken with her.

"For a long time I thought I must be pretty unlovable if my own mother didn't want to stick around. I never wanted you to feel that way." He placed a kiss on the top of her head. "A lot of people love you very much. Your mother included."

The silence became more companionable. After a time, Andie lifted her good hand and swiped at her cheek.

"I really like Mrs. Smith," she said.

Blake froze. Once again, he'd rather teach a course in stamens and pistils than delve into his relationship—or lack of one—with Miranda.

"You like her, don't you?"

"Um, yes, she's very nice."

"No, I mean *like* her, like her. The way I like Jake."

"Well, now, I—"

He looked around, but there were no holes in the gym floor to crawl into, then gave her a minute to accept the fact that he wasn't going to answer. "So," he said by way of transition. "Have you asked someone else to be your escort for the ball?"

"No."

"I'm sure there are lots of boys who'd like to go with you." He'd finally accepted the idea of her going with a boy. He just wanted that boy to be short and homely and totally lacking in social skills. The direct antithesis of Jake Hanson would be about right. A eunuch would be perfect.

"Grandpa offered, but I think Mrs. Richards already invited him."

"I'd be happy to escort you, sweetheart. I haven't been to a dance in a while, but I think I still remember how to shag."

Andie rolled her eyes, but at least he'd made her smile. "Only old farts do the shag, Daddy. If you're going to come with me, you absolutely cannot dance."

Blake stood and offered Andie his arm. "Gus and I will take you shopping for a dress. Then we'll be quite the elegant couple," he said with a straight face. "And you don't have to worry about me not having the right clothes. I'm pretty sure I still have the blue velvet tux I wore to my high school prom."

Now that Miranda actually *wanted* to run into him, Blake Summers was nowhere to be found. She looked for him at Hyram's and at the counter of the Dogwood, but he was either avoiding her or visiting another planet. She tried to tell herself that what they'd shared was just sex, a much-needed weekend of R&R, but she was not feeling at all good about her impact on men.

Perhaps not too surprisingly, Blake appeared as soon as she stopped looking for him. It was the Thursday evening before the Guild Ball, and Miranda and the members of the decorating committee were in the process of turning the Masons' Hall into a full-fledged faux garden. Green indoor/outdoor carpet had been laid and wrought-iron fencing used to create flower beds around the perimeter of the room.

One minute she was sorting clay pots for the planned terrace; the next she was staring into Blake Summers's face. Andie stood next to him.

It was embarrassing the way just being near him made her heart pound. She'd replayed their night together so many times that seeing him clothed came as something of a surprise.

"Look, Mrs. Smith." Andie held out her right arm and raised her sleeve. Her hand and lower arm were unnaturally white, but they were no longer covered in bright orange.

"You got your cast off. That's so great."

"Yeah." Andie flexed her fingers and smiled. "It was getting awfully itchy in there. I'm glad to have my hand back."

"Congratulations." She kept her gaze locked on Andie, but every ounce of her being was aware of Blake. "Why don't you help—"

"Someone else," Blake cut in smoothly. Taking Andie by the shoulders, he turned her toward the group of girls on the far side of the room and gave her a gentle push.

He took a step toward Miranda and the rest of the room receded. He was standing so close she could smell the woodsy scent of his aftershave. A flush of heat shot up her neck and stained her cheeks. Only he could do this to her.

"I've been trying to find Tom," he said.

"Oh." She braced herself to hear that her husband was shacked up with some woman on the other side of the world, or modeling women's underwear for an underground fashion magazine. Or that Blake had already forgotten about their weekend at the Ritz.

"I promised myself I was going to stay away from you until I found him, but the man seems to have dropped off the face of the earth."

"Oh." She looked up into his blue eyes.

"In fact, there's no evidence that he ever left the country. I can't find him on an airline manifest anytime in January. And given the amount of money he had apparently taken out of your joint accounts, he could have bought a whole slew of airline tickets."

Miranda winced.

"You know, you could have actually told me things instead of forcing me to find everything out myself. I shudder to think what else you might have decided wasn't important enough to mention."

"Could he have just driven somewhere?" Miranda did *not* want to discuss her sins of omission; she was teetering between relief that Blake had not taken their weekend lightly and confusion over what so much difficulty in finding Tom might mean. So far, Harrison Maples hadn't fared any better. "I saw a story about a man who had two wives and two separate families living within a twenty-mile radius of each other." Her stomach twisted into a knot. It was bad enough knowing Tom had probably fooled around with Helen St.

James. What if he had another wife somewhere? She swallowed. What if he had a child?

"I don't know, Miranda. But something definitely doesn't feel right. I've filed a missing persons report and I've entered him into the National Crime Center computer. If it was his intention to disappear, he's done a hell of a job of it."

Miranda's brain raced. Legally, she could file even if they couldn't find Tom or serve him with papers, but she'd feel a lot better if she could look Tom in the eye and ask what had happened. Divorcing someone you couldn't find felt an awful lot like winning because the other team had to forfeit; you got what you wanted, but without the satisfaction of beating your opponent.

Blake looked down at her and Miranda felt the intensity of his gaze ripple through her. "I'm going to talk to the PI you hired and see if we can't work this between us. This staying away from you is not going to cut it. I want you free and available." He leaned in closer. "And I wouldn't mind naked, either."

Miranda felt a thrill shoot through her. It was almost enough to make her forget that just two nights from now she was going to walk up on that stage, sit in the throne they were moving into position, and rule over the faux palace garden they were creating. *Alone.* She could have refused the crown and the throne, but her pride wouldn't allow her to back down.

"You are going to let Andie come get dressed for the ball with me, aren't you?" she asked now. "At the moment it's the only potential bright spot on Saturday's humiliating horizon."

Andie's new ball dress lay in the center of Miranda's king-size bed. Miranda circled it slowly while Andie looked on anxiously.

"Okay," Miranda finally said. "It's, it's . . . interesting." She thought about the perfect ball dress hanging in her closet and wished she could give it to Andie right now. But she couldn't do that to the two men who had braved three junior departments in their quest for the perfect gown. Blake and Gus had beaten her to the punch and this was the unfortunate result.

"It's got so many flowers." Andie worried her lip between her teeth. "And doodads."

That it did. Miranda narrowed her eyes, trying to imagine the dress without all the distractions.

"I know they meant well, and I don't want to hurt their feelings," Andie said. "But . . ."

"It's not what you were hoping for."

"No. It was so frustrating. Every time I liked a dress, one of them found something wrong with it."

Miranda murmured sympathetically, but her mind was on the dress. Andie was right; it definitely had too much . . . stuff.

"The black ones were too sophisticated. The strapless ones were 'asking for trouble.'" She mimicked Blake's voice so perfectly, Miranda had to laugh.

"Then they had this loud debate in the middle of

Dillard's dress department about whether I should be allowed to dance with a boy if one actually asked me. I wanted to die."

Miranda nodded in sympathy.

"This was the only one they could agree on. And that's because it looks like it was designed for a ten-year-old." Andie groaned. "I mean, look at it. Give me a bonnet and cane and I can lead a flock of sheep."

Miranda looked. The dress had two very distinct parts. The undergown was a sleeveless floor-length sheath made out of an ice blue taffeta that would set off Andie's blue eyes and blond coloring to perfection. The sheath was simple and elegant, with spaghetti straps and a scooped neckline—not all that different in line from the dress Miranda had chosen for her. The overdress was a disaster.

"Here." Miranda scooped the dress off the bed and placed it in Andie's arms. "Go put it on. I have an idea."

They stood side by side in front of the full-length mirror.

"Oh, God," the girl wailed. "I look like an FTD bouquet."

"There *are* a lot of flowers," Miranda agreed. In fact the chiffon overdress, which covered every scrap of skin the gown left bare, was covered in them. A row of ice blue bows circled her hips and held the chiffon in place. When Andie raised her arms the bell sleeves made her look like she was doing a Dracula impression.

"Picture it without the chiffon," Miranda said.

"What?"

"The blue taffeta underneath is beautiful. It's just right for your figure. If we removed the floral chiffon . . ."

"Can you do that?"

"I don't see why not."

"So I'd still be wearing the dress my dad bought me."

"Technically . . . yes."

"Is it complicated?" Hope shone in Andie's eyes; Miranda would have sewn a new gown from scratch to keep it there.

"No. All I have to do is remove the bows, they're what's holding the chiffon in place. I don't think we'll miss them, do you?"

"Nope."

"And I can cut a big rectangle out of the chiffon and stitch it around the edges to make a wrap."

"Awesome."

Fifteen minutes later the overdress had been surgically removed, and Andie stood in front of the mirror in the taffeta sheath. The dress clung to her slim figure, and its thin straps emphasized the graceful slope of her shoulders and the long column of her neck.

Miranda took the chiffon overdress into her sewing room and came back ten minutes later with Andie's new wrap. Slipping it around the girl's shoulders, she showed her how to twine it through her arms for a careless look.

"Is that really me?" Andie breathed.

"It most certainly is. And we're just warming up. We

have appointments at Chez Nous for hair and nails. Then we're going to come back here, put on fresh faces, and suit up. I'll let your dad know you'll meet him there."

Andie brightened further. "Once I'm at the ball it'll be too late for him to try to change anything."

"Now you're getting the idea," Miranda said. She waited for Andie to change back into street clothes and then slipped her arm companionably around the girl's waist. "When you're dealing with the opposite sex, sometimes it's smarter to maneuver around their defenses instead of trying to plow through them. There's less bloodletting that way."

By 5:00 P.M. they were back at Miranda's, coiffed, buffed, and ready to apply the finishing touches. Showered and gowned, they giggled in front of the lighted mirror while Miranda did Andie's makeup, carefully explaining each item as she applied it—thoroughly enjoying passing on the knowledge gleaned in front of decades of lighted mirrors. The girl's cheeks already glowed from their outing, and her blue eyes shone with excitement. Miranda kept the painting to a minimum, simply blending and highlighting so that her natural assets stood out. Then she brought out the necklace and earrings she'd bought for Andie in the Atlanta boutique and helped her put them on.

"Oh . . . my . . . gosh," Andie breathed when Miranda

pronounced her done. "Is that really me?" she asked again.

"It is." Miranda slipped into a black strapless gown and fastened diamond studs at her ears, but her own appearance seemed unimportant compared to the transformation she'd wrought in Andie. For her, the evening was a trial to be gotten through, one more test of her newfound resolve.

"You are absolutely beautiful." Miranda smiled. "And I sincerely hope your father's going to forgive me for it."

chapter 23

Miranda stood between her mother and grandmother in the Guild Ball receiving line, taking the shots aimed her way and smiling so brightly she was afraid her face might crack.

"Thank you, yes, the hall really does look like a garden, doesn't it?" she agreed for the hundredth time, happy to be telling the truth about something. With stage lighting that included an overhead projection of the night sky and painted backdrops courtesy of the Truro Theatre Company, the room had been transformed. A faux-brick patio with a container garden served as a second stage for the band, and Grecian columns and statuary formed a walkway that led to the throne on the center stage. Her Miss Rhododendron crown sat on a gilded table beside it.

If she didn't know that in a matter of minutes she was going to have to ascend the steps to that throne and become the first Guild Queen since the husband-flattening Adrian Wright to do so without a king by her side, Miranda would have been relishing the ball's success.

"Hello, Button." Her father kissed her on the cheek and squeezed her hand in his. "You've done a wonderful job. As always." He held her hand and looked her in the eye. "The three of you took me by surprise at the meeting last week, but I was very proud of you." He glanced at his wife, who was chatting with a guest to Miranda's left. "I don't know what's come over your mother, but I kind of like it." He gave her hand a final squeeze. "I'm here if you need me, and ... well, your mother told me 'Button' probably wasn't the best nickname for the president of the company. I guess she has a point."

She bussed her father back on the cheek, touched. "Oh, Daddy, you can call me Button any time you want," she said with a smile. "As long as you're voting my way and you keep taking care of yourself. I'm counting on you to be around for a long time to come."

Her father moved on to her mother and she saw them lean toward each other and kiss. Watching them, she offered up a prayer that one day someone would love her like that. She thought, as she did too often lately, of Blake Summers, then pushed the thought away. When her gaze strayed to the crowd in search of him, she chided herself and pulled it back.

The receiving line broke up and Miranda was alone. Around the garden, gowned women and their tuxedo-clad escorts chatted and danced. Vivien Mooney walked up to whisper something to the bandleader, and Miranda knew that the crowning ceremony would begin soon. She was heading toward the ladies' room to freshen up her makeup when she spotted Blake walking toward her.

He looked magnificent in the black tuxedo and crisply pleated white shirt. As he approached she felt a familiar stir of anticipation that bordered on . . . well, okay, it might have been lust. This man moved her in a way she didn't understand and was afraid to explore. She was trying not to think about how good he looked without any clothes at all when he came to a halt in front of her. He didn't speak at first but took her by the arm and propelled her away from the crowd.

"What are you doing?"

"I'm calming down," he said, although it didn't look as if that were the case at all. "And I'm telling myself you weren't just tweaking your nose at me, that there's a reason for what you did."

"What in the world are you talking about?" Miranda asked through the public smile that was still plastered on her face.

"I'm talking about my daughter. And that dress." He ran a hand through his already rumpled hair, then pointed toward the stage. "She looks exactly like my mother. And she has a whole hiveful of boys buzzing around her."

Andie kept her shoulders back just like Miranda had told her and was very careful not to slouch. She knew from Miranda's mirror, and the eye-widening that took place every time someone caught sight of her, that she had broken through some invisible barrier and taken Truro by surprise. The other girls, who'd been buzzing with self-importance in their juvenile ruffles and bows, fell silent when she approached. The boys looked equally stunned.

Only Jake commented on her transformation. "Wow, Andie," he said, stepping forward and welcoming her into the group. "You look great."

"You look pretty good yourself," she said. And he did, in his simple black rental tux with his dark hair curling just above his broad shoulders. "ML." She nodded regally, for once feeling that her height was an advantage somewhere other than on the court. The other girl barely reached Jake's shoulder and wore a pink cap-sleeved dress with an unfortunate ruffle that wound from her waist across her thighs.

Andie was admonishing herself for being so uncharitable, when Steve Carrington and Earlene Johnson arrived. Steve clapped Jake on the shoulder and the couple stepped into place next to Mary Louise.

"Ahchoo!" Mary Louise sneezed, and the massive ruffle quivered.

Earlene leaned across Steve. "Do you need a Kleenex, ML?"

"Ahhhhhchoooo!" Mary Louise doubled over with that one. Earlene fished in her bag for a tissue and ML sneezed again. As a group they watched Mary Louise's face begin to swell.

"Oh, no!" she wailed. "Is somebody wearing Libido?" She sniffed and stared at Jake accusingly.

"It's not me, ML. I gave that bottle away to . . . Jake's voice trailed off and he winced. "Steve. I didn't know he was going to be here tonight, or I would have warned him."

"Ahhhchooo!"

Tears ran down Mary Louise's cheeks. Andie knew she should feel bad for her, but there'd been a few too many catty remarks to feel truly sympathetic. "Do you want me to look for an antihistamine?" she asked.

Mary Louise's eyes were starting to disappear into the swollen blob of her face. "No, somebody find my mother. Oh, God, I look like Miss Piggy when this happens."

"Do you want me to try to find Doc Pritchard?" Jake asked.

"No!" Mary Louise shrieked. "Don't look at me. Oh, God." Her hands skimmed over her misshapen face. "I'm all swollen and ugly!"

ML's mother swept up and pulled her shrieking baby bird under her wing.

"Should I drive her home, Mrs. Atkins?" Jake stepped forward, looking shaken.

"No!" ML shrieked again. She glared at Andie and Jake from behind the hands she'd cupped over her face as if they'd planned her humiliation intentionally. "I want my mother to drive me home! I'll never forgive you for this, Jake Hanson, never!"

With a final sneeze and shriek they were gone.

Miranda followed Blake's finger to the group assembled near the stage, the one Mary Louise Atkins and her mother appeared to be fleeing from.

"Those boys are buzzing all around her. The next thing you know, that one"—he pointed at Jake Hanson—"will be trying to suck her nectar. Excuse me." He took hold of her shoulders and tried to set her out of the way. "I'm going to arrest him."

"Don't be ridiculous." Miranda stood her ground. "She's absolutely magnificent. And if you leave her alone she'll have the time of her life."

"That's what I'm afraid of."

She laughed and tugged on his shoulder to pull him around to face her.

"Andie is a—" he began.

"Very smart levelheaded girl," Miranda finished. "She's not going to rush out and do something stupid. And Jake Hanson is a very nice boy."

"That's just what he wants us to think. Believe me, I know what's going through his mind right now, and—"

"Shhh," she hushed him. "Vivien's going up to the microphone. It's almost time to take the tumbrel up to the guillotine—I mean, the stage." She closed her eyes briefly to gather her strength. One last humiliation and the Guild Ball could be put behind her.

The girls from her prep class moved sedately into line on either side of the platform as they'd been instructed, their escorts beside them. Jake stepped into place beside Andie, and the girl shot her father a look.

"Just leave them be," Miranda urged. "You can put the fear of God into Jake *after* the presentation. Let her enjoy her moment. Look—" She pointed to the other side of the dance floor, where his grandfather and her grandmother stood. "Gus is taking a picture of them now. They look so unbelievably sweet together."

Blake growled under his breath, but he stayed put.

Miranda ran a nervous hand over the front of her gown and drew in a steadying breath as Vivien began to speak into the microphone. She wished she were anywhere but here. She wished the night were behind her, the embarrassment of being crowned without her husband by her side already lived through and forgotten. She looked over at Blake. She wished a lot of things.

"And now," Vivien said, "without further ado, I present you with this year's Guild chairwoman and reigning queen..."

There was a drum roll, and then a spotlight skidded around the room searching her out. "Miranda Smith."

A trumpet sounded, and Miranda felt the hot glare of the spotlight skim over her face. For a moment she was paralyzed by fear and embarrassment; the room practically echoed with the all-too-true whispers that her husband wasn't coming back. Then the knowledge washed through her: She'd been abandoned and left to face what had seemed like insurmountable problems, but she hadn't run from them and she hadn't let them beat her. She might be alone, but she knew now what she was made of, and what she was made of was more than enough.

Miranda drew herself to her full height and stepped forward into the light. She felt the warmth of the spotlight on her face and felt the smile come naturally to her lips. She walked slowly and regally, trying to calm her racing heart, pretending it was just a pageant, letting herself walk the walk, reminding herself she didn't need a man by her side.

She had covered only a few steps when she felt someone step up beside her.

"Would you like an escort?" Blake's smile was both warm and confident as he bowed smartly before her. Heads bent toward each other and the murmuring grew louder, but she ignored it. She was moved by Blake's gesture and tempted by the idea of having his solid strength at her side. She looked into his eyes and smiled her thanks, but shook her head slightly.

"I really appreciate the offer," she said softly. "But I think it's time to prove I can go it on my own." Her smile grew, and her voice got even softer. "But if you'd like to come over later . . ."

Blake bowed again, his acceptance clear in his eyes. Lifting her chin, Miranda walked between the double line of Rhododendron girls and up the steps to accept her cape and crown. As the applause swelled, she surveyed her domain with new eyes and felt a calming sense of acceptance settle over her. For better *and* for worse, these were her people.

When you got right down to it, it was good to be queen.

It was long past midnight by the time Blake was able to extract Andie from the swarm of young bees and spirit her and Gus home, and after one by the time he'd shucked the monkey suit and judged the town tucked in enough to drive over to Miranda's.

He'd stayed clear of her since their night at the Ritz, knowing they had no business being anywhere near each other until Tom Smith was found and dealt with. But he'd never thought finding the man would take so long, or that staying away would be so difficult.

Getting through the evening without dragging her off to a broom closet or some deserted corner had required every bit of restraint—something that seemed to have deserted him completely as soon as she'd whispered her invitation.

Miranda answered the door in the long velvet cape and nothing else, and his entire body snapped to attention. The red velvet swirled around her bare legs and provided glimpses of smooth white skin. She looked regal and sensual all at once and the look in her eyes told him she was as eager as he was.

"No crown?" Blake stepped into the foyer, lowered his mouth to Miranda's, and kicked the door shut behind him.

"Do I need one?"

He slipped his hands inside the velvet and pulled her up against him. "No."

Her skin was warm and ripe and, at her short gasp of excitement, he walked her backward until they came to a halt against the foyer wall, their bodies pressed intimately together.

He let his hands roam freely, and somehow his coat came off and his shirt was untucked and her fingers were fumbling with his belt.

Moving his hands beneath her buttocks he lifted her in his arms and headed for the stairs. Her legs wrapped around his waist and a bare breast brushed against his lips. Her tongue teased his ear.

"I want you *now*." She nibbled on his earlobe and her teeth grazed his neck as the velvet cape swirled around them.

"Then you've got me, Your Majesty." Stopping midstep, Blake undid the tie at her neck and let the red velvet puddle on the landing. Then he placed her gently on top of it and prepared to service his queen.

"You're a loyal subject." She smiled as he kneeled in front of her and brought his mouth down to her breast. "And if you keep that up, I see a knighthood in your future."

He woke at four in Miranda's bed and told himself he should go home, move the car, do something other than lie there feeling so good. She lay curled beside him looking decidedly unqueenlike. The last vestiges of her makeup had disappeared, and so had the sophisticated façade she presented to the world. Without makeup the dusting of freckles scattered across the bridge of her nose stood out in stark relief, and her lips looked even more inviting without the shiny gloss of lipstick.

"I like you this way," he said as her eyes fluttered open. "Without all the ... props and lighting."

She smiled and moved closer.

A wave of real feeling washed over him and he beat it back. Miranda Smith had a husband who was still missing, and a host of secrets she hadn't seen fit to share. The last place he should be right now was here. "I need to go," he said. "Your neighbors ..."

"Have probably already called Clara Bartlett to report seeing us strip in the foyer." She snuggled closer and reached for him, and he stopped worrying about her neighbors and her secrets.

When his cell phone rang an hour and a half later, he was in a postcoital fog and it took him a couple of minutes to track the phone down to his pants pocket on the stairs. He pulled it out and saw the phone number of one of his deputies scrawled across the small screen, but then phone calls at 5:30 A.M. almost never came from Publishers Clearinghouse. He answered, and stood naked on Miranda Smith's stairway as Ed Beagley's voice came over the line.

"Chief?" The deputy's voice was hushed. "I just got a call from Earl West—he was up fishing at Lake Carraway on Ballantyne Bald."

Blake stared out the fanlight above Miranda's front door as Ed went on speaking, and his whole body tensed as he replied. "Get ahold of Gabe Holcomb and have him bring the tow truck up there. Then you take Earl's statement and ask him to wait until I get there. I'll call the GBI."

Blake slipped on his pants and put the cell phone back into his pocket. He carried his shirt and the velvet cape back upstairs with him and placed them next to Miranda on the bed.

"You'd better get dressed, Miranda," he said quietly. "That was Ed Beagley. It looks like we've found Tom."

chapter 24

She was a widow. The word reverberated in Miranda's brain. She was a widow, because her husband was dead. Kaput. As in no longer alive.

She could not get her brain around it.

She'd spent the last three and a half months hardening her heart and telling herself that she was better off without Tom. Stunned by both his departure and betrayal, she'd spent those months whipping up her anger, shoring up her backbone to do what needed to be done. She'd even dedicated numerous hours to picturing Tom with a world-class wedgie and more than a couple wishing him dead. But she'd never really thought about what that would mean, or truly considered the permanence of it.

And never, even in her worst nightmares, had she imagined that he might die in the front seat of his car wearing nothing but ladies' lingerie. Or that he and his car, which was packed and ready to blow town, would be found in the lake in front of their vacation house. And that all of Truro would know it.

"I'll need to file a report," Blake said when he came back that afternoon to give her the official news.

She looked at him through her tears, unable to bear the distance in his eyes. Less than twenty-four hours ago they'd been as intimate as it was possible for two people to be. Now he was looking at her as if he'd never seen her before.

"I'll have the coroner's findings by midweek, and then the body can be released for burial."

That thought had produced a fresh flood of tears.

"It can wait until after the funeral," he said in that professional voice of his, "but you're going to have to cooperate with this investigation."

"Investigation?"

He sighed and ran a hand through his hair, but he didn't step closer and he didn't take her in his arms. "Your husband's dead, Miranda," he said. "Under very strange circumstances. And you've been pretending he's away on business."

She blinked back more tears and looked for some vestige of the man who'd knelt at her feet just the night before, but all she saw was the chief of police.

"It doesn't look good," he said. "In fact, it looks like a damned movie of the week."

"You don't actually think I . . ."

"It doesn't matter what I think," Blake countered.

But of course it did.

"What matters is finding out the truth and piecing together the events leading up to Tom's death. That means questioning any and all potentially involved parties." He looked at her out of blue cop eyes. "And that would include you."

"Got some more for you, Chief." Anne Farnsworthy waved a stack of pink message slips four times the usual size at Blake. "And the coroner's holding on line two."

Blake took the slips and headed for his office. Closing the door behind him, he leafed through the messages and shook his head. Word of his cross-dressing underwater corpse had spread through the law enforcement grapevine like lightning. By his reckoning, he'd heard from every officer he'd ever met in his twenty years in law enforcement, and some he'd never heard of. And Tom Smith had been pulled out of Lake Carraway less than a week ago. He picked up the receiver and brought it to his ear.

"What you got goin' on up there, Chief?" Truro didn't produce enough dead bodies to warrant its own coroner, so Clyde Bartell in Claymore did the honors.

"Just your usual Sunday driver who wandered off the highway."

"And ended up in the lake in his wife's skivvies?"

Bartell laughed. "If this guy was seeking sexual pleasure he picked a piss-poor place to find it."

Blake was too tired of the jokes to laugh. And he needed to know whether there was any evidence linking Miranda to her husband's death.

A GBI mechanic had confirmed that the Mercedes' accelerator had stuck, and investigators had discovered frozen skid marks, preserved under a protective layer of snow, on the shore. With no smudge marks on the car's exterior to indicate a push from a third party, all evidence pointed toward an accidental death. What Blake needed to know now was whether the autopsy results supported that evidence.

Blake switched ears and opened the legal pad on his desk to a fresh page. "What have you got for me?"

"I'll be faxin' my report over in the morning," Bartell replied. "But there's no sign of foul play. No marks on the body that can't be accounted for. It looks like he died after the car went into the lake."

Blake felt relief course through him. "Yeah?"

"Yeah. The cause of death'll be listed as death by drowning. Drownings are always tricky, but based on the evidence I'd say he was alive when the car went under and trying to get outta there. Must've had his panties in a real uproar." The coroner chuckled. "To tell you the truth, he might have made it out if his brassiere strap hadn't gotten hung up on the gearshift."

Blake gave a short bark of surprise. "Are you telling me that if Tom Smith had gone strapless the night he died, he might be alive today?"

"It's possible."

Blake snorted at the pure ridiculousness of it.

"The water was probably about four degrees Fahrenheit, so the body was well preserved. Guy was in pretty good shape, definitely an athlete. I'd give my left nut to hear how he happened to be up there driving around in below-freezing weather in that bra and panties."

So would Blake.

The man chuckled. "Yep, officially it's a drowning, but you might also call it a DBC."

Blake didn't bite. He doubted there was a lingerie joke he hadn't already heard.

"That's a Death by Cleavage in case you're wantin' to know."

Okay, so maybe there were a few he hadn't heard yet. "That's very creative of you, Clyde. You think of that one all by yourself?"

"Naw. One of the GBI guys came up with it. Kinda catchy, don't you think?"

Blake groaned as he hung up. He'd be a very old man before he lived this one down.

Anne Farsworthy poked her head back in his doorway. "I've got Seymour Butts and Titty Twister on lines one and two. Which one do you want to take first?"

"Neither. But the sooner I get to the bottom of this mess, the better."

He was more than relieved that he didn't have a murder case on his hands, but while the coroner and the GBI might be ready to sign off on this, it was his job to find out how in the hell Tom Smith got into that lake in that underwear.

Somebody had to know something, and the logical somebody to start with was Miranda. Despite her claim that the wife was always the last to know, she knew a hell of a lot more than she'd been letting on. Which didn't say a lot for the effectiveness of Operation Bad Penny.

He was putting on his jacket when Anne put a hand up to stop him.

"Tell those guys I'm not interested in—" he began.

"You'll want to talk to this one, Chief. It's her, our anonymous caller. She's calling from her favorite location."

Blake motioned to the deputy at the next desk. "Ed, go on down to the pay phone near the Dogwood. Walk real slow and easy, don't look right at it, but make sure you see who's inside. Then come right back."

Ed nodded and took off.

"Tell her I'll be right there," Blake directed Anne, but he took his time, wanting to give Ed a head start. In his office he closed the door and took a while getting seated. "Chief Summers," he finally said into the phone.

"I told you there'd been foul play. I knew he wouldn't have left me without a word." She was still disguising her voice, but he could hear a very real anguish in it.

"And why is that?"

There was a silence and then a quiet, "Because he loved me."

"Is that right?"

She sniffled. "Yes, that's right. And here he's been dead all this time, while she's been running around acting as if he was away. As if she was talking to him and seeing him."

"By she you mean his wife?"

He waited, wishing to hell Ed would get back here and tell him who he was talking to.

There was another sniff and then the voice grew harder. "It was me he loved. We were supposed to go away together."

"Did Miranda Smith know that?"

"I don't know. He said he was going to tell her, but I'm not sure."

"And did you know he liked to . . ."

"Dress up?" She laughed, the sound dry. "Such a big dark secret. He wasn't gay, you know, no matter what all the ignoramuses are saying."

"But he was going to leave his wife for you?"

"Yes."

"You do realize . . ." he paused, but she didn't rush to fill in her name, "that he only had one airline ticket. His car was packed and ready to leave town, but he was traveling alone."

She cried, and her distress sounded genuine. "I don't believe it. But I'll tell you something I bet you don't know."

Blake wished there were only one thing he didn't

know, but he stayed silent and waited for the woman to speak.

"Miranda Smith was at the lake the night of January eighth. I was supposed to meet him that afternoon and couldn't get there. When I finally made it to the lake road later that night, she was coming down that mountain like a bat out of hell."

He waited, holding his breath.

"When I got up to the house there was no sign of Tom or his car." She sniffed again and her voice quivered. "He must have already been in the lake."

The line went dead as Ed Beagley raced into Blake's office, out of breath. "It was Helen St. James," he whispered, the surprise evident on his face. "The bookkeeper from Ballantyne. I saw her clear as day."

On the day of Tom's funeral, Miranda sat in the family pew between her mother and grandmother and stared at the casket that held her husband's incredibly well preserved mortal remains. Tears rolled down her cheeks as she stared at the brass-bound box while memories, the ones she'd held at bay while she struggled to maintain her charade and salvage what she could of Ballantyne, assaulted her.

The day they met, their first kiss. The holidays and vacations. Their increasingly frantic efforts to produce a child.

She didn't know how to reconcile the man she'd married and loved with all the things she'd discovered about him. Nor did she know when he'd begun to change. Or how he'd ended up in the lake.

Floating in and out of the turmoil were her undefined feelings for Blake Summers and the crushing formality with which he'd handled her as the legal end of Tom's death unfolded.

Behind her, Helen St. James sobbed brokenheartedly, and Miranda had no doubt most of the mourners were busy trying to guess whether the corpse had on hundred percent cotton or beige cream satin under his burial suit.

It was a funeral the residents of Truro were unlikely ever to forget.

$\mathbb{M}$iranda?"

"Hmmm?" Miranda blinked and looked up from the condolence card she was reading to stare up at her mother. She was so tired. Tired of pretending she was okay, tired of trying to get the details of Tom's death out of her mind, tired of being the subject of everybody's delighted speculation. She wanted to curl up in a ball and go to sleep and wake up in a couple of years when all of this was over.

She stared unseeing at the kitchen with its endless Tupperwared offerings and paper plates covered with foil. A vase of tissue-paper flowers from Andie sat in the center of the table, and Carly had brought one of Lindsey's crayon masterpieces for the front of her refrigerator. Everything she looked at made her want to cry. Or sleep.

"Miranda, can you help me carry these things out to the car?" Her mother pointed to a group of casseroles she'd separated from the rest. "You won't even be able to make a dent in all this food. I thought I'd take some to Gran."

"Sure." Miranda balanced a disposable baking dish of macaroni and cheese in one arm and a tuna-noodle bake in the other and followed her mother outside onto the front porch.

Her grandmother's Cadillac sat in the drive, bathed in swaths of dark and moonlight.

"Why do you have Gran's car?"

"Mine's in the shop and she didn't need hers. I thought I'd just leave these off for her and then walk on home from the cottage."

Her mother's voice receded as Miranda stared at the car; something about the way it looked in the dark jiggled at her brain. She'd replayed the night of January eight in her mind countless times, trying to remember something that might make a difference. She'd passed two cars on the gravel road that night, one while she was going up and one while she was coming down, but she'd only looked to assure herself that neither was Tom's white Mercedes; she hadn't bothered to try to figure out who was in them. Until now.

Flipping on the porch light, she trailed her mother down the drive. There was a slight chill in the air.

Nothing like the bitter cold that night in January, but...

Her mother popped the trunk on Gran's dark blue Cadillac, and Miranda stopped as the image she'd been trying to call up became clearer. The first car had been a dark sedan about this size.

No. She cocked her head and looked at the car from another angle. What would Gran have been doing up there that night? And if it had been Gran on that gravel road, surely Miranda would have recognized her. Or Gran would have said something.

Her mother bent into the backseat and started re-arranging things. "I think you'd better put those casseroles in the trunk, Miranda. Just make sure they're flat and secured in some way."

Miranda opened the trunk and slid the casseroles toward the back, then looked for something to prop against them. She wedged them in place with a black umbrella and a pair of galoshes she found in the recess, then felt around for something softer to wrap around them.

Her hand closed around something promising and she pulled it out to examine it for barrier-building potential.

Glancing down, she saw the Izod logo, noted the size was too big to be Gran's. And froze when she recognized Tom's sweatshirt. In disbelief she rooted around until she came up with a pair of his pants.

Miranda closed her eyes and tried to picture the car

she'd whizzed by on her way up, but her head was swimming with thoughts she didn't want to think.

What would her grandmother have been doing up there that night? And more importantly, what was she doing with Tom's clothes?

Miranda's heart dropped down around her knees as she tried to come up with an answer that didn't require Gran being responsible for Tom ending up in the lake. With what she hoped *wasn't* evidence crumpled to her chest, Miranda waved good-bye to her mother and hurried back into the house. She was going to have to have a little talk with the wrinkly wise woman.

Miranda wasted several valuable days trying to come up with a tactful way to broach the subject with Gran. She definitely couldn't do it by phone, and she couldn't for the life of her figure out an opener that would smooth the way into such a conversation. A "My, the weather's getting lovely, you didn't have anything to do with Tom's death, did you?" simply wasn't going to cut it.

When she finally accepted the fact that she was simply going to have to get her grandmother alone and dive right in, having that private conversation proved much trickier than she had anticipated. Having it before Blake forced her to "cooperate with his investigation" proved trickier still.

The night she knocked on her grandmother's door primed for truth-seeking, Gus Summers opened it and

invited her in for drinks. The next day she drove into
town and tracked Gran to the post office, but she had
barely finished parking her car when Blake came
strolling down the sidewalk toward her. Panicked,
Miranda ducked into the first doorway she came to—
and learned how to count Weight Watchers points
while she waited for him to move on.

For days she skittered out of Blake's way while un-
successfully trying to get her grandmother alone. In
her fear and frustration, she vowed she'd answer every
one of Blake's questions—just as soon as she was able
to stop worrying about Gran having a hand in Tom's
death.

On Friday evening, determined to put her fears to
rest, she caught up with Gran in the bakery aisle of the
Piggly Wiggly.

"Hello, darling." Gran smiled as Miranda pushed
her cart up next to her grandmother's. "I'm so glad to
see you out." She stopped in front of the bakery case,
and Miranda stopped with her. "Oh, just smell those
cinnamon buns. Why don't we take some to the cottage and . . ."

"Gran, I'm not here for baked goods. I need you to
tell me exactly what you were doing at . . ."

Gran picked up a wax bag, opened the case, and
used the tongs to slip the buns in. Out of the corner of
her eye, Miranda spotted Blake and Gus. She didn't
think they'd noticed her and Gran yet, but they were
only two aisles over and closing in fast.

Taking the bakery bag out of Gran's hands, Miranda

set it down on the display table. "Let's not fuss with any of this," she said as she grabbed the handle of Gran's cart and began to push toward the next aisle. "Let's go to the Dogwood and get a slice of pie instead."

Miranda navigated both carts around the end cap and down the next aisle, intent on staying out of sight. "Or we could go to Hyram's for coffee and a piece of cake."

"Darling, what are you..." Gran began but Miranda pushed faster, desperate to get away before the Summers men caught up with them. She moved as quickly as she could without actually dragging Gran's feet off the floor.

"Miranda, what on earth are you doing?"

What she was doing was sprinting toward the front of the store so that they could abandon their carts and make their getaway.

Gus's voice carried over from the next aisle and Miranda slammed to a halt. Putting a finger to her lips to warn her grandmother, she peeked around the end and held her breath while Blake and Gus finished and split off to their left.

"Gran," she whispered as she crouched next to the Cap'n Crunch, "the Summerses are here, and Blake wants to question me. But first I need to know what you—"

"You're *hiding* from Blake?"

"I'm not... hiding. I'm just"—she straightened and moved them forward again—"delaying the questioning until you assure me you had nothing to do with Tom's—"

"Me? Why, I thought . . ."

Miranda tried to listen to Gran while looking over her shoulder and pushing forward at the same time. The crash of metal and the jolt of impact were apparently God's way of telling her she wasn't that great a multitasker.

Blake Summers looked down at his dented grocery cart and at the cans that now covered the floor, then back up at Miranda. "I'm trying real hard not to make any obvious comments about women drivers."

Gus grinned. And so did Gran. Miranda was too stunned to speak.

"I don't think I've ever written a ticket in the grocery store before, but I'm pretty sure we've got speeding." Blake's tone was incredibly dry. "And probably reckless endangerment."

Miranda closed her eyes, tried counting to ten, opened them. "I'm sorry," she said. "We were in a hurry and I wanted to check out."

Blake's gaze dropped to her and Gran's empty carts.

"But since we're all okay, I'm, uh, going to have to go." She was babbling but she didn't care. She had to get out of there now. "I've got an, um, important, uh, weigh-in at, uh, Weight Watchers." She swallowed. "Gran, would you ask Mr. Tyndale to send me a bill for the damage? I've really got to go."

With a parting nod to Blake and Gus, she leaned close to her grandmother and whispered in her ear,

"I'm coming by first thing tomorrow morning. I'll expect you to be home." She looked her grandmother straight in the eye. "And I'll expect you to be alone."

Early the next morning Miranda drove to the cottage and found Gran on her knees in the dirt. She was digging holes and had a flat of red-and-white geraniums next to her. Miranda knelt on the grass and began to remove the flowers from the flat, loosening the soil around the roots as her grandmother had taught her when she was a child, handing them over to be inserted in each small hole. "I found Tom's clothes in your trunk, Gran."

Her grandmother placed a geranium in its newly dug hole and gently patted the topsoil around it. Miranda handed her another plant and waited. "We definitely need to talk."

Gran shook her head. "I forgot they were in there. Can you believe it? I'm starting to get old." She stuck her hand out for another plant, but Miranda didn't pass one over.

"I don't think you're old enough to cop an insanity plea, if that's where you're going with this. And I hope to God you don't need one." She set the plant back in the flat. "Why didn't you tell me you were up there that night?"

Gran looked up, her gaze steady. "Maybe I should be asking you the same question. There are a lot of things we haven't discussed."

They were so intent on each other that they didn't hear the car drive up or the slam of a car door. Their first clue that they weren't alone was the black boot tips that came to a stop at the edge of the flower bed.

Still kneeling, their gazes traveled up the pant legs to the face of the man who towered above them. Miranda's heart slid somewhere down near the pit of her stomach.

"Ladies." Blake Summers tipped his hat, then crouched down across from them. "Planting flowers, are we?"

Miranda's brain went into warp speed but all that came out was, "Yes, geraniums." Gran did the smarter thing and remained silent.

"Beautiful." He was looking at Miranda. "But tricky. Not as obvious as they appear on the outside. Not always forthcoming."

Miranda swallowed and waited. Gran, too, kept her silence.

"Well," Blake said. "I have a few questions that need answering. And I'm thinking I'd like to ask them down at the station."

Gran stood, brushing off her knees as she straightened. "I'll just go get my wallet and keys and meet you down—"

"No, I want to talk to Miranda first. Alone. She can come with me. Why don't you come by in about an hour?"

"But I don't . . ." Miranda stood, too, her mind racing.

Gran looked Blake right in the eye, and she appeared a lot calmer than Miranda felt. "Should I be calling an attorney?"

Blake actually seemed to think about that one, which did not bode well for the line of questioning. "I don't know. You tell me."

Miranda placed herself between Blake and Gran, trampling a couple of geraniums on the way. He looked tall and serious and coplike, not at all like the man who'd laid a velvet cape under her and made love to her on the stairs. "You can't just show up here and 'take me down to the station for questioning.'" She lowered her voice in an imitation of a TV cop.

"Actually," he said, folding his forearms across his chest, "I can."

Miranda shot Gran a look. "Why don't I just come down with Gran? We can..." She was frantic to talk to her grandmother before she had to talk to Blake.

"Nope." He took her gently by the elbow and steered her toward the waiting jeep, and she offered a small prayer of thankfulness that he hadn't felt the need to shove her in the back of the cruiser like a criminal.

Miranda looked out the passenger window as they pulled away. Gran stood with her gardening tools clutched to her chest and a thoughtful expression on her face. Miranda sincerely hoped Gran wasn't planning to reveal all without revealing it all to Miranda first.

The new police station wasn't exactly a hubbub of activity. In fact, on a Saturday morning it was downright quiet. Miranda's heart thudded in her chest as she followed Blake through the empty reception area to an office at the back. His shoulders were broad, and right now they were completely rigid. She was too nervous to appreciate his back view. When he motioned her to the chair across from his desk, he didn't crack a smile.

She'd been hauled into the police station and the chief of police had seen her naked. The thoughts had nothing to do with each other, but were equally disturbing. A picture of her Gran being led away in chains was more disturbing still.

"Are you allowed to plead the fifth in a chief of police's office?"

"No."

God, she wished she'd studied law instead of business. She was scared for Gran, and unsure of her ground. A deep knot of hurt and anger lodged itself in her chest. How could he look at her so dispassionately? "Are you accusing me of having something to do with Tom's death?"

"I'm not *accusing* you of anything, Miranda. I'm looking for answers, and I need you to provide them. Today. We know *how* Tom died, but we don't know *why*. And I'm not signing off on this case until I understand what happened that night."

She tried to push back the hurt; tried to figure out

how in the world to proceed. Maybe he'd ask her things she wouldn't have a problem answering. Maybe none of his questions would implicate her grandmother, and she could just come clean. So that he would stop looking at her like she was some speck of dust on the wall.

"Did your husband ask you for a divorce?"

Miranda blinked, surprised. This wasn't at all what she'd been expecting, but at least she could answer honestly. "No."

"Did you know your husband liked to dress up in women's underclothes?"

"No."

He shot her a look.

"Well, not until recently."

"And you found out, when?"

She swallowed. "The night he left—when I accidentally found the pictures."

"Of?"

"Of him dressed up in Ballantyne's best-sellers."

"Did you know your husband was having an affair?"

"Sort of."

"Did you or didn't you?"

"Well, when you find a picture of your husband in women's lingerie with another woman's hand on his butt, you kind of have to figure she's not some innocent passerby. But I didn't officially know he was having an affair, no." And had hoped she'd never have to.

"So you didn't have reason to believe he was having an affair with Helen St. James?"

Miranda winced. The man had been doing his homework. "Not exactly."

"So you *sort* of knew?" His tone was dry and not at all amused.

"I kind of figured it out from her hostility and her, uh, manicure. But it was never actually discussed." *Because then I would have had to fire her.*

It was Blake's turn to blink.

"And you found the pictures on . . ."

"January eighth, the night I found the note from Tom that said he was leaving. And, uh, a letter that made me think something might be wrong at Ballantyne." She'd be as helpful as possible, as long as it didn't implicate Gran.

"January eighth was a pretty big night for you."

"You could say that."

"You find pictures of Tom in ladies' lingerie with another woman, and?"

"A letter," she filled in obligingly.

"From?"

"Our lender, Fidelity National."

"Indicating?"

Once again she wished for a law degree, but in the end decided the fraud probably was no longer relevant, since Tom was dead and she'd pledged her assets to guarantee the line of credit. "That there was a possible problem with our receivables."

"And *then* you found the note from Tom, saying?"

Miranda cleared her throat, embarrassed. "Well, he

apologized for some things and told me to 'Have a nice life.'"

She squirmed in her chair while Blake watched her and waited. She thought she saw a brief flash of sympathy in his eyes, and to her horror her eyes filled with tears and the urge to explain became almost overwhelming. Unloading all the stuff she'd been carrying around would be such a relief; she felt lighter just thinking about it. But she wasn't Catholic and Blake Summers was no priest.

But maybe she could pull this off, without sending any members of her family to prison. Surely Gran's involvement was innocent and explainable. She just had to give him enough to make him leave them alone so she could hash this out with Gran.

She averted her gaze and tried to look reluctant. "Somewhere in there my mother called. Because my parents were expecting us for dinner, and when she said my father had seen Tom—" Her mouth clamped shut as she remembered what had happened next. If she told him she'd gone up there, he'd want to know if she'd seen anyone else while she was there, and this would lead to Gran.

She resettled in her seat and folded her hands in her lap. "I'd like to plead the fifth."

"I told you, you can't do that."

"All right, then. No comment."

"I'm not a reporter, Miranda, I'm a cop. No comment doesn't cut it."

"Fine." The whole confession idea was really stupid

anyway. She'd just shut up like she should have from the moment she'd come in here.

They contemplated each other over the desk that separated them. She wanted to believe that the Blake who'd made love to her so beautifully was inside the police chief she was facing. And she really hoped Andie's doting father was in there, too. She had feelings for this man whether she wanted to or not, damn it, and he was grilling her like a steak.

"So what did you do then? When your mother told you your father had seen Tom—I'm assuming you were going to say up at the lake?"

She remained silent.

"You don't really expect me to believe you just sat there and did nothing?"

She absolutely was not going to say anything else, no matter what.

"The Miranda Smith I know wouldn't have taken all that without dishing out a little herself. And I happen to have an eyewitness who saw you coming back down that mountain like a—I believe the expression was 'bat out of hell.' "

Her shoulders slumped. Very tricky, this guy, baiting her that way. But he didn't know whom he was up against.

"You've been lying and covering for months, Miranda. The time has come to tell the truth."

Miranda narrowed her eyes. In an incredibly childish gesture, which she hoped she'd live to regret, she put two fingers to her lips and pretended to zip them shut. There was nothing in the world he could do that would make her say another word.

Blake sighed and stood. Taking her by the elbow, he led her out of his office and down a hall away from the lobby.

"Where are you taking me?"

"I really hate to do this, Miranda, but you leave me no choice. I'm hoping some time alone to . . . reflect . . . will help you see the advantages of talking."

Before she realized what he was doing, he'd walked her through a door that swung shut behind them, and stopped in front of an open cell.

She pulled her arm from his grasp. "But that's a jail cell!"

"Maybe a little solitary contemplation will help jog your memory."

Then he put an arm around her shoulder and walked her into the cell.

"You can't possibly be serious," she said as he stepped around her, pulled the cell door shut, and turned the key so that he was on the outside looking in.

The man had locked her in a cell!

"This is NOT Mayberry and you're NOT Andy Griffith," she sputtered. "There is no way in the world you can get away with . . ."

He walked to the outer door and opened it before turning back to face her. His lips turned up in a smile. "I think I hear Aunt Bea calling. You just let me know when you're ready to talk."

chapter 26

There was something about being locked in a jail cell that made a person want to sing "Nobody Knows the Trouble I've Seen." Or learn how to play the harmonica in a really woeful way. Or get their hands around the chief of police's neck.

An hour later, the outer door clicked open and Miranda heard footsteps approaching. "Blake," she shouted through the bars. "You have absolutely no legal right to keep me here." She took the Diet Coke he'd brought her and dragged the can back and forth across the bars, producing a hugely satisfying cacophony of sound. "I'll have your badge for this. I'll—"

Blake appeared. With Gran. She supposed she should be glad he hadn't brought her in in handcuffs.

"I'll post bail, Miranda," Gran said. "I'll have you out of here in no time."

"Don't think so." Blake shook his head and tried to appear regretful, the louse. "She's not under arrest, so bail isn't really an option."

"This is the most ridiculous—" Miranda began.

"There is such a thing as due process, young man," Gran pointed out.

"Yes," he replied dryly. "And there's also obstruction of justice, and lying to a police officer." He leveled a look at both of them, then began to unlock the cell door. "Don't you want to know why Tom was in the lake in his car in nothing more than a bra and panties?" He looked at Gran and then at Miranda. "Or is it that you already know and just don't want to tell *me?*"

"Now see here, Chief." Gran's imperious tone didn't seem to phase Blake in the least. You had to respect a man who didn't cave in to Gran. "This is highly irregular, and . . ."

He opened the cell door. Miranda breathed a sigh of relief and moved toward the opening. "Thank goodness you've regained your senses," she said. "I'm sure we can . . ."

But instead of letting her out, Blake put a hand to Gran's elbow and gently escorted her in. Then he closed the cell door and relocked it, leaving the two of them staring out at him in shock.

"Now," he said calmly. "If you're done complaining, I think we should begin with the afternoon of January eighth. Your grandmother can go first."

"Ha!" Miranda said. "Don't say a word, Gran. Someone will notice we're missing and send help. He can't keep us in here indefinitely."

For the next thirty minutes Miranda and her Gran sat side by side on the cot in the corner of the cell and imitated clams, their green eyes glaring, their chins pointed upward, their lips clamped together as they refused to speak.

Until Ed Beagley showed up with Helen St. James and locked her in the cell with them.

"I want out of here *now*," the bookkeeper said as Blake stepped back to examine his handiwork.

"Don't waste your breath," Miranda told her. "He's waiting for some big confession." She turned to the other woman. "Do you have something you want to confess?"

"I do not." Helen turned her back on Miranda and rattled the bars. "You can't leave me alone in here with them, Chief. It's not safe. I mean, who knows what they did to poor Tom?"

Gran hooted. "*Poor* Tom? Is that really what you think?"

"Shhh, Gran." Miranda shot a look in Blake's direction. "That's just what he wants, some kind of catfight where we all tell him what he wants to know. I don't plan to give him the satisfaction." She shot her grandmother a worried look. "And you shouldn't, either."

"No, satisfying men has never been your thing, has it?" Helen St. James said.

"Ouch," Blake said, but was smart enough to hide his grin.

Miranda rounded on the other woman. "And what's *your* thing, Helen? Besides having sex with other people's husbands? What did you get out of your relationship with Tom besides a chance to play dress-up and the opportunity to help him bankrupt Ballantyne?"

Gran gave Miranda a high five.

"I saw you coming down off that mountain," Helen shot back. "And when I got up there Tom wasn't there. And neither was his car."

"So you say," Gran said.

"*Gran*," Miranda said with a warning glance toward Blake.

There was a ruckus out in the hall and then the door to the holding area burst open. At her first sight of the three women in the cell, Joan Ballantyne Harper skidded to a stop. Brow furrowed, she whipped back around to face Blake. "Have you taken leave of your senses?"

"I think we can safely answer yes to that one," Miranda said.

Her mother turned back to Miranda and Gran. "What's going on here?"

"We're hashing out the chain of events leading up to Tom Smith's death," Blake said reasonably. "Maybe you'd like to tell us what *you* were doing on the evening of January eighth."

The shock on Miranda's mother's face was almost comical. "But you can't just put people in a cell and tell them they have to talk."

"Actually, I can." Blake left and came back with two chairs, which he placed in the cell. Then he escorted Miranda's mother to one of them. "If it helps, you can just think of this as an interview room."

"With bars."

"That we're not allowed to leave."

"Right."

"What if we have to go to the bathroom?"

Blake nodded to the toilet in the far corner of the cell. "It's got all the amenities."

The four of them stared at him in openmouthed horror. Blake settled back against a wall and tried not to enjoy himself too much. There was no way the four of them were going to be able to pull off "the clam." He'd stake his reputation on it.

"What's Helen doing here?" Miranda's mother asked.

"She was having an affair with Tom," Gran said.

"Oh, God," Joan Harper groaned. "Like the underwear and the being dead weren't bad enough."

"Don't forget the fraudulent receivables," Helen pointed out.

"Fraudulent receivables?" It was Gran's turn to groan. "I wondered why Miranda needed to pledge all those assets."

"Thank God your father's away fishing," Miranda's mother said. "He'd be lying on the floor right there, dead of a heart attack."

Miranda stepped forward and wrapped her hands around the bars of the cell, the expression in her eyes steely. "We're entitled to a phone call." She motioned toward her cellmates. "Actually, by my count we're entitled to four. Mother, did you call Reuben?"

"He's fishing with your father. They didn't take cell phones because the reception's so spotty."

Miranda turned back to Blake. "This has gone far enough. You've done your big bad cop thing; now let us out."

"Sorry." He tried to look like he meant it. "All of you have information pertaining to Tom Smith's death. All of you have been...reluctant...to step forward and share that information. I'm giving you the opportunity to do that now. When you've explained things satisfactorily, you can go."

"This is absolutely absurd," Miranda sputtered. "I'm sure even *you* have heard of the Constitution of the United States. There are laws preventing this very thing. You can't simply leave us in here as long as you like."

He kept his voice calm and under control and the smile off his lips as he settled back against the wall. "It would appear I'm doing just that."

Lunch was delivered from the Dogwood Café. And despite Blake's earlier threats, they were allowed to go, one at a time, to the ladies' room. The afternoon dragged by in silence. Blake came and went, but mostly he stayed and waited. At one point Miranda dozed. About four o'clock in the afternoon, Gran shook her awake. Her mother and Helen St. James appeared to be sleeping. Blake had left his post.

"He hasn't accused anyone of murdering Tom," Gran whispered. "Why aren't we talking?"

Miranda kept her voice equally low. "Are you kidding? I saw Tom's clothes in the trunk of your car. What were you doing at the lake?"

"It sounds so ludicrous now," Gran said, "but I went up to my place to look for the yarn I bought for that new afghan I'm working on."

She smiled ruefully at Miranda's snort of disbelief. "It was about four-thirty and it hadn't started snowing yet, so I ran on up there." Gran sighed. "I figured I'd do a quick search for the yarn and come home before it got too dark. But when I got up there I saw Tom's car at your place."

Miranda leaned closer though she wasn't sure she really wanted to hear what was coming.

"I found the yarn and checked to make sure everything was closed up. It was already getting dark and it had started to snow, but he was still there. So I waited a while longer—I didn't put on my lights or anything—and when he didn't come out, I, uh, went over and let myself in."

"Oh, Gran." Miranda tried to imagine who had been more shocked.

Gran shook her head. "When I found Tom dressed in that lingerie waiting for some other woman I was so shocked I couldn't even think. And then I just got so mad." Gran lowered her voice further and looked around to be sure the others were still asleep. "I yanked his clothes off the bed and shouted at him to get the hell out of your life. And then I left." She shook her head again. "When I saw you coming up as I was going down, I thought it would be good for you to see him as he really was so that you could tell him off and throw him out. I thought that's what you'd done."

Miranda remembered Gran's prophetic statements, her unwillingness to push for details.

"But then you started pretending he was away on a business trip, and I didn't know what to think," Gran said. "When his body turned up I started worrying that you had . . ."

"But he wasn't there when I got there," Miranda said. "The house was empty and I didn't see his car . . ."

They looked at each other in surprise. "You mean you didn't do it?" they asked in unison.

Miranda closed her eyes as relief washed through her. When she opened them she saw that her grandmother's face reflected the same emotion.

"I knew you'd never intentionally hurt anyone," Miranda said. "But it's all been so bizarre."

"Ditto," her grandmother agreed. "I did shriek at him like a crazy woman when I barged into the cabin and found him in that bra and panties, and I *did* take his clothes. He must have just wanted to get the hell out of there, and figured he'd get dressed once he was off the property. But it had gotten icy and he was parked right next to the lake. Maybe his high heels slipped on the gas pedal. The car must have gone under awfully fast if you didn't see it."

There was a long moment of silence while they both pictured the icy waters of the lake closing around Tom. It was not an ending Miranda would have wished on anyone.

Gran interrupted the reverie. "Where do you think Helen fits into all of this? If she came up *after* you, she couldn't have been responsible, either."

Miranda reached out a tentative hand and shook Helen awake.

"What?" Helen St. James opened her eyes, still groggy.

"Are you sure you didn't see any sign of Tom up at the lake?" Miranda asked.

"Me?" Helen sat up. "Hey, are you trying to pin something—"

"No, we're just trying to figure this out." Miranda threw a glance over her shoulder. "*Without* police supervision."

Helen shook her head and dug sleep out of her eye. This time when Miranda looked at the other woman she saw another victim, one who'd been abandoned just as surely as she had. "Did you see Tom that night?"

"No." Helen shook her head. "I was supposed to meet him that afternoon and couldn't get away, and he didn't answer his cell phone. I saw you coming down on my way up, and I thought maybe you'd finally found out about us." She scrubbed at her eyes again. "The chief told me Tom was going away, but he'd only booked one ticket." She looked as weary as Miranda felt. "When I let myself into the cabin—"

"You had a key to my lake house?"

Helen nodded sadly. "I think the best part for him was using the place you cared about the most."

Miranda closed her eyes as she absorbed this latest blow. "How could I be married to him for fifteen years and know so little about him?"

Helen regarded her carefully. "I don't think he knew you too well, either," the bookkeeper replied. "He said a lot of things I'm starting to realize weren't true." Helen's smile was grim. "He underestimated you. We all did."

Footsteps sounded in the hallway and they shook Joan awake. "I'm ready," she muttered, still half asleep. "Are we going to make a break for it?"

"No," Miranda said. "We're going to tell Chief Summers what he wants to know. But if he gloats even the tiniest bit, we're going to have to kill him."

It was dusk by the time they'd provided enough information to satisfy Blake.

It was only then, while they were all still reeling from the hours spent locked up with the ugly details of January 8, that Blake had admitted Tom's death had already been ruled an accident.

After a shocked silence Helen St. James left. Miranda's mother went shortly after that. Gran got a ride home from Gus and left her car for Miranda.

Tired and deflated, like a balloon whose slow leak had finally emptied it of its last ounce of air, Miranda faced Blake in the empty office. She still couldn't believe he'd locked them up. Or that he'd withheld such critical information in order to get them to talk.

"Do you feel better now?" Miranda asked. "Now that you got the truth, the whole truth, and nothing but the truth?"

Blake leaned back against Anne Farnsworthy's desk. Stubble darkened his cheek and shadowed his jaw. He looked almost as tired as she felt.

"We could have avoided all of this if you'd just stepped forward at any point and told me what was going on." He folded his arms across his chest, and she saw the anger simmering underneath the iron control. "After Tom left would have been a good time. After we slept together would have been even better." A tick appeared in his cheek. "Even after Tom's body was found would have worked for me." His blue eyes pierced right through her. "How well do you have to know someone before you think they can handle the truth, Miranda?"

She fell back a step. He knew why she'd kept silent, and still he used it against her. "That's not fair and you know it. There was too much at stake. It wasn't just about us. And you weren't exactly up front yourself. Showing up every time I turned around. Tailing me to Atlanta. Failing to mention the outcome of the investigation until you got everything you wanted."

He snorted and ran a hand through his hair. "You didn't leave me much choice. This whole mess needed to be cleared up. For everyone's sake." The blue eyes held her fast, and his voice softened. "I know what it is to be left, Miranda. Believe me, it's better to know what happened than to spend a lifetime wondering."

She looked at him, saw that he was sincere, and knew just how dangerous that made him. "So you're saying, what? That this little fiasco today was staged on my *behalf?*" She shook her head, thinking of the lengths he'd gone to. "Frankly, I think the *truth* is highly overrated." Tears welled up and she swiped them away. "Because now I know all kinds of things I could have gone a lifetime without knowing. And you're crazy if you think I'm going to thank you for rubbing my nose in them."

Miranda looked at the man who'd made love to her so thoroughly then held her so gently; the one who had just locked her in a jail cell with her mother, her grandmother, and her dead husband's mistress. Blake Summers was too big and his personality was too commanding. And for some reason, he thought he had the right to decide what was best for her.

She stoked her anger because it felt better than the bone-crunching weariness. She stoked it until it flamed up and burned a hole through her fog and allowed her to see things she'd been afraid to see before.

"You know what else is overrated?" she asked.

"No." He was starting to get that amused glint in his eyes, which really pissed her off. "But I have a feeling you're going to tell me."

"*Men* are overrated. And relationships. In fact, I

don't even see how those two things are supposed to go together."

She felt suddenly freed of all the rules and expectations that had governed her life. At the ripe old age of thirty-eight, after fifteen years of playing the dutiful wife, her slate had been wiped clean. In the aftermath of her husband's betrayal and her public humiliation she'd discovered the one truth her mother had neglected to tell her: The only person a woman could count on was herself. Period. Which made her the only one she had to answer to.

Not Blake Summers with his arrogance and his primordial urge to set everyone straight. It had taken thirty-eight years to figure out who she was and what she wanted; she wasn't going to get hooked up with some man who'd want to tell her who to be and what to do.

Miranda pressed a finger to Blake's chest and felt a burst of electricity at the contact. But what was electricity when compared to insight? And what was an ache in the heart compared to hard-won independence?

Miranda left her finger where it was. Careful to keep any sign of the hurt and regret she felt off her face and out of her voice, she tilted her chin up and looked him right in the eye. "It could be centuries before I believe anything a man has to say to me again," she said. "Possibly eons."

She took her finger back and let her hand drop to her side. "It's time for me to be my own person. I'm not in the market for guidance or unsolicited advice. And I

think we're better off ending whatever it is that's between us before anybody really gets hurt."

She couldn't help taking a small bit of pleasure from
the look of surprise that spread across his face. It was
kind of hard with the damned tears welling up again,
but she kept her tone flip as she moved toward the
door. "As someone I know once wrote on leaving," she
said as she placed her hand on the doorknob, "you be
sure and have a nice life."

Impressed despite himself, Blake watched Miranda
leave. He'd fully expected to have it out with her over
the importance of honesty in a relationship. He'd figured if he was lucky, he might even win a chuckle or two
for this afternoon's imitation of the folksy Andy
Griffith.

But while he'd been braced for a certain amount of
anger, he'd never anticipated Miranda Smith's Emanci-
pation Proclamation.

He didn't regret the action he'd taken. If he hadn't
staged today's lockup, Miranda would still be ducking
and hiding from him all over Truro, while she and her
Gran each worried that the other had somehow done
Tom in.

Blake closed up the office, smiling over Miranda's
rendition of "Nobody Knows the Trouble I've Seen."
Then he walked through the gathering darkness to his
car, trying to figure out what to do next.

On the drive home, he realized he had no choice but

to give Miranda the space she'd asked for. He'd just have to bide his time and hope that once she got over her anger at him and the shock over Tom's death, she'd recognize what she was turning her back on.

She did have one thing right, though, he decided as he parked and let himself into the house. He did think he knew what was best for her. What was best for Miranda Smith was him.

chapter 27

The spring was tinged with sadness as Miranda grappled with the feelings of loss and grief that ambushed her when she least expected them.

The spring was also full of firsts and lasts. Miranda's first official Ballantyne board meeting as acknowledged president and CEO, her first feature article in the industry publication *Underneath It All*. At the end of May her Rhododendron Prep class met for the last time, and the girls spent it guessing who would be chosen to represent Ballantyne in this summer's Miss Rhododendron Pageant.

"Does the contestant really get a whole set of handmade underwear?" Mary Louise clearly relished the thought.

"And personal coaching? And a brand-new evening gown?"

The girls were flush with excitement over the up-coming announcement. All except Andie Summers, who slumped in her chair and stayed there after the rest of the girls had left.

As she slipped into the desk beside her, Miranda noted the changes in the girl's appearance with satisfaction. Andie's blond hair was pulled back in a smooth French braid that accentuated her high cheekbones and finely arched brows. Over the months her makeup technique had steadily improved, and she now wore the minimum to maximum effect, just a subtle enhancing of the gifts she'd been given. She and Mary Louise were the top contenders for Ballantyne's sponsorship.

"What's wrong?" Miranda asked.

"It's my dad."

"Is he all right?" Her imagination rushed to provide images of an auto accident, or something incurable.

"Yeah, he's just being a pain."

Miranda let out a small sigh of relief. She would shoot herself before she'd admit it, but Blake Summers was blowing a great big hole in her superfluous-man theory. Now that she'd sworn off men, he'd begun to look increasingly attractive. Sort of like chocolate when you were on a diet; you knew it wasn't good for you and you'd probably regret it later, but staying away from it took increasing amounts of willpower.

"He won't let me date, he won't let me meet Jake at

the Tastee-Freez, he won't let me take calls from boys period. The number of things he won't let me do gets longer every day. And he's gotten all grumpy and growly, like a bear who thinks someone's stolen all his honey."

"And this is different, how?" Miranda smiled.

"Just different. Grandpa says he needs to stop pussyfooting around and go after what he wants, and then they clam up whenever I walk in." She sighed. "I'm considering putting myself up for adoption. I don't suppose you'd be interested?"

Miranda smiled and slipped an arm around Andie's shoulders. "I've been wanting a daughter since I was a little older than you." She paused as if seriously considering the idea. "You're taller than what I was planning to bring home from the hospital, but I'm game if you are."

Andie gathered her things and they moved toward the front of the classroom. At the doorway Miranda stopped and turned Andie around to face her, then placed a hand gently on the top of the girl's head. "By the power vested in me as a beauty pageant coach and all-around girlie-girl, I hereby adopt you and make you my own."

She kissed both of Andie's cheeks and wrapped her in a less-than-ladylike hug. "That means any time the testosterone level in your house gets too high, you can call me and I'll come whisk you away to my bastion of femininity."

"Bastion of femininity?" Andie looked delighted. "I

love the sound of that. Maybe we can build our own clubhouse or something."

"Yeah," Miranda laughed. "And we'll post a sign out front that says 'No Boys Allowed.' "

"You know, I hardly miss men at all."

"That's good." Carly held the straw hat tighter to her head to keep it from flying off as the convertible rounded a curve. They were on their way to Ballantyne's Memorial Day Picnic and the Miss Rhododendron contestant naming. For obvious reasons, this year's event was NOT being held on the banks of Lake Carraway at the top of Ballantyne Bald, but at another lake site several miles away.

Miranda glanced in the BMW's rearview mirror to where an excited Lindsey was also dressed in full picnic regalia. "Do you? Miss Lindsey's daddy, I mean?"

Carly looked out the window at the scenery rushing by. The wind whipped her blond hair back from her face and lifted the collar of her cotton shirt. "Sometimes," she said. "When the day's been really long and I'm bone tired and I don't have anyone to talk to about it."

Miranda knew the feeling all too well. Those were the times when Tom's absence was a tangible thing and no amount of dredging up his betrayals eased the emptiness.

They rode in silence for a minute.

"Or when my boss is especially difficult and I don't have anyone to gripe to about her."

They looked at each other, then threw back their heads and laughed. A short time later they pulled into a makeshift parking area and followed the music to this year's picnic grounds.

"Oh, Mommy, look!" Lindsey dropped Carly's hand and jumped up and down.

A bright yellow-and-white-striped tent perched on the far side of the clearing. Beside it, Sam Skinnard's All Mountain Man Band played on a makeshift wooden stage; the twang of their banjos and fiddles rang off the surrounding mountains and echoed through the woods. Beyond them, lines of children waited for a turn on one of four ponies being led around a circle. It was toward a white one with a brightly ribboned tail that Lindsey now ran.

"Oh, my," Carly breathed. "We really outdid ourselves this year."

As they drew near, Miranda squared her shoulders and raised her chin. Things were going well at Ballantyne, she was seeing to that, but it wasn't what Andie would have called a "slam dunk." There were pockets of resistance, and the occasional muttering about how Mr. Smith would have done things. No one came out and argued with her, but they didn't exactly welcome her with open arms. Even with the change of venue, she wouldn't be the only one noting Tom's absence today.

Miranda spotted Gus in a group of suspendered

old-timers pitching horseshoes while Gran cheered him on, and she located Andie in the middle of a group of girls chattering excitedly while Jake Hanson and several of his buddies buzzed nearby. She automatically began to scan the crowd for Blake Summers, but stopped herself in mid-scan. Much better to keep that box of chocolates closed; she'd never be able to eat just one.

Inside the tent, women set out food on buffet tables already groaning with delicacies, and eyed what others had brought. Ballantyne had provided the site, the entertainment, and the drinks, but plates would be filled to overflowing with homemade fried chicken, potato salad, and cornbread. Her mother blew her a kiss as she directed the rearrangement of the dessert table with a seriousness normally reserved for invasions of troublesome countries, while her father, who looked wonderfully fit and tan, swapped fish stories with a couple of his cronies nearby.

Miranda forced herself to stroll around the edge of the crowd, moving from group to group with a friendly nod or wave; but while people nodded back or raised a hand in greeting, no one called her over or invited her to linger. Everyone seemed to be a part of something except her.

Slipping out the back flap of the tent, Miranda leaned against a support pole and stared out at the lake.

Only a few teenage boys had braved the still-cool waters; a few of the younger ones amused themselves splashing water at any girl who ventured close enough to be a target. The girls' delighted shrieks swirled up into the mountain air and blended with the pickin' and singin'. A good time was being had by all.

"Having fun?"

Blake's voice took her completely by surprise. Her heart started dancing its own little jig, which she did her best to hide.

"Sure," she said too quickly. "How about you?"

"I'm having about as much fun as it's possible to have while keeping bees away from the hive." He nodded toward the crowd of boys surrounding Andie. "It was a lot easier before you turned her into such a . . . girl."

For a moment she considered warning him about her upcoming announcement, then decided he deserved it. The man had locked her in a jail cell and threatened to throw away the key. "She's a very attractive young woman; being attractive should be a positive, not a negative."

Blake didn't argue the point. "I don't think she's going to last in your man-haters' club. How many members you up to now?"

Miranda blushed. "Our numbers are legion. Converts are born daily."

He looked down at her with a knowing look. Kind of like a Twinkie planting himself outside a Weight Watchers meeting.

A voice reached them from the other side of the tent

wall. "Don't ya'll think this party should have been cancelled out of respect for Tom Smith?"

An angry buzz of voices joined in, though their words couldn't be discerned. Miranda's shoulders tensed, and she froze in place.

Wanting to end the uncomfortable silence surrounding them, she turned her attention to the relay teams being formed on the other side of the meadow. "Excuse me," she said as she stepped away from the tent, "I'm going to go check on things."

"There you go, Carly," Sam Skinner boomed into the microphone as Miranda neared. "If you add Miranda and the chief you'll have an even number."

"What?" Blake reached her at the same moment Carly stepped up. And began to tie Miranda's ankle to Blake's.

"Hey, wait." Miranda protested, but Carly had already moved around them to start on the other line. "If you want to keep that promotion you'll come back here and untie us."

Before Carly could respond, a white flag flashed downward and their team's first couple lurched forward.

Miranda and Blake stood tied together at the back of what was now their team's line. Blake's heat pressed against her side and his arm hung behind her back.

"Sorry." He lifted his arm, letting the hand trail casually up her rear end before slinging it across her shoulder. He didn't sound at all apologetic. "I have to put my hand somewhere."

The first couple returned laughing and out of breath and the next took off. Blake and Miranda moved forward, and he used the hand on her shoulder to weld her more tightly to his side.

"You know, if you ever decide to fraternize with the enemy . . ." he began as their teammates went down in a tangle of arms and legs. A groan went up from their side.

"Me?" Miranda made the most of her tone since she was wedged too tightly to him to risk serious shoulder movement. "Fraternize with someone who investigated me, then slept with me, and then locked me up and interrogated me? I'm surprised you didn't come right out and ask me whether or not I killed my husband."

She risked turning under his arm and her breast smashed against his chest. "How could you make love to me the way you did and then grill me like that?"

The duo in front of them swiveled around. At Blake's glare, they spun back toward the front, and then took off in a practiced skip.

"Miranda, I have to ask the questions whether I think I know the answer or not. I'm also required to investigate any death in this town to the fullest extent of my ability. And it's not like you didn't tell a few lies along the way."

They were busy staring into each other's eyes and neither of them saw the white warning flag go up. "You are the most confusing and irritating woman I have ever known. And I can't seem to get you out of my head."

"Go!" There was a push from behind, and Miranda and Blake hurtled forward in reaction—pretty much all feet at once. They clutched at each other in an effort to regain their balance. The other team's couple took off in a smooth, coordinated lope.

"Middle foot!" Blake shouted. "Pick it up!"

Before she could argue, Blake's arm clamped tighter around her shoulder and he surged forward, pulling her along with him. The other team waved as they raced by.

They were moving now, in a rough and totally unco-ordinated way. Actually Blake was moving; she was being hauled along like a sack of potatoes. She jounced against his side as they moved.

"This is ridiculous!" she shouted.

"Yeah!" He yanked her closer and increased his speed. "But I hate to lose. Let's move!"

His arm was a vise on her shoulder; she rammed against his rock-hard edges with every step.

The other couple rounded the end marker and began to head back.

"Ow!" She yelped as Blake's hip rammed into her waist and all five of his fingers dug into her upper arm.

"Can't you move any faster?" he asked.

"Good grief." Their thighs knocked as they half walked, half skipped toward the turnaround point. They'd been left in the dust, but had finally managed to find some semblance of a rhythm. She slipped her arm around his waist and held on.

"This race is starting to remind me of our relationship."

"What relationship?" She shouted as her foot dipped into a hole and her knee buckled beneath her.

Blake hauled her up tighter against his side and lengthened their stride.

"We've spent the night together twice and we argue a lot," she pointed out. "Last time I checked, that was not the foundation for a relationship."

The couple who'd been about to pass them slowed down to listen. Blake kicked up their pace a notch and they shot past them.

"Don't be stupid, Miranda. We have enough chemistry to blow up a small country. You don't walk away from something like that."

"I'd be happy to walk at all."

They were skipping toward the finish line now; he'd given her absolutely no choice about that. But she was not going to be led or dictated to. She'd already been there and done that. Testosterone and tingling were not enough.

Miranda dug in her heels and applied the brakes. Through sheer surprise or some law of physics she'd failed to learn in school, she brought them to a screeching halt. Blake shouted in surprise and his body slammed backward into hers. The air whooshed out of her lungs as they crashed to the ground and then tumbled, still joined at the ankle, down the slight incline toward the finish line, where they landed in a much-too-intimate heap.

Enmeshed from the top of their grass-strewn heads to the toes of their tied-together feet, they lay in their own personal pile while something sprang up between them.

Cringing with embarrassment, Miranda lay flush on top of Blake as a crowd gathered around them. She could feel their curious stares on her backside and hear the whir of a motor drive as Clara Bartlett moved in closer to capture the *Truro Gazette*'s page-one photo.

chapter 28

Blake rolled them onto their sides and reached down to untie the rope around their ankles. Miranda's breathing was still ragged, and he considered offering mouth-to-mouth resuscitation, but he suspected they'd already commandeered enough attention.

"You're supposed to signal before you stop," he pointed out as he pulled her to her feet. "I'm pretty sure that's rule number one in the three-legged race strategy book."

"I'll keep that in mind." She yanked her hand back and swiped at the seat of her jeans. He considered offering to help with that, too, but her sense of humor seemed to have disappeared when they hit the ground.

The murmuring swelled around them as he followed her out of the circle of onlookers and into the fresh afternoon air.

"Are you all right, Miranda?" Her mother and grandmother claimed places on either side of her and glanced over at Blake suspiciously, as they brushed grass off her clothes and removed twigs from her hair.

"I really don't think rolling around on the ground with the chief is advisable right now, Miranda," her mother admonished. "And it's time to name Ballantyne's contestant for Miss Rhododendron. Sam sent me to bring you up to the stage."

Miranda turned back to look at Blake, and he thought for a moment she was going to say something. Instead she bit her lip and hurried toward the stage. Like a massive herd of cattle scenting water, everyone else followed. Andie and her friends formed an excited knot on the far side of the platform, and the older folks left the tent to mill around beside them. The relay contestants surged forward, too, many of them still chewing over the spectacle of Miranda rolling in the grass with the chief of police, and there was an edge to their muttering that Blake didn't care for one bit. Concerned, he elbowed his way forward and took a position in front of the stage where he could spring into action if necessary.

The music ended as Miranda stepped up to the microphone. A light breeze off the lake teased at the stray tendrils of dark hair on her neck, and her nose looked red from an afternoon in the sun. A large grass stain covered the right breast of her white Ballantyne T-shirt.

Only the slight flutter of the sheet of paper in her hand betrayed her nervousness as she waited for the talk to die down.

He watched her carefully, even as he monitored the whispering behind him. Her gaze rested on him briefly and then swept across the crowd toward Andie. Blake braced himself and felt a faint glimmer of unease.

"Thank you all for coming today. We hope you're having a good time," Miranda said into the microphone.

There was a groundswell of applause and shouts of "Best one ever" and "Let's hear it for Ballantyne," but there was grumbling, too, and an undercurrent of negativity that had Blake scanning the crowd.

"So," Miranda said. "The time has come to announce the name of the young woman Ballantyne will sponsor in this year's Miss Rhododendron Pageant, which as you know takes place in August." She nodded to Sam, and the Mountain Men broke into the opening chords of "Pretty Woman."

Miranda waited for the song to get established, then she looked directly at Blake and said, "This year, Ballantyne Bras will be sponsoring a talented and multifaceted young woman. It was a difficult decision, one the selection committee devoted a lot of time and thought to." She paused. "I'm pleased to announce that this year's contestant is...Andrea Summers. Come on up here, Andie, and accept your applause."

Girls shrieked, not all of them with pleasure. His daughter stood in a circle of shouting teenage girls who were jumping up and down around her like the working parts of a washing machine. Jake Hanson gave Andie a brilliant smile as she made her way up onto the stage.

As he'd been forced to admit at the ball, she looked just like the dog-eared pictures Blake had of his mother. She had the same sleek blond hair, the same bright blue eyes, the same elegant cheekbones. He'd been trying to deny the resemblance since Andie's childhood, had almost managed to obscure it by turning her into a boy. But there it was, staring right at him.

Andie threw her arms around Miranda and then stepped up to the microphone. His daughter *was* beautiful; Miranda had been right about that. And as he listened to his daughter speak, he acknowledged that she was a lot more than that. Unlike his mother, her beauty ran deep beneath the surface.

"I'm honored and thrilled to be given this opportunity to represent Ballantyne and Truro." She looked directly at Blake, and her smile was so full of promise that it broke his heart. "I promise ya'll I'm going for a full-court press on this. And I promise my father I won't break any more bones while I'm at it."

Mary Louise stood to the side of the stage trying to smile through her tears. Her mother looked mad enough to eat nails. "Don't you worry, Mary Louise," she said loudly enough to be heard. "We can all see what kind of favoritism is going on here. It doesn't hurt to have a relative on close and personal terms with the sponsor, now, does it?"

Miranda fixed the woman with a stare as Andie walked off the stage. Blake moved closer and prepared to step into the fray if necessary.

"Well, Miranda Smith knows about beauty pageants all right," someone shouted. "But why is she making so many changes at Ballantyne?"

There was a more pronounced murmuring in the crowd, and people started to surge toward the stage. Blake glanced up to see how Miranda was handling things and saw that her hands were clenched at her sides, just like his, and her gaze was steady. He felt a burst of pride as he watched her stand her ground.

Most people saw the beautiful package and never bothered to untie the bow and look inside. Which was pretty much what he had been doing right up until the moment she'd told him to take a hike.

He looked now at the *real* Miranda, not at the dark hair and the green eyes he liked so much, or the long legs and lithe body. Those were nice, more than nice. But they were nothing compared to what lay inside; like his daughter, she was so much more than he'd given her credit for.

Their eyes met and he recognized, clearly, who she was and what she was made of. And realized just how much he wanted to walk up there and tell her so.

He wanted Miranda to resign as president of the Truro Man Haters' Club and give whatever was between them a chance. Because he cared for her, cared deeply. Might even be in love with her. He could just imagine what she'd have to say about that.

From the stage, Miranda studied the employees and townspeople before her. "You're right," she said clearly into the microphone. "There have been a lot of changes. They were made to preserve our company. And the jobs it provides here in Truro."

There were a few cheers but the grumbling continued. She saw Blake step closer to the stage, and for a mad minute she thought he was planning to rush it and—what? Take her in his arms? Declare his love? She must have hit her head harder than she'd realized during the three-legged race, because her imagination was running wild. Not at all appropriate for a woman who had sworn off men, and this man in particular.

Her mother stepped up onto the stage beside her. Her mother, Miranda thought, had come a hell of a long way. Then her father was there, too.

"What happened to Tom Smith? Why isn't anyone being held responsible for his death?" The words were hurled at the stage.

"The chief is covering up for her," someone else shouted. "In this town, Ballantynes can get away with anything." There was a pause. "Even murder."

Clara Bartlett scribbled madly, clearly intent on capturing every word for the *Truro Gazette*.

"Oh, pshaw." Gran climbed up the stage steps and elbowed her way toward the microphone. Gus clambered up behind her.

Miranda looked down into the crowd. The only one not on the stage was . . .

"Oh, for Heaven's sake!" Not bothering with the steps, Blake sprang onto the stage and strode toward the group in its center. Taking the microphone from Miranda's hand, he turned to face the folks he had sworn to protect and defend. "What in the world is wrong with you people?" he demanded.

No one responded, which Miranda figured was a good thing.

"This woman," he said, gesturing toward Miranda, "has lost her husband. And while I don't like to speak ill of the dead, I think we all know Tom Smith wasn't the prize he tried to pass himself off as."

There were murmurs.

"Tom Smith was running around with other women," Blake said. "And he stole money from his wife's company, from *your* company. He ran it badly and then he stole from it. And when he realized the truth was going to come out he made plans to run away. Right after he took all the money out of his and his wife's personal bank accounts." He watched their faces as his words sank in. "He didn't get real far, but he ran without a thought for his wife, his girlfriend"—he looked pointedly at Helen St. James—"or you all." He didn't bother to mention the lingerie Tom Smith ran in. Miranda figured everybody was busy filling in that blank for themselves right now.

He let them mutter and mumble for a bit, and then he continued. "For almost five months, *this woman*"—

he pointed at Miranda again, and she began to think maybe in the excitement he'd forgotten her name—"has carried the weight of her family's company and our town on her shoulders."

There was more murmuring, but it felt decidedly less hostile.

"She had *no* money, *no* one to confide in, and *no*where to turn. A lot of people would have given up, shrugged you all off, and moved on. But she didn't turn her back on you. She found a way to keep Ballantyne intact and all of your jobs safe."

Blake looked at her, and though he continued to speak into the microphone, his words were clearly meant for Miranda. "This woman we've shrugged off as a beauty queen has more grit and determination than any ten men put together." He smiled. "If this is what a Miss Rhododendron is capable of, then I hope my daughter has what it takes to win a crown."

"And what about her husband's death? Are you just going to let her wiggle off the hook for that?" someone shouted.

"Every shred of evidence gathered by the GBI, the coroner, and my office supports an accidental drowning," Blake said.

"But he was leaving her," Clara Bartlett broke in. "How did he end up in the lake?"

Blake paused, then looked the gossip columnist in the eye.

"Tom Smith's car slid into the lake. The GBI found skid marks preserved under the snow, and when the car was pulled out they found the accelerator stuck. There was no sign of foul play—just a malfunctioning accelerator and an icy bank. He was alive when the car went in and if his"—Blake cleared his throat— "clothing hadn't gotten caught on the gearshift, he might have made it out alive."

He shook his head and got a strange look on his face and concluded, "According to the coroner who handled the autopsy, Tom Smith died of something we law enforcement personnel refer to as a"—he cleared his throat again—"DBC."

The crowd dispersed, and with a sigh of relief Miranda turned to Blake. "Thanks, I, uh, appreciate the vote of confidence and the public explanation."

She wanted to throw her arms around him and bury her face in his chest, but she kept her arms anchored to her side. She'd missed him, missed his quick intelligence and dry wit; she'd even missed tangling with him. Blake Summers could be annoying and arrogant, but he was a good man and a well-intentioned father. And just being around him sent her into sensory overload.

"I wondered if you might like to go to a movie or get a bite out one night?" he asked now. "Maybe we could start fresh, take some time getting to know each other."

Miranda looked into the blue of his eyes and wanted nothing more. Little voices in her brain stood up and shouted, "yes, oh yes," and tried to find their way to her lips. But she'd only just managed to find her way, had only recently begun to know herself; if she let him into her life he'd take it over without even trying.

Miranda shook her head and forced herself to maintain eye contact. "I know how keen you are on the truth, so I'm going to give it to you right now."

She bit her bottom lip, mauled it for a while before plunging ahead. "I'm still dealing with the failure of my marriage and the fact that Tom died wanting to leave me." She shrugged. "And you," she smiled sadly, "you're not someone I can just go out with now and again. There's too much there, Blake. And you're too . . . big . . . to be contained."

He looked like he wanted to argue, but he didn't interrupt.

"I don't feel quite as . . . militant about it as I did that day at the jail, but nothing's really changed. I'm still figuring out what I want and where I'm going, and I can't afford to get sidetracked. I need you to leave me alone."

They stared into each other's eyes for a long moment. His were filled with disappointment and disbelief, and she suspected hers were filled with the same.

Then he took a step back, and he was the one shaking his head. "You may call that honest, Miranda, but I call it bullshit." His eyes locked with hers and wouldn't let go. "No one takes over your life unless you roll over and let them. And from what I can see, your rolling over days are *over*." He ran a hand through his hair and shook his head one last time. "I'll stay away, but you're making a big mistake. Going it alone's not all it's cracked up to be. That I know for a fact."

It was July, and the Ballantyne parking lot sparkled under a bright summer sky. The scents of summer drifted on the breeze and the Truro High School Marching Band stood at attention, their instruments raised, ready to blow their hearts out at the awaited signal.

Miranda, the attending board members, Ballantyne's Miss Rhododendron contestant, the company's three hundred and twelve employees, and a crowd of townsfolk stood beneath the spot that the old sign declaring Ballantyne's support of Truro had once spanned. With a nod to Andie and the band director, Miranda pulled the end of rope in her hand and felt Andie do the same with hers. The first note of the trumpet fanfare rang out as they unfurled the new banner.

With held breath, she read the new sign along with the crowd. BALLANTYNE BRAS, HOME OF CUSTOM CLEAVAGE: CREATING THE PERFECT BRA ONE STITCH AT A TIME.

There were murmurs, and the fanfare died in midnote. Like a precision drill team, hundreds of pairs of eyes clicked from the banner to Miranda. Not exactly the enthusiastic reaction she'd been hoping for.

She stepped forward into the surprised silence and surveyed the crowd.

"You're right," she said. "This is not your parents' Ballantyne." She looked at her own parents' surprised faces and then back at the crowd. "Or my parents', for that matter."

There were a few guffaws.

"What this *is*," she said, "is our opportunity to create something entirely new out of a long and proud history. And it's going to take each and every one of us pulling together to make it happen."

Scanning the assembled faces, Miranda saw pockets of doubt. She understood their fear of the unknown but refused to let it hold her back. She intended to build consensus where possible, and drag the unwilling along when necessary. The resurrection of Ballantyne had become so inextricably linked to the reshaping of her own life that she could no longer envision one without the other.

Miranda stepped off the podium as the band pulled itself together. Carly sent her a thumbs-up and Helen St. James, with whom she had forged a surprisingly effective working relationship, signaled her approval. For all his failings, Tom Smith had had great taste in women.

Gran stepped up beside her and gave her a hug. "You've done well, Miranda."

"It feels right, Gran, to try to repair what Tom destroyed."

"Yes, I can understand that." She paused. "And it fills your days. You run to New York and Atlanta. You torture the store designer and the fabric suppliers. Your energy is boundless. You've accomplished so much." She took Miranda's face in her hands. "But at some point you're going to have to slow down and look at the other part of your life."

Over Gran's shoulder, Miranda spotted Blake Summers at the back of the crowd. He was tall and commanding in his khaki uniform and dark-billed cap. He wore sunglasses, so it was hard to know where his gaze was aimed. As she always did in his presence, she felt that tiny frisson of electricity. And as always she pushed it away.

He hadn't approached her since the Memorial Day picnic two months ago, for which she told herself she should be grateful.

"You're getting that wrinkly-wise-woman look again, Gran," she said, still looking at Blake. "And we all know how that turned out last time."

Following her gaze, Gran spotted Blake and gave him a small wave. "I don't understand why you two keep doing this strange tango."

"Believe me, we're not dancing. The man locked me up in a cell and forced me to talk. I'm still thanking my lucky stars he didn't haul out the naked lightbulb and the rubber hose."

"We had lunch from the Dogwood and regular potty breaks, darling. I don't think that constitutes cruel and unusual punishment."

"He could have just taken my word and not dragged us all through that ludicrous charade."

Gran raised an eyebrow.

"Well, okay, maybe I'd omitted a few things up until then."

The other eyebrow went up.

"Well, he should have known I didn't have anything to do with Tom's death."

"He's the chief of police, Miranda. He couldn't exactly write a report that said 'I didn't bother to ask because I know she's innocent.' And in case you've forgotten, he stood up in front of most of the town and defended you quite eloquently."

Miranda remained silent.

"But that's not really the issue, is it, Miranda? I don't think you're being honest with yourself or Blake."

When she looked next, Blake had disappeared into the crowd and Miranda felt the usual surge of disappointment. "It doesn't really matter," she said as they walked under the new banner and back toward the main offices, though she sounded less certain than she intended. "My life is finally my own, Gran. And I'm living it the best way I know how. I really don't need a man to complicate it."

"Oh, pshaw." Gran's face registered her impatience. "We're not talking *any* man here, we're talking Blake. And for such a smart woman you're being incredibly stupid."

"Thanks, Gran. Your vote of confidence is overwhelming."

"I know you've been hurt, Miranda, and after all that's happened I understand you being afraid. But loving someone, the *right* someone, doesn't obliterate who you are. It enhances it." Gran smiled in that wrinkly wise way and lifted her hand to Miranda's cheek. "A smart woman knows when she's found that someone."

Miranda tried to shrug off her grandmother's words, but they took hold deep inside her and wouldn't let go. She spent the rest of the summer sidestepping her grandmother's attempts to draw her into Blake's circle through Gus, and she did her best to keep her pageant coaching and friendship with Andie as separate as she could. And slowly she let go of Tom, keeping only the best memories tucked deep inside.

When being without Blake got tougher instead of easier, she told herself that she'd get over it one day soon. Only that day never came. She was horribly afraid she might actually be in love with him.

It was September now, and boxes of engraved invitations to Custom Cleavage's grand opening were stacked on the conference table in front of her. Pages of the proposed guest list were strewn across the tabletop.

Her mother, her grandmother, and Carly, all of whom had contributed to the list, sat at the table with her while she went through it one last time.

"Is this Selena's whole Atlanta client list?" she asked Carly.

"Yes."

"And we've got the symphony guild, the Junior League, the private clubs, and all the volunteer groups that she suggested?"

"Check," her mother said.

"We've got family, friends of family, Ballantyne board members, and friends of board members."

"Definitely," Gran said.

"There is not a woman with enough money to buy a custom bra within a hundred-mile radius of Phipps Plaza who is not on this list," Carly assured her.

Miranda shifted uncomfortably in her seat.

"Is there someone you'd like to add, darling?" Gran eyed her knowingly, but Miranda refused to rise to the bait. Whether or not she invited Blake Summers to her grand opening was nobody's business but her own. And what would inviting him to the opening mean anyway, when the whole world appeared to be coming?

After all the attempts he'd made and she'd rejected, any gesture from her would have to be grander than that. She pulled an invitation out of the stack and slipped it into her purse. Or maybe the scale of the gesture no longer mattered. Maybe it was just too late.

chapter 29

Ballantyne's first Custom Cleavage opened in Atlanta's Phipps Plaza on a bright fall morning.

Outside, the crapemyrtles had deepened to a burnished gold and the Japanese maples were the color of a rich merlot, but in this carefully created corner of Selena Moore's flagship store, colors were muted and a quiet elegance prevailed.

Cream brocade covered the walls and twined around brass finials, while mahogany display pieces and antique lingerie chests showcased finely sewn samples. The richness of the wood furnishings gleamed brightly against the faded beauty of the Aubusson carpet on which they sat.

Miranda took a final walk through the showroom,

then did a last check of the two oversize fitting rooms. She plumped pillows, polished the already spotless mirrors, and rehung the silk dressing gowns on their antique brass hooks. Every choice reflected her taste; no decision had been too small to require her input. She knew she'd driven the interior designer crazy, but in the end she'd gotten exactly what she'd envisioned.

In these rooms, customers would be measured within an inch of their lives and then led to a formal sitting alcove to sip champagne while they selected the components and fabrics that would make their undergarments completely custom. The surroundings promised quality and pampering, and Miranda intended to make sure those promises were kept.

In the alcove, Carly perched on an elegant slipper chair beside a Louis XV commode, her smile radiating the satisfaction Miranda felt. "You did it, Boss. You really did it," she said.

"*We* did it," Miranda corrected, as she used her sleeve to wipe a small smudge from the burled wood. "I'm going to miss you outside my office when you move to the design department full-time." She nodded toward the bookkeeper, who had already moved to Atlanta to oversee their expansion there and who was busy fussing over the big gold appointment book. "And we won't have Helen around to torture anymore."

Surveying her newly created kingdom, Miranda knew a deep stirring of satisfaction. She *had* made this happen; she had looked adversity in the face and triumphed over it.

So she had no personal life, and today her "grand gesture" might be thrown back in her face. What was that compared to all she had achieved?

At 9:58 A.M. she joined Selena on the main sales floor.

"Ready?" Selena asked.

Miranda rubbed her palms down the sides of her skirt. "Ready as I'll ever be."

Together they stepped forward to unlock the glass doors of Selena Moore and welcome the crowd of well-heeled women who waited, invitations in hand.

They'd been chosen for their buying history and their standing in the community, and Miranda had vowed to make sure they all left with scheduled fitting times and a taste of the luxury and personal service that awaited them at Custom Cleavage.

Two hours and twenty appointments in the schedule book later, Miranda glanced up to see her mother, Andie, and Gran approaching.

"It looks marvelous." Joan Ballantyne Harper surveyed her daughter's domain while Gran and Andie bussed Miranda on the cheek.

"But?" Miranda waited for the thing she'd overlooked, the way in which she might have made it better.

"But nothing," her mother said. "It looks perfect. I wouldn't change a thing."

Miranda exchanged glances with Gran. "It's the suite at the Ritz I treated her and Daddy to, isn't it?"

"It most certainly is not." Her mother blushed. "Though I must say that in-suite massage was especially nice." She smiled, her love and approval so obvious and genuine they nearly knocked Miranda over. "I'm very proud of you, sweetheart." Her mother glanced over at Andie. "And I must say you're doing a fine job of teaching this girl how to shop." She patted Miranda on the cheek before heading toward the hors d'oeuvres. "Keep up the good work."

"So?" Miranda turned her attention to Andie, unable to halt the quick peek over her shoulder for some sign of the girl's father, or to keep her face from falling when Andie confirmed her fears.

"Daddy, uh, didn't think he'd be able to make it." She cleared her throat. "Is it okay if I hang out?"

"Always." Miranda took in the girl's flawless makeup, the artfully styled hair, the high-top sneakers, and squashed her disappointment. She could hardly have expected Blake to wait all those months for her to signal her interest. Her invitation to a candlelit supper following the opening had obviously been too little, too late.

"Why don't you go help Carly pass canapés. Be charming."

Andie grinned her father's grin. "And what *else* would the reigning Miss Rhododendron be?"

"Good point." She watched the girl head over to Carly and saw the two confer.

"She's a good girl," Gran observed. "Lots of spunk. I can still see her strutting across the stage in that gown you chose for her." Gran's eyes twinkled. "I understand

Blake's putting in a special holding cell at the police station for all her suitors."

Miranda smiled, but it felt strange to have everyone else on such a friendly footing with Blake when she herself was so ... *left out?*

"Hasn't he come by?" Gran asked.

Miranda pulled an order form from the desk drawer. There was a steady stream of women coming through the front doors. She had bras to sell and a company to rebuild. "No." She tried to keep the hurt out of her voice. She'd asked the man to leave her alone and he'd obliged. Then she'd changed her mind and he hadn't. End of story. She was not going to moon about in the middle of her big day. She didn't need Blake Summers or any other man to make her life complete.

"Well, enjoy yourself, darling." Gran gave her a hug. "I'm going to see what Lindsey's up to back in the office. Gus and I may take her for an ice cream. We'll see you back at the hotel."

Miranda went back to chatting up customers and making sure all went smoothly, while out in the boutique Selena did the same. The afternoon passed in a blur of smiles and handshakes and a truly satisfying number of appointments. Custom Cleavage was off and running.

So why did her heart feel so damned heavy?

When the last invited guest had left, Miranda kicked off her heels and shared a celebratory glass of champagne with the jubilant Selena. Watching her new partner leave through the back entrance, Miranda chastised herself for letting her disappointment over Blake steal the luster from the day, but she was at a loss as to how to make that disappointment go away.

From beneath a back counter, she pulled out a beribboned picnic basket and specially stocked cooler and began to unpack their contents. She set the candlesticks, the bottle of red wine, and the carefully chosen cold supper for two out on the table in the alcove, and contemplated what she'd intended to be the first of many romantic meals she'd share with Blake.

Lighting the tapers, she took a seat at the table, folded her hands in her lap, and stared into the flames, knowing he wasn't coming, but unable to stop wishing the man she'd finally admitted she wanted would somehow walk through the door and tell her he still wanted her.

She lost track of how long she sat there, but the candles had burned low by the time her remaining glimmer of hope finally sputtered out and died.

Miranda blew out the candles and turned her back on the alcove. Not yet ready to face her family, she sank into a fitting-room chaise, closed her eyes, and let the events of the last nine months tumble through her consciousness. She tried to push the sadness away and focus, instead, on how much had been accomplished, how fortunate she was. But she couldn't stop thinking that in the jigsaw puzzle of her life, one very critical piece was missing.

She was still thinking about Blake Summers when the fitting-room door opened.

"Ah, what is this I see?" Blake stepped inside and closed the door behind him. "Could it be a delicate flower in need of pollinating?"

Miranda looked up. She'd started tingling at the sound of his voice, and as he crossed the dressing room and sat on the edge of the chaise, relief and a surge of hope shot through her. Her insides turned all warm and gooey; there was a chance she might actually be producing honey.

Without asking permission, Blake lifted her foot onto his lap and started massaging it with strong fingers.

"Blake, I . . ."

"Even with the invitation, I wasn't sure if you were really ready," he said quietly. "I wasn't going to come." He ran a hand through his hair in a gesture that had become as familiar to her as his face. "But I didn't want to miss your opening." He said it simply, sincerely. His smile was rueful. "And I couldn't make myself stay away."

The rightness of his being here settled over her, and as he continued his massage, she searched for the words that would convey all she felt.

"I've learned a few things since I took over the business," she finally said as she offered her other foot for his ministrations.

He cocked his head, interested.

"And now I know that a good bra is like a good relationship. It lifts you up and helps you stand on your own. And it's right there in your drawer when you need it."

The massaging stopped and the corners of his mouth tilted upward. "I think I hear a new banner in the making."

She used her foot to silence him but smiled back as she followed through with the analogy. "Some women want lace and some want cotton. Some of us need a little padding. But when it comes right down to it, we're all just looking for the perfect fit." She looked at him, willing him to understand what she was trying to say.

"Okay," Blake said. "It may be a little long for a banner, but it's very profound all the same."

He wasn't going to make this easy.

"What I mean is..." She paused and gathered her courage. "If you're willing to give me some time, maybe we could, um, try each other on for size."

He didn't respond and her heart thudded in her chest. He considered her carefully, weighing something—she had no idea what—in his mind. Maybe she had misread his intentions; maybe he'd only shown up to be polite. Maybe...

"Okay," he said while his smile grew. "But I get first dibs on the measuring tape."

With her feet still in his lap, he leaned over and brought his mouth down to hers. And then he kissed her until all she could think about was taking him to her hive.

He nibbled on her earlobe and the nape of her neck.

"I'm sorry I missed our candlelit supper. We can go have it now if you'd like."

But dinner wasn't at all what she had on her mind right now. She nudged him with a big toe. "So is that a stinger in your pocket," she asked in a passable Mae West, "or are you just glad to see me?"

She looped her arms around his neck, and when she nudged her foot more tightly against his crotch he made a buzzing sound that reverberated in his chest. He pressed her down into the chaise, and she shot a look toward the fitting-room door.

"It's okay," Blake said as he stretched out on top of her. "I locked the back door, and the worker bees have all gone home."

His lips moved down to the hollow of her throat and on to the V between her breasts. His hair tickled her chin as Miranda closed her eyes and sighed with pleasure.

"You know, I promised you a knighthood that time on the stairs," she said as his fingers moved to the buttons of her blouse. "And in appreciation for your loyal service and the service I hope you are about to provide, I hereby dub you"—she thought a moment, then smiled as it hit her—" 'Sir Stings-A-Lot.' "

Blake laughed and brought his lips back up to hers. Good God, the man could kiss. She sighed again and gave herself up to him completely.

It was a damned fine thing to be queen.

Acknowledgments

One of the great things about writing is all the cool stuff you get to learn and the even cooler people you get to learn it from. This time out I'd like to thank Rob Vann, Purchasing Manager, VFIntimates, for teaching me more about bras than I ever expected to know, and for always being just an E-mail away. I'd also like to thank Angela Dotson, former pageant coach and Miss Telfair County, for helping me see how well pageant training translates to the corporate world.

Additional thanks go to James Butts, Jack Berry, and Wally Lind for sharing their knowledge of small-town law enforcement. I hope they'll forgive me for any liberties I've taken. Any errors or mistakes are definitely my own.

Thanks also to the Highland Gap contingent, Cheri and Mike Madsen, Earl and Diane West, and Julie Hilliard for introducing me to mountain life and helping me create the fictional town of Truro. For financial and basketball info I have to thank my husband, John Adler, and Amy L. Kaye, Esquire, for the details of divorce.

Thanks, too, to the members of the Georgia Romance Authors Network and all the other women I coerced into sharing their feelings about their bras.

No acknowledgment would be complete without a very large thank-you to fellow writers Karen White, Jennifer St. Giles, and Karen Kendall, without whom I'd still be beating my head against a blank computer screen. You're the best!

About the Author

Wendy lives with her husband and two sons in a testosterone-laden home in the suburbs of Atlanta. When not at one ballpark or another, she spends her time either writing or attempting to invent an automatic toilet-seat—dropping device.

Leave It to Cleavage is her second romantic comedy for Bantam. Readers can contact her at 1401 Johnson Ferry Road, Suite 328/(-70, Marietta, GA 30062 or through her website at www.authorwendywax.com.

The Bestse
TOM

RAINBOW SIX

John Clark is used to doing the CIA's dirty work. Now he's taking on the world. . . .

"ACTION-PACKED."

—The New York Times Book Review

EXECUTIVE ORDERS

The most devastating terrorist act in history leaves Jack Ryan as President of the United States. . . .

"UNDOUBTEDLY CLANCY'S BEST YET."

—The Atlanta Journal-Constitution

DEBT OF HONOR

It begins with the murder of an American woman in the back streets of Tokyo. It ends in war. . . .

"A SHOCKER CLIMAX SO PLAUSIBLE YOU'LL WONDER WHY IT HASN'T YET HAPPENED!"

—Entertainment Weekly

THE HUNT FOR RED OCTOBER

The smash bestseller that launched Clancy's career—the incredible search for a Soviet defector and the nuclear submarine he commands . . .

"BREATHLESSLY EXCITING."

—The Washington Post

continued . . .

RED STORM RISING

The ultimate scenario for World War III—the final battle for global control . . .

"THE ULTIMATE WAR GAME . . . BRILLIANT."

—*Newsweek*

PATRIOT GAMES

CIA analyst Jack Ryan stops an assassination—and incurs the wrath of Irish terrorists. . . .

"A HIGH PITCH OF EXCITEMENT."

—*The Wall Street Journal*

THE CARDINAL OF THE KREMLIN

The superpowers race for the ultimate Star Wars missile defense system. . . .

"*CARDINAL* EXCITES, ILLUMINATES . . . A REAL PAGE-TURNER."

—*Los Angeles Daily News*

CLEAR AND PRESENT DANGER

The killing of three U.S. officials in Colombia ignites the American government's explosive, and top secret, response. . . .

"A CRACKLING GOOD YARN."

—The Washington Post

THE SUM OF ALL FEARS

The disappearance of an Israeli nuclear weapon threatens the balance of power in the Middle East—and around the world. . . .

"CLANCY AT HIS BEST . . . NOT TO BE MISSED."

—The Dallas Morning News

WITHOUT REMORSE

The Clancy epic fans have been waiting for. His code name is Mr. Clark. And his work for the CIA is brilliant, cold-blooded, and efficient . . . but who is he really?

"HIGHLY ENTERTAINING."

—The Wall Street Journal

continued . . .

And don't miss Tom Clancy's fascinating nonfiction works . . .

SPECIAL FORCES
A Guided Tour of U.S. Army Special Forces

"CLANCY IS A NATURAL."   —*USA Today*

CARRIER
A Guided Tour of an Aircraft Carrier

"CLANCY IS A MASTER OF HARDWARE."

—*The Washington Post*

AIRBORNE
A Guided Tour of an Airborne Task Force

"NOBODY DOES IT BETTER."

—*The Dallas Morning News*

SUBMARINE
A Guided Tour Inside a Nuclear Warship

"TAKES READERS DEEPER THAN THEY'VE EVER GONE INSIDE A NUCLEAR SUBMARINE."

—*Kirkus Reviews*

Tom Clancy's
NET
FORCE®

POINT OF IMPACT

Created by
Tom Clancy and Steve Pieczenik
written by Steve Perry

BERKLEY BOOKS, NEW YORK

TOM CLANCY'S NET FORCE®: POINT OF IMPACT

A Berkley Book / published by arrangement with
Netco Partners

PRINTING HISTORY
Berkley edition / April 2001

All rights reserved.
Copyright © 2001 by Netco Partners
NET FORCE® is a registered trademark of Netco Partners.

This book, or parts thereof, may not be
reproduced in any form without permission.
For information address: The Berkley Publishing Group,
a division of Penguin Putnam Inc.,
375 Hudson Street, New York, New York 10014.

The Penguin Putnam Inc. World Wide Web site address is
http://www.penguinputnam.com

ISBN: 0-425-17923-0

BERKLEY®
Berkley Books are published by The Berkley Publishing Group,
a division of Penguin Putnam Inc.,
375 Hudson Street, New York, New York 10014.
BERKLEY and the "B" design
are trademarks belonging to Penguin Putnam Inc.

PRINTED IN THE UNITED STATES OF AMERICA

10 9 8 7 6 5 4 3 2 1

ACKNOWLEDGMENTS

We would like to acknowledge the assistance of Martin H. Greenberg, Larry Segriff, Denise Little, John Helfers, Robert Youdelman, Esq., and Tom Mallon, Esq.; Mitchell Rubenstein and Laurie Silvers of Hollywood.com, Inc.; and the wonderful people at Penguin Putnam Inc., including Phyllis Grann, David Shanks, and Tom Colgan. As always, I would like to thank Robert Gottlieb, without whom this book would never have been conceived. But most important, it is for you, our readers, to determine how successful our collective endeavor has been.

PROLOGUE

Saturday, October 1, 2011
Atlantic City, New Jersey

"We should go outside and enjoy the sunny weather," Mary Lou said.

Bert snickered. "Right. We'z drove alla way from da Bronx to Atlantic City to take the goddamned sun? I can sit onna stoop at home, I want to get hot. No thankyuz, I'm happy right here."

Bert fed another dollar into the slot machine and pushed the button. He didn't like the new electronic machines as much as the old mechanical ones, like those in the back rooms of the New Jersey bars where his father used to sneak off with him when he was a kid. Those had been fun, with the big arm you pulled down and the real wheels going round and round. Cost a quarter, was all. He didn't quite trust the new ones to pay off—it'd be too easy for some computer geek to rig 'em so they'd keep every damned dime you put in—but it was what it was. Hell, he was up seventy-five bucks, he should complain?

Around him, the machines flashed colored lights,

hummed and whirred and played crappy music, and now and then dropped tokens into a metal tray.

Mary Lou said, "There's something you don't see every day."

The slot's computer screen whirled to stop on a cherry, a bar, and a picture of some dead rock star. Crap. Only seventy-four dollars ahead now.

Irritated, Bert said, "What?"

"Over there. Lookit."

He glanced in the direction Mary Lou was pointing. He saw right away what she meant. There was a fat, white-haired old guy, maybe sixty-five, walking into the casino. Way he moved, he was like a man with a mission, nothing real unusual there, except the dude was in a tiny red Speedo and nothing else.

"God, I'm trying to win money here, you wanna make me puke? There ought to be a law against a suit like that if you're thirty pounds overweight."

"Prolly there is. I'm pretty sure the casino rules say no swimsuits without a robe and some kind of sandals or shoes. There you go, see, the security guard is gonna toss him out."

A big uniformed guard, six five, two sixty, easy, angled toward the fat guy in the red Speedo. This might be worth watching. You didn't get to see a guy in a bikini bottom get bounced up by a casino guard real often. In fact, Bert had never seen it before.

Speedo smiled at the giant guard, grabbed him by the arms just under his shoulders, picked him up, and threw him like the guy was a toy. The guard smashed into a slot machine with a loud, rattling crash.

"Holy shit!" Bert said.

He wasn't the only one to notice Speedo at this point. Two more guards came running, pulling out those expandable steel batons they carried as they ran.

Speedo didn't seem concerned. He took a couple of steps to the nearest slot. It was bolted to the floor, so Bert didn't know what the guy thought he was gonna do with it.

Still smiling, Speed wrenched the slot from the floor with a sound like a nail being pulled from wet wood, and threw that, too. Made a helluva noise.

Bert stared, frozen. This wasn't possible. He hit the gym two or three times a week, kept in shape for a man pushing forty, could bench two fifty for reps, and there was no way this flabby old Q-Tip–haired dude had the muscle to do what he'd just done, no way! Nobody was that strong.

The second security guard to get there let fly with his expandable night stick, took a good crack at Speedo's white head. Speedo reached up, almost in slow motion, grabbed the baton as it came down, jerked it from the guard's grip, and threw it. The thing whistled as it whirled away, so fast Bert couldn't even track it. Speedo shoved the guard one-handed, and the guy just *flew* into two by-standers and knocked all three of them down.

Mary Lou stared at Speedo, frozen like a deer in head-lights. Bert understood that. It was like he was hypnotized himself. He couldn't look away.

The third guard, seeing what had happened to the other two, dropped his baton and went for his pistol. Bert thought this was a real good idea.

Speedo took a couple of quick steps—really quick steps—and caught the guard's wrist before he cleared leather.

Thirty feet away, Bert heard the sound of the man's arm bones breaking.

Oh, *man!*

The guard fell to his knees, screaming in pain, and

Speedo stepped around him like he was doggy doo on the sidewalk.

Then things really got going. Speedo waded through the casino like Sherman through Georgia, breaking stuff, throwing it, tearing the place up. He knocked over slots, he upended card tables, he flipped a roulette wheel table completely over. People scrambled to get out of his way.

He was a human wrecking ball, he was *smiling* while he did it, and Bert couldn't begin to understand how he was doing it. He just stood there and watched.

It seemed like a long time, but it couldn't have been more than a minute or two before the local cops showed up. Six of them in full battle array.

The first couple of cops to reach Speedo tried to whack him with their batons and collar him. You'd think, after seeing what the guy had done, they'd have better sense, but they didn't, and Speedo grabbed one and used him like a club on the second.

The other four cops were smarter. One of them fast-drew his pepper spray, another pulled an air taser, and both let loose.

Speedo ran at the cops. Through the pepper fog, and from where he stood, Bert saw the two electric taser needles in the old man's chest, and if either the fog or the juice bothered him, you couldn't tell. Either one should have stopped him, had him gagging or jittering like a spider on a hot stove, but he never slowed. Speedo slammed into the next two cops, knocking them sprawling. He went down himself, but he was up in a heartbeat. He looked pissed off now, and he scooped one of the cops from the floor—a big black dude who probably went two hundred pounds—and shot-putted the cop at a thick plate glass partition that separated a cafeteria hall from the casino floor.

The partition had to be six, eight feet away, easy.

The partition shattered, shards of glass flew everywhere, and the cop who went through it would be lucky if he wasn't slashed to hamburger.

"Everybody down!" one of the two remaining cops on his feet screamed. "Down, down, down!"

People hit the floor, but Speedo wasn't one of them, and Bert stayed up watching, too.

The two cops had their pistols out by now—big ole Glocks—pointed at the old man.

Speedo looked at them and smiled, a kind of sad smile. Like he felt sorry for them. He started walking toward the cops.

"*Stop,* asshole!"

He didn't.

Both cops fired, couple, three times each.

Speedo kept coming, and they kept shooting.

Bert *saw* the hits on the old man, saw dark puckers appear in his arms and chest, wounds that oozed blood, but he kept going.

People screamed bloody murder, but the cops kept blasting away. In some corner of his mind, Bert tried to keep count of the shots, but there were too many of them. How many rounds did those guns hold? Fifteen? Eighteen? They were going to town.

It was like some monster movie. The old guy in the red bathing suit just kept shambling toward the cops. He was hit at least six or eight times, but he wouldn't stop.

"Fuck!" one of the cops yelled. He turned and ran.

The other cop clicked empty, then, when Speedo was almost on top of him, he threw the Glock at the old man.

Yeah, right. Guy takes a whole shitload of bullets and a plastic pistol is not gonna bounce off him like a cotton ball? Bert stared at the cop. Whaddayuz, stupid?

The old man grabbed the cop, managed to get him five or six inches off the floor—

—then the old man finally ran out of gas. He dropped the cop and fell, landing on the floor facedown.

It got real quiet in the casino then.

"Ho-ly *shit,*" Bert said softly.

"Amen, sweet Jesus," Mary Lou said. "Amen."

1

Alex Michaels grunted as the socket slipped off the hex nut and his hand shot forward, scraping his knuckles on the rocker-arm cover.

"Ow! Crap!"

At such times, he was wont to blame the nut or the wrench, but since he had put the bolt in himself, and the wrench and socket were both fairly new Craftsman tools, he knew he had nobody else to blame.

From the kitchen, he heard Toni call out. "You okay?"

Must have yelled louder than he'd thought. "Yeah, yeah, I'm fine. Stupid piece of crap Chevrolet!"

Toni drifted into the garage doorway. He was leaning over the fender on the passenger side, under the hood, so he saw her. Five months pregnant, in one of his T-shirts and a pair of drawstring sweatpants, she was, if anything, more beautiful than ever.

She smiled. "That's not what you said when you were convincing me you needed to have it. 'A fifty-five Bel Air convertible,' you said. 'A classic.' "

"Yeah, well, that was before I had a chance to spend time with it. Thing is engineered like a tank."

"Also a selling point, if I recall."

He looked at the nut. It was tight enough, he decided. He put the wrench down, grabbed a red rag and some of the pungent lanolin hand cleaner and started wiping grease off his fingers. Well, it *was* a classic car. Created by the chief engineer of General Motors in the post World War II years, Edward Coles, with legendary designer Harvey Earl, the '55 introduced the small block V-8 engine, the 265, later the 283, and then the 327. These engines became the standard against which all others were measured for more than forty years. A convertible in top condition would cost $60,000 to $75,000, easy. Even one in so-so shape like this one wasn't cheap.

He smiled back at her. "I thought it was your job to keep me from running off half cocked."

"I don't recall that part of the marriage vow."

He walked toward her. "How did your *djuru* practice go?"

Her smiled disappeared, and frown lines wrinkled her forehead. "Terrible. I'm all off-balance! I try to do the turnaround, I almost fall down. When I sweep, it's all I can do to keep from falling over. When I dropped into the squat for *djuru* five, I *farted!*"

He couldn't help it; he laughed.

Her face clouded up, tears welling. "It's not funny, Alex! I feel like a big fat *cow!*"

Michaels hurried to her. He hugged her to him. "Hey, it's all right."

"No, it's not! Nobody told me this was going to happen! If I can't practice my *silat,* I'll go crazy!"

This was not the time for him to point out that her doctor had told her to avoid exercise because of some bleeding early in the pregnancy. Everything seemed to be all right, but just to be sure, Toni was supposed to take it easy. That theoretically included Toni not doing the short dances of the Indonesian martial art in which she was an expert. No, definitely not the time to bring that up. A wrong word, and she'd start crying, which was so unlike her that it still amazed him every time. It was just hormones, the doctor had said, a normal part of pregnancy, but Michaels still hadn't gotten used to it. Toni could kick the crap out of most men, even some who were fairly good martial artists themselves—he had seen her do it a few times—and for her to well up and cry at the drop of a hat was, well . . . it was spooky.

"Maybe you should just, you know, take a break from *djurus*. It's only another four months until the baby is born."

"Take a *break?* I've done *djurus* almost every day since I was thirteen. Even when I had pneumonia, I only missed three days. I can't just *give them up* for four months!"

"Okay, okay, it was just a suggestion."

Maybe it was better if he just kept his mouth shut. It had been a long time since he'd been around a pregnant woman. When his first wife Megan had been carrying their daughter, Susie, he had still been working in the field and was gone quite a bit, sometimes for a couple weeks at a time. He'd missed a lot of the experience, and at the time he'd been sorry he had. Now he was the commander of the FBI's elite subunit Net Force, and maybe he might be spending a little more time at the office until things settled down at home.

He immediately felt guilty at that thought.

"I know it's not your fault," Toni said. "Well, okay, it *is* your fault, technically speaking." She grinned. "But I don't blame you."

He smiled back at her. Her mood swing was instant, zap, just like that, from angry to happy.

"Go on back and finish installing your carburetor," she said. "You putting in the four-barrel?"

"I decided to go with three deuces," he said. "You know, pep it up a little."

She shook her head. "You've been watching that old movie *American Graffiti* again, haven't you? Boys and their toys. You won't be able to afford to run it, you know. It'll get what? Ten miles a gallon? You'll have to take out a loan to fill the tank."

"Well, I really am going to sell it. Eventually."

"Uh-huh. Go on, go scrape some more skin off your hands and curse the guys who made that big chunk of Detroit iron. I'm going to sit down and see if I can't get your son to stop kicking my bladder."

"You sure are pretty when you're pregnant," he said.

"Forget it. One baby: That's my limit."

Toni went to her computer and slid the VR band down over her eyes, adjusting the earplugs and olfactory bulbs so they were comfortable. The set was wireless and had a pretty good range, so if her ankles started to swell, at least she could go lie down and prop her feet up on a cushion while she was on-line. She put on the tactile gloves and was ready.

She allowed the system's default scenario to play, and there was a small moment of disorientation as the virtual reality program took over and constructed a shopping mall in place of the small office that had been the guest bedroom. She found herself in front of a virtual elevator, the door of which opened. She stepped inside, along with other shoppers.

"Arts and Crafts, please," she said.

Somebody tapped a button.

The sensation was of rising rather than falling. After a moment, a chime sounded and the door opened. Toni alighted from the elevator and looked at the sign a few feet away. YOU ARE HERE pulsed in a pale green light. *No, I'm at home in my office with my shoes getting tighter.*

But the suspension of disbelief that was VR was easy enough to accept. She found the place she was looking for listed: Hergert's Scrimshaw. It was not far away— though it could have been if she wanted a long walk in VR—and she headed toward it.

When she and Alex had been on their honeymoon in Hawaii, they'd gone to an art gallery in Lahaini, on the island of Maui. There had been some world-class work in the gallery, in all kinds of media and materials—everything from pencil drawings to oil paintings to sculptures in wood or bronze or even glass. Seascapes and dolphins and whales were big, but what had impressed her the most was a small display of microscrimshaw. There were pictures engraved on small bits of fossilized ivory, old piano keys and billiard balls, even a couple of sperm whale teeth. Some of the images were smaller than her thumbnail but, when viewed under magnification, showed a wealth of detail she would not have thought possible. There were sailing ships and whales, portraits, nudes, tigers, and several with fantasy elements. She had been particularly impressed by a tiny black-and-white rendering of a long-haired, naked woman sitting in a lotus position and gazing up at the heavens, but floating two feet above the ground. The image had been done on a pale ivory disk the size of a quarter.

"How do they do that?" she'd asked Alex.

He'd shaken his head. "I dunno. Let's ask."

The gallery manager was happy to explain: "There are different ways," she said, "but in this case, what the artist did was to polish the ivory smooth, then use a very fine-pointed instrument, probably something like a sewing needle, to put thousands of tiny dots into the material, it's a process called stippling. Then he rubbed the color onto it. This is a Bob Hergert piece, and he prefers oil paint to ink. I believe he uses a shade called lampblack.

"Once the piece was covered with paint, he wiped it clean, and the oil paint filled up the stipple marks but came off the polished part. It has to be done under magnification, of course, and it is, as you might suspect, rather painstaking work."

"I can only imagine," Toni said. "It's beautiful."

"Yes, Bob is one of the better artists working in the medium. We handle some other scrimshanders who are also very good—Karst, Benade, Stahl, Bellet, Dietrich, even Apple Stephens—but Bob's work is not only beautiful, it's still reasonably priced. He does a lot of custom commissions on things like knife handles and gun grips."

"How much?" Alex asked.

"Eight hundred for this one."

"We'll take it," he said.

"No, Alex, we can't—"

"Yes, we can. It'll be your wedding present."

"But—"

"I made a good profit on my last car restoration. We can afford it."

As she packaged the scrimshaw and ran Alex's credit card, the manager said to Toni, "If you are ever interested in seeing how he does it, Bob teaches an on-line course."

At the time, Toni had nodded and murmured something polite, not thinking such artwork would ever be something she'd have time for.

As she walked through the virtual mall, she smiled to herself. Well, she had time now. Plenty of time. She was supposed to sit around and twiddle her thumbs for the next four months, and even if she wanted to practice her *silat,* she was, for all practical purposes, a beached whale. She'd just flop around on the sand if she tried to do anything physical, she could already see that, and she was only five months along. At seven or eight months, dropping into a *djuru* turn was just not going to be in the cards. But sitting at a table and scratching on a piece of faux ivory with a pin? She could do that, and the idea of creating something anywhere close to as beautiful as that tiny scrimshaw Alex had bought for her was appealing. Of course, she didn't really have much artistic talent, but maybe she could learn. It was worth a shot.

She arrived in front of a small shop. On the window it said, Bob Hergert, Microscrimshaw—www.scrimshander .com.

Toni took a deep breath, let it out, and walked into the shop.

Inside, the place was neat and well laid out. There were glass-topped cases with pieces of ivory on black velvet, everything from knife handles, gun grips, and billiard balls to larger framed pieces. Several magnifying glasses on little stands had been set up on the glass so that the smaller pieces under them were easier to see.

An electric guitar hung on the wall behind the longest counter. Toni didn't know from guitars, but there was an ivory plate on the body of the instrument, and she recognized the man's face lovingly engraved upon the plate.

A medium-sized man with a thick mustache came out of the back and smiled at Toni. "The King," he said. "When he was in his prime. About 1970 or so, the television concert where he wore the black leather suit."

Toni nodded. "I bought one of your pieces in Hawaii," she said. "A naked woman sitting in a lotus pose, floating in the air."

"Ah," he said. "Cynthia, the Goddess of the Moon. I enjoyed doing that one. How can I help you, Mrs. . . . ah . . . ?"

"Michaels," she said, still feeling somewhat strange about using Alex's name that way. "Toni."

"Toni. Nice to meet you."

"I understand you give lessons in how to do this." She waved, taking in the shop's interior.

"Yes, ma'am, I surely do."

"I'd like to sign up, if I could."

"No problem at all, Toni."

They smiled at each other.

2

"You look like hell, Julio."

"Thank you, General Howard, sir, for your astute observation."

"What happened?"

"I was up half Sunday night feeding the baby. Your godson."

"I thought Joanna was breast-feeding."

"Yeah, she is. But somebody told her about a little pump that lets you take mama's milk out of the original container and put it into little bottles. That way the father can be part of the suckling process."

"Don't look at me, I didn't tell her."

"No, it was Nadine, your lovely wife, who was the snake in the garden."

Howard laughed. "Well, you know how women are. Never let a man spend too much time getting by with something."

"Amen."

"So, what are we looking at this fine morning, Sergeant Fernandez?"

"Three new items of field gear unrelated to weaponry, sir."

Howard glanced around the inside of the small storage warehouse. There were crates, boxes, and items covered with tarps, the usual.

"Proceed."

"Over here, we have our new tactical computer units, supposedly shockproof backpackers that will plug into the SIPEsuits. Seven pounds, more FlashMem, DRAM, and ROM than a high school computer lab and faster than greased lightning. Ceramic armor and spidersilk webbing, all bullet-resistant and waterproof and like that. I turned one on and dropped it on the floor from chest height, and it still ran fine. Twelve-hour batteries the size of D cells, so you can carry a few days' backup without recharging, no problem."

"Good, about time they came up with something that didn't go down every time somebody sneezed. What else?"

"Right this way. This here is our emergency broadcast jammer, which will supposedly make any radio inside a ten-kilometer circle spew static and nothing else. Doesn't work on LOS infra or ultra headcoms. They say it'd stop KAAY in Little Rock at its peak, but I haven't tested it yet."

"Bad guys use LOS, too."

"What can I say? This is RA stuff. You know how they are."

Howard nodded. Regular Army did have its own whys and wherefores. He'd been there, done that, and was much happier being the head of Net Force's military arm, such as it was. He had expected it to be a lot more quiet than when he was a colonel in the RA, but in the last year or so, it sure had been anything but that. In fact, after his last fracas, he'd been thinking about retiring. He still ached from his wounds when it got chilly, and the idea of not being around to see his son grow up bothered him a lot.

Julio kept talking:

"And under this here cover, we have the toy of the week. Ta-da!" He pulled the lightweight tarp off, revealing what looked like a table with four jointed arms sticking up from it, two in the corners at one end, two more in the middle. The thing had wheels and a closed compartment under it.

"And what is this? A high-tech electric golf cart?"

"No, sir, this is Rocky Scram—that's R-O-C-C-S-R-M, the acronym standing for Remote-Operated, Computer-Controlled Surgical Robotic Module."

Howard frowned. "We talking about a doc-in-the-box?"

"Actually, a surgeon-in-the-box, only this is just the box. You're gonna love this one, it actually might be useful."

"Talk to me."

"Here's the deal. You need a surgical PA, couple nurses, and orderlies. They set this sucker up in a field hospital. Guy comes in, all shot up, needs fixin'. The PA—that's physician's assistant, for those of you who missed the medical personnel lecture—does a triage, examines the guy, and makes a quick diagnosis. They plunk him on the table, get him prepped, and dial up a first-class REMF surgeon, who can be up to a thousand miles away, give or take. He cranks up his unit—that part is over here, come look."

They walked to another covered unit, and Julio removed a tarp from it. There was a chair, a computer screen mounted in front of it on a platform, and some odd-looking appendages on the arms of the chair.

"Your surgeon sits here and slips his fingers into the surgical controls, that's these rings here. He uses his feet on pedals down on the floor, one each, with a freeze pedal in the middle, kind of like a brake."

Julio sat in the chair and slipped his fingers into the jointed ring arrangements. The computer screen lit up. "These control the waldos, those are tools you can connect to those arms on the operating table. Left foot runs the endoscope, which holds your light and your camera. Right foot works various clamps and suction things. The hand tools will hold scalpels, hemostats, suture needles, scissors, and a bunch of other things."

"You're telling me a surgeon can operate on a patient from a thousand miles away using this gadget?"

"Yes, sir, that's what the RA medicos say. The surgeons who qualify have to cut up a bunch of pigs and cadavers and RA soldiers before they let them work on real people. They've repaired bowels, done blood vessel grafts, stitched up torn hearts, all kinds of things. Nurses and the PA assist, just like in a regular OR. RA medicos say a guy good with this toy can pick up number-six BBs and never drop one."

Julio waggled his fingers, and there was mechanical hum from the nearby table as the surgical arms moved around.

"It's all self-contained, battery backup if you can't get a generator going. Wheel it out there, slap 'em on the table, and you cut and paste."

"Good Lord."

"Yessir, I expect He is impressed."

"Downside?"

"Heavy, expensive—million and half a copy—and you need a repair tech who's qualified to service 'em if they break down. Still, RA figures it's cheaper than training and replacing a surgeon who catches a stray round on the way to do his cutting."

"Good point."

"There's a civilian model been around for a while, but it's not so compact, and it ain't portable."

"Amazing."

"Ain't it, though? Now, if the general is through being impressed with modern hardware, I'd like to go catch a nap."

"Go ahead, Sergeant. Oh. Wait. Hold up a second. I got something for you." Howard grinned. He was going to like what he was about to do. He was going to like it a whole lot.

Julio paused, and Howard tossed the small plastic box at him. Julio caught it, started to open it. "Not my birthday. What's the occasion?"

Howard didn't say anything, just kept grinning.

When Julio got the box open, his eyes went wide. "Oh, shit. No!"

"Oh, shit, yes. And we're skipping right over shavetail and going to right to first.

"Congratulations, *Lieutenant* Fernandez."

"You can't do this, John. Gunny'll never let me live it down."

"Already done, Julio. Paperwork is signed, sealed, and delivered."

"John—"

"More money, which you need with a new baby. Plus now you don't have to take orders from your wife. Well, no more than any of the rest of us have to take orders from our wives." Julio's wife was Joanna Winthrop, and a lieutenant in Net Force herself, although she was on extended leave at the moment.

"But . . . but . . . who can you get to replace me?"

"Nobody will be able to replace you, Julio. But there

are some new recruits who can manage a top's chores if you show them how it is done."

Julio shook his head. "I'll be damned."

"No doubt, but at least you can tell the devil you earned your money for part of your career before you got the free ride."

Julio nodded slowly, then looked up. "All right. Thank you, sir."

"Don't look so sour, Julio. Welcome to the officer-and-a-gentleman club. Or at least the officer part of it."

"Yeah, right."

Under the bitching, Howard was pretty sure that Julio was pleased. They'd been working together for more than twenty years, first in the regular army, then in Net Force. Julio had known about Howard's promotion to general before Howard himself had, and there were times when the two of them were practically telepathic. Julio didn't have the educational background of a lot of officers, but when a situation went hot, he was the man you wanted covering your back. He had another few years before he was going to think about retiring, and the higher his grade, the bigger his pension. He was a married man with a baby; he needed it.

"Go take your nap, Lieutenant."

"Yes, sir."

Washington, D.C.

Normally, at seven in the morning, Jay Gridley would be at Net Force HQ, plugged into his computer and making war on the bad guys. He'd be hunting lubefoots who'd dumped the latest ugly virus into the world's e-mail, or searching for clues to some computer fraud, or trying to track down some sicko posting kiddie porn on church web sites. Now and then, there'd be a big shark cruising the virtual waters of the net, like the mad Russian or the crazy Georgia redneck or the British genius who'd been using a quantum computer to try and restore England's lost glory, though those were relatively rare. But a few months ago, Jay had finally met his on-line guru who had been helping him recover from a stroke, an old Tibetan monk named Sojan Rinpoche. And as it turned out, the old man was actually a young and beautiful woman. Saji, she liked to be called, and one thing had led to another, which had led to another, which had led to her lying beside him in the bed.

Now, there were days when he called in sick and never left that bed except to pee.

He giggled.

"What is funny?" Saji asked.

He smiled at her. "You. Me. This. Us."

"What time is it?"

"Who cares?"

"No, you don't, goat-boy. I'm teaching an on-line class this morning."

"You don't have to get up to do that. You can lie right there."

She laughed. "I don't think so. I remember the last time I tried to do that. Somebody kept distracting me."

"You're a master Buddhist, you're supposed to be able to meditate and tune out little distractions."

"Yeah, but the problem was, the little distraction kept getting bigger every time I looked at it."

They both laughed.

"Work is dead. I could stay home. It's totally boring there these days. Seriously."

"Seriously," she said, "no, you can't."

"You are a party pooper."

"Life is full of suffering, haven't you learned that yet?"

Jay rolled out of the bed, scratched his chest, and padded toward the bathroom. "You'll be sorry when I'm gone. You'll finish your class and be all alone in this big old condo, and you'll wish I was here."

"I'll try to be brave."

"You want to shower?"

"Yes. After you leave."

"You don't trust me. I'm hurt."

"I can see that. Go on. I'll cook supper when you get home."

"What, roots and twigs?"

"You said you liked my cooking."

"That was before you threw me out into the cold," he said.

"It's supposed to hit seventy-two today," she said. "Not so cold."

"I was speaking metaphorically."

"Go and shower, Jay."

He grinned at her. Boy, did he like having her around. Really. A lot. More than anything he could think of. He headed for the shower and considered for the hundredth time the proposition he'd been working on in his head for the last couple of weeks. Was it possible to make it permanent? Legally permanent? As in getting married? Would she go for it?

There was only one way to find out, but he was hesitant. What if she said no?

That would be . . . bad.

The hot water began to steam up the bathroom. He called out to Saji: "Hey—?"

"No," she cut him off. "Definitely not."

But he was rinsing the shampoo from his hair when the shower door slid open and Saji followed the draft of cool air in, gloriously naked and grinning.

"Why, Sojan Rinpoche! What are *you* doing here?"

"I came to wash your back is all."

"Uh-huh."

"Turn around."

"Yes, ma'am."

He turned around. She reached out, and her soapy hand began rubbing him.

However, the hand was definitely *not* stroking his *back*, nope, no sir, no *indeedy!*

He laughed, and she laughed with him.

Yep, he was going to be late to work, no two ways about it.

"Hey, I think you missed a spot there."

"I didn't miss it. I was ignoring it. Easy to do, it's so . . . small."

"Ooh. You are a cruel woman. Cruel."

"Suffer, big daddy, suffer. . . ."

3

Malibu, California

Robert Drayne looked up from his mixing bench in front of the big picture window as a pair of young women in thong bikinis jogged past on the hard-packed wet sand, just at the water line. No rain today, the sky was clear, the Pacific Ocean a nice blue and fairly calm, and the two honeys were blond and tan and bouncy. Not bad for a Monday. He grinned. He loved this town.

He looked back at the bench. He had a batch ready to time and encapsulate, only six hits, and where the hell was Tad? You didn't want to start the clock ticking and then have the stuff sit on the table for an hour or two. That might cut things a little close. Even with a master such as himself, the timing could get a little tricky, could be an hour either way.

As if in response, the door alarm *ching-chinged* as somebody disarmed it and entered the house.

That had better be Tad. . . .

Drayne dumped a bit of catalyst into the white compound, stirred in the fine red powder so that the resulting mix started turning pale pink. Drayne worked by sight and smell, he kept adding catalyst until the right shade was achieved—a shade somewhere between titty and bubble gum—and that sharp, cherry-and-almond odor drifted up and told him it was about right, too.

Ah, there we go....

"About fucking time," Drayne said. There was no real anger in his voice, just making a comment was all.

"Traffic is bad on the Coast Highway," Tad said by way of explanation. "The tourists are all slowing down to look at the house coming down in the mud slide. How's it coming?"

"Catalyst mixed, as of thirty seconds ago."

Tad looked at his watch.

Drayne grabbed one of the big purple gel caps, a special run he'd had made three years ago by a guy in Mexico who was, unfortunately, no longer among the living. Well, what the hell, he had more than a thousand caps left. Worry about it when he ran out.

He opened the cap and scooped up the mix with both halves, expertly judging how much so that he could put the cap together again without overfilling it. He looked up and smiled. This was the easy part. The real work was in the creation and mixing of the various components. That had to be done in a lab, and the current one was an RV parked in a dinky burg on the edge of the Mojave Desert, a couple of hours away from here. By tomorrow, it would be parked a hundred miles away, the old retired couple driving it looking about as illegal and dangerous as a bowl of prunes. In this biz, appearance counted for a lot. Who'd pull over Ma and Pa Yeehaw in their RV with Missouri plates for anything but a traffic ticket? And Ma could talk her way out of that by making a cop think about his sweet little ole granny. And if the cop got really horsey, Pa would cap him with the .40 SIG he kept under the seat.

Tad Bershaw was Drayne's age, well, actually, he was a year younger at thirty-one, but he looked fifty, rode hard and put up wet, like Drayne's grandma used to say. Tad was black-haired, skinny, pale, and had dark circles under his eyes, a real heroin-chic kinda guy. He always wore black, even in the middle of summer, long sleeves, long pants, pointy-toed leather boots. And sunglasses, of course. He looked like a vampire or maybe one of the old beatniks, because he also had a little patch of hair under his lip.

Drayne, on the other hand, looked like a surfer, which he had been: tanned, sun-bleached dishwater blond hair, still enough muscle to pass for a gymnast or a swimmer. He had to admit, they made an odd-looking couple when they went out. Not that they went out that often.

Drayne put the finished cap down and picked up another empty. He had enough mix for six. Five for sale and one for Tad. At a thousand bucks each, it wasn't a bad day's work, not bad at all, given that their costs were about thirty-five dollars a cap.

"You heard about the guy in Atlantic City?" Tad asked.

Drayne worked on the third cap. "Olivetti?"

"Yeah."

"No. What happened?"

"Hammer ate him. He ran amok, tore up a casino, beat the shit out of some rent-a-cops and local police before they cooked him. DOA."

Drayne shrugged again. "Too bad. He was a good customer."

"We got a guy coming from NYC says Olivetti referred him. Are we interested?"

Drayne finished the fourth cap. Found one of the special-special empties for number five. "No. If Olivetti is dead, the reference is dead. We don't sell to him."

"I figured," Tad said. "Just checking."

"You shouldn't have to check. You know the deal. A vetted customer vets a newbie, always. First time we get a guy we can't check out, that will be a narc, you got to figure it that way."

"I hear you."

Drayne finished the fifth cap, reached for Tad's empty. "How are you working today's produce?"

"Three off the net, FedEx Same Day as soon as we get the payment transfers to the dissolving account. One is a pickup, three-messenger drop. One is hand-to-hand."

"Who's the hand-to-hand?"

"The Zee-ster."

Drayne grinned. "Be sure to tell him we want tickets to his next premiere."

"Already in the pipe."

"Okay, here you go. Last one is yours, be sure the double-special, that's number five, goes out."

"You're crazy, you know that," Tad said, as he took the caps.

"Yeah, so what else is new?"

The two men smiled at each other.

"What's cold?" Drayne said. "I need to sit on the deck and watch the waves roll in."

"Got a bottle of the Blue Diamond, one of the Clicquot, and one of the Perrier-Jouët in the little fridge. Dunno what's in the garage."

"The Diamonte Bleu, I think," Drayne said. "You want a glass before you take off?"

"I'm not rotting my liver out, thank you."

They laughed again.

"I'm gone."

"See you later," Drayne said.

Tad left, and Drayne went to open a bottle of cham-

pagne. He had three-quarters of a million cash in a suitcase hidden in a floor safe under his bed, another two
hundred and some thousand dollars in a safe-deposit box
in a bank in Tarzana, and five cases of assorted but all
high-quality champagne in the cool room downstairs.

Life was pretty damned good.

Tad swung his souped-up, reconditioned Charger R/T
Drayne had given him out into the road the locals called
the PCH and stomped the gas pedal, heading south toward
Santa Monica. The big motor roared and laid five hundred
miles worth of expensive rubber compound behind it, tires
squealing and smoking. Tad grinned as the car acceler-
ated. No big deal. The radials were good for fifty thousand
miles, and he didn't expect either the car or himself to be
around when the tires' warranty ran out.

He never expected to live past thirty, maybe thirty-five,
max. Depending on how you looked at it, he was either
four years shy or a year overdue for the big sleep, and it
didn't much matter to him which it was. He'd been on
borrowed time for years.

He roared past a white four-runner with out-of-state
plates, a middle-aged couple in the front, and a pair of
big old German shepherd dogs looking out the windows
in the back. Goddamned tourists. He cut sharply in front
of the car, but the tourists were too busy looking at the
ocean to even notice. Dogs were probably smarter than
the people in that car.

That Bobby, now there was a smart one. He was a
certified fucking genius, no shit. IQ way up in Mensa
territory, one sixty, one seventy, something like that,
though you'd never guess he was anything more than a
big ole dumb surfer dude by looking at him. He could
have gone into any kind of legit work and made a mint,
but he had these quirks: One, he hated his old man, who

was a retired FBI agent, and two, the guy he most wanted to be like was some flower-power drug guru from the sixties, a guy named Owsley, who came out of the psychedelic movement. Owsley was so long ago that when he started making LSD, it was still legal. Problem was that he kept making the stuff after it got to be illegal, and got busted, but Bobby thought the sun rose and set in the guy's shadow.

Bobby wanted to be the Owsley of the twenty-teens. An outlaw to the core.

Tad patted his pocket for the fourth time, making sure the five caps were still in there. The other cap—*his* cap— was tucked away in his private stash bottle in the special pocket in his right boot, right next to the short Damascus dagger he carried there.

He lit up a cigarette, inhaled deeply, and coughed. His lungs were bad, never had gotten much stronger after the TB was cured and he got out of the sanitarium in New Mexico, and smoking only made 'em worse, but the hell with it, he wasn't gonna live long enough for cancer to get him anyhow.

The air conditioner blasted the smoke away as he reached for the music player to crank up some volume. Something with a lot of bone-vibrating bass, but none of that techno-rap junk the kids were listening to today.

He glanced at his watch. Still had half an hour before he had to make the first delivery.

He rolled the window down, took a final drag off the cigarette, and thumbed the butt out the window. He couldn't do the Hammer today, too much work, so it would have to be tonight or tomorrow. He knew when he needed to drop to get off. He didn't want to miss that window. Sure, Bobby would make him another, but it would be such a waste there was no way Tad was gonna let it happen.

Tonight, definitely. He could become Thor, and he would swing the Hammer high, wide, and anywhere he damned well pleased.

Oh, yeah—

Some asshole in a low-slung Italian something or the other whipped around Tad, caught rubber as he upshifted, and blew past. Guy looked like a movie star, might even be one: tan, fit in a tank top, designer shades, and a big expensive smile when he flashed his caps to show Tad there were no hard feelings.

The way he felt right now, Tad wouldn't bother chasing the guy. Even if he caught him, the guy would certainly be able to stomp his butt for his trouble.

Come back and see me tonight, pal. See how your SoCal pretty-boy tough-guy act plays when I'm swinging Mjollnir high, wide, and repeatedly. Be a different story then, old son, a whole different story.

4

Michaels was on the way to his office when his virgil blared out the opening chords for "Mustang Sally." He smiled at the little electronic device. Jay Gridley had been at it again, reprogramming the attention call. It was one of Jay's small delights, to do that every so often, usually coming up with some new musical sting Michaels never expected.

He shook his head as he unclipped the virgil—for virtual global interface link—from his belt and saw that the incoming call was from his boss, Melissa Allison, director of the FBI. Her image appeared on the tiny screen as he said, "Answer call," and activated the virgil's voxax control.

"Good morning, Alex."

"Director."

"If you would please stop by my office on your way in, I would appreciate it. Something has come up that I think Net Force needs to address."

"Yes, ma'am, I'm on my way. I'll be there in fifteen minutes."

She looked at something off-screen, then said, "I see you're on the freeway. You might want to take an alternate route. There's an accident a couple of miles ahead of you. Traffic will start backing up pretty fast."

"Thank you," he said. "Discom."

It used to bother him that they could GPS him that way, using the virgil's carrier sig to tell exactly where he was. Then he reasoned if he wanted to keep his whereabouts secret, all he had to do was kill the unit's power. That is, if there wasn't some hidden internal battery that kept the carrier going, even if the thing looked like it was turned off.

He smiled at his thought. Paranoid? Maybe. But stranger things had happened in the U.S. intelligence service, and he wouldn't put anything past certain factions, nothing.

The man was big, he was stark naked, and he had an erection. He walked through the hotel hallway, got to a window at the end, and stopped. The window was closed, one of those that couldn't be opened, and from the skyline visible in the distance, it was fairly high up.

The man put his hands on the window and shoved.

The window exploded outward. The man backed up a few steps, took a short run, and dived through the shattered window, looking like he was diving off the Acapulco cliffs or maybe pretending to be Superman.

Melissa Allison said, "Agent Lee?"

The man who'd been introduced to Michaels as Brett Lee, of the Drug Enforcement Administration, shut off the InFocus projector and his laptop computer, and the image of the broken window faded.

"This was taken by security cameras in the new Sheraton Hotel in Madrid," he said. "The man was Richard

Aubrey Barnette, age thirty, whose Internet company License-to-Steal.com earned him fourteen million dollars last month. He fell twenty-eight stories onto a cab, killing the driver and causing a traffic accident that killed three others and injured five."

Michaels said, "I see. And this is related to the casino owner who trashed his competitor's place of business before being killed by local police?"

"Yes."

"And to the woman who attacked a gang of construction workers who whistled at her and put seven of them into intensive care?"

"Yes," Lee said. "And to others of a similar nature."

Michaels looked at his boss, then at Lee. "And I take it that, since you are DEA, you think drugs were somehow involved?"

Lee frowned, not sure if Michaels was pulling his chain or not. Which, Michaels had to admit to himself, he was, a little. Lee seemed awfully stiff.

Lee said, "Yes, we are certain of that."

Michaels nodded. "Please don't take offense, Mr. Lee, but this concerns Net Force how?"

Lee looked at Allison for support and got it. She said, "My counterpart at DEA has asked for our assistance. Naturally, the FBI and any of its subsidiaries are happy to help in any way we can."

"Naturally," Michaels said, knowing full well that interagency cooperation was more often like competing football teams than the least bit collective. Rivalries among the dozen or so agencies that comprised the intelligence community in the U.S.—everybody from CIA to FBI to NSA to DIA to NRO—were old, established, and more often than not, nobody gave up anything without some quid pro quo. Yes, they were all technically on the same team, but practically speaking, an agency was happy to shine its own star any way it could, and if that included using another agency's shirt to do it, well, that's how the game was played. Michaels had discovered this early in his career, long before he left the field to take over Net Force. And DEA wasn't a major player anyhow, given its somewhat limited mission.

Michaels said, "So how is it that Net Force can do something here DEA can't?"

Lee, a short man with a fierce look, flushed. Michaels could almost see him bite his tongue to keep from saying what he really wanted to say, which was undoubtedly rude. Instead, Lee said, "How much do you know about the drug laws, Commander Michaels?"

"Not much," he admitted.

"All right, let me give you a quick and rough overview. Federal drug regulation in the United States comes under the authority of the Controlled Substances Act—that's CSA—Title II, of the Comprehensive Drug Abuse Prevention and Control Act of 1970, with various amendments since. Legal—and illegal—drugs are put on one of five schedules, depending on what uses have been established for them and on how much potential for abuse they have. Schedule I is reserved for dangerous drugs without medical applications that have a high potential for abuse, Schedule V is for stuff with low abuse potential."

"We're talking about the difference between, say, heroin and aspirin?" Michaels said.

"Precisely. The CSA gets pretty specific about these things."

"Go ahead, I'm still with you."

"In the last few years, there has been a resurgence in so-called designer drugs, that is to say, those that don't slot neatly into the traditional categories. Variations and combinations of things like MDA and Ecstasy and certain new anabolic steroids, like that. The government realized that certain individuals were trying to circumvent the intent of the law by adding a molecule here or subtracting one there to make a drug that wasn't technically illegal, so there is a provision for analog drugs not addressed by the code.

"So, basically, any salt, compound, derivative, optical or geometric isomers, salts of isomers, whatever, based on a drug that is regulated become automatically de facto regulated the moment it is created."

Michaels nodded again, wondering where this was going.

"And in case we have a really clever chemist who comes up with something entirely new and different— which is pretty much unlikely, if not impossible, given the known things that humans abuse—the attorney general can put that on Schedule I on an emergency basis. This is done if the AG determines that there is an imminent hazard to the public safety, there is evidence of abuse, and there is clandestine importation, manufacture, or distribution of said chemical substance.

"Basically, the AG posts a notice in the Federal Register, and it becomes valid after thirty days for up to a year."

Michaels nodded again. He thought Lee was a stuffed shirt, and he decided to give another little tug on his chain. "Very interesting, if you are a DEA agent. Are we getting to a point anytime soon?"

Lee flushed again, and Michaels was fairly certain that if the director hadn't been sitting there, the DEA man would have lost his temper and said or maybe even done something rash. But give him credit, he got a handle on it.

"What it means is, we have some pretty specific tools we can use to get dangerous, illegal drugs off the street. But in this case, we can't use them."

Ah, now that was interesting. "Why not?"

"Because we haven't been able to obtain enough of the drug to analyze it properly. We know what it does: It makes you fast, strong, mean, and sexually potent. It might make you smarter, too, but that's hard to say from our samples, since if they were that smart, they ought not to be dead. We know what it looks like; it comes in a big purple capsule. But we can't make it illegal if we don't know what it is *in* the cap."

Michaels grinned slightly. He could hear that conversation: *"Yes, sir, this is the vile stuff, all right. Could you put it on the list so we can bust the guys who made it? What's in it? Uh, well, we don't exactly know. Can't you, uh, you know, just make big purple capsules illegal temporarily?"*

Be interesting to hear the AG's response to that one.

"And where does Net Force come in?"

"We have evidence that the makers of the drug—they call it Thor's Hammer, by the way—are using the Internet to arrange delivery."

"If the drug isn't illegal, then using the net to distribute it isn't illegal, either," Michaels said.

"We know. But if we can find them, we can damn well ask the miscreants making it to give us a sample. So to speak."

Miscreants? Michaels didn't think he'd ever actually heard that word used in a conversation before. He said, "Ah, pardon me for asking a stupid question, but wouldn't it be easier just to buy some on the street and analyze it?"

"Believe it or not, Commander, that thought did occur to us, it being our job and all. It isn't a common street drug. The cost of it is extremely high, and the sellers are very selective about who they sell it to. So far, none of our agents have been able to make a connection.

"We did manage to seize one capsule after the death of one of the people that we know took the drug. Unfortunately, the chemist in this case is very clever; there is some kind of enzymatic catalyst in the compound. By the time we got the stuff to our lab and analyzed, the active ingredients had all been somehow rendered . . . inert. There is some kind of timing mechanism in the drug. If you don't use it fairly quickly, it turns into a bland, inert powder that doesn't do anything but sit there."

"You can't tell what the drugs were?"

"Our chemists can infer what they were, sure. There are residues, certain telltale compounds, but we can't document for certain what the exact precursor drugs and percentages of each were, because they are essentially gone."

"Huh. That must be frustrating."

"Sir, you do not know the half of it. The common thread running through all the sudden insanities is money. Every one of the twelve people we feel certain died as a result of having ingested this drug is—or was—rich. Nobody on the list made less than a quarter million a year, and some of them made fifteen or twenty times that much."

"Ah." Michaels understood that. You might lean on a criminal street pusher, threaten him, rough him up a little, to get what you wanted from him, but millionaires tended to come equipped with herds of lawyers, and a man with big bucks in the bank didn't get hassled by street cops who wanted to keep their jobs. Not unless the cops had enough to go into court and get a conviction, and even then, they tended to walk with more care. Rich people had recreations denied to the common folk.

"Precisely. So until we can get a sample before the enzyme is added, or get to one fast enough to beat the decomposition, we're stuck. We need your help."

Michaels nodded. Maybe the guy wasn't that bad. In his place, he could understand how he might feel. And things around Net Force were as slow as he had ever seen them. "All right, Mr. Lee. We'll see if we can't run your dope dealers to ground."

Lee nodded. "Thank you."

5

Toni smiled at the UPS man as he left—he was late today—then took the latest packages into the garage. Alex
had told her she could have half the workbench, though
she only needed maybe a quarter of it, and she had already
started putting her stuff there. So far, she had the magnifying lamp set up, the alcohol burner and wax cauldron,
a couple tubes of lampblack oil paint, and some rags and
cleaning supplies. There wasn't really much else left she
needed. The new packages should have the pin vises,
some assorted sewing needles, lens paper, lanolin hand
cleaner, and a couple of X-Acto knives and some blades.
Plus the jeweler's special wax and some polishing compound. She already had some fake-ivory slabs, some old
piano keys, and some little rectangles of micarta, which
looked like real ivory but was much harder. She didn't
need the heavy-duty saws and buffing wheels, Alex had
a Dremel tool that would work for polishing small stuff.
And while the stereomicroscope like the one her teacher
used was really neat, she couldn't justify spending eight

or nine hundred dollars on it—not unless she got to the point where she was selling pieces, which would probably not ever happen—especially given she wasn't sure she even wanted to try that.

Toni had never thought of herself as having much artistic talent. She'd done okay in art courses in school, could draw a little, but according to Bob Hergert's online VR class, while being a world-class artist wouldn't hurt, it wasn't absolutely necessary. Given the wonders of the modern computer age, there was a lot technique could do to make up for talent. And given what she'd learned so far, you'd be able to fool a lot of people into thinking you knew what you were doing when you didn't.

She opened the packages, removed the tools and supplies, and set them out. Being pregnant wasn't at all like she'd thought it was going to be. Sure, she'd heard about morning sickness and mood swings, but the reality of those things was something else. And it wasn't as if she were really a whale, not at five months, but she'd always been in shape, her belly flat and tight, her muscles firm, and having to lie around and watch herself balloon up was, well, it was scary. Having something to do that needed concentration and skill, like scrimshaw, might be just the ticket to help her get past this. The morning sickness—which lasted almost all day and any time she was around any food more spicy than dry soda crackers—had finally stopped. Supposedly, the hormone swings got better after the sixth month.

Supposedly.

She had some ideas of what she might like to try first, and for that she needed to go back to her computer. There were lots of places to find pictures in the public domain, and if those weren't good enough, lots of places where you could license an image for personal use for a small fee. Later on, if she got better at it, she could try some freehand drawings of her own, but at first, she wanted to keep it simple.

Toni looked at her corner of the workbench. The rest of it was covered with Alex's tools and car parts, all laid out neatly. He was much more orderly than she was about such things. So far, her investment in scrimshaw supplies had run less than what it cost Alex for a good set of wrenches. If it turned out to be a total waste of her time, at least she wouldn't be out much money.

She sighed. Before she sat down at the computer and went shopping on-line, she needed to go pee again. And that, she understood, was not going to get better as her pregnancy progressed. She sure hoped having Alex's son was worth all this aggravation.

John Howard bent from the waist and tightened the laces on his cross-trainers, finishing with the double-loop runner's knot that theoretically kept the laces from coming untied. Finished, he straightened, bent backward and stretched his abdominals, then shook his arms back and forth to loosen them.

Normally, he ran at the base or around the Net Force compound, but today he felt like taking a tour of his own neighborhood. It was warm for early October, and muggy, so he wore running shorts and a tank top, though he did have a fanny pack holding his virgil, his ID, and a small handgun—a little Seecamp .380 double-action auto. The tiny pistol made the Walther PPK look like a giant, it only weighed maybe eleven or twelve ounces and was awfully convenient if you were wearing summer clothes or workout gear. True, the .380 wasn't exactly an elephant-stopper; the gun didn't have any sights, liked only one brand of ammo, and it tended to bang your trigger finger pretty good when it recoiled. No way it compared with his primary side arm, the Phillips & Rogers Medusa, but it did fulfill the first rule of a gunfight: Bring a gun. Point it at somebody in your face with a knife or a broken bottle and pull the trigger four or five times, and it certainly would offer them major incentive to back off. With the fanny pack strapped on tightly enough so it wouldn't bounce around much, it was doable. He used to carry a little can of pepper spray to discourage loose dogs, but realized that if he stopped running and said "Bad dog! Go lie down!" in a loud voice, the dog would stop, frown, and leave. At least they had so far.

A bit more limber, Howard started to jog up the street.

The leaves were falling—they'd all be down by Halloween, first good wind that came along any time now would finish 'em—and while the sun was warm, there was that subtle difference between spring and fall, that sense of impending winter.

He passed old man Carlson working in his yard, using the blower to herd leaves into piles. The old man, eighty if he was a day, smiled and waved. Carlson was a tanned, leathery old bird who was the ultimate Orioles fan. He'd retired after forty years with the Post Office, and there wasn't a street in the district he couldn't locate for you.

Howard reached the corner and turned right, planning to loop in and out of the cul-de-sacs that fed the main road through the neighborhood, staying on the sidewalk and ducking low, overhanging trees.

Tyrone had called today from his class trip to Canada. He was going to be gone for another ten days, two weeks in all, on a visit for his international relations class, something new at his school. Howard thought it was a good idea, getting to know other cultures. Better than learning it the Army's way. He smiled, remembering the old slogan his first top kick had posted over his desk when he'd first joined up: "Join the Army and See the World! Travel to exotic, unusual locales! Learn about other cultures!

Meet diverse and interesting people—and kill them."

He picked his pace up a little, stretching out, getting into a longer stride and rhythm. Just inside his breath, barely.

The scars were formed up pretty good where he'd had surgery after the shooting in Alaska. Pretty much nothing hurt most of the time—well, no more than usual after he worked out—but the memories hadn't faded at all. Being out in the middle of nowhere, exchanging gunfire with some real bad men, giving better than he'd gotten, but almost dying—those kinds of memories didn't go away in a few months. Every firefight—and he hadn't had that many—was as clear in his mind as the day or night it had happened. The thought that he might have bled to death in the woods and been eaten by scavengers wasn't so horrifying in itself. Hell, he was a professional soldier, getting killed went with the territory. But dying and leaving his son, just hitting his teens on his way to manhood, that bothered Howard more than it ever had. All it took was a real possibility he might actually buy the farm. Before, he'd been lucky. Never made it to a real war, and when he finally started seeing some action in Net Force, the bullets had zipped here and there, missing him. Julio had taken a round in the leg during the recovery of the stolen plutonium from the sons-of-whoever. Some of his troops had eaten frags from a mine or bullets from the mad Russian's hit man, Ruzhyó, the former *Spetsnaz* killer. Intellectually, he knew it was just chance and maybe a little skill that he'd never gotten hit; emotionally, he'd felt invulnerable, at least to a degree. Like God was watching over him because he was worthy. Yeah. Until that long shot in the darkness had plowed into him. A round from a handgun at rifle distance had killed that feeling of being bulletproof, oh, yes, indeed, it had.

Even Achilles had his heel, and waking up in a hospital

full of tubes did make a guy stop and consider the idea
he wasn't gonna live forever.

And while he wasn't afraid to go into battle—at least
he didn't think so—he didn't want to die and leave his
wife and son. They had become more precious to him
when he'd realized he might lose them. He believed in
the Kingdom of Heaven, and he tried to live his life in a
moral and upright manner, but going there wasn't at the
top of his to-do list for this year.

He opened up a little more on the run, starting to
breathe through his mouth more heavily now, as he
looped into the next street over from his and headed for
the circle at the end.

He remembered another joke his father had told him:

"So the preacher stands up in front of the congregation
and says, 'How many of you want to go to Heaven?'

"And all the hands in the church except Brother
Brown's go up.

"And the preacher looks at Brother Brown, who was
known to drink a little even of a Sunday morning, and he
says, 'Brother Brown! Don't you want to go to Heaven
when you die?'

"And Brother Brown says, 'When I die? Well, sure,
Reverend.'

"And the preacher says, 'Then, how come you didn't
raise your hand?'

"And Brother Brown says, 'Well, I thought you was
gettin' up a busload to go *now*.' "

He looped around the circle and headed back up toward
the main street. A toy poodle in a fenced yard raced back
and forth inside, barking wildly at him. *Fish bait,* his
Daddy would call it. *A waste of dog space.*

He could, Howard knew, become an armchair general,
an REMF who directed operations at a distance. Net Force
would prefer it that way, and probably nobody would

think less of him for it, not those who had been on ops with him before, anyway. But sending a man somewhere he wasn't willing to go himself didn't seem right, never had.

That left the other option, which was to retire. He could muster out with his current rank of general, draw a fair retirement, and get a job consulting somewhere, teaching, whatever. Probably do better moneywise than he was doing now. And be a lot more certain of being around when his son graduated from high school, from college, got married, and brought home grandchildren. Sure that was ten, fifteen years away, maybe, but he didn't want to miss it. And he didn't want to leave Nadine. If something happened to him, he'd always told her to remarry, find a good man, because she was too precious to waste away alone. And he meant it, too, but on a real, deep level, he had to admit to himself that the idea of Nadine laughing and loving another man wasn't at the top of his list of fun thoughts, either.

But he was a soldier. A professional warrior. This was what he did, who he was, and he liked it.

So he had to puzzle this out. It was important. Not easy, maybe, but something he had to do.

He picked up his pace again, now close to top speed for his run. He tried to get in four miles a session, at least four or five times a week, and while he was past the days when he could run 'em in five or even six minutes a mile, he could still manage six and a half or seven minutes.

That is, if he didn't get to thinking so hard he forget to keep the speed up.

Run, John. Think later.

Malibu, California

Tad Bershaw drove back to the beach house, poking along, in no hurry now. He had made his deliveries, collected the money, and decided what the hell and taken the purple cap half an hour ago. It would be another few minutes before it started to come on full force, but even now he was getting patterns, geometric overlays of complicated, pulsing grids on everything. That was from the psychedelic components of the drug. It made driving real interesting.

Bobby was cagey about his chem, he never told *any-body* exactly what was in it, but Bershaw had sampled enough illegal stuff over the years to have some pragmatic knowledge about such things.

There was some kind of MDMA/Ecstasy analog in the Hammer's alloy, with maybe a bit of mescaline; the body rushes got pretty intense an hour or so in, and just *breathing* was orgasmic when it got to circulating.

His experiences were not based on any formal knowledge of chemistry, but he knew it when he felt it. Though it didn't really matter, he had poked at it mentally a few times, what he thought Bobby had created. The psychedelics—*entheogens,* Bobby called those—for sure. That would be the MDMA, mescaline, or LSD, or maybe even some psilocybin from magic mushrooms. Maybe all four. That gave you that sense of being in contact with your inner self and loving the world and all, *entactogenesis* and *empathogenesis,* Bobby called them. Also picked up the sensory input, made everything feel really, really intense.

It had smart drugs in it, he knew that, because he was quicker, sharper, able to make choices better when the Hammer was at full pound, no question. He didn't know much about nootropics, stuff like deprynl, adrafinil, provigil, shit like that, but Bobby did, and he knew how to tweak 'em for an immediate response.

For sure it had some kind of speed—cylert, ritalin, dex, maybe; some tranq to balance it so you got the fast mind but not bad jitters. It definitely had painkiller in it, or a way to kick in the body's own opiates, and Tad guessed some kind of animal tranq and steroid mix, though he didn't see how those would do much in the short run. And something like Viagra was in it, too, because it gave you a hard-on that wouldn't quit. The Zee-ster once took six women to bed while tripping, and none of them could walk the next day. Supposedly made women horny, too.

Past that, Bobby definitely had some secret ingredients about which Tad knew zip. He knew what they did to him, but not why or how.

The total combination was synergistic—that meant more than the sum of its parts—and the bottom line was, it didn't really matter how it did what it did, only that it *did* do it.

There was a bright flash of orange to Bershaw's left but, when he glanced over that way, no cause for it. He grinned. Yeah, he was coming on. Hallucinations, real hallucinations you could talk to and have them answer back, he'd never had those while riding the Hammer, but light flashes, visual distortions, little shifts in reality, those were par for the course. Your motor ran at full speed, no governor and no idle.

He took a deep breath, and chills frosted him all over, despite the still-warm late afternoon Santa Ana wind blowing in through the open window.

Hoo, what a rush!

Seventeen times he had swung Thor's hammer, and not once a bad trip. One in five or so went bonkers, like the guy in the casino. Something in their body chemistry maybe, or the way their brains were hardwired, Bobby didn't know which, but whatever it was, Tad didn't have it. Seventeen times he had become more than he was, practically turned into a superhuman. Stronger, faster, smarter, pain-free, fatigue-free, a guy who could walk into the local kung fu school and kick its collective ass.

And, oh, yeah, there was the sex, though that never seemed to call to him much. Yeah, he got the iron woody and all, but he never seemed to have time to put it into anybody, too much else to *do* to lie down and be still . . . or relatively still.

Though right at the moment, he felt pretty mellow, the desire to shuck the car and get physical was ahead, he knew. Maybe he'd go for a walk on the beach after it got dark. Or a swim. He was usually a crappy swimmer, but once he'd swum out half a mile or so and back without any problem with the riptide or anything. He'd been looking for a shark; he'd had a kitchen knife in his hand, and he wanted to see if he could take a shark out with it. Hadn't found one, which was probably good. Away from the Hammer, you knew you had limits. Swinging it, you didn't. But hell, maybe he could have sliced Jaws up into cat food. Who could say?

Another rush enveloped him, and he was glad the house wasn't too far away. It wasn't that he couldn't maintain control enough to drive during the early stages of the trip 'cause he could, but it took too much effort, and he didn't want to waste effort on piddly shit. He would get home, shuck the car, and go outside. After all, outside was only a bigger inside, right?

He grinned. It was like the time he realized that chocolate wasn't the opposite of vanilla. They were just two different flavors. That had hit him like the secret of the universe. Shit, for all anybody knew, that *was* the secret of the universe.

6

Michaels was almost home and wishing he was already there. What he had in mind was a nice, cold beer, his bare feet propped up to watch the news hour, maybe falling asleep on the couch. Might make a sandwich, if he felt up to it. He was tired. It had been a long day, made longer because it was dull and mostly uninteresting, and just as he was about to leave, they'd had a small crisis over some hacker who was flooding every church web page his autopost-bot could find with obscene pictures taken during an orgy in a Thai whorehouse.

There was a threat to the republic.

Graffiti had certainly changed from simple spray-paint tags on the fence next to the local drugstore when it went electronic, but it was still stupid. Who gained anything by such foolishness? Did the idiot posting think people were going to see the pictures and abandon their faith? Run screaming into the streets?

No, probably he just thought it was funny. Which right off indicated a somewhat retarded sense of humor.

The church fathers and mothers were not the least amused, of course, and there were plenty of them in high enough government positions to get Net Force's attention in a hurry, including the president himself, and what was worse, a minor annoyance suddenly became a priority project.

Find whoever was doing this and stop him. Now.

Turning the other cheek didn't apply when the cheek was below the waist, so it seemed.

The e-tagger called himself The Tasmanian Devil, and as it turned out, that was a major clue. Net Force ops traced the postings to the north coast town of Devonport, Tasmania, overlooking the cool waters of the Bass Strait. The tagger was clever, he'd found some meltware that got him through a lot of firewalls, but he slipped up. His anonymous reposter was six months out of date, and in this business, six months was ancient history. Jay Gridley's team ran the cable sig to a house, informed the local constabulary, and they went round and knocked on the door. There they found a sixteen-year-old kid running a six-year-old IMac.

The boy was the son of a local minister, which probably explained a lot.

It had taken a while, and when it was done, Michaels called several heavyweights and told them they could rest easy, then left the building.

He was only a mile or so away from home when his virgil came to life.

He was tempted to ignore it, but it might be Toni, so he pulled the device from his belt and looked at the ID sig.

It was blank.

Michaels frowned. FBI com-watchware was supposed to circumvent any commercial ID blocker, so the only people who could reach out and touch him at this number without him knowing who they were would have to be somebody with federal-level blockers. He thumbed the connect button.

"Yes?"

"Commander Michaels, this is Zachary George, with the National Security Agency. Good evening. I hope I'm not interrupting your dinner?" The voice was smooth, even, just deep enough to sound authoritative. There was no picture transmission. The tiny screen was blank.

"Not yet. What can I do for you, Mr. George? Oops, can you hold on a second? I have another call."

This was not true, but it gave Michaels a few seconds to key in a trace, which he did. He didn't like not knowing to whom he was talking.

"Sorry about that. Go ahead."

"Sir, we understand your agency is involved in a joint investigation with the DEA. We'd like to speak to you about this, if we could."

"You can set up an appointment with my assistant, Mr. George. Although I'm not sure why NSA would have any interest in such a thing if it was so . . . and I wouldn't confirm it over the com in any event."

The incoming diode lit, that would be his trace. He tapped it, and a number scrolled up on the view screen, with an ID: George, Zachary, National Security Agency. Well. At least that much was true.

"I understand your reluctance, sir, and I will be happy to explain it all to you when I see you. This was just a courtesy call to let you know of our interest." There was a pause. "Ah. I see you've traced the call and confirmed my ID. Excellent. I'll be contacting your assistant for an appointment at your earliest convenience, sir. Thank you. Discom."

He went away. Michaels frowned again. What did NSA want with the drug investigation? And why was their stealthware better than the FBI's, to know they had been traced? He was going to have to talk to Jay about that. Maybe he could come up with a better program.

He dropped the virgil onto the seat and shook his head. Two more blocks to go.

Beer. Couch. Television. Soon . . .

Not that easy, of course. When he walked in, Toni was all aglow over her new hobby, so of course he had go into the garage and admire her toys.

Well, what the hell, it made her happy, that made him happy. With all the mood swings lately, anytime she was smiling was good, better make the most of it.

". . . and this is the pin vise, see, you put the needle in here and twist it, like so, and it holds it. I glued a fishing weight—this lead ball here—onto the end to give it some heft, so when I stipple, I won't have to use so much muscle."

"Such a clever girl," he said, smiling.

She smiled back at him. "And look here, this is the magnifier. . . ."

He listened with half an ear, not being that interested in the artwork per se. When she ran down, he smiled again. She couldn't drink, given her pregnancy and all, but maybe she could take some vicarious pleasure out of watching him enjoy a cold one.

"Not yet," she said.

"Huh?"

"You need to work out first. Do your *djurus.*"

Michaels wanted to say a bad word, but he wisely refrained. Toni wasn't just his wife, after all, but also his *silat* teacher, and that was the hat she had just put on. If he tried to beg off, that would be bad.

"Oh, yeah, sure, that's what I meant. *After* I work out."

That didn't fool her for a second, she was way too

sharp, but hey, you had to give it a shot. Might catch her dozing.

She said, "It takes a few thousand repetitions to get the moves down, Alex. Latest scientific research I read says somewhere in the fifty- to one-hundred-hour range."

He did the math mentally. "So, for eighteen *djurus,* I need to practice for nine hundred to eighteen hundred hours before I get them? At thirty minutes a day, that works out to about one hundred and eighty hours a year, so we're talking about ten years?"

"Well, to get them really smooth, it'll take maybe another five years."

"I'll be retired by then."

"Good. Give you more time to practice."

He laughed. "You are a slave driver."

He went to the bedroom, shucked his street clothes, and put on a pair of sweats and a T-shirt. He didn't need any shoes since he was inside. He went back and sat down in the living room and began to do some basic yoga exercises Toni had showed him. Stretching was a luxury you wouldn't get in a real fight, but for somebody over forty, it was better to do it before working out than not. A street fight might last ten seconds; a workout was gonna run thirty minutes to an hour, depending on how ambitious you were, and the older he got, the longer it took for a strain to heal.

As he was doing spinal twists, Toni wandered back in from the garage. "So, how was your day?"

Given that she had been his assistant and knew as much about his work as he did—more in some areas—it was natural for her to ask and just as natural for him to tell her.

"Dead calm," he said. "Except for a flurry at the end with a kid hacker posting porno."

"Oh, boy. And me here missing it all."

"Well, there were a couple of things mildly interesting." He told her about the drug stuff and about the cryptic call from the NSA guy.

She watched him, said, "Keep your back straight when you turn." Then, "So what does Jay say about tracking down the dope dealer?"

"He said it was going to be a bitch. Apparently, drug sales over the Internet have always been a problem. Back in the early days, a lot of it was technically illegal but not prosecuted."

"How so?"

"Well, suppose you were seventy years old and living on social security in North Dakota or maybe south Texas. If you got sick and needed medicine, a prescription might cost, say, fifty bucks a bottle. Suppose you had to take two or three bottles a month for years. That could cut way into your food budget. So you'd hop a bus to Canada or to Mexico, where the same drug might cost sixteen or eighteen dollars. A local doc writes you a scrip based on your existing one from the U.S., and even with twenty bucks for that, you still come out way ahead in the long run."

"Yeah?"

"So with the net and cheap home computers or access through cable TV or whatever, you don't even have to take the bus ride. You log onto a site, order what you need, maybe answer a couple of questions over the wire to keep things more or less legal in Canada or Mexico, and your prescription shows up in your mailbox in a day or two, assuming you are dealing with a reputable outfit."

"All the way down," she said. "And keep your knees straight."

He chuckled. "Being pregnant has made you mean, woman."

"Oh, you think so? Just wait. So the DEA didn't leap

all over these folks for importing medicine illegally?"

"Ha! Think about that for a second. Here's somebody's little old granny on a pension who's got a bad heart after working forty years teaching grammar school kids. Would *you* want to be the DEA guy in charge of arresting her for buying her nitroglycerin or whatever across the border to save enough money so she doesn't have to eat dog food? Imagine how many federal prosecutors would want to hop on *that* career bandwagon. The press would swarm you like a cloud of starving locusts. Can't you just see the headlines? 'Grandma Busted for Heart Meds!' "

"It could be a political problem," she said.

"Oh, yeah, it could. Then there are the drugs that are legal in other countries but not approved by the FDA, which, according to Jay, is another whole can of worms. Let's say you want to take Memoril, one of the new smart drugs that improves your short-term memory something like seventy percent. The FDA is still out on that one, but it's been legal in most of Europe for a couple of years. So, you log onto a web page in Spain, give them your credit card number, and order a hundred tabs. A few days later, you get a package from Scotland that looks like a birthday gift from your Uncle Angus, and inside is your drug, made by a pharmaceutical company in Germany. And all of this is perfectly legal in Spain, Scotland, and Germany, and it's not their concern about laws in the U.S.

"If Customs happens to guess what's in the package, they'll confiscate it, because technically it is illegal, but it's a gray area. If you went to Spain and got the stuff from a doctor there, you could bring it home for your own personal use. What's the difference if it comes by mail or you carried it home in your pocket? It's *malum prohibitum*—bad because it's illegal—not *malum in se*—bad in itself."

"When did *you* start speaking Latin?"

"Since I asked our lawyers about all this."

"Watch your shoulder."

"And then we get to the illegal stuff, which is easier to prosecute, assuming you know what it is and know for sure that it *is* illegal, which is the problem here. Big purple caps aren't illegal in themselves."

"Ipso facto," she said.

"Talk to me about Latin," he said. "So, there you have it. It's really the FDA's problem, only the boss made it mine. She probably owes somebody over there a favor, and this is it. And the NSA listens to everything on the air or over the wire, so I can understand how they know about it, but I don't see why it should interest them. Fortunately, I have plenty of time to think about it, things being slow. I wish you were still working there. It would be more interesting. We all miss you at the office. Me most of all."

"You're loose enough. Up. Do your *djurus*. You'll feel better after you work out."

He came to his feet. That was true. He almost always did feel better afterward. It was the damned inertia that was so hard to overcome sometimes. Good that he had Toni here to prod him. Among her many other virtues.

7

Naked, Drayne padded into the kitchen to get the rest of the bottle of champagne from the freezer. He really ought to get a little fridge for the bedroom, save him a walk.

Life was *so* hard.

Not that the girl would miss him. What was her name? Misty? Bunny? Buffy? Something like that. He'd say, "Honey," and call it good. She was out, and she ought to sleep pretty hard, too, given the athletic encounters and the first bottle of bubbly they'd just split. She was an actress—all of them around here were actresses—early twenty-something, tight, fit, perky. A natural redhead, he had discovered to his delight, once the itty-bitty black silk bikini undies had come off.

Ah, youth, nothing like it.

He'd picked her up at the gym, which is where he found most of the girls he brought home. Jocks tended to be fitter, had less risk of disease, and were able to play longer before they wore out. He didn't like his women with too much muscle, so he stayed away from the hard-core lifters, but there was always a Misty-Bunny-Buffy working the aerobic bikes and the light weights, and it never took long for him to make a connection with one. He wasn't bad-looking, and the twenty-thousand-dollar diamond ring and drop-top Mercedes two-seater usually impressed them. He even had some business cards that said he was an independent movie producer—Bobby Dee Productions—and that would usually be enough to clinch the contact if they were about to walk away. "Oh, sorry we couldn't get together. Here's my card. If you are in Malibu, give me a call sometime."

Sex was always available, and not just to movie guys in this town. And Mama Drayne's little boy Bobby had more than a little endurance in that area, and without any chemical assistance, either—well, unless you counted good champagne. He didn't use the drugs he made, never had. Maybe someday when he got old and couldn't get it up anymore, he'd whip together a batch of some custom-made dick hardener, but frankly, he didn't think that was ever gonna happen. He'd never once had a failure in that particular arena, thank you very much, and four or five times a night was nooo problem. Then again, he was not thirty-five yet. Maybe when you hit sixty or seventy it *was* different.

As he turned from the hallway toward the kitchen, he saw Tad standing on the beach, staring at the ocean.

Drayne shook his head. Tad rode the Hammer, crazy fucker that he was. It was gonna kill him someday, no question. He was in such crappy shape, it was a miracle it hadn't killed him already, should have long since blown a blood vessel in the man's brain, stroked him blind, crippled, and stupid, not necessarily in that order. A night running with Thor was worth a week's recovery for somebody in pretty good physical condition, maybe more. Tad ought not to be able to recover at all, and yet he had swung the Hammer more than anybody alive and some-how managed to keep breathing. Of course, Tad had a portable pharmacy he gobbled, snorted, or shot up after he came off a Hammer trip. Probably more drugs than blood circulating in him at any given time. Somehow, he had managed to stay a step ahead of the reaper. Pretty damned amazing.

Drayne opened the freezer, pulled the second bottle of champagne out. He lifted it to his lips, thought better about that, and grabbed one of the chilled glasses on the freezer rack. Drinking it from the bottle was for barbarians. The bubbles didn't get released.

Had to be civilized about this, didn't we?

He poured the icy wine into the icy glass, watched the liquid turn to foam and fountain up, then slowly begin to settle down.

Time waiting for champagne bubbles to settle didn't count.

Out on the beach, near the water line, three hulking big jocks ran past, working on their aerobic fitness. Drayne glanced at Tad, worried. If Tad decided he didn't like the way the guys looked, he'd go for them, and big and strong as they were, they wouldn't have a prayer, Tad would twist them up like soft pretzels, if that's what he felt like.

But the trio jogged past, and if Tad even saw them, Drayne couldn't tell it from here. Watching Tad when something like this happened was like watching a Roman emperor. Thumb up or thumb down, and nobody knew which it'd be.

He shook his head. Sooner or later, Tad was going to step wrong and draw the law's attention. It had been a while since he'd done it last, and fortunately, it hadn't led back to Drayne that time. Plus, the house was clean, that wasn't a problem, he never kept anything illegal on hand for longer than it took to mix it and get it out again, but he didn't need the local deputies knocking on his door and asking about the crazy asshole dressed in black who suddenly turned into the Incredible Hulk and laid waste to the beach. Low profile was the way to go. If they didn't know about you, they wouldn't be able to bother you.

He finished filling up the glass, topped it off, and put the bottle back into the freezer. He walked to the deck, sipping at the cold champagne. Yeasty, with a hint of apple, good finish, no bitter aftertaste. Not the best, but after five or six glasses, there was no point in wasting the best; you couldn't taste the really exotic flavors and subtle stuff anyhow. As long as it was good enough not to irritate your stomach, that was all you needed for the second bottle.

There was a guy they called the Wine Nazi, up just north of San Francisco, way out a winding road in Lucas Valley, who made the best champagne on earth. Grand Brut, dry as the Sahara, and he sold *futures* in it, you bought what you could afford, he would call you when it was damned well ready, and if you didn't like it, too fucking bad. Worked out to about five hundred bucks a bottle—if you bought a case—and you couldn't buy more than one case a year. Six thousand bucks a case, and that was the nonvintage stuff. Sometimes it took eighteen months for the last batch to ripen to his satisfaction. The *really* good stuff ran two grand a bottle, and you had to get on a waiting list for that, too. Drayne's name hadn't gotten to the top of that list yet, but next year, he was pretty sure it would.

Drayne had done a tour there once. The winery was tiny, a hole-in-the-wall place, and before he was done, the Wine Nazi had him climbing up on barrels to taste the whites and reds right out of the casks, sucked it out with a long rubber tube and dribbled into a glass. And after a few sips of that, the guy had him helping hand-riddle the champagne bottles. They had to be turned so much every day, so the silt would settle and all.

Drayne was an appreciative audience. The guy was a certified genius when it came to wine, no question, and the champagne was the best of the lot. Of course, the Wine Nazi wouldn't let him call it champagne, since technically that meant it had to come from that particular region of France, so he called it sparkling wine. Even though it made the average good vintage of the French stuff taste like stale ginger ale.

That was the stuff you saved for special occasions, definitely first-bottle, and not something you shared with Misty-Bunny-Buffy just to get laid. He had six bottles left, and six months left before he could buy another case. If he was lucky. So he had to ration it, one bottle a month, no more, and even then, he might have to wait. Terrible situation.

He grinned. He sure had a lot to complain about, didn't he? Living in a big house on the beach in Malibu, good-looking naked woman in his bed, a shitload of money, six bottles of the best champagne anybody in *this* town had. Hell, it really didn't get much better than that, did it?

Since it didn't look like Tad was going to go ballistic and destroy the neighborhood, maybe he should go back to bed and nudge Honey awake. He was sure he could think up something new for them to try.

Yep. That seemed like an *excellent* idea. He lifted his glass in a toast to his own cleverness. *Hi, ho, Bobby. Away!*

He headed back toward the bedroom.

Tad felt the power.

It coursed through him like an electric current, filling him with pulsing flashes of juice, set him humming like a dynamo at full spin.

He was a god out here, deciding the fate of all who passed. At his whim, he could strike them down, become Shiva the destroyer, changing the very configuration of the planet with a mere wave of his hand. At his whim, which was how gods operated, far as he could tell.

He took a breath, and the sensation made orgasm seem pale in comparison. The thrills ran through his entire body, he could feel it everywhere at once, in his hands, his body, even his toes. *Man. What a rush!*

He was a god. Able to do anything he wished.

And what he wished to do right now was . . . walk. To stride down the beach, to pass among his people, disguised as a reedy, tubercular man all dressed in black, but beyond comprehension to mere mortals.

As far above them as a man was above an ant.

They couldn't know. He felt sorry for them, being so weak, so stupid. So pitiful.

He started to walk, feeling the sand like a living thing under his boots, hearing the soft *chee-chee-chee* squeaks it made with each step. He was aware of the evening breeze touching his skin, the smell of salt and iodine from the sea, the taste of the very air. He was aware of *every*-thing, not just on this beach, but radiating out to galaxies a billion light-years from where he walked. It was all his territory, all of it. If he reached up his arms, he could encompass it all in his grasp.

He laughed.

Ahead, somebody finished up a Frisbee game and headed for their towels. A beach volleyball game wound down. Traffic roared past on the highway, the cars and trucks taking on the aspect of dragons: fearsome creatures in their element, but creatures who knew better than to cross his path. He was Tad the Bershaw, and any being with enough sense to see him would know he was to be feared.

He walked through his kingdom, feeling for the moment benevolent in his omnipotence. He would suffer them to live.

For now, anyway.

Jayland/Quantico, Virginia

Jay Gridley had always been a man who enjoyed moving fast. When he slipped into his sensory gear and the net blossomed before him, infinite in its possibilities, he had always chosen speed as his vehicle. If he drove, it was a Viper, a rocket with wheels that smoked everything else on the road. Sometimes he flew—rocket packs, jets, copters, whatever. He created virtual scenarios that he zipped through like rifle rounds, clean, fast, slick as a tub full of grease.

Oh, now and then he would do period. He'd make a Western town and mosey into town on a horse. Or a boat. But getting there in a hurry was his pleasure, and most of his programs reflected that. Getting business done had always been about getting it *done,* not about the trip.

Not today. Today, Jettin' Jay was out for a stroll, through an Eastern garden. It wasn't strictly accurate, his program, it had mixed elements in it: Right where he was at the moment stood a Japanese tea house with a little brook running past it. Just ahead was a Zen garden, three rocks in a bed of raked sand. But over to the left was a Shaolin temple, monks out front doing kung fu, and to the right, a second temple, straight out of Bangkok, with traditional Siamese dancers moving like snakes. The Taj Mahal was past that, and there were even some pyramids off a ways behind him. It was a veritable theme park of Eastern religious thought.

The sun shined brightly, the day was warm with a little breeze, and the smell of jasmine and sandalwood mixed with roses and musk.

Welcome to the land of the happy, nice people, Jay. Your kind of place.

He smiled, walking slowly, not in the least bit of a hurry. What he wanted was here somewhere, but you know what? He would get to it when he got to it.

To be honest, he hadn't exactly embraced the tenets of Buddhism. The eightfold this, or the four ways of that. But there was an energy about what Saji did and how she related to it that he did find worth thinking about. He'd never considered himself much of anything, other than a computer jock, but this go-with-the-flow stuff—that was Taoism rather than Buddhism, right?—well, here of late, it had a whole bunch of appeal.

Thank Sojan Rinpoche for that, along with her other, more earthy talents.

A bee flew past, buzzing, looking for pollen.

Ah, yes, what could be better than a stroll in the cosmic gardens—

"Hey, Jay, you awake?" came the somewhat dissonant voice, intruding on his scenario.

Jay dropped out of VR, and was at once back in his office at Net Force. Standing in the doorway were two coworkers, Alan and Charlie.

"That door is supposed to be locked," Jay said, mildly irritated.

"Yep, and if you hadn't wanted somebody good enough to rascal the sucker, you'd have hired somebody other than us," Charlie said. He waved his key card. "You ought to change the codes every year or two, Jay."

"Would that do any good?"

"About as much good as me changing the codes on my bike did," Alan said.

Jay laughed. He had broken into the comp on Alan's fuel-cell scooter and programmed it so it wouldn't go faster than nine miles an hour. Well, that was the old Jay. He was a new man these days. No more sophomoric games.

"C'mon, we're going to Pud's for burgers and beer."

Jay spoke without thinking. "Nah, I'll pass. I'm giving up eating flesh."

Both Alan and Charlie stared for maybe two seconds before they cracked up. They laughed. They laughed harder. They fucking *howled*.

"Flesh? *Flesh,* you said? Ah, hahahaaa!"

"Gee, Jay, we wouldn't want you to kill and eat the waitress or anything. Flesh? Oh, yeah, 1 can hear that: 'Excuse me, ma'am, could I get a fleshburger on an onion bun, and could you sprinkle it with a little ground-up human skull?' "

"I dunno, Charlie, come to think of it, maybe we ought to skip Pud's and go to that new place, you know, Cannibal Moe's, instead. I hear they have a real good chicken fried thigh there."

"Nah, Alan, I think we should go to the new Donner's Pass Pizza, and pick up a pizza with fingers and nipples. Or maybe the spaghetti and eyeballs."

"Fuck off and die," Jay said. "You know what I mean."

The two men looked at each other and shook their heads in mock sadness.

"Tsk, tsk, tsk," Alan said. "The man is in *love.* Next thing you know, he's gonna be wearing a cowled robe to work and doing Gregorian chants up and down the halls."

"Yeah, and sprinkling rose petals everywhere and smiling at everybody like a fool."

"Go away," Jay said.

They did, cackling down the hall as they went.

Well. That certainly went well, didn't it? Maybe you

*might want to be a little bit more low key in your con-
version to vegetarianism, hmm?*

Too late now. By tomorrow morning, this would be all
over the building. He knew the jokes would be coming,
and he had better recode his lock and his access, or his
computer would be full of crap, too.

Still, he grinned. He could stand a little ribbing. He
was, after all, the new, improved Jay Gridley, much more
mellow than the old Jay had been. Much more.

8

Washington, D.C.

Toni came up from sleep all of a moment. She looked at the clock on the bedside table. Two A.M., and she was wide awake, not a trace of drowsiness. Well, wasn't that terrific?

What, she wondered, had awakened her? Another hormone-fueled dream she couldn't remember?

She glanced at Alex, who slept soundly, tangled in the sheet and a couple of pillows. Sometimes he snored, and that might do it, but while he was breathing deeply, he wasn't making any noise to speak of.

She listened carefully, but the house was silent. No footsteps skulking down the hall, no creaks of doors being stealthily opened. No feeling of intrusion.

Was it because she needed to go pee?

No, not really, she *always* needed to go pee these days, and the urge wasn't particularly strong. She had fallen asleep plenty of times needing to go more than now. Still, as long as she was awake . . .

She got up, went to the bathroom, did what she needed

to do, and padded back to bed. Alex didn't stir. You could come in and walk off with the place, and he wouldn't wake up, he slept heavy. He had told her he hadn't done that before they got married, but now that she was here, he could could relax. That amused and pleased her on one level; on another level, it was mildly irritating. So she had to be responsible for their safety after hours? Not that she wasn't qualified, but still . . .

She slipped carefully back into bed and began practicing her *djurus* mentally, going through them step by step in her mind's eye, striving to capture all the details of each move. That usually would put her to sleep before she got very far along, but it wasn't working tonight. She managed to go all the way through the eighteen on the right side, and was halfway through doing them on the left when the phone rang.

It managed less than half a cycle before Toni grabbed it. "Hello?"

"Toni? It's me, Mama."

Toni felt her bowels and belly twist suddenly. Mama would never call at two in the morning unless somebody was seriously injured or dying. "Is it Poppa?"

"No, dear, Poppa's fine. But I'm afraid it's Mrs. DeBeers."

"Guru? What happened?"

"She had a stroke. About fifteen minutes ago."

Toni glanced at the clock again. Exactly when she had awakened. Was this some weird coincidence, or were she and her elderly teacher psychically connected as Guru sometimes said?

"She's on the way to the hospital," Mama continued. "When it happened, she managed to reach her medical alert button, and the paramedics and ambulances woke us all up. Poppa is going to the hospital with your brother. I thought you'd want to know."

Alex finally woke up. "Toni?"

She waved him quiet. "Which hospital, Mama?"

"Saint Agnes."

"Thanks for calling me, Mama. I'll talk to you later."

She cradled the phone. Alex was sitting up. "Who—?"

"Guru had a stroke," she said.

"How bad?"

"I don't know."

He nodded. "I'll drive you to the airport."

She blinked at him. Just like that, no question, he knew she was going. "Thank you, Alex. I love you."

"I know. I love you, too. I'll call and get you a flight while you get dressed."

Toni nodded, already up and headed for the shower. Guru had been her teacher for more than fifteen years. Toni had started learning the art of *pentjak silat* from the old lady when she was already past retirement age, and she was eighty-three now. Guru was still built like a squat brick, but even so, she was not a young woman. *A stroke.*

Dear God.

She turned the shower control on and waited for the water to warm up. Was she supposed to fly in her condition? Well, supposed to or not, she was going. Guru was like her own grandmother; whatever was happening to her, she wasn't going to suffer through it alone.

Alex was mostly quiet during the drive to the airport, though he did offer to go with her.

"Nothing you can do to help," she said.

"Not her. But I can be there for you."

She smiled at him. "I knew there was a reason I married you. Keep the home fires burning. I'll call as soon as I know what's happening."

It was hard to think about Guru dying. She had been so much a part of Toni's day-to-day life from her early teenage years until she left for college. Every morning, they'd practice before Toni went off to school. Every afternoon, after she had done her homework, Toni would head across the street to the old woman's place, and they would practice the Indonesian martial art for an hour or two. Guru DeBeers had become part of the family, was included in all the gatherings: Christmas, Easter, Thanksgiving, birthday parties, weddings, graduations. She had finally given up smoking that nasty old pipe, but she still drank half a gallon of coffee a day and ate whatever she pleased. And even though she was in her eighties, Guru could still give most big strong men fits if they bothered her enough. She was slower and frailer, but her mind and skills were still sharp.

Toni hadn't been to Mass except with Mama on home visits for a long time, but she offered a silent prayer: *Please let her live.*

9

Michaels hadn't managed to get back to sleep after Toni left for New York, so he was a little tired. Fortunately, as slow as things were, he could probably take off early.

He had a partial staff meeting scheduled, and when he got there, his people were already at the conference table. John Howard, Jay Gridley, and the just-promoted Julio Fernandez. A few months ago, Fernandez's wife, Joanna, would have been there, as would Toni. He missed seeing them.

"Good morning," he said.

"Commander," Howard and Fernandez said in unison.

"Hey, I thought it was your turn to bring the doughnuts, boss," Jay said as Michaels sat. This was an old joke; they never ate doughnuts at the morning meetings.

"You didn't give up sugar when you gave up flesh?" Fernandez said.

"Very funny, Julio."

Michaels raised an eyebrow.

Fernandez answered the unasked question: "Our computer wizard here is turning Buddhist. No more eating *flesh* for him. Gonna step around ants on the sidewalk, too, I expect, chanting *om mani padme hum* while he does."

Michaels shook his head. *Never a dull moment around here.*

"Okay, what do we have? John?"

General Howard led off with his weekly report. New gear, new troops, old business. Things were slow. They'd be taking various units out on training runs over the next couple of weeks, unless something came up.

Jay didn't have a lot to report, either. "Nothing on your dope dealers," he finished. "The DEA's info was pretty sparse and dead-ended quick. I'll run some other things into the mix and see what comes up."

Michaels turned to Howard. "I sent a report your way, but in case you haven't had a chance to read it, we're helping the DEA run down some kind of new designer drug that turns the users into temporary supermen. And sometimes it makes them jump off tall buildings."

Howard said, "Yes, sir, I saw the report. Thor's Hammer."

Michaels said, "Here's another little twist. I got a call from an NSA guy yesterday. He's made an appointment to come see me today, in about an hour, my secretary tells me. He says it's about this designer drug thing. I'm curious as to why."

"What's his name?" Jay asked. "The NSA guy?"

"Last name, George, first name, Zachary."

Jay shrugged, but tapped it into his flatscreen's manual keyboard. "Never heard of him, but I'll scope him out."

"John?"

"Doesn't ring any bells with me, either," he said. "I can check with my Pentagon contacts."

"Why would the National Security Agency be interested in this?" Michaels asked. "Dope isn't in their mission statement, is it?"

Howard said, "Mission statements aren't worth the paper they are written on, sir. Everybody stretches them to fit whatever they need."

Michaels smiled. He had done that himself more than a few times, and everybody here knew it.

"I suppose I can wait until the man gets here and ask him, but I somehow doubt he'll be entirely forthcoming. Anybody have any thoughts I might pursue?"

"Overspent their budget and need a little extra cash?" Jay said. "Wouldn't be the first time an agency sold drugs to make up a shortfall."

"I thought Buddhists weren't supposed to be cynical."

"Nope, not according to Saji. You can be pretty much anything and still be a Buddhist. Cynical works."

"Except, apparently, a flesh-eater," Fernandez said.

"Well, actually, that, too. Some parts of the world, like Tibet, where food is scarce, meat is okay. As long as you do it with the right attitude."

Fernandez laughed. "Yeah, I can see you praying over a Whopper, chanting and all. Bet they'd love that at BK."

"You obviously have never been to a D.C. Burger King," Jay said. "You could do a Hawaiian fire dance over your fries there and nobody would look twice."

Fernandez laughed. He looked at Michaels and said, "Maybe one of their people is into drugs. Could be they are looking at some kind of internal security."

Howard blew out a small sigh. "There's another possibility that springs immediately to mind. Military applications."

Michaels looked at him.

Howard continued. "If you have a compound that makes a man think he's faster than a speeding bullet and more powerful than a locomotive, when you put a weapon in his hands and point him at an enemy, you could have something of military value, assuming there are controls in place."

"Didn't the Nazis try that kind of thing?"

"Yes, sir, and other armies have tried it since, from speed to steroids. Nobody has come up with something cheap and dependable enough yet, but if they did, it would certainly have useful applications."

"Would you use such a thing, General?"

"If it was safe, if it was legal, and if it would give my people an advantage over an enemy? Bring more of them back alive? Yes, sir, in a heartbeat."

"From what the DEA has given us, this stuff is neither safe nor legal."

"But it might be made both. Legal is the easy part, if it's useful enough. Safe might be harder, but it might be possible to make it so, and a lot of services would be willing to explore the possibility. And there are some armies with fewer scruples about testing things on their own people than we have."

Jay said, "When did the U.S. military develop scruples, General? Remember *The Atomic Café*? 'Here, men, put on these goggles when you look at the nuclear explosion. And don't worry about that glowing dust if it gets on you, just brush it off, you'll be fine.' "

"That was a long time ago," Howard said.

"Yeah? What about Agent Orange in Vietnam, or the vaccines against nerve gas and biowarfare in Desert Storm? Or the new, improved, supposedly safe defoliants in Colombia?"

Before Howard could respond, Michaels said, "Give it a rest, Jay. We didn't come to argue about the military's checkered history. And whatever happened, we can hardly blame General Howard, can we?"

Jay shut up, having expressed his standing liberal attitude.

"All right. If there's nothing further, I've got a ton of files to review."

Forty-five minutes later, as Michaels sat developing eyestrain scanning computer files using his new sharpgoggles, supposedly designed to keep the letters so clear you wouldn't get eyestrain, there was a tap at his door.

"Jay."

"Boss. I uploaded what I could find on this George guy. I didn't know if you'd get to it before he showed up."

"Thanks, Jay, I appreciate it."

After Jay left, Michaels found the file and read through it. Not much. There was a brief bio on Zachary George, place and date of birth, education, family, and shorter work history. Seemed Mr. George had been with the NSA since leaving college fifteen years ago, and the only references to his status there was a GS number only a grade below Michaels's own before he was booted upstairs.

"Sir?" came the voice of his secretary over the com. "Your nine o'clock is here."

Well, speak of the devil. "Show him in."

Mr. George wasn't particularly impressive upon first look. Average height, average weight, brown hair cut short but not too short, fair skin, and clothes that were standard midlevel bureaucrat: a gray suit expensive enough to look decent, not so expensive as to stand out in your memory. Black leather shoes. Put him in a room with four other people, and he'd be invisible. The guy in the corner who looked totally average? No, no, not him, the guy *next* to him.

Michaels stood and extended his hand. "Mr. George."

"Commander. Good of you to see me."

"Well, we like to keep relations good with our fellow agencies. Spirit of cooperation and all."

"With all due respect, sir, bullshit. Almost anybody at my agency would cut the throats of everybody at yours if they thought it would gain them two brownie points at review time. And that's pretty much my experience with all the security agencies I've dealt with."

Michaels had to smile at that. "Don't sugarcoat it that way, tell me what you really think."

George returned the smile, and whatever he was up to, he was interesting.

"Have a seat."

The NSA man sat, leaned back, crossed his ankle over his knee. "You figured out what it is I'm up to yet?"

"I have some thoughts. Why don't you just tell me?"

George smiled again. It started on the right side and worked its way across his face. "Well, sir, I don't want to make it too easy for you."

"Much as I'd like to fence with you, I do have a couple of other things on my plate. Twenty questions isn't high on the list. Talk or walk."

George nodded, as if that was what he expected to hear. "Sir. You may be aware that there are qualities connected to this drug we spoke of that might be of use to certain of our military organizations."

"That thought has crossed my mind."

"As it happens, my agency has a . . . research facility engaged in studying certain pharmaceutical aids for possible use in . . . field operations."

"Really?"

"More information is need-to-know, I'm sorry. Suffice it to say, we would be very interested in speaking with the chemist who has come up with this compound when you find him."

"Why aren't you talking to the DEA?"

George smiled. "We have. Frankly, we don't think the DEA has much of a chance of catching the guy."

"It is their area of expertise, isn't it?"

"Then why did they come to you for help?"

That was a good point, but Michaels didn't speak to it. Instead, he said, "And why didn't you just go after the dealer on your own? NSA has a finger in just about every pie there is, don't they?"

"True. And as a result, we are stretched somewhat thin. Net Force has had some excellent results in its short history, and continuing to speak frankly, your computer operatives are better than anybody else's. Including ours. You probably know we've tried to, ah . . . recruit some of them."

Michaels smiled. He knew. "No luck?"

"Oh, yes, plenty of luck . . . all bad. Your organization seems to engender a very high degree of loyalty."

"We try to treat our people right."

"So it seems. But the bottom line is, we think you'll uncover this dealer before either the DEA or our own ops will, and we'd like you to keep us in mind when you do."

Michaels leaned back in his chair and steepled his fingers in front of his face for a second, then quickly put his hands down on the desk. He'd read somewhere that steepling your fingers was a sign of feeling superior, and while he certainly felt he had the upper hand in this discussion, he didn't want to give anything away. He said, "Even if we did, what good would it do you? DEA has jurisdiction. We turn the information over to them, they make the arrest. End of our participation."

George hesitated for a second, then said, "Of course. We wouldn't want to usurp the DEA's legal position. But a heads-up from you would allow us to, ah . . . begin negotiations with that agency from a position of knowledge. I'm sure we can convince them that the nation's best interests would be served if we were allowed to question the criminal before he was locked away to await a long, drawn-out trial."

Michaels smiled again. George would know this conversation was being recorded, and he didn't want to say anything that sounded remotely illegal, but it was easy enough to read between the lines here. One developed a certain expertise in verbal fugue working in Washington. You said one thing, you meant something else, and you used expression or tone or gestures to make sure your listener got it. Tape recordings missed visual clues, and even videos couldn't pick up between-the-lines stuff.

George's fugue was simple: You give us the dope dealer, we rattle his cage real good and get what we want, *then* we turn him over to the DEA.

Interesting.

Michaels's immediate gut reaction was to tell Mr. Zachary George to scuttle back to his NSA hole and not let the door hit him on the way out. But he had learned a thing or two about political survival in this town, and peeing in somebody's corn flakes was not a smart move, especially when they had clout. NSA knew where a lot of bodies were buried, some figurative, some no doubt quite literally, and a direct confrontation, while it might be emotionally satisfying, was not the smart move. It wasn't just Michaels, it was his agency, and he had to keep that in mind. A hard lesson, but one he was learning better and better all the time.

"Well, I suppose we could keep you in the loop," Michaels finally said. "As a courtesy to a brother agency." There was no real fugue here, he wasn't going to give them squat, but he strived to leave that impression: *Why, sure, we'll scratch your back. What will you do for us?*

George flashed his crooked smile again. "We would

appreciate it, Commander. I'm certain we can return the favor in some small way."

The meeting was over, George had said what he came to say, and it was but the matter of another minute to exchange good-byes before the man left.

Interesting, indeed. So the National Security Agency had some kind of clandestine operation involving drugs. Not really that big a surprise, when you thought about it. There were more sub-rosa operations going on at any security agency than you could shake a stick at, some well-known in the trade, some hinted at, and some surely buried so deep that nobody had happened across them yet. Net Force was fairly public, but they didn't air certain articles of their laundry in public. And for sure the FBI had its own black-bag ops skulking about in the shadows. It was all part of the game. You couldn't sneak up on somebody if you had to yell at him through a bullhorn and flash your warning lights. Even local police departments knew you sometimes had to use unmarked cars.

When and if they came across the drug dealer, then Michaels could decide whether to let NSA know about it. Probably they wouldn't. Almost certainly not in time to do anything nasty with the knowledge. If NSA swooped in and grabbed the dope dealer from under the DEA's nose and someone figured out that it was Net Force who gave the guy up, heads would roll.

Right now, it was a moot point anyhow. They didn't have anything to give.

Before he could get back to his reading, the intercom cheeped again.

"Sir, Agent Brett Lee is here. He doesn't have an appointment, but he seems, ah . . . quite insistent on seeing you."

"Show him in."

Lee arrived in a huff, glowering. "What the hell is Zach George doing here?!"

"Nice to see you, too, Mr. Lee."

"You didn't answer my question!"

"Nor do I intend to. What goes on in my office is none of your damn business."

Lee stepped forward, as if he planned on doing something physical.

Michaels was tired and cranky. He came to his feet, ready to move. *Go for it, pal. Let me show you what my wife taught me!*

But Lee stopped, having apparently realized that throwing a punch at the head of Net Force might not be a smart career move.

Too bad. Michaels felt like decking him. This clown had no right storming into his office demanding anything.

"You and George are up to something, and I'm warning you, it better not get in our way! My boss will be calling yours," he said, still red-faced and angry.

"I hope they have a pleasant conversation, Mr. Lee. But right now, I'm busy, so if you'll excuse me, I have work to do." He sat and reached for his viewer.

In another second, Brett Lee was gone, leaving an angry wake behind him.

This was a *very* interesting development. Much more fun than reading reports on a dull morning.

10

When Drayne shuffled into the kitchen with just the tiniest headache from drinking most of two bottles of champagne, he saw Tad sprawled on the couch and dead to the world.

Good. One of these trips, Tad wasn't gonna come back, but he was glad it wasn't this time. He'd miss the guy. Tad was balls-to-the-wall and full-out, not too many like him. And loyal; you couldn't buy that.

Drayne opened the cabinet over the microwave oven and dug through the vitamins until he found the ibuprofen. He shook four of the brown tabs into his palm, swallowed them dry, and put the bottle back. There were rows and rows of vitamin bottles there, he was a big believer in such things, but he wouldn't take those until he had some food in his stomach. He took so many vitamins and minerals and assorted other healthy supplements that doing so on an empty belly was apt to make him nauseated. His normal intake each morning amounted to maybe twenty, twenty-five pills, caps, caplets, or softgels.

Two grams of C, two caplets; three E's, 1200 IUs; 120 mg of ginkgo biloba, two caplets; two Pain Free tabs, that was 1,000 of glucosamine and 800 of chondroitin combined; couple of fat-burners, mostly chromium picolinate and L-caritine; 705 mg of ginseng, three softgels; 50,000 IUs of beta-carotene in two gelcaps; 100 mg of DHEA, that was four pills; couple of saw palm—he didn't really need that yet, but better to get a head start on prostate problems, as much screwing as he did—two gels, 320 mg; five mg of Deprenyl to keep the gray matter from rotting; and however many creatine caps he thought he needed when he was on the cycle, those varied from day to day, depending on how hard he hit the weights.

He waited until bedtime before he took the multiple and his melatonin, plus a couple of other odds and ends. That many pills down the hatch every day, dry-swallowing four ibuprofen was nothing. The stack seemed to work for him, and as long as it did, he'd keep it up. Prevention was better than a cure.

Champagne was his only vice—well, unless you counted sex—and he made sure he was covered on the health stuff. He ate pretty well, exercised regularly, even wore sunblock these days. He planned to live a long, rich, full life, unlike Tad, who'd be dead in a year, tops, and probably a lot sooner.

He'd tried to talk Tad out of them, the Hammer trips, but Tad was who he was, and if he did quit, he'd turn into somebody else. Drayne could live with the guy running at half speed, but Tad couldn't, and that was that.

Misty-Bunny-Buffy was gone, slipped out in the night sometime. He figured she had a steady boyfriend or a husband she had to get back to, sleeping with a producer to maybe get a job didn't really count, especially not if you were home before dawn. He was done with her, anyhow. She'd been great, but she'd only be new once, and there was no point in going spelunking in caves where he'd already been, was there? Unless they were spectacular—and past a certain point, they didn't seem to get much better—why bother? Might be a better one just ahead.

He looked at his watch, one of those Seiko Kinetics that you never had to wind or replace the batteries in; it ran off some kind of tiny generator that charged up a capacitor or something every time you moved your wrist. Watch would run as long as you could wiggle your arm a little, guaranteed for life. And if things got to the point where he couldn't wiggle his arm a little, there wouldn't be any reason to worry about what time it was.

At the moment, it was almost ten A.M.

He sighed. Too late to get in a workout or a jog on the beach. Better go take a shower and then get rolling. He had to drive out to the desert to restock his mobile lab, and it was a couple hours each way, even if the traffic was good. He could take his vitamins with him, get something to eat later. He needed to be back by six, he had a dinner with the Zee-ster, that was always good for some laughs. If Tad had been mobile, he'd have sent him, but he wasn't and that was that, too.

Well, at least it looked as if the weather was okay. Once he got past the smog curtain, he could drop the top and enjoy the sunshine. Great thing about SoCal was that you could pretty much do that year round. Yeah, it rained in the winter and actually got chilly a couple times in season, but he'd spent many a January day lying on the beach cooking under a warm sun. Sure, the water got colder, but with a wet suit, you could surf any time. Not that he'd done much of that lately. Too busy working. Have to remedy that pretty soon.

He grinned. He wondered what his father would say if he knew how much money little Bobby had tucked away.

Or how he had earned it. The old man would blow a gasket, that was certain, you'd be able to see the steam coming out his head for fucking miles. Thirty years with the Bureau, as straight an arrow as ever put on a suit, his old man, a guy who'd always paid his own parking tickets rather than flash his FBI badge at a meter maid.

And for what? What had all that nose-to-the-grindstone, johnny-be-good crap gotten his old man?

It had gotten him retired to a condo in Tucson, Arizona, just him and that little terrier of his, Franklin, living on a pension and bitching about how the world had gone to hell in a handbasket. Actually, Drayne kinda liked the dog. Best thing his old man had done since Mom died was get a dog, not saying much. First week he'd had the beast, it had come back inside carrying a big ole dead rat it had caught. Rat almost as big as the dog, and you'd have never thought by looking at the little barker that he had it in him. Drayne liked that.

It had been more than a year since he had gone to visit his father. Franklin must be pushing nine or ten by now, probably middle-aged in dog years.

Drayne often wondered, if his old man found out what he was doing, would he turn him in? Some days he was sure that former Special Agent in Charge Rickover Drayne, RD to his friends, most of whom were feds, would do it, no question. Other days, he wasn't so sure. Maybe the old bastard had a soft spot for his only son. Not that Drayne had ever been able to see it.

As far as the old man knew, Bobby worked for a small chemical company that produced plastic polymer for use in industrial waste containers, earning a decent salary, just a hair more than his father had made in his last year before retirement. This was done so the old man would think all that tuition money for the chemistry degree hadn't been wasted. He might have his differences with his son, but at least he could say the boy had a legitimate job making decent money.

Of course, that was as much for Drayne's protection as for making his father proud. He had gone to some lengths to create the PolyChem Products company, duly incorporated in Delaware, to set up a modest history in a few selected computer banks, and to make sure he was listed as an employee. Just in case his father checked it out. He wouldn't put it past the old man to do that. Paid taxes on the paper job salary he showed, too, and FICA and all that shit. IRS didn't care what you did as long as you paid taxes. He could have declared his income from dope sales and paid the feds their cut, and the IRS would never say anything to the DEA about it. People had done it before.

The government, in whatever form it manifested, was plainly stupid. He could dick around with them all he wanted, and they'd never catch him.

Drayne wandered into the bathroom and cranked up the shower. It was a big sucker, room enough for four or five people, all pale green tile and glass bricks, with a dozen shower heads set all over: high, low, in-between. With the jets turned on full blast, it was like being stabbed by wet needles. Used a shitload of water—he had a pair of eighty-gallon water heaters in the garage—but when you came out of it, you felt clean and rejuvenated, that was for sure.

He stepped into the shower and gasped at the force of the spray.

Tad would be out for probably eighteen or twenty hours, maybe longer. He'd still be on the couch when Drayne got back. Maybe even still breathing. And he'd spend most of the next week or so on the couch, lying on the floor, or, if he made it that far, a bed. Recovering from the Hammer was a chore. It got harder each time.

Drayne stopped thinking and let the hot water take him.

The Bronx, New York

Toni sat in the chair next to Guru's bed, watching the old woman sleep. Mrs. DeBeers had been lucky, the doctor told her. The stroke was mild, and she was in otherwise remarkable health for an eighty-three-year-old woman. There was only a slight effect on her grip and speech, no real paralysis, and they expected she'd make a full recovery. There were still tests they had to run and medications they had to administer and monitor for a couple of days, but pretty much they thought she was out of the woods.

The doctors only told her that because Guru had listed her as next of kin, even though that wasn't true.

Toni was more than a little relieved. Guru DeBeers had been a part of her life since Toni had seen her, at sixty-five, clean the clocks of four neighborhood toughs who tried to give her a hard time. Toni had been amazed at the sight and had known immediately she wanted to learn how to protect herself against physical attacks that way. Men tended to take women for granted physically, and even at thirteen Toni had known she did not want to be at the mercy of some man who decided he wanted something from her she didn't want to give. The training in *pentjak silat,* starting with the simple *bukti negara* style and progressing to the more complex *serak,* had been a part of Toni's world ever since. She still went over to see her teacher whenever she went home to visit her parents, and the trip across the street had never gotten dull.

Old as Guru was, it was impossible to imagine her gone.

"Ah, how is my *tunangannya* today?"

Toni smiled. *Best girl.* There was the smallest slur to Guru's voice, hardly noticeable. "I'm fine, Guru. How are you feeling?"

"I've felt worse. Better, too. It would be nice to have some coffee."

"The doctors won't let you do that, not after a stroke."

"I have outlived three sets of doctors so far. I will outlive this set if they wait for coffee to kill me. And if does kill me, at least I die happy."

Toni smiled again, and reached into her purse. She brought out a small stainless steel thermos.

The old woman's smile was radiant, if a trifle saggy on the left side of her face. "Ah. You are a dutiful student."

"It's not fresh," Toni said. "I didn't have time to go by your place and grind your grand-nephew's beans and make it. I got it at Starbucks more than an hour ago. I'm sorry."

Guru shrugged. "It will do. Raise the bed."

Toni operated the controls, and the motor hummed and raised Guru into a more-or-less sitting position. Toni poured the coffee into the thermos's cup and passed it over.

Guru inhaled deeply through her nose. "Espresso?"

"Of course. The darkest they had."

"Well, stale or not, it is welcome. Thank you, my best girl." Guru brought the cup to her lips and took a small sip. "Not bad, not bad," she pronounced. "Another hundred years or so, and Americans might learn how to make a decent brew. And certainly it is better than nothing." She took another sip, then smiled again. "And how is our baby doing?"

"Fine, as far as I can tell. Mostly he elbows me in the bladder or rolls around and tries to boot my stomach inside out."

"Yes, they do that. And he is tiny yet. Wait until you are eight or nine months along, and he kicks you so hard your pants fall down." She chuckled.

"There's a pleasant thought."

"You are worried because you cannot train," Guru said.

Toni shook her head. How could she know exactly what was going through her mind?

"I had four children," Guru said. "All after I began my training. Each time, I had to alter my practice."

"So I'm discovering."

"You can do *djuru-djuru* sitting down," she said. "Your *langkas* will need to be sharpened, but there is no reason to stop upper body movements."

Toni nodded. The Indonesian martial art forms Guru taught were divided into two parts, upper body, or *djurus,* and lower body, or *langkas.* You usually lumped them together and called the whole thing a *djuru,* though that was not technically correct.

"I have some things in my house for you to take home with you when you go. I have packed them into a big box by the front door."

Before Toni could protest, Guru continued, "No, it is not my time yet, and I am not giving you your legacy before I go. These are merely things I think you will enjoy and that I no longer have a need for."

"Thank you, Guru."

"I am proud of you as a student and as a woman, best girl. I expect I will live long enough to cuddle your child."

Toni smiled. She certainly hoped so.

11

Quantico, Virginia

The woman was young, maybe twenty-two, twenty-three, and dressed in jeans, a black T-shirt, and running shoes, nothing that unusual about her appearance. She was nobody you'd cross the street to get a better look at, but nobody you'd cross the street the other way to avoid because she was hideous, either. Average-looking.

The woman approached an automated bank teller, put in her card, and stood back. Apparently there was some malfunction. The woman smiled, then, without preamble, drove her fist through the teller's vid screen. Shattered glass flew every which way, and even before it finished falling, the woman was grabbing at a garbage basket on the sidewalk. She picked up the basket and began hammering at the teller, smiling all the while.

Alex Michaels leaned back in the chair and said, "There's something you don't see every day."

Jay Gridley said, "Actually, it happens quite a lot, according to Bureau agents I've talked to. Although the level of violence is usually much less. People tend to spit at the screen or camera, slam it with the edge of their fist once or twice, even kick at it. Sometimes they scratch the glass with their car keys. Nobody's ever seen one quite this . . . ah . . . *active* before."

"What happened after she trashed the videocam recording it?"

Jay said, "According to witnesses, the destruction continued until she *really* got pissed off, whereupon she somehow managed to rip the machine free of its mountings, scattering several thousand dollars in twenty-dollar bills all over the sidewalk. A small riot ensued as concerned citizens sought to . . . ah . . . recover the money for the bank."

The boss laughed. "I bet. How much of it was turned in?"

"About fifteen percent."

"Well, at least there are still a few honest citizens left. So we have another drug berserker who destroyed a bank machine. Why is this more special than the others?"

"The woman is Mary Jane Kent."

"Related to the arms and chemical companies Kents?"

"Yes, sir. She's the secretary of defense's daughter."

"Oh, my."

"Slumming in those clothes," Jay said. "Way I hear it, she could paste her diamonds all over herself and show less skin than in jeans and a T-shirt. With enough left over to make a cape."

"The family has a bit of money."

Jay nodded. *There* was an understatement. The Kent family had become modestly rich during the Spanish Civil War in the '30s, running guns into Spain via Portugal. They made out like bandits in World War II, and had done quite well in assorted revolutions and border wars, since. The men in the family generally took turns managing the family fortune and tended to became ambassadors, cabinet officers, or U.S. senators; the women did charity work, ran foundations, and tended to marry badly. Every now and then, a couple of the scions would switch roles, and the girl would manage the company while the boy ran a foundation.

Certainly, the rich had their problems, too, but Jay couldn't feel too sorry for somebody with half a gazillion dollars tucked away waiting for them to come of age. It was one thing to start poor and earn your way to luxury, another thing to be born with a platinum spoon in your mouth.

He said, "She beat the crap out of four of LAPD's finest before she ran out of steam. A passing doctor happened along during the struggle and sedated her. Hit her with a hypo full of enough Thorazine to knock out a large horse, according to the reports, and it slowed her down, but not completely. She isn't talking about what drug she took or where she got it, but she was apparently on a shopping trip, and she used her credit card until it maxed out. That was why the bank machine wouldn't give her any cash."

"Ah," the boss said. He thought about it for a few seconds, then said, "Just how much does a billionaire's daughter have to spend to max out a credit card?"

"Take a look."

He handed Michaels a ROM tag, and the boss thumbed the pressure spot and looked at the number that appeared on the tag.

"Good Lord!"

"Amen. Enough to buy a yacht and an island to sail it to," Jay said. "I got most of the credit card company's tags. If we can backtrack her and find out how and where she spent her money, the DEA guy you sicced on me says they are willing to put more bodies on the street to check everything out. It's not much, but it's what we have."

Michaels nodded. He looked at the tag again.

"Never fear, boss, Smokin' Jay Gridley is on the case." He gave Michaels a two-finger Cub Scout salute and headed for his office.

Michael's com chirped, and the caller-ID signal told him Toni was trying to reach him. He grabbed the headset. "Hey."

"Hey."

"How's Guru doing?"

"Doing okay," Toni said. "Doctor says she's gonna be all right."

"Good. I know you're relieved to hear that."

"Yes, I am. Anyway, I'll be catching a shuttle back this afternoon. I should be home when you get there."

"Great. You want me to stop and pick up something for supper?"

"Nah, we can just call the Chinese place when you get home, if that's okay."

"If you promise not to get the octopus/squid special again," he said.

She laughed. "I get cravings, what can I say? It's part of the pregnancy."

"Me eating in the other room is going to be part of the pregnancy, too, you keep slurping that slimy stuff down."

She laughed again. "How's work?"

"The usual. Got a lead on that drug thing we talked about. It's not much, but Jay is running with it. Other than that, it's pretty quiet around here. A yawn in the park. Be nice if things picked up a little."

"Careful what you wish for. I miss you."

"I miss you, too. Fly safe."

"I will. See you tonight."

She hung up, and he blew out a relieved sigh. With all the pregnancy stuff, having her *silat* teacher kick off would have been another brick on Toni's load, and she didn't need any more weight right now.

A nice, quiet evening at home with Chinese take-out would be fine by him.

"Sir. You have a call from Richard Sharone on line five."

Michaels shook off his daydream of supper and Toni. "Who is Richard Sharone, and why should I talk to him?"

"He's the president and CEO of Merit-Wells Pharmaceuticals."

Michaels blinked. Why would the head honcho at one of the world's largest drug companies be calling him?

Oh.

Michaels stared at the com's headset. He might not be the sharpest needle in the package, but he wasn't completely dull. What did Net Force have to do with drugs? Nothing, until the DEA asked for their help with this esoteric dope they were trying to find. First it was NSA, now the overlord of a drug company. Man. Somebody wanted this stuff bad.

Probably get a call from the Food and Drug Administration next.

"This is Commander Alex Michaels. How can I help you, Mr. Sharone?"

But he was pretty sure he already knew.

Net Force Shooting Range, Quantico, Virginia

John Howard stood on the line at the firing range, ready to start. He said, "Eight meters, single. Go."

A three-hundred pound crazed biker blinked into existence eight meters down the alley. The biker held a tire iron, and he lifted it and charged right at Howard, no hesitation.

Fast for a fat man, he was, too.

Howard slipped his right hand under his Net Force windbreaker, cleared the jacket, caught the smooth wooden grips of his side arm, and pulled the weapon from the custom-made Fist paddle holster. He brought the Phillips & Rodgers Model 47 Medusa up and shoved it one-handed toward the biker as if punching him.

The biker was less than four meters away now, three, two . . .

Howard pulled the trigger, once, twice . . .

The gun roared and bucked hard.

Two rounds hit the biker five feet away. The running man collapsed and slid to a stop inches from Howard's spit-shined, patent-leather-bright shoes.

Cut that a little close, John.

The biker disappeared, like turning off a lamp.

Which, in essence, was what happened. The hologram was, after all, just a particularly coherent brand of light. But the computer cams that watched it all calculated the flight path of Howard's two .357 slugs as they zipped down range, and having decided they would have struck vital areas on a real human target, gave him the ersatz victory.

Score one for the good guys.

Howard reholstered the handgun and looked at the score screen. He saw the image of the biker there and noted the pulsing red spots where the bullets hit. The one marked with #1 was in the heart, the #2 round was slightly higher and to the right. With the best .357 Magnum or .40 rounds, one-shot knockdowns hovered right about 94 to 96 percent with a solid body hit, as good as a handgun got—and it didn't even have to be to a fatal area. The first shot would have done the trick, and probably a real attacker would be dead or well on the way there by now. Dead wasn't the thing, though, it was the stopping power that was important. You could shoot somebody in the leg with a .22 and it might nick a big blood vessel and eventually kill him. Thing was, *eventually* wouldn't do you much good if the guy kept coming, beat you to a pulp with his tire iron or crowbar, then went home and died in a few days, a few hours, even a few minutes. No good at all. When you shot somebody, you wanted them to fall down *right now;* anything less was bad. They lived or died, that was something to worry about later. You didn't have time to ponder on it in the moment.

Handguns were lousy weapons for instant stops, relatively speaking. A shotgun was better, and a good rifle better still. He smiled as he remembered the old story about a civilian who carried a handgun. A friend asked him, "Why do you have a pistol? Are you expecting trouble?" And the guy answered, "Trouble? No. If I was expecting trouble, I'd be carrying a rifle."

Then again, it was kind of hard to slip a scoped .308 sniper rifle under your Gore-Tex windbreaker. And the first rule of a gunfight was . . .

Come on, John. You gonna shoot or stand here daydreaming?

"Reset," he said.

The screen went blank.

"Ten meters, double. Thirty-second delay. Go."

This time, the scenario computer gave him two attackers. One looked like a pro wrestler holding a long knife, the other an NFL lineman with a baseball bat. They charged.

Howard drew, gave the wrestler two, shifted his hand, and gave the lineman two. The last of the four cartridges in the revolver left the barrel at about the same time the lineman got within bat range.

Both attackers fell.

Howard thumbed the cylinder latch open with his right, pointed the gun at the ceiling, and used his left hand to slap the extractor rod hard enough to punch the empties out of the chambers. The hulls fell to the range floor. He pulled a speed loader with six more cartridges from his left windbreaker pocket. Reloading the P&R was trickier than doing it with his old S&W. There were spring-loaded clips in each chamber of the black-Teflon-coated P&R, to allow for using various calibers—the thing would shoot .380s, .38s, .38 Specials, and 9 mms, as well as .357 Magnums—and you had to keep the extractor partway out to make the speed loader work, and even so, it was slower than the Smith was.

Still, if you couldn't get the job done with six, you probably weren't going to be able to get it done at all.

He managed to get all six of the reloads into the chambers. He dropped the speed loader on the floor, hit the cartridges with the heel of his right hand a couple of times to get them fully seated, closed the cylinder, then brought the gun up into a two-handed grip as the third attacker appeared.

The attacker was a naked woman with a samurai sword.

Well. Somebody was getting creative with their programming. He wondered who Gunny had doing the scenarios. He'd have to ask.

Since he was ready when the woman came to life, he had plenty of time. He lined the front sight up on her nose and fired one round.

One to the head was plenty.

He looked at the score screen. Three for three. Not bad for an old man.

Gunny's voice came over the intercom, easy to hear with the smart earphones that kept loud noises out but let normal sounds in. "General, we have a troop of Explorer

Scouts coming by in a few minutes. Okay if they watch you shoot?"

Before he could respond, Gunny said, "That's 'cause we want to show them how *not* to do it."

"You want to come out here and let me show you how it *is* done, Sergeant?"

Gunny chuckled, and Howard had to smile. That was less than an idle threat. Gunny could shoot the pants off Wyatt Earp, Wild Bill Hickok, and John Wesley Hardin all at the same time, either hand, and you pick it. He was outstanding with anything you could pick up and fire. Came from being a full-time range officer and daily practice. Too bad Gunny didn't want to compete anymore. They could use him in the annual shoot against the other services. He claimed he was too old, and as he was only three or four years past Howard's age. Howard didn't much like hearing that.

Howard himself was lucky if he got to the range three or four times a month. Usually Julio came with him, but with a new baby at home, he was doing father duty, and that cut into his practice time.

Julio was about to learn that a baby changed all kinds of priorities.

Gunny said, "*Thirty* seconds for a reload? Two-plus seconds to take out two goblins you started halfway to Los An-ju-leeez? Lord, we could have gone out for dinner and a movie and gotten back before you finished. I don't guess you're about to threaten the Ragin' Cajun's records anytime soon, sir."

Howard chuckled at that. The Ragin' Cajun was Jerry Miculek, a pro shooter who'd set the modern revolver record a dozen or so years ago, down in Mississippi. Using an eight-shot .38 Special revolver, he put all eight rounds on a target in one second flat. He also fired at four different targets, two rounds each, and hit them all just

0.06 of a second slower. And with a six-shooter, he was
was able to put six hits on one target, *reload,* and put six
more there in just over three seconds. By those standards,
thirty seconds was a couple of eons.

Howard had had his revolver fitted with a set of grips
designed by Miculek, but it hadn't helped that much.

Of course, more than sixty-five years before Miculek,
the legendary Ed McGivern fired five shots from a 1905
Smith & Wesson Hand Ejector Military and Police .38
into a playing card in a mere 0.4 of a second.

No way Howard could ever get close to any of that,
not if he practiced every day of the week and twice on
Sunday. Still, for his purposes, he was good enough for
government work. Tests had shown that a fair-to-middling
shooter took between a second and a second and a half
to draw a handgun from concealment and get a shot off.
If a man with a tire tool or a knife was inside twenty or
so feet and was in a hurry, he'd get to you before you
could shoot him. If he was closer than that, and your gun
was in the holster, best you make some space or be ready
for hand-to-hand to hold him off long enough to draw
your piece.

Of course, if Howard went somewhere expecting trouble, he was sure going to be carrying a rifle. Maybe a
submachine gun, and it would be pointed in the general
direction of any trouble, too.

Then again, he had gotten shot when he hadn't been
expecting it, so this was a skill he needed to hone.

"Don't forget to stop and have your ring reprogrammed
on the way out, sir."

Howard nodded. All Net Force guns were smart technology now. You wore a ring with a code that changed
every month or so. If somebody not wearing a properly
coded ring picked up a Net Force weapon and tried to use
it, it wouldn't fire. Howard still didn't trust it, but so far

there hadn't been any failures of the system, at least not with his people. It was a good idea in theory, but if one of his team ever pointed a gun that didn't go bang! when it was supposed to, there would be hell to pay, and he'd be leading the devil's collection team himself, assuming it wasn't his gun that malfunctioned and got him killed.

"Reset," he said. "Seven meters, one."

Make it a little more challenging, this time . . .

"Go!"

He reached for his gun.

12

The gag came to Bobby as he was driving back from the desert.

It happened because a year or so ago, he had concocted about a quarter kilo of something he called GD, short for Giggle Dust. At the time, he'd had a customer somewhere interested in it, but something must have happened, and he'd stuck it into a drawer in the RV and completely forgotten about it. When he'd been there today talking to Ma and Pa Yeehaw, who actually were married and from Missouri originally, he happened to open that drawer, and son of a bitch lookit, there it was. Eight ounces of the gray green powder, worth an easy four grand if he wanted to bother with it. Free money.

GD was a blend of MMDA—an analog of MDA, or Ecstasy—some psilocybin from a batch of dried baeocystis mushrooms he'd bought from a guy in British Columbia, and a little dexadrine. Everybody didn't react to it the same way, of course, but in most people, it tended to make for a really happy trip, laughing, giggling, speeding their asses off, beaming at everybody, and having a fun time in general. Problem was, the mix was iffy, and it was hard to get the recipe exact. This batch worked pretty good—he'd let Tad try a hit way back when—but the next mix might not. The mushrooms were the key, and they varied all over the place. Only real side effect was it tended to make you thirsty but not able to pee, so when it wore off, you'd be spending a lot of time in the john.

The gag would take all the GD he had, but what the hell, if you couldn't have fun, why bother? He had precursor for another batch of the Hammer, he already had orders for fifteen grand or so lined up, and probably another five or eight thousand would be in by the time he got ready to mix. Money wasn't a problem. He had money to burn.

The more he thought about it, the better he liked it. So he might be late for his dinner with the Zee-ster, no big deal. Zee was gonna be out of it anyhow, if he'd swung the Hammer last night. He wasn't in as bad shape as Tad, Zee was a jock, but even with chemical assistance, he was gonna be dragging ass today. And he was usually late, even when he was straight.

Drayne grinned. Yeah. He was gonna do it. He could cut over to the 405, get off at Westwood, and it would be right there, just up Wilshire, no problem. It was still early enough he could beat most of the traffic. Thirty, forty minutes, he'd be pulling up next to the Federal Building. He been there enough times when his old man had still been protecting the republic.

The building was the home of the Los Angeles office of the Federal Bureau of Investigation.

Oh, yeah, this was gonna be a hoot, all right.

Malibu

Still hardly able to move, Tad managed to sit up on the couch to stare at Bobby. There weren't many days when he thought Bobby was crazier than he was. This was one of them. He said, "You're shittin' me."

"Nope."

"You blew four thousand dollars' worth of Giggle Dust to *stone* fuckin' FBI HQ in L.A.?"

"Yep."

"You're friggin' nuts, Bobby."

"I'd have spent that much more to have been a fly on the wall. Maybe we can get one of the security recordings of it someday. See all those uptight fuckheads laughing and holding hands and being in tune with the universe and all."

"Jeez, Bobby, you have to let that go. They are just doing their jobs, you know? That's why they hire 'em."

"You don't know what you're talking about, Tad."

"Yeah, yeah. Okay. How'd you pull it off?"

"Easy. They got great security, but I went to fill out an application for a job on the floor above them. Got out to the roof, up to the air conditioners, found the right vents, moved a couple of filters, voilà! the air is full of magic."

"Four grand. For a practical joke."

"Tad, Tad, Tad. Let me tell you a story."

"Aw, geez, not another of your shaggy dog stories!"

"Shut up, Tad. Listen and learn:

"So there's this couple in Vegas, see, and after a long day, they go upstairs and go to bed. Wife drops off to sleep, but the husband can't, so he gets up, gets dressed, and goes down to the casino with ten bucks. He goes to the craps table, puts it down, throws a natural, and he's a winner!

"So he lets it ride, and wins again. And again. And yet again!

"This is incredible stuff. He's throwing naturals, he's making points the hard way, he can't lose.

"Next thing you know, the guy has parlayed his bets up to almost a million bucks. And he's feeling unbeatable, so he lets it ride one more time. If he wins, he's gonna leave rich.

"He throws snake eyes and loses it all.

"He goes back to his room. As he's getting into bed, he wife wakes up. 'Where you been?' she asks.

" 'I went down to play a little craps,' he says.

" 'How'd you do?'

"Guy slips under the covers, shrugs, says, 'I lost ten bucks.' "

The conversation sat still for a moment. Tad said, "Okay, funny. And, uh, what exactly is the point?"

"Point is, it's all gravy, Tad. This morning, I didn't know the GD existed, so when I came across it, it was like something for nothing. I used it up, I had a big laugh, it didn't cost me anything. Hell, I didn't even lose ten bucks. I came home with as much in my pocket as when I left this morning. Except what I paid for the tofu burger for lunch."

"You go a long way to make a point, man. And I don't know how you can eat that tofu shit."

"Yeah, well, getting there is half the fun, isn't it?"

Tad had to nod. "Yeah. I guess you're right. But you're still a crazy motherfucker."

"So who's arguing with that?"

"Jesus." A beat, then, "So how is the Zee-ster?"

"Probably as burned out as you are. He didn't show. How you holding up?"

"I've been worse."

"Want to eat something?"

"Nah, not yet. Maybe in a day or two. I'll just pop a few pills."

"Keep it up, Tad, pretty soon nothing short of tanna leaves is gonna bring you back."

"Karis, the mummy, with Boris Karloff," Tad said. Like half the people in L.A., Tad was an old-movie buff. He especially loved those old black-and-white Universal monster pictures.

"Well, at least part of your brain still works. I'm gonna get some champagne. You want some?"

"And rot my liver? Shee-it."

Bobby laughed and said, "I'm gonna miss you, Tad."

Tad nodded. "I know. But that was always in the cards, man. Always in the cards."

13

Hemphill, Texas

Jay Gridley hiked down a country road, not far from the Toledo Bend Reservoir on the Sabine River, just across the state line from Louisiana, a place he had once visited as a child. Long-leaf pine and red dirt and lazily buzzing flies completed the summer scene. When he'd actually been here in real time, he'd been eight or so, walking with a couple of his cousins, Richie and Farah. Richie was his age, Farah was four. They had seen a long reddish snake wiggling on the road, and all excited, he and Richie had run back to tell their parents. Jay hadn't been able to understand why his mom and Aunt Sally had jumped up in such a panic. *"Where is Farah!"*

"Hey, don't worry, we left her to watch the snake, she won't let it get away."

He smiled at the memory.

Just ahead, a white-haired old man in a dirty T-shirt and overalls—no shoes—sat in the shade of a tall pine tree and whittled on a long stick with a Barlow jackknife. Jay liked to get the small details right in his scenario work.

"Howdy," Jay said.

"Howdy, yo'self," the whittler said. A long wood shaving curled up from the edge of the knife blade.

In RW, Jay was querying a server for information that would be downloaded into his computer spool; but in VR, it was much more interesting.

"What's happenin'?" Jay asked.

"Not much," the whittler allowed. "This and that. You heard about them FBI guys got poisoned?"

"Stoned," Jay said, "not poisoned." He smiled. Yep, that had been a funny one. Something to wave at the Bureau boys when he ran into them in the cafeteria. The regular feebs were always ragging on Net Force about one thing or another, so any ammunition Jay could gather to pop off at them in return was good, especially since the L.A. incident hadn't hurt anybody, only embarrassed 'em.

"Anybody come through selling snake oil lately?"

In this case, "snake oil" was a representation of the mysterious purple cap the DEA was all hot to run down. And not just them, so it seemed.

Along his way, Jay had stopped to chat with several local characters, and so far, he hadn't turned up anything. But this time, it was different.

"Well, yes, sir, there was this fellow come through a little while ago had some of that stuff, I do believe."

Jay's laid-back Zen attitude vanished. "What? When? Which way did he go?"

Whittler spat a stream of something dark and icky and pointed with the knife. "He headed on up the road, over toward Hemphill, I reckon."

Jesus! Could it be this easy?

"Was he walking?"

"In a horse-drawn wagon."

Speed, he needed to get moving if he was going to track and run down the dope dealer. He looked around. He could drop out of this scenario and switch to another, or do it in RT with voxax or a keyboard . . . No, wait, he had a toggle he could use, a backup. He did it, and suddenly there was a moped leaning against a tree, just there.

"Mind if I borrow the bike?"

"He'p yo'self."

Jay ran to the moped, essentially a heavy bicycle with a motor that you started by pedaling the bike. It wasn't a Harley, but it was faster than a horse-drawn wagon, and a lot better on a gravel road than a hog would be anyhow, at least the way he rode, even in VR.

He hopped on the moped and started pedaling.

This contemplative Buddhist stuff was all well and good, but when things started to break, you needed to be able to *move!*

The little two-cycle motor belched, emitted a puff of white smoke via the tailpipe, and started up.

The boss would be really happy if Jay could wrap this up.

Washington, D.C.

Michaels was moving the boxes Guru had sent home with Toni when he came across a small, highly polished wooden one that gleamed, even under the dust. "Very nice," he said, holding it up.

Toni glanced over from where she was piling shoes. She already had a molehill of them in the hall, the mound threatening to become a small mountain completely blocking the door to the bedroom. "Oh, I forgot all about those."

Toni came over to where Michaels stood and took the

box from him, flipped the brass catch up, and opened the lid, then turned it to show him.

"Wow," he said.

She removed a pair of small knives from velvet-lined recesses in the box, then pulled out a shelf to reveal a hidden space under it. There was a thick leather sheath in the bottom section. It looked like somebody had chopped a third or so off the end of a banana and flattened the sides. She took the sheath out and inserted the two curved blades into it so that they rode side by side, separated only by a center strip of leather. They were all metal, the knives, and the pommel end of each consisted of a thick circle with a big hole in the middle. With a quick move, Toni pulled both blades, dropped the sheath onto the carpet, and brought her hands together. When she pulled her hands apart, each one wore a knife, with short and nasty-looking curved blades extending point forward, maybe two inches from the little finger sides of her palms. Her forefingers went through the rings on the end.

"These are a variation on *kerambits*," she said. "Sometimes called *lawi ayam*. Indonesian close-quarters knives."

She turned her hand over, palms up, to show him.

He took a closer look. The things were short, maybe five or six inches long, and most of that was the flat handle with the hole in it. The cutting hooks themselves looked like little talons. The steel had an intricate pattern of lines and whorls in it.

"The traditional ones are usually longer and sharp on both edges. Guru had these made for her by a master knife smith and martial artist in Keenesburg, Colorado, a guy named Steve Rollert. I guess it must be ten, twelve years ago, now. They are forged Damascus, folded and hammered to make hundreds or thousands of layers in the steel. Edge is heat-treated differently than the body, so it's hard and will stay sharp, while the body has a little more flex to it.

"See, you put your forefinger through the hole and grip it so. You can also turn it around and use your little finger, with the blade coming out on the thumb side, like this."

She demonstrated the move, then moved it back to the first grip.

"And perfectly legal to carry around, I suppose?"

She grinned. "Actually, you can in some states if you wear them on your belt, out in the open. Not most places if you conceal them."

"Kind of like brass knuckles," he said. "Or maybe knuckle, singular."

"But much better," she said. "The blades are extremely sharp, and you can hit with the ring end without hurting your finger."

"Great."

She missed the sarcasm, or more likely, ignored it. "Aren't they?" She did a little series of moves, whipping the two knives back and forth.

A slight error and there was gonna be blood everywhere. His or hers. He took half a step back.

"They aren't very long," he said, and even as he spoke, he was glad they weren't longer.

" 'Cause they are slashers rather than stabbers. All the major peripheral arteries are fairly close to the skin's surface. Carotids, antecubitals, femorals, popliteals. These will reach all of those. Cut a big artery, and you bleed out pretty quick if you don't do something. Kill you quicker than not breathing will, and blood is lot harder to replace than air."

"How nice."

"I remember this guy Rollert has a sense of humor, too. These are custom work, but he makes a tool-steel version of these coated with black Teflon. He calls them box cutters, and that's how he markets them. 'Why, what's the problem, Officer? This is a box cutter, see, it says so right there on the handle.' I've got a set of those tucked away somewhere. Of course, those cost about a twentieth of what these did."

She waved the knives again, getting into it. It was spooky to watch those things blur as she whipped them around.

"What'd the cheap ones cost?"

"About fifty bucks each."

"You mean these two little pieces of steel cost a thousand dollars?!"

"Quality doesn't come cheap."

Michaels shook his head. His darling bride, carrying his unborn son, was a mistress of death and destruction. She talked about such toys the way other women talked about getting their hair done.

"You can do your *djurus* holding one of these in each hand, and with only a slight adjustment, do them the same."

"Yeah, and slice off my nose if I make a mistake."

"Better your nose than some . . . other extremity." She grinned. "Don't worry. By the time you know all eighteen *djurus,* you'll be able to use these or a longer knife or a stick, no problem. Might nick yourself if you get sloppy, but as long as you keep proper form, you won't. *Silat* is weapons-based, remember. Only use your hands if nothing better is available."

She waved the little knives back and forth, crossing and uncrossing her hands in patterns that looked damned dangerous to him.

But she was excited, and as upbeat as he'd seen her lately, and he liked seeing that.

"These were the first knives Guru showed me how to use. Traditionally, they were backup. Women carried them a lot. You could wind one into your hair or tuck it into a sarong. These have a leather sheath, but the old-style ones made in Java usually have wooden scabbards. Supposedly, there were guys in the old country who could grip them between their toes and turn your legs and groin into hamburger while you were still checking their hands for a weapon."

"Lovely."

She kept twirling and slicing the air as she talked. "They make them longer, but the short ones are best for *djurus*. Even though *djurus* are practice and knives are for application, you can do the moves with steel hands. Watch."

She stopped moving, and then did *djuru* three. Her hands didn't move any slower than they did when she did the form unarmed, at least not that he could tell. "See? You block or punch like usual, only these give the moves more of a sting."

" 'A sting,' right. I'd be careful on *djuru* two," he said. "Way your boobs are getting big, you come across your chest on that inside block, you'll shear off a nipple."

She laughed, then put the knives back into their little velvet nests. "Thanks. I feel better. Now I can go back and finish sorting my shoes."

She handed him the box. "Put these somewhere we won't forget them, and I'll show you how to play with them when we get a chance."

She went back to her chore, and he looked at the box. Well. He knew what she did for fun when he married her. She had saved his life with the art once, and he had learned enough to use it himself, a little. He had been training seriously for almost a year, and he seldom missed a day of practice, thanks to Toni's proximity. After nearly being brained once by an assassin using a cane and pretending to be a little old lady, Michaels could hardly bitch about the down-and-dirty side of fighting. *Pentjak silat* was about as dirty as it came, and when somebody was trying to bash your head in, all bets were off. When you reached into your bag of tricks, *this* was the stuff you wanted to come up with. A guy charging at you with mayhem in mind might think twice if he saw you whirling these nasty little claws around with a demented grin while you did it. He sure as hell would.

Rules? In a knife fight? No rules!

He smiled at the wooden box and went to put it on a shelf in the living room. It would make a great conversation piece at a dinner party. Or a conversation stopper, depending on what you wanted to do.

It would be very interesting to see what the two of them decided to teach their son when he got old enough to wonder about all those funny dances Mama and Daddy did. For certain, they would show him how to protect himself. Michaels's father had taught him how to do a little boxing when he'd been about six or seven, and while he'd never been very good at it, at least he had developed a sense of self-confidence in his ability to protect himself.

Once he'd started learning *silat,* he realized how much he didn't know, but since he hadn't spent a lot of time fighting, it had worked out okay anyhow.

Funny to think about, teaching your son how to fight, when he wasn't even born yet. Next thing you knew, he'd be buying him baseball gloves and electric trains.

14

Michaels had left the director's office, feeling a nagging sense of unease. Director Allison had ostensibly called him in for a progress report, but the real reason was, he was sure, that she had been given the word to light a fire under his ass. His backside certainly felt warm enough when she was done talking. She wasn't exactly dumping on him for what the agency had or had not done so far, but she must have used the term "interagency cooperation" ten times during their conversation. As much as he hated politics, Michaels knew what *that* meant.

Pee flowed downhill, and the director's drain was right above his head . . .

Unfortunately, business was slow, and because it was, this was rapidly becoming *the* case to solve, and quickly. If there had been some major e-terrorism going, some big-time computer frauds, or even more bored hackers, he could beg off, point to those, and wash his hands of this crap fobbed off on them. But his people were good, they were on top of the day-to-day stuff. Even though it was the DEA's problem, had almost nothing to do with computers, and Net Force was just helping out, if they didn't do something pretty quick, it could get ugly.

A couple more millionaires going bonzo, and the powers that be would be looking for a scapegoat to roast, and while it should be the DEA, it could well turn out to be a major barbecue, with Net Force on the spit, too.

As he got back into the hinterlands and his own office at Net Force HQ, he saw Jay Gridley standing in the door, grinning.

"Tell me you have good news, Jay."

"Oh, yeah. I think I got a solid lead on our dope dealer."

"Really?"

"Yes, sir, boss."

"How?"

"The rich man's daughter. I backtracked her spending spree. Somebody remembered that she used a public computer in one of the shops for some kind of on-line transaction. I sieved the computers she might have operated, found all the e-mail for the time she would have been in the shop, and did some cross-references and keyword hits, in case she used a phony name . . . which, by the way, she did."

"Go on, impress me."

"I had the searchbots looking for a long list of pointers, about forty keys, including Thor, Thor's Hammer, and all like that. I got a hit on one and followed it up."

"And this keyword was . . . ?"

"Purple."

"Purple?"

"As in the color of the caps. Here's the e-mail I ran down."

He handed Michaels a hardcopy print. It said, "Yo, Friday Girl—I'll have that purple thingee for you when you come by."

It was signed, "Wednesday."

"No offense, Jay, but this is a reach. A 'purple thingee'? It could be some kind of plush kid's toy for all we know. And days of the week as code names? Why would that be our rich woman and her dealer?"

Jay grinned. "That's the key, boss. *Friday* was named for the Norse goddess Frigga. *Wednesday* comes from *Woden*, which, as I'm sure you must know, is the way the Norse in the southern countries spelled *Odin.*"

"Fascinating. So?"

"Frigga and Odin were Thor's mom and pop."

Michaels thought about that for a few seconds. "Ah. That would seem to be a bit of a coincidence, wouldn't it."

"Yeah, I'd say so. Doesn't mean it's the chemist himself, but I'd bet my next month's pay against a week-old, road-killed possum this 'Wednesday' guy has something to do with this drug."

"Good work, Jay."

"I didn't spook the guy, stayed well back, but I can run him down to an addy."

"Better still."

"Well, the thing is, this is good *and* bad. If I found it, the NSA people will find it, too, if they haven't already."

"How do you figure?"

"Well, their mission is to monitor communications outside the U.S. for possible terrorist activity, assorted plots, and things it would be good for us to know in general. So they have a whole list of words which, if they come up in a telephone conversation, a com-radio, telegraph signal, or e-mail, stuff like that, it kicks in a recorder. The message is taped and downloaded into one of a shitload of mainframes NSA operates, and rescanned, then routed to a computer program that reads the message and assigns it a priority code on a scale of one to ten. Anything above five gets sent to a human, and the higher a number, the faster it gets there. So if you put the words *Suicide mission* and *bomb* into your e-mail heading in any one of a hundred major or twenty minor languages, and NSA happens across it, somebody checks it. Most of the time it's nothing, guys screwing around or whatever, but sometimes it pans out. A message that says something like 'Shoot and kill the president and blow up Washington D.C.' had better be a line from a TV show or an upcoming techno-thriller novel."

"Nobody could be that stupid."

"Oh, yeah they can. Dumb crooks are legion."

Michaels said, "All right. I know this, in general, about NSA. So?"

"So you think NSA confines its eyes and ears to *outside* our borders? Yeah, home court's supposed to be FBI territory for such things, but everybody in the biz knows which way that wind blows. NSA has the tools, and how would anybody know they were doing it if they didn't tell us? Sheeit. If they are as hot to run down these dopers as the DEA, they will have assigned anything having to do with Thor a high priority. If we want to beat 'em to this Wednesday, we better get somebody on the street PDQ. The dealer might get taken, and that'd be good, but it's better for us if we get some credit, right?"

"Right," Michaels said. "Let me step into my office and make a call. Thanks, Jay."

"Info is in your in-file under the name 'Rich Girl.' Remember me when you give out the bonuses."

Malibu, California

When Tad woke up again, he looked at his watch. Not so much for the time as for the date. Sometimes after a Hammer trip, he would be more or less unconscious for three or four days.

He had been awake a couple times before, to go pee and get some water and pain pills, and he thought he remembered Bobby telling him a story about stoning FBI HQ in L.A. all to hell and gone. Maybe that had been a dream. Make more sense if it was.

Not too bad, if the watch was right, only a couple days since he'd crashed. If he remembered the day he'd done it right.

And if it hadn't been a week and some.

He hurt all over. It was like he'd been dropped off a tall building and then bounced like a superball for a couple of blocks, slamming a different part of his body against the concrete each time. The slightest movement stabbed him with hot needles, cut at him with cold, dull razors. He managed to roll to a sitting position, then up to his feet. He swayed there for a moment, fought for balance, then headed for the shower. Moving slowly. After he got clean, he'd feel a little better, though a little better wasn't going to be much compared to how crappy he felt. Still, that was the price you paid. You could bitch after the first time, but after that, you had no excuses; you *knew* what it was gonna feel like. You couldn't blame anybody but yourself.

He managed to achieve the bathroom without falling, though he had to lean against the wall a couple of times along the way. He stripped, then got into the shower and cranked the water up full blast from all the nozzles. Had to; water coming from only one direction would probably knock him down.

Halfway to using all the hot water in the house—and that was saying something—Bobby stuck his head into the steamed-up bathroom and yelled: "Still alive? Amazing."

"Fuck you," Tad yelled reflexively.

"You okay enough to work?"

"I'm up, aren't I?" He shut off the water and stepped out, grabbed one of the beach towels, and started drying off.

Bobby watched him, shaking his head. "You look like hammered dog shit."

"Why, thank you. So what?"

"Business is picking up. I've got a dozen orders I need to send out today, eight more tomorrow, and four more the day after that."

"Got me a cap for the first run?"

"Jesus, Tad, you do want to die, don't you?"

Tad didn't answer but finished toweling off. He looked at himself in the foggy mirror. Skinny as hell, yes, but in the blurry, soft-focus mirror reflections, he didn't really look that bad.

Bobby blew out a theatrical sigh. "Yeah, I got one for you."

Tad nodded, managed a grin. He'd never gone riding with Thor twice in a week before, it always took a long time to recover completely, but with enough chemical assistance, he could get past the aches and injuries he collected while tripping. They were still *there,* of course, but he didn't feel them. Well, not as much. Thing was, he'd built up a pretty good tolerance to Demerol and morphine over the years. He could take a handful of 50 mg tabs and walk around like it was nothing, a dose that would put much bigger guys on the floor in a dreamy trance for six or eight hours. Morphine was a better painkiller than Demerol, heroin better still, but of course, those had their own problems—he wasn't a big fan of needles or gas-powered skin-poppers that blasted the drug into you. Getting addicted wasn't a problem he worried about, and he used morphine or smack sometimes, when it got really bad, but only as a painkiller, not for the high. Some people liked downers, which was what the opiates were. Tad liked uppers. Being able to *move,* to do things. The months he'd spent in a bed coughing up bloody sputum when he had active TB never left him. He didn't plan to die in bed. Live fast, die young, and if the corpse was ugly or good-looking, what did that matter? You weren't gonna be around to hear praise or revulsion, were you?

Time was running out. Take the trip now, or miss it. You get to be dead a long time, right?

Even with the Demerol tabs he'd taken last time he was up, and the shower, he felt like Bobby said he looked: like shit. So a little of the Mexican white was called for, to dull the edges. Some muscle relaxants, some steroids for the swelling and inflammation, and a little speed to balance things, he'd be able to get around. And once he picked up the Hammer again? Well, then it would all go away.

Superman don't need no pain pills.

"I'm on it," Tad said. "Give me ten minutes."

Bobby nodded. "I'm going to start final mix now."

Tad waved him off. His stash was in his car, parked at the sandwich place. He'd have to go get it, come back, and hope he could find a vein he could hit. What a bitch.

Washington, D.C.

Toni spent an hour playing with the scrimshaw, then had to quit. Her ankles were swelling, her right thumb and forefinger had gone numb from gripping the pin vise, and she was going blind looking through the magnifying lamp's lens. That stereoscopic microscope would sure come in handy.

Yeah. So would some artistic talent and a lot more patience. Putting in a thousand tiny dots, each the size of a flea's eye, was extremely exacting work. A couple of times, she had lost her concentration and put a dot outside the lines. Those would have to be sanded out and polished, and that was tricky, she'd already found out.

Maybe this wasn't such a good idea, taking up something this precise. Maybe she was just wasting her time and a lot of effort.

She went to the bathroom, washed her hands and face in cold water, and went into the living room. She sat on the couch. She could do her *djuru* hand work sitting down, most of it. The footwork was getting harder and harder to add in, and while Guru's advice had been not to worry about it, it would all come back after the baby was born, she did worry about it. It had never occurred to her it would be like this.

The Indonesian martial art had been the core of who she was since she'd been thirteen. She hadn't gotten into team sports, school clubs, or other extracurricular activities as a young woman in high school and college, not to speak of. No, she had dedicated herself to learning how to move in balance, to being able to deliver a focused attack against an aggressor, no matter if he was bigger, stronger, faster, or even well-trained. Yes, she had school, in which she did well, and yes, she had friends and lovers and a job, but in her own mind, she was a warrior.

A warrior with, she had to admit, some control issues.

Now a big, fat, pale, pregnant warrior with control issues, hey?

Shut up!

Putting scratches and itty-bitty dots on fake ivory instead of kicking ass. Some warrior.

Tears rose and threatened to spill, but Toni angrily wiped her eyes. No. She wouldn't give in to this emotional turmoil. Hormones, that was all it was, goddamned hormones! She'd learned how to control PMS, and she never let her periods keep her from work or working out. She could beat this, too! It was a matter of will!

Sure, sure, it is, as long as you watch out for peg-legged guys with eye patches carrying harpoons, whale-girl. Thar she blows!

She was more angry than she was anything, but now the tears did flow, and she couldn't stop them.

The com chirped. She stared at it. It kept on cheeping. Finally, she picked it up.

"Hello," she said.

"Hi, babe, it's me. How are you doing?"

Alex. Oh, boy. Was *that* the wrong thing for him to say.

"I hate my life," she said.

He didn't say anything, but he didn't have to say anything. She had more. Much more.

15

"You want me to go along on a *drug* raid?" John Howard said.

Michaels nodded. "Yes. We have a vested interest here, even though it is officially a DEA matter. I just got off the com with Brett Lee. They are willing to allow a Net Force liaison to tag along . . . if he's field-qualified. In the interests of interagency cooperation, of course."

"Let me see if I can translate that. We need credit for this, right?"

"Damn straight. This is going to be a high-profile bust. There is a lot of interest in catching these folks, from way up the food chain. When the media figures out what this is connected to, we don't want to be left out in the cold. You standing there conspicuously in your Net Force blues on the six o'clock news will make sure nobody accidentally 'forgets' to mention that it was us who located this evildoer and gave his location to the DEA."

Howard smiled. "You're getting a lot better at this political in-fighting, Commander."

"I'd say thank you, but I'm not sure I consider that a compliment."

Howard shrugged. "Goes with the job. Same with any organization. Once you get above the rank of major in the army, most of what you do requires one eye on the chain of command, the other eye on the internal and external politics affecting your unit. Makes it hard to see what you actually want to accomplish. You don't watch out for us, you sure can't expect anybody else to do it. Certainly not the DEA or NSA."

"I wouldn't order you to do it. Strictly voluntary, General."

"Well, sir, I'd be happy to go along and help our fellow crime fighters take down this dope peddler. It's been a little slow around here anyway."

"Knock on wood," Michaels said, rapping his desktop. "In case there are any bored angels watching who want to give us something to worry about."

"Amen."

After Howard left, Michaels's secretary told him he had a call.

"From?"

"Gretta Henkel."

"Why do I recognize that name?"

"She's the CEO and largest shareholder of Henkel Pharmaceuticals, which is headquartered in Mannheim, Germany."

Michaels rolled his eyes. Jesus, word was definitely out about this drug thing. He reached for the phone.

The conversation didn't take long, and when it was done, Michaels leaned back in his chair and shook his head. Ms. Henkel, of Henkel Pharmaceuticals, the largest European drug manufacturing company and the fourth largest in the world, had offered him a job.

Ostensibly, Ms. Henkel was looking for somebody to run their computer security department, and who better than the man who ran the computer security service for the United States government? She had, she had said, heard great things about him. Would he be interested in speaking with her personally about this? She could have one of the corporate jets pick him up and fly him to Mannheim for a chat. She mentioned a starting salary that translated to roughly four times what he was making as a government employee, plus stock options and a medical and retirement package that would, in twenty years, make him a fairly wealthy man. He could also bring two or three of his best people with him if he elected to accept the job, of course, and with hefty increases in their salaries, too.

It was tempting to think her offer was exactly what she said. A recognition of his ability to manage a complex technical operation. An offer tendered on merit. A deserved and great opportunity.

Michaels smiled at that. He had never considered himself the brightest light on the string, but neither had he thought he was the dimmest.

What this was about, of course, was this damned purple capsule everybody wanted so badly. Probably Ms. Henkel wanted it to move her company from fourth largest to third or maybe even first place. Or maybe she wanted it so the Germans could gear up for another war with supersoldiers. It didn't really matter. But she was assuming that if she paved a road with platinum for him to get there, Michaels would bring the secret of the stuff with him. It would be interesting to see if the job offer became real if he didn't happen to have that information at hand or didn't want to give it up. Or even how long his new job would last if he did.

He smiled again as he thought about telling Toni: "Hi,

honey, I'm home! Guess what. We're moving to Germany!"

Deutschland, Deutschland, über alles . . .

He chuckled at that thought.

He'd declined the offer with appropriate regrets and thanked Ms. Henkel politely.

Whatever the hell was in that mysterious capsule must be very interesting indeed.

Beverly Hills, California

He could have requisitioned a Net Force jet, but having risen on merit as a colonel in the regular army before taking command of the Net Force military arm, John Howard had a few friends still active in other services. An old Air Force buddy who had likewise risen high in the ranks got him second seat on a fighter going across the country. The training flight had to refuel midair, of course, but since it didn't land, Howard was more than two hours ahead of Mr. Brett Lee's commercial flight and waiting at the airport for him when he got off the plane. A small victory but worth the effort for the look on the face of a man who had left Washington, D.C., an hour before Howard had and well knew it.

Lee filled him in on details as they drove toward Beverly Hills.

"The suspect's name is George Harris Zeigler, age thirty-one." He looked at Howard as if expecting some response, but the name didn't mean anything to him, and Howard said so.

"He's a fairly well-known actor," Lee said. "A pretty boy who plays action heroes, has the teenage girls all hot for him. They call him the Zee-ster."

"There you go," Howard said. "I'm neither teenage nor female. And not much of a movie fan."

"In any event, we have the warrants, and our surveillance teams have him at home. He lives in a big, gated estate in Beverly Hills."

"Of course he does."

"We're going in hot and fast. We need to do this quick enough to get samples of the drug. He has bodyguards and a commercial security system. It is unlikely he is the chemist. He flunked out of high school before becoming an actor, but we think he either sells or gives the stuff to his friends, especially his female friends. He doesn't need the money; he gets fifteen or twenty million dollars each for the movies he stars in. And you've never heard of him?"

"I guess I need to get out more," Howard allowed.

Lee glared but then forced a smile. It was his operation, and he would be giving Howard his assignment. He'd have the last word. "You will be assisting the agents covering the *garage*," he said. "In case Mr. Zeigler decides to try to escape. It's a twelve-car garage, but he only has ten in it at the moment. The usual toys, including a Ferrari, a Land Cruiser, a Ford Cobra, a Dodge Viper, and a couple of antique Rolls-Royces."

"Must be nice. How many agents do you have going into the house?"

"Sixteen."

"Ah. Well, if he gets past you, we'll do our best to try to stop him."

Lee didn't speak to that, and Howard leaned back in the seat, looking out the window. *Smoggy out here today. Big surprise.*

When they got to the staging area, a local park, Howard pulled his gear out of his tactical duffel bag. He had his side arm, the Medusa, his blue coveralls, and the spidersilk vest with "Net Force" stenciled in big phosphorescent yellow letters across the back. He strapped on his revolver, slipped into the coveralls, and tabbed the vest into place. It was class-one armor with full side panels and a crotch drape. The tightweave silk and overlapping ceramic plates would stop any handgun round and most rifle bullets, assuming the shooter went for the body and not the head or legs. Somehow, he didn't think an actor who let himself be called the Zee-ster would be doing much blasting. Rich folks generally fought with lawyers, not firearms. And his chances of getting past a whole slew of DEA agents armed with subguns were slim and snowball.

Howard had wanted to bring his old Thompson, the ancient .45 submachine gun his grandfather had gotten when he was an unofficial deputy in the preintegration days, but he thought that might be a bit ostentatious in front of the cameras. And there were sure to be news copters flitting around pretty quick in this kind of operation. Dead-eye John Howard and his Chicago typewriter might not provide the image Net Force wanted.

During the briefing, Howard memorized the maps, met the two agents who'd be watching the garage with him— their names were Brown and Peterson, a tall woman and a short man, respectively. Lee, despite his quick fuse, gave a pretty good sitrep and assignment layout. Everybody synchronized their watches and slipped into tactical radio headphones set to a narrow-band opchan. Whatever the DEA's political agendas, they had done enough drug busts to know how to enter a secured residence efficiently.

They'd borrowed a tactical truck from the local police force, and it went through the heavy steel gate as if it were paper. The cars followed the truck in, five vehicles, and made for their assigned locations. Howard wasn't sure, but it seemed to him there were more than sixteen agents leaping from cars and hurrying toward the house.

Brown, Peterson, and Howard alighted and moved to the garage. Brown had an electronic master key she triggered, and the signal worked; the garage doors rolled up, all six of them.

Peterson moved to stand behind the door from the garage into the house, his handgun pointed up by his ear.

Brown crouched behind the car closest to the door, a seventies Charger, a muscle car lovingly painted in maybe twenty hand-rubbed coats of metalflake candy-apple red. *Be a shame to see that paint chipped by a bullet,* Howard thought.

He looked around. Which car would he take if he was in a real hurry? Probably the Cobra. Nah, better would be the Viper, which was essentially a rocket with wheels. They'd have to use roadblocks; nobody would be catching that sucker from behind.

He walked over to the Viper and looked into the little convertible. *Had to be a real wood dash and steering wheel. Hello? What's this?*

Lying in plain view on the passenger seat was one of those zippered plastic bags, like for sandwiches.

Inside the bag were four big purple capsules.

Howard grinned. Son of a bitch!

Brown and Peterson were intent on the door. Orders from Lee rattled over the operations channel on the headset. They had crashed the front door, after some effort, and were entering the residence.

Howard reached down, picked up the bag, opened it, and shook one of the capsules into his palm. He looked at the two DEA agents. He could have been invisible as far as they were concerned.

He slipped the cap into his coverall pocket, zipped the bag closed, and dropped it back onto the car seat.

The sounds of fully automatic weapon fire and Lee

screaming over the headset came simultaneously: "Return fire, return fire!"

Well. Looked like the bodyguards were earning their money.

More full-autos came on-line. The DEA assault team carried MP-5s, and the distinctive sound of those chattered, joining the other guns. All pistol-caliber stuff, Howard thought, nothing loud enough to be rifle. The suspect's bodyguards must have MAC-10s, Uzis, something like that. Didn't sound like H&Ks.

". . . all available agents, they're heading for the kitchen!"

The kitchen, Howard recalled from the maps, was just up a short hall from the garage.

Brown and Peterson took this as a sign they should go in. Peterson jerked the door open, Brown stepped in, pistol leading. They didn't look for Howard but vanished into the house.

Howard, whose side arm was still in the holster, considered his options. If sixteen DEA agents couldn't take out a pretty-boy movie star and his bodyguards, he wasn't going to be able to add much firepower. He'd stay right here, just like he'd been assigned.

More shots echoed from the house. Somebody screamed, two or three different voices.

"Shit!"

"Fuck!"

"Ow, ow, I'm shot!"

Ten seconds later, a man emerged from the house into the garage. In one arm gathered to his chest, he held a young woman in a maid's uniform. From her face, the girl was in mortal terror, and rightly so, since in his other hand, the guy held a short knife pressed against her neck. He was a handsome young man.

This would be the Zee-ster, Howard guessed.

He pulled his revolver, brought his other hand up, clasped the weapon in a two-handed grip, and pointed it at the knife man.

"Hold it right there, Zeigler," he said.

The man froze.

Howard forced his hands to relax a hair. Holding the revolver tightly was necessary for the shot, but clenching the thing in a death grip for any length of time past a second or two would cramp his hands pretty quickly. And he might be here a while, you never could tell.

Zeigler, with the knife held at the hostage's throat, tried to make himself smaller, but there was no way a five-foot-tall, hundred-pound woman was going to completely shield a six-foot-tall, two-hundred-pound man. Howard had all kinds of targets, including the only one that meant instant incapacitation, a head shot.

"Put the gun down! Put it down, or I'll kill her!"

He had the shot. Sights square, lined up on the man's left eye. At fifteen, maybe sixteen feet, he wasn't going to miss. Unless the guy jerked at the last second and put the hostage where his head had been. Not much risk to the woman, but some. And he'd have to kill the movie star, a head shot would do that, right into the brain.

Well, maybe not on a movie star . . .

"Listen," Howard said, "let's discuss this."

"No fucking *discussion!* Put the gun down, or I'll cut her throat!"

The maid whimpered.

"You don't want to do that. You kill her, you're standing there unprotected with a knife in your hand. Think about that. She's all that's keeping *you* alive. She dies, you die, simple as that."

"You can't do that. Do you know who I am?"

"I'm not a cop, son, I'm a soldier. They trained me to kill, not capture. I see blood on that blade, it's a done deal. I don't *care* who you are. God doesn't love men who murder innocent women, and I expect He sent me here to teach you this."

The man was on the edge of panic. "Let me go, I let her go."

"What, do I have the word *stupid* tattooed on my forehead? Put the knife down, you get to tell your story to a judge. Maybe a good lawyer can even get you off, it happens all the time. You're a millionaire. Rich and famous men don't go to the gas chamber. You cut that woman, I guarantee you'll be dead before she is. Game over."

"You might hit her if you shoot!"

Howard blew out a theatrical sigh. "Let me explain some things to you, son. This weapon I am holding in my hands is a Phillips & Rodgers .357 Model 47 Medusa. It's about as well-made and accurate a double-action revolver as you can get, and with the hammer back in single-action mode like it is now, it's *extremely* accurate. I can hit an apple at twenty-five meters all day long, and you are less than one-third that far away. You understand? You want to think about how much of you I can see that's not behind your hostage?"

Zeigler didn't say anything.

Howard continued. "There are six one-hundred-and-twenty-five–grain semijacketed hollow point rounds in this handgun. If I shoot and hit you solidly anywhere with only *one* shot—and I *will* hit you, son, you can bet the farm on that—the bullet will thump you at around twelve hundred feet per second. That means it gets there before you hear the sound of it going off. That hypersonic bullet will expand to maybe twice its size and it will put a big hole most if not all the way through you. Based on documented shootings with this caliber and particular brand of ammo, you will go to the floor ninety-six point four times out of a hundred, and no longer have any interest in anything but trying to breathe. And probably not that for long."

Zeigler swallowed dryly.

"Now, here's the deal. I don't give a rat's ass if you walk out of here or if the DEA drags your dead body out; it's all the same to me. But if I have to shoot, this gun is going to make a terrible noise inside this garage, and probably my ears will ring for a couple of days, because I didn't think to put my plugs in before I came through the door. I'd just as soon not damage my hearing any more than I have to.

"So if I have to shoot, I am going to be real pissed off. I might as well shoot again. You following me? You put the knife down right now, or I will punch a hole in you, and when you fall, I'll pump a couple more in you for making my ears hurt. Your movie career might survive an arrest. You don't put that knife down, you won't. Simple as that. Your choice. Either the knife hits the floor or you do."

Somebody was listening on the radio, because Howard heard, "Don't shoot him! Don't shoot him! We're on the way!"

Howard tongued the radio's off switch. He couldn't turn off his mike, but he silenced the earphones. He didn't need the distraction.

He took a deep breath and let part of it out, held the rest, preparing for the shot. You never bluffed in a situation like this. He put his finger inside the guard and onto the trigger. Wouldn't take much, just under three pounds, a nice, crisp pull, like breaking an icicle.

"Don't! Don't kill me! Please!"

Ziegler's left hand came away from the maid, releasing her, and made a pushing motion toward Howard.

"Come on, we can make a deal here! I'll . . . I'll give you my supplier! That's what you want, isn't it?"

The knife moved away from the maid's neck. Ziegler hadn't dropped it yet, but he was about to. His knife hand had already relaxed, and he had taken a half step away from his hostage.

Howard let out another sigh, quieter this time. *Thank you, Lord.* That would have been all he needed, millions of teenage girls hating his guts for killing their screen idol. He'd dodged a bullet himself when that knife dropped—

Somebody ran around the corner from outside and into the garage and fired a handgun twice, hitting the suspect square in the chest.

Zeigler collapsed. The maid screamed and fell to the floor, onto her hands and knees, scrabbled for cover behind the muscle car.

Instinctively, Howard spun toward the shooter, gun leading.

It was Brett Lee.

Lee quickly pointed his gun toward the ceiling, his other hand open and raised. "Easy, easy!"

Howard said, "Why did you shoot, you fucking moron? He had dropped his weapon!"

"Sorry. It looked like he was about to hurt the hostage."

"I thought you wanted him alive!"

Lee didn't say anything else. He put away his weapon.

Howard shook his head, went to check on Zeigler. One in the heart, one in the upper chest, he'd be dead before the paramedics could get him to the ambulance. Shit!

Howard stood, holstered his revolver, helped the crying hostage to her feet. "It's all over, ma'am. You're safe now." He glared at Lee. *Sweet Jesus.*

He heard the sound of helicopters moving in and swore under his breath. He was gonna take the vest off. No way he wanted the name "Net Force" to show up on the evening news after this fiasco.

Commander Michaels would surely agree with that idea.

More DEA agents boiled out of the house, guns waving around. *Day late and a dollar short.*

What a snafu.

Sweet Jesus.

16

"So, the only lead we had to the dealer is cooling on a slab at the morgue in sunny L.A.?"

"Yes, sir," John Howard said. "Apparently to the regret of teenage girls everywhere."

"Jesus," Michaels said.

"My feelings exactly. My guess is, Mr. Lee of the DEA is going to have some tall explaining to do to his superiors."

Michaels shook his head. John Howard and Jay Gridley both looked at him as if expecting some wisdom, and he didn't have any on tap. He said, "Well, at least our information helped the DEA beat the NSA to the target."

"Might have been better the other way," Jay observed. "I kinda liked the Zee-ster's movies myself. He had a certain style."

That the first part of Jay's observation was a thought Michaels had already had didn't make it sit any better. And while he'd seen the actor in a couple of movies and hadn't been that impressed, dead was dead, and shooting somebody with his hands up was bad juju, no two ways about it. Especially a rich and famous somebody.

He said, "Well, if you give folks a knife and they cut themselves with it, that's their problem. The director can't fault us for what DEA screws up. What is the deal with NSA and DEA, anyway? Some kind of ongoing bad blood?"

Jay said, "Not that I know of. No more than any other interagency rivalry. CIA, FBI kind of thing. You get the ball, you don't pass it, you shoot, even if we're all on the same team."

"What about personal histories? Agent Lee and Mr. George go to competing schools? Sleep with each other's girlfriends?"

Jay looked surprised. "Hmm. Never thought of that."

"Maybe it's not relevant to the situation, but why don't you poke around a little and see what you can find. From our meetings, it doesn't seem as if these two have any great love for each other, and I'd just as soon not get Net Force splattered with incidental mud if these two are going to keep throwing it at each other."

Jay nodded. "Good idea, boss. I'll do that."

"Even though it's primarily their problem, we can't just wash our hands of it. We have to help them keep looking, and right now, all we've got is a dead movie star and a dead end."

"Not altogether," Howard said. He grinned, showing bright teeth against his chocolate skin. "There is the matter of the recovered capsules. Unfortunately, they were near the end of their life span; the movie star could afford to buy them and let them go bad if he wanted, and by the time the DEA got the things to their lab, they were so much inert powder internally."

"Which doesn't do us much good, does it?" Michaels said.

"Well, sir, probably not. But while you'll notice that the report says there were three of the capsules, that is actually in error."

Michaels looked at him, waiting.

Howard reached out and dropped a purple cap onto his desktop.

Jay grinned. "General! You swiped one?"

"Liberated it," Howard said. "It won't do us any more good chemically than the ones the DEA's got, but I figured what they could learn from four, they could learn from three."

Michaels picked up the cap and looked at it. "Doesn't seem like it's worth all the trouble, this little thing."

"Diamonds are small, too, boss, and so are wetware and lightware chips."

"Well, as it happens, we have a friend in the FBI lab who would like to get his hands on this," Michaels said. "That way, at least we'd know as much as the DEA about what's in it, for whatever that is worth. Maybe some rare herb found only in bouillabaisse served in a certain bad section of Marseilles, France."

"Sir?"

"Sorry, General, it's from an old spy comedy vid I once saw. But the regular FBI boys have a huge database and long memories, and their lab techs are second to none. Might be they could come up with something. I'll run this past them and see what they can find. Good work."

"Thank you, sir."

"And I was very happy not to see you on the news."

"I thought you might be," Howard said.

After Howard and Jay were gone, Michaels put the capsule into an empty paper clip box and stuck it into his pocket. Chain of evidence was no good, given how they'd come by it, but he was just looking for information. This whole mess was still the DEA's bastard child, and the sooner he could get Net Force out of helping take care of it, the better. He'd drop by the lab and have a chat with the assistant section head, a man he knew from his field days. They could work something out.

Malibu, California

"Don't take the Hammer," Bobby said.

Tad, whose last little hit of heroin was wearing off, frowned through the start of a headache. "Why not?"

"Because I need you straight."

Tad grinned his lopsided grin.

"Well, okay, *relatively* straight. We got problems."

"We're rich and good-looking, how bad could it be?"

Bobby smiled, but it vanished quickly. "The Zee-ster's dead."

"No way! I just saw him. Gave him the caps from that last batch. He looked great. He can't be dead."

"I got a contact in the police who says his body's in a big drawer at the new county morgue and the doctors are flipping coins to see who gets to slice and dice him. He's past tense."

"Aw, geez, that's too bad. I liked him. He knew how to party. What'd he do, wrap one of his cars around a tree? He never could drive worth a crap."

"He was shot twice in the heart by a DEA agent leading a drug raid on his mansion."

"Whoa. You're shittin' me."

"No. Storm and Drang put up a fight when the narcs kicked in the door. Word is, the Zee-ster's house walls got more holes in 'em now than a colander. Both body-guards are shot half to pieces, too, but Storm will probably make it. Drang is still in surgery, and they don't think he'll survive, or if he does, he'll be a big hamburger patty . . . he took a couple rounds in the head."

"Fuck."

"Yeah, it's awful and all, but stop and think about what that means. Why would the feds be going after the Zee-ster? He's a user, not a dealer."

"He spreads it around some," Tad said. "I mean, he did. Could be they caught somebody he ran with, they gave him up."

"Whatever. But this puts us in a kind of bad spot. We ran with him, too. Somebody might remember us."

"Remember me, you mean. You look like ten thousand other surfer dudes. Me, I kinda stand out."

Bobby waved that off. "The point is, we let ourselves get public with him more than we should have, because he was a movie star and cool and all. If he had the Hammer caps on him when they took him out of the game, they are gonna go over his background with a microscope . . . everywhere he went, everybody he saw. A guy like that can't move in this town anonymously unless he wears a bag over his head, and Zeigler never was one to hide his pretty face. The cops and the feds will burn many shoe soles tracking every move the man made. Somebody will cover all of the trendy places where the Zee-ster liked to party."

Tad nodded.

"All right, here's what I want you to do. You search your memory and dig up every time you saw Zee in public, anywhere might have had a security cam lit. Get to those places before the feds or the local police do, get the recordings or wipe them or whatever."

"Yeah. I can do that."

"He never came here, and when I bought drinks or dinner, I paid cash, so there's no e-trail on me. I've made up a list of the places where I went with him alone, or where

you and him and me were. Add those to your list. Crowd
he traveled with, they don't know us well enough to send
anybody here, hell, they were usually too stoned to know
who *they* were, much less us, but vids are different. If
we're on a tape, a RAM drive or a DVD, that's bad. If
that's gone, we're clear."

Tad nodded again. "Yeah, I got it. Only a few places
they might have captured images of us."

"We can't do shit about some tourist who snapped a
few frames of Zeigler while we were at Disneyland or the
beach or whatever, but the feds probably won't find them,
either. I think we can ride this out, we do it right."

"I wonder how they did figure out to go for him?"

"He fucked up. He liked to brag about doing five girls
at a time while he was on the Hammer, and like you said,
he passed out dope to the people around him like it was
chewing gum. Doesn't matter how they found him. What
matters is, they don't find us."

"I hear that." Tad had no desire to finish out his little
remaining time on earth in a cell. He'd punch his own
ticket before he'd let that happen.

"So we're on vacation for the next couple months,"
Bobby said. "No production, no deliveries, we are shut
down. Maybe we'll go to Maui, drive the crooked road
out to Hana, kick back on the black sand beach and watch
the girls awhile."

Tad nodded absently. "Yeah." But what he was thinking was, he had Thor's Hammer in his pocket, the last
one Bobby had made, and it still had a few more hours
of shelf life left. If he didn't take it, it was going to go
to waste, and Bobby wasn't gonna be making any more
until he felt safe.

Tad might not have a couple months left in him, you
never could tell.

Should he take it? He and Bobby hadn't spent that

much time with the Zee-ster out in public. Half a dozen spots in the last couple of months, no more, and most places didn't keep vid records more than a day or two, maybe a week, before they recorded over the old stuff. He could shave it close, check out the first few places, drop the cap, and finish the last few before it came on full blast. And even after it came on, he could maintain enough to take care of the security stuff, he was pretty sure. For a couple hours, anyway.

There was some risk, sure, but what the hell, he didn't have much to lose, did he?

There was one other possibility, something he hadn't ever tried, but he'd held in reserve, just in case something happened to Bobby before it did him. He could let the cap croak, clean up the security cam stuff, and head out to the islands with Bobby. Then, in a week or two, he could find some reason to split with Bobby for a couple days. Tell him he was gonna go camp out by the Sacred Pools or something—Bobby hated camping—then catch a flight back to L.A.

He'd been with Bobby a long time. And while he wasn't in Bobby's league as a chemist, he knew a fair amount about drugs. He had managed, over the time they'd been dealing the Hammer, to be around Bobby at one point or another during every step of the creation and blending of the ingredients for the drug. Yeah, he didn't even know what they all *were,* but he knew where to find the powders and how much to use of each.

He wasn't a genius like Bobby, he couldn't create the stuff from scratch, no way. But while not everybody could create a major symphony from nothing, like Mozart, a whole lot of people could play the sucker if they had the sheet music. Tad knew Bobby's routine; he'd watched it, memorized it, and he could do that much. Ma and Pa out in the RV had all the stuff for Thor's Hammer, neatly stored in little bottles. He could pay them a visit. They'd never think twice about it. He'd collected the stuff for Bobby several times.

Of course, when Bobby found out, he'd be pissed, so maybe Tad might have to eliminate Ma and Pa, torch the RV, and hope Bobby would blame it on rival dealers or the law. Then again, maybe Tad wouldn't be around when Bobby found out. The hole he had to climb out of each time was deeper and deeper. One day, he'd hit the bottom and not be able to make it back, and that was gonna be sooner rather than later.

It was something to think about.

"You gonna sit there staring into space all day or what?"

"Huh. Oh, yeah. I'm going. I need to, uh, freshen up a bit, then I'm good."

"Fine. Do what you need to do, but don't get pulled over for a ticket or whatever, be careful, okay?"

"Yeah, yeah, don't worry."

"I have to worry, Tad, for the both of us."

Tad headed for the bathroom and another hit of the Mexican white. As he walked, he fingered the capsule in his watch pocket to make sure it was still there. As long as he took care of business, what could it hurt to take it? It would be a crime to just waste it.

And even if he did take it, a few weeks from now he could *still* come back to L.A. And if he skipped the final step when he mixed the stuff, left out adding the self-destruct catalyst, the resulting caps maybe wouldn't be quite as potent, but they wouldn't go bad, either. He could take one every day until it killed him, and that wouldn't be the worst way to go out, now would it?

He smiled at himself in the bathroom mirror.

It was like looking at a grinning skull.

• • •

Drayne was pissed off at himself. He knew better than to associate with people he dealt to, he *knew* better. He'd talked to a lot of dope dealers over the years, had wrangled access to a lot of FBI files via his father, without the old man knowing, of course, and he'd learned a whole lot about the biz before he had ever sold his first pill.

The upside of things were big bucks and big thrills. Dopers who were smart made fortunes, and they got to make the assorted varieties of cops look stupid while they did it. Big money, big rushes, the thrill of victory, and all that green to feed the machine.

There was a downside, of course. Stupid dopers could get killed by a rival dealer. Or ripped off and maybe killed by a customer. Or busted and sent to the graybar hotel for twenty years on a heavy federal rap. Or busted by the local yokels. Lot of minefield in the illegal trade, and you couldn't complain to the cops if somebody pointed a gun at you and stole your dope or your money.

The thing was, if you were a dealer, and if you did it long enough, and if you didn't move around a bunch while you were doing it, you were sooner or later going to get caught. Ninety-nine point ninety-nine percent of dealers who stayed in the biz for more than a few years in one place eventually got nailed. Sometimes it was a distributor who gave 'em up, sometimes it was an ex-wife or girlfriend, sometimes the cops found 'em on their own.

Once you got a lot of cash in your hands, it sometimes made you stupid. You bought expensive, flashy toys, you got to thinking because you were rich you were invincible, and just like Zeigler, all your money didn't mean squat when the bullets started to fly. You couldn't take it with you.

So Drayne had always kept a low profile. No yachts, no car that couldn't be leased by half of L.A. No bodyguards with muscles and bulges under their jackets to make people wonder who you were who needed body-guards. Absolutely minimal risks in sales, delivery, taking on new customers. Never more stuff in the house than necessary. Nobody knew what he did except for three people: Tad and the old couple who drove the RV. Tad would never give him up, and Ma and Pa Yeehaw were lifetime criminals who would go down with guns blasting before they let themselves be taken. If not, he'd have them bailed out and gone before the feds knew what they had.

Not perfect, no ironclad guarantees, but he had been very careful. Until he got sucked into the glitz of Zeigler's movie-star circles. Even then, Drayne had stood in the back on the Zee-ster's coattails, and what the hell, it had been fun, watching every door open in front of them, women falling all over themselves to get close to them, and the reflected feeling of celebrity.

It had never occurred to him that Zeigler would be the target of a raid. Feds just didn't kick in famous million-aires' doors; it just wasn't done.

Well, it was now. And while they were *probably* okay, going to ground and turning invisible until all the heat died down was the way to play it. No reason to push things. He was ahead of the game. The feds were plod-ders, but they were like the tortoise: While the hare was taking a nap, they might creep up on him and bite him on the ass. Drayne wasn't going to give them that chance, no sir, thank you very fucking much.

A month or two in Hawaii in the fall? You could do a lot worse. And worse was not the way to go.

Soon as Tad got things taken care of, they were gonna hop on one of those big honkin' jumbo jets and zip on out to the islands. By the time they got back, all this other stuff would be old news.

Old news.

17

Toni was going stir-crazy, she had cabin fever big time, and she had to get out of the house before she went totally bonkers. Yes, the doctor had told her to stay home and confine herself to light activity. Because, the doctor had said, if there were any more problems with cramping or bleeding, and she wanted this baby, she was going to wind up spending the rest of the pregnancy in bed, so best she not cause things to get to that state by being overactive.

Toni's mother had, of course, agreed entirely with the doctor's assessment. Sure, she hadn't slacked off any when her babies were growing, Mama said, but that was different. She was healthy as a horse, and besides, all that fighting stuff Toni did was probably upsetting the baby anyhow.

Toni didn't really have any place she wanted or needed to go, and she would window-shop in the mall if nothing else, as long as she didn't have to sit here alone in the place while Alex was off at work for one more day.

She missed work more than she'd expected, and it

wasn't the same doing little piddly consulting things on the net. There was no interaction with real people, no matter how good the virtual scenarios were. Yes, the state-of-the-art ScentWare ultrasonic olfactory generators gave some pretty authentic smells. The latest-generation haptic program from SensAble Technologies allowed you to feel pressure and touch, and of course, everybody's visuals were getting better every day, but the differences between the best VR stimware and reality were like light-years compared to millimeters; there was a long, long way to go.

On a whim, Toni called Joanna Winthrop.

"Hey, Toni! How's the pregnancy going?"

"Awful. I feel like a bloated cow."

Joanna laughed. "I hear that, and I sympathize completely. No matter how many times Julio told me I was beautiful, I knew I could stand next to the hippos at the zoo and nobody could tell us apart."

"Alex doesn't understand. I know I'm whining, I can't stop myself, and as soon as I start, he runs and hides in the garage. That old car he's working on is going to be the most overbuilt classic in all creation. I think he's leaving early and coming home late from work just to stay out of my way."

"Bet on it."

Toni sighed. "So how is your baby?"

"The demon child from Hell?"

"What?"

Joanna laughed. "He's great. That's just what we call him when we can't figure out why he's crying."

"Does that happen a lot?"

"Not really. But every once in a while, none of the usual things work. He's not hungry, he's not wet, he doesn't need to burp, he doesn't seem tired, he's too little to be cutting teeth. So far, the little battery-powered swing mostly does the trick, and if that fails, we put him in the car seat and take him for a ride in the car, and that pretty much calms him down. Or Julio takes him for a long walk. By the third or fourth mile, Julio says, he's usually okay."

"Jesus," Toni said. "What have I done?"

Joanna laughed again, louder. "I'm kidding, sweetie. He's a terrific kid, worth every penny. How are you doing, really?"

Toni explained about her scrimshaw, and about how she was feeling cooped up.

"Why don't you come on over and visit us? The baby is asleep, he'll be out for another couple hours, and I'd love to see you again. I've missed the crew at work."

"Me, too," Toni said. "You're sure it's okay?"

"Of course I'm sure. I'm a new mama and you're gonna be in a few months. If we can't help each other, who will?"

Toni felt as if her load had been lightened immeasurably.

"Thanks, Joanna. I'm on my way."

Bobby's "work" phone jangled as he was looking for his suitcase in the garage. He frowned. Only a few people had the number, which was supposedly a direct line to his "office."

He went to the kitchen and touched the com's caller ID button.

Nothing; whoever was calling was blocked. Probably a wrong number. He tapped the speaker button.

"Polymers, Drayne," he said.

"Hello, Robert."

Jesus Christ! "Dad?"

"How are you?" his father said. He sounded old.

"Me? I'm fine. How, uh, are you? Everything okay?"

"I am well."

"How's the dog?"

"He's fine."

There was a long pause.

"What, uh, what's up, Dad?"

"I have some bad news, I'm afraid. You remember your aunt Edwina's son, Carlton?"

Aunt Edwina's son. He couldn't have just said, "Your cousin"?

"Yeah, sure."

"Well, he was in a boating accident yesterday. He passed away in the hospital this morning."

"Creepy's dead?" *Jesus.*

"I asked you not to call him that, Robert."

Drayne shook his head. His father would remember that. Still worried about the name, even though the man was dead.

Carlton Post had been called Creepy as long as Drayne could remember. He was three years younger than Drayne, and whenever his folks had come to visit—Edwina was his old man's younger sister by five years or so—they'd brought their four kids along. Creepy was the only boy, and Drayne had usually been stuck watching him. Drayne didn't know who had nicknamed him in the first place; the oldest girl cousin, Creepy's sister, Irene, had passed the name along to Drayne once when she and Drayne had been teaching each other how to play doctor. The name came from the way he stared at people. He'd been a shrimpy little black-haired boy who looked at you crooked without blinking for what sometimes seemed like ten minutes.

"What happened?" Drayne said. He hadn't known Creepy that well, but hearing about his death left him feeling oddly distressed.

"He was waterskiing on Lake Mead. Apparently he fell and was run over by another boat. Knocked unconscious, then cut by the boat's engine propeller. He lost a lot of blood before he was fished out, and there was extensive head trauma."

His father related the information as if talking about the weather, no excitement, no grief, deadpan and almost in a monotone. Fell. Run over. Cut. Always the cool federal agent.

"Oh, man. That's awful. How's Aunt Edwina holding up?"

"She is, of course, greatly distressed."

Creepy was dead. It was hard to imagine. The kid had grown up, gone to school at UNLV, married a girl he'd met there, gotten a degree in history, then stayed to teach high school somewhere outside Salt Lake City. Orem? Something like that? Him and—what was her name?— oh, yeah, Brenda, probably the only two non-Mormons for as far as the eye could see. They'd gotten a divorce after a couple years, and Creepy stayed there. It had been five, six Christmases since Drayne had seen his cousin. He'd actually turned out okay, a nice guy.

"The funeral will be day after tomorrow at Edwina's church in Newport Beach. I'll be driving up for it."

Edwina and her husband, Patrick, were Presbyterians. God's frozen people.

His father was coming to L.A. Well, shit. So much for jetting off to Hawaii. Drayne said, "You, uh, need a place to stay?"

"No, I'll stay at Edwina's or get a hotel room nearby. She'll need family support. The funeral will be at ten o'clock. Can you get off work to attend?"

That was the kind of man his father was. If he'd still been working for the FBI when his nephew had been killed, he would have worried about shit like that. Sure, he'd have taken a personal day and gone, but he would have fretted over missing work. Duty was his reason to get up in the morning.

Drayne said, "Sure, no problem, I can take off."

"I'm going to be at Patrick and Edwina's at nine and then drive over to the church. You can meet me either place. You remember how to get to her house?"

It had been a long time since he'd been there. "She still at that place overlooking the highway?"

"Yes."

"I can find it."

"Good. I'll see you then. Good-bye, Robert."

Drayne tapped the speaker button and shut the com off. That was his old man. Just the bare facts—who, where, what, when—and he was done. No emotion in his voice that his sister's only son, his nephew, was dead; it was just a flat recitation: *"Your cousin is dead. We're going to bury him. We'll see you there. Good-bye."*

Jesus fucking Christ.

Drayne sighed. Well, okay, this was gonna put a small crimp in his plans, but Creepy had been his cousin. He was family. You couldn't just not go, not if you ever had to bump into the rest of the family again. Traffic would be a bitch that time of day, he'd have to get up and get rolling on the PCH early, by seven, at least. Maybe six-thirty. You didn't want to be caught in a traffic jam on the way to a funeral.

Shit. First it was Zeigler, then Creepy. Bad things came in threes. He hoped the next one wouldn't be Tad.

Or himself . . .

December 1991
Stonewall Jackson High School Cafeteria, Cool Springs, Georgia

Jay Gridley stood in the cafeteria line. The woman behind

the counter slopped a big ice cream scooper full of mashed potatoes onto his compartmentalized baby blue Melmac plate, turned the scoop over and pressed it against the creamed spuds to make a concave indentation, dipped the scoop into a pan of greasy brown liquid, and said, "Chon'tgravyth'thet?"

Jay made the translation mentally: *"Do you want gravy with your mashed potatoes?"*

By the time he'd figured out what she said, the server had already poured the warm goo all over the plate, slopping into the green beans, the hamburger steak, and the little empty slot where Jay had planned to have a piece of cherry pie. Forget that.

"Uh . . . sure," he said, way late.

She handed him the plate back, under the angled glass sneeze guard.

This was where Mr. Brett Lee of the Drug Enforcement Administration had gone to high school, graduating at age seventeen, third in the class of '91, before going off to Georgia Tech to get his master's in criminology. He'd gone to work for the DEA the year after he had graduated college and had thus spent nearly thirteen years working for them.

In the real world, Jay would be looking at the school yearbooks, talking to teachers and fellow students, downloading pictures and stats, and putting together an education history of Mr. Lee. In VR, he had built a scenario that would let him walk through the school itself—or rather what he imagined a place named after a Southern Civil War hero might look and feel like—and absorbing the information in a much more interesting manner.

Lee had been well-liked, had gotten good grades, and had hung with jocks, having been a middle-distance runner on the school's track team.

Jay had come as far back as high school because he

had not been able to discover any connection between Brett Lee and Zachary George either in their work careers or college. While the two men were only a year apart in age—George was thirty-seven, Lee, thirty-six—Lee had been born and raised in Georgia, while George had grown up in Vermont. When Lee was at Georgia Tech, George had been at New York University. They had not crossed paths that Jay could tell until they were both working for the federal government, and while there was no record of their first meeting there, there was some kind of friction apparent by the time both had been in harness for a few years.

Jay had all that—the two didn't like each other, maybe they just rubbed each other the wrong way or something—but the cause of the conflict had not come to light. He could pass on what he'd come up with to Michaels, but it didn't tell them anything they didn't already know.

The young Lee, sitting at a table with four guys and two girls from the track teams, dipped a French fry in catsup and ate it as Jay moved to sit at a conveniently empty table behind the group.

Convenient, hell. He had designed the setup that way himself.

The conversation was hardly enlightening. They talked about things of interest to teenagers: music, movies, who was going out with whom, teachers they hated, the usual. And in the twenty-year-old jargon, it was pitifully dated. Lee was close to Jay's age, and if he'd talked like this, he must have seemed a terrible dweeb to any passing adult. Or dork. Or dickhead. All phrases the boys used fast and furiously, mixing and matching as needed:

"Yeah, well, Austin is a dickhead dweeb," one of the boys said. "He gave me a fuckin' *C* on the midterm because I didn't use the right color ink!"

"Yeah, Austin's a dork, all right," another boy said.

One of the girls, a pretty bottle-blond in a gray T-shirt held together with safety pins, said, "Yeah, but he's kinda cute."

The other girl, a brunette with hair worn so short as to almost be a crew cut said, "Yeah, too bad he's gay."

One of the boys said, "Gay? Shee-it, he ain't gay. I seen him lookin' up Sissy Lou's skirt and gettin' a hard-on in debate one, you know how she sits with her knees apart. You're just pissed 'cause he don't look at you that way. Maybe if you wore a skirt instead of jeans all the time, you'd see."

"I don't think Jessie here owns a skirt," the third boy said, poking the short-haired girl on the shoulder. "But I hear she's got some black bikini panties."

Jessie slapped at the third boy. "*You* won't never find out, dickhead."

"What*ever,*" the safety-pinned girl said, dismissing the topic.

He could die of boredom here, Jay thought. Or worse, start laughing so hard he'd spray milk out of his nose.

Brett Lee said, "He's not queer, he's just smart, is all. He got us that trip to the Debate Finals in Washington, D.C."

"Pro'lly had to give somebody a blow job to do it," Safety-Pin said.

"I'm tellin' you, he's not queer," the second boy said.

"Hell, Hayworth, maybe he was lookin' at you instead of Sissy when he got the hard-on," Jessie said.

"Your ass!" Hayworth said.

"What*ever,*" Safety-Pin said.

Jay shook his head. Oh, yeah, he was gonna learn a lot here. Jesus.

"So," Jessie said to Brett, "you going to the debate thing?"

"Yeah. There's gonna be people from all over the country there."

"Mostly Yankees," Hayworth said. " 'N' queer Yankees, at that."

"I'm goin'," Lee said. "I'm not gonna live the rest of my life here in Hickburg. I'm gonna meet people, make friends, get myself a job where I can make a shitload of money and retire by the time I'm forty."

"Your ass," Hayworth said.

Jay shook his head. He'd heard enough of this.

Then, as he was about to leave, he had a thought.

Maybe Zachary George had been interested in debate in high school?

Hmm. Well, he could take a little run up to Montpelier High and check that out. Easy enough to do when you were Jay Gridley, master of virtual space and time.

18

Michaels walked into the Columbia Scientific Shop, not expecting much from the small size of the storefront. An error, he quickly found.

The place didn't have much frontage, but it opened up once you were inside. It wasn't the size of a Costco or anything, but it was a lot bigger than he'd expected.

There were racks and racks of items, ranging from Van de Graaff generators to home dissection kits to chemistry sets to huge telescopes.

Lord, he'd wander around in here forever.

"May I help you, sir?"

Michaels turned to see a woman who looked as if she might be the perfect TV grandmother smiling at him. She was short, slight, wore her gray hair in a bun, a pair of cat's-eye reading glasses hung from a string around her neck, and she had a white sweater draped over her shoulders. The blue print dress she wore went almost all the way to the floor. She looked to be late sixties.

"Yes, ma'am," he said. "I'm looking for a stereomicroscope."

"Ah, yes, aisle nine. What kind of working distance would you need between the lens and object?"

Michaels didn't have a clue. "I don't know."

"Perhaps if you told me the purpose?"

"Um, it's for my wife. She's pregnant and has to stay at home, so she's taken up scrimshaw."

Granny beamed and nodded. "Congratulations! Your first child?"

"Yes." Well, it was his and Toni's first child. And their last, too, according to Toni.

"If you'll follow me."

He did, and in due course, they arrived at aisle nine and a rack of optical equipment, most of which he couldn't put a name to. None of it looked cheap, however.

Granny said, "Your wife will need a focus distance at least the length of her inscribing tool, eight or nine inches. This unit here will give her a foot, so that will do it. It's a Witchey Model III, and it comes with ten times and twenty times. Much more power than she needs, but if you put an oh point three times auxiliary lens on it, right here, that will give you three times and six times, which should be sufficient for scrimshaw. Just to be sure, we can add in another lens that will ramp it up to five times and ten times."

Michaels nodded, not really understanding what she was talking about.

"We could use an articulating arm, but probably a standard post mount would be fine." She looked around and leaned a little closer toward him. "My supervisor would just as soon I sell you a fiber-optic shadow-free ring light to go with it, but frankly, you can get a gooseneck lamp and a hundred watt bulb and save yourself three hundred dollars."

Michaels blinked. "Uh, thank you."

She gave him a perfect grin, full of smile wrinkles and

dimples. "The basic scope is eight hundred dollars, and the two lenses normally retail for about one hundred dollars each, but I can knock a bit off that. Say, nine hundred and fifty dollars all total? And I'll throw in a gooseneck lamp at a discount, too."

Michaels blew out a small sigh and nodded. The profit he'd made on the Miata rebuild was pretty much shot after the honeymoon and the Chevy, but he had a thousand or so left. Toni wanted this but wouldn't buy it for herself, and the truth was, he was feeling guilty about not being more supportive about the pregnancy. It was his son she was carrying, after all, and the least he could do was try to make her enforced inactivity more bearable.

"I'll take it," he said.

Granny laser-beamed another smile at him. "Excellent. If you'll follow me, I'll have one brought up to the check-out counter."

Michaels followed her toward the front of the store. On the way there, a pair of small boys ran past on the cross aisle in front of them. A second after they passed, there was a crash, yells, then what sounded like glass shattering.

Granny said, "Shit! You little bastards! You're *not* supposed to be running in here!" Whereupon she herself took off at a good sprint. The long dress's hem kicked up enough for Michaels to see that Granny wore a pair of flaming red Nike SpringGels, high-end running shoes that went for almost two hundred bucks a pair.

He had to smile. Another example that things were not always what they appeared to be.

Quantico, Virginia

John Howard, in shorts, a T-shirt, and his old sneakers, was working up a pretty good sweat on the obstacle course near Net Force HQ. There were a few Marine officers he recognized running the course, a few FBI types, and there, just ahead on the chinning bars, none other than Lieutenant Julio Fernandez.

Julio saw Howard but kept doing his chins, palms forward and hands a little wider than his shoulders.

Howard stopped and watched. He counted eight before Julio gutted out the last one and let go, then leaned forward and started rubbing at one bicep.

"How many did you do?"

"Twelve," Julio said.

Howard raised an eyebrow.

"Yeah, yeah, I know, I used to do fifteen, sometimes twenty on a good day. I haven't been getting out here as often as I should."

"The joys of family life," Howard observed.

"Yes, sir, that's for sure. I wouldn't trade it for anything, but it does change things some. Before I met Joanna, if I woke up in the middle of the night and felt like it, I could suit up and hit the gym or go run a couple miles, whatever. Now when I wake up in the middle of the night, it's to the sound of a crying baby. Changing a diaper full of gooey yellow poop at three in the morning was never in my flight plan. I don't think I've had three hours of sleep at any one stretch for three months.

"How'd you do it, John? How'd you live through a tiny baby?"

Howard laughed. "I stopped working out. I stopped going to have a drink with the boys after dinner because I was falling asleep in my chair watching TV. You have to change your priorities."

"Yeah, I hear that. I can see it all now: I'm gonna wind up like a certain fat old general, too stiff and tired to walk from the couch to the bed. It's a pitiful thing to think about."

"Fat old general? You want to run the course, Lieutenant, and see just how fat and old I really am? Perhaps I should give you a handicap. Ten seconds? A minute?"

"Your ass, General, sir. I might be in terrible shape, but that's compared to a twenty-five-year-old SEAL, not a man your age."

"I'm not a man my age, Julio. I'm getting better every day."

"You got your stopwatch?"

Howard smiled. "As it happens." He pulled the watch from under his shirt where it hung on a loop of old bootlace.

"Start it. I'll see you at the end. Time you get there, I can probably shower, shave, and catch up on my sleep."

"Go, Lieutenant. The clock is ticking. But be careful of your heart."

Julio smiled, and took off.

On the way home, Michaels's virgil played a few bars of Franz Liszt's *Les Preludes,* a somber, regal musical sting that, according to Jay Gridley, was the basis for the theme that announced the Emperor Ming in the old Flash Gordon movie series in the '30s. Buster Crabbe, the swimming champion, had starred in those, Jay had told him. Jay had been to what had once been Buster's house, as a boy in SoCal. It had a big swimming pool in the backyard. Talking a bigggg pool . . .

It was Susie. He saw her tiny picture appear on his virgil's screen, and he activated his own minicam so she could see him.

"Hey, yo, Daddy-o!"

" 'Daddy-o'? What happened to 'Dadster'?"

"Oh, that's *so* yesterday," she said. "You really did go to school with the dinosaurs, huh?"

"It's true. I had to hike a prehistoric trail ten miles long every morning, in the tropical heat, uphill both ways, and be careful of stepping into the tar pits. You have it easy, kiddo."

"So Mom says."

"How are you?"

"Fine."

"Everything going okay with, ah, Byron?"

"Yep. He's a good guy, really."

Michaels felt his belly clutch. He had thought he was going to lose contact with her after the nasty business with Megan, but somehow, his ex-wife had relented. Thank God for large miracles.

"I'm glad to hear it," he said. Boy, that came hard.

"He argued with Mom something awful about letting me see you."

Michaels felt the heat begin in him, threatening to rise and shut off his breathing and vision. *That bastard!*

"Didn't like the idea, huh?" he managed to say, faking a smile. She could see him, after all.

"Oh, no, Daddy-o, it was *Mom* who didn't like it. Byron said it wasn't right to keep a father from seeing his daughter. He wouldn't give up until she agreed."

Michaels's anger turned to wonder. "Really?"

"Yeah, he doesn't like you much after you insulted Mom and knocked him down, but he tries to be fair. He's just not you. I miss you, Dad."

As always, that broke his heart. "Me, too. You tell Byron thank you for me, would you?"

He debated for a moment about whether to tell his preteen daughter that she was going to have a new little brother. Well, half brother. Then he decided she ought to hear it from him.

"I have some news for you. Did you know you're going to have a baby brother in a few months?"

"Mom told?" she said. "She told me I couldn't say anything to you. But it's not a brother, it's a sister."

For a moment, he couldn't track what she said, it was as if she had spoken words he understood but arranged them wrong. What she said made no sense.

Then it came to him:

Megan was pregnant!

"Daddy-o, where'd you go?"

"Huh? Oh, sorry, sweetie, I'm in my car, I had to, uh, switch lanes."

"Pretty cool, huh?" she said. "A baby sister. Almost none of my friends have any that little. Chellie's got a brother who's two, and Marlene's got a sister who's like one, but nobody else's mom is preggers."

"Pretty cool," he said. "Congratulations."

Susie's slip brought up a whole wave of things he didn't want to think about. He loved Toni, and she loved him in a way Megan never had. He was over his ex-wife, finally. Well, almost over her. There was always that little wonder about the road not taken, even though the roads they had traveled the last few years had been pretty ugly. But she was Susie's mother, and there had been some good times. Wonderful times, at the beginning.

Now that she was having another man's baby, the old jealousy tried to rear its viperlike head, and for a moment, he almost let it.

No. That serpent was dead.

And now what did he tell Susie about her half brother? Should he say anything? He didn't want to get into any kind of competition with Megan for his daughter's affection as much as he didn't want to lose it.

And yet, if he was going to continue to be part of Susie's life, Toni was also going to be a part of it, as would their unborn child.

Sooner or later, word would get back to Megan; somehow it always did, and he would rather Susie hear it from him.

"Well, Li'l Bit, it looks like you are going to be *really* cool."

"Huh?"

He smiled into the virgil.

19

The Safari Bar and Grill was first on Tad's list. This was an old but little-known watering hole not far from Santa Monica City College. The food was good, the drinks generous, and the place was far enough off the main drags so the locals had mostly kept it hidden from the tourists.

Tad approached the assistant manager on duty and gave him the bullshit story he'd worked up.

"Say, man, I got a problem maybe you can help me with?"

The assistant manager, a smiling black guy of thirty with nice teeth, dressed in khaki safari shorts and matching shirt, said, "What's the problem, bro?"

"Okay, look, a while back, my brother and his wife were having some difficulties. I uh, got together with her to, you know, help them out. We had lunch here a few times."

"Uh-huh, so?"

"One thing kinda led to another. My sister-in-law and I, well, we, ah, stepped over the line, you know what I mean?"

"You punching your brother's wife? That's bad biz, bro. Gonna make Thanksgiving dinners a bitch."

"Yeah, yeah, I know. It just happened, you know. Anyway, they got their shit worked out okay, they're back together. But my brother, he's a jealous type, and he suspects that while they were on the outs, his wife maybe did some stuff she shouldn't have done."

"He's right, too, idn't he?"

Tad looked at his boots. "Yeah, and I feel like shit about it, okay? But he only suspects, he doesn't *know,* and he sure as hell don't know about *me.* The thing is, my brother is big and kinda mean, and he's with the cops, and if he starts poking around and finds out his wife and I spent any time together, I'm fucked."

"I hear that."

"So like I said, we were in here a few times, had a few drinks and a few laughs, and if he shows up here somehow and gets his hands on your security tapes, I could be in deep shit."

The assistant manager smiled. "Not to worry, my man. You here further back than a week, he won't find nothing. We record three days at a time. Nobody sticks up the place or starts a fight the police need to see, we start the disk over again. No permanent records."

Tad smiled. "Hey, man, I appreciate you tellin' me this." He pulled a couple of tightly folded twenties from his pocket and extended his hand. When they shook hands, the twenties pressed into the assistant manager's palm, and he grinned and nodded. "No problem, bro. You be more careful now, you hear? That pussy will kill you, you not careful."

After the Safari, Tad rumbled the big Dodge along surface streets to two other restaurants within a few miles of each other and ran the same story.

At the Sun 'n' Shore, it played pretty much the same, except for the time. The security cams there recorded over the old stuff after only twenty-four hours. Not to sweat it.

At the Irish Pub, they had cams, but all they did was feed a couple of show monitors, no tapes or disks.

Tad was feeling pretty good about this. He had three more places to hit, and he was done. He could take the Hammer cap and get the trip rolling, they were all gonna be this easy.

But of course, just to fuck up that plan, the Berger Hotel, on the hill overlooking the ocean, was more of a problem. A lot of well-off people with well-known faces came here and got a room to get laid in, and the bar was dark and quiet. And when you had folks with fame and money in your house, you were smart to spend a little more on security to make sure the rich and famous didn't get ripped off. That was bad for business.

So at the Berger, they kept their recordings for a year on long-running superdense video diskettes, SDVDs. The system wasn't full-frame twenty-four-a-second vid, but blink cams that snapped stills every few seconds. You didn't get full motion stuff that way, but you could store a lot more time on a lot less space, and the cams were set to take snaps often enough so you couldn't walk across the lobby without being caught. A still picture that showed faces would do the trick.

Tad ran the sister-in-law number on the assistant manager of the hotel, some kid who looked like he was just out of college with a degree in hotel management, and got sympathy, but that was all.

The kid, a pale, green-eyed, dishwater blond in a dark suit and tie, said, "I'm sorry, sir, it is against hotel policy to allow anybody to see the security recordings."

"Even the cops?"

"Well, of course, we cooperate with the police in criminal matters."

"So if my brother shows up and flashes his badge, he gets the SDVD? And my sister-in-law and I get drummed out of the family? Not to mention by brother kicks the shit out of me, maybe breaks an arm or two?"

"I . . . I wish I could help, really."

"Look, if I knew the date we were here, couldn't you get that diskette out and, uh, misfile it? Accidents happen, right? Somebody could have put that into the wrong file drawer or something, couldn't they? It would have been like a month ago. If anything had happened on that day, the cops would have come looking for it by now, right?"

The kid was wavering.

Tad brought out the heavy artillery. "C'mon, man, I made a big mistake, but it's done. Nobody got hurt, and as long as it never gets out in the open, nobody ever will. I love my brother. What he don't know won't hurt him. Or me. Put yourself in my shoes."

The kid wanted to help, but he was skittish.

Tad went for the throat: "Enter it . . . nobody will ever *know*. I sure won't tell, and it's not like you'd be doing anything *criminal*. It would be worth a lot to me to keep my brother from finding out. Look, I just sold my car. I got enough for a down payment on a new one, plus about a thousand bucks extra. You get me the diskette, I give you the thousand. Everybody comes out ahead. My brother doesn't find out I screwed up, he and his wife live happily ever after, and even if anybody ever comes looking for the recording—which they probably won't—all they'll think is that it got mislaid. Hell, you could even put a blank one in the slot, and they'd probably just think the cams were out of whack . . . if anybody ever bothered to look. Cut me some slack here, please."

Everything Tad said made a certain kind of sense. And

the bottom line was, who would know or ever find out? Not to mention that a thousand bucks tax-free cash was surely more than this kid took home in a week. A week's pay and then some for a thing nobody would ever miss? How tempting was that?

The kid licked his lips. "What was the date?" he asked.

Tad kept his face serious, even though he wanted to smile. One born every minute.

When Tad got back into the Dodge and cranked it up, he had the SDVD, a little silver disk about the size of a half-dollar coin. He broke it in half, broke those pieces in half, and stuck them in the ashtray. He lit a cigarette with a throwaway Bic, dialed the flame up to high, and torched the diskette pieces. They smoked but didn't catch fire, just melted into sludge after a minute. The greasy smoke coming off the molten diskette did stink up the car something fierce, so he rolled down the windows to let the smoke escape.

So much for that.

Two places left on Bobby's list, and neither one of them was going to be as tough as the hotel. One was a movie house the Zee-ster rented to show one of his pictures to a hundred of his closest friends at the moment, the other was a gym where Bobby and the Zee-ster had worked out together a couple of times. Probably neither of them even had security cams, but if they did, between his sister-in-law story and a pocket full of cash, he didn't foresee any problems. People would help you out if the story was good enough, and if they were a little reluctant, a fat wad of green went a long way to moving things along. Everybody had a price; you just had to find it.

So there was no reason not to pick up the Hammer that Tad could see.

He swallowed the big purple cap, washed it down with a swig of bottled water, and headed for the movie theater.

April 1992
Washington, D.C.

The ballroom at the hotel was crowded, mostly fairly well-dressed teenagers, with a sprinkling of teachers and employees here and there. Jay walked through the twenty-year-old scenario, looking at the students as they headed for their seats.

This was the quarter-final round for the debate, whose topic this year was: "Resolved—Imminent Threats to National Security Should Supersede Habeas Corpus."

Boy, didn't that sound exciting?

Jay had learned in his research that debate teams were given an issue at the beginning of the year, and that this issue would be the same nationwide. The teams—two on a side—had to be able to argue both sides of an issue, and the reason for that was that sometimes they might not know which side they were going to be assigned until the last minute. The topic, which certainly sounded like ends-justify-the-means to him, spoke to the idea of the scope of legal protection, habeas corpus, being a shortened version of the full term habeas corpus ad subjiciendum. Technically, he had just learned, it meant something like, "You can have the body to undergo the action of the law," or some such. What it meant was, you couldn't be thrown into jail without due process of the law. If you were suspected of a crime, then you had to be arrested, charged, given access to legal counsel, arraigned, and eventually brought to trial. The authorities couldn't just throw you in a jail cell and leave you there without offering a reason. As such, habeas corpus was the cornerstone of British and U.S. law.

To Jay, such a debate was a yawner, about as exciting as eating a bowl of cold oatmeal while watching paint dry, but the buzz in the room was certainly enthusiastic.

The reason Jay was here was because the DEA agent Brett Lee and the NSA agent Zachary George had both attended this conference as teenagers. It could have been a coincidence—there were hundreds of students here, one team from the small states, and multiple teams from the bigger ones—but maybe this was where the two had run afoul of each other originally.

That would make sense, Jay reasoned. Being on opposite sides of a debate would mean that one would lose and the other would win, and maybe arguments had gotten heated to the point of personal anger.

However, a check of the records once he got to looking revealed that Lee and George had not been on teams that debated each other. In fact, neither of their teams made it to the finals. Georgia got blown out in the first round. Vermont did get to the quarter-finals, and had argued the affirmative position against a team from Nebraska, the result of which was that they had also been eliminated. Georgia and Vermont had not even been staying on the same floor of the hotel.

Jay's scenario was based on old news footage, hotel records, and camcorder tapes and photographs taken by students and teachers, as well as the official society recordings that had been compiled and sold commercially. The net was still in its infancy in the early nineties, but there were some old debate web pages in WWW archives, and some BBSs. Jay had set his searchbots and blenders and strained it all, feeding it into a simple WYSIWYG view program. Added a few bells and whistles, of course.

So there he sat, with the Nebraskans and the Vermontians—the Vermontinese? the Vermin?—about ready to go at it.

Zachary George was the leader of his duo, and he was the opening speaker for the round.

He got up, defined terms, and began his introduction to his reasoning.

George said, "In times of war or national disasters, the country as a whole must come before individuals. While we are a nation based on liberty for all, destruction of the national structure could easily result in liberty for none.

"If a man has a cancerous finger, is it not wiser to cut off the finger than allow it to spread and destroy him? Is a single finger worth the whole man? No, of course not. Likewise, if the life of the nation is threatened, a single or a few individuals cannot be allowed to cause such destruction. As the great Roman general Iphicrates said two thousand years ago, 'The needs of the many must outweigh the needs of the few.'"

Huh. Jay thought that quote came from the Vulcan *Star Trek* character Spock, in one of the old movies from the eighties or nineties.

George continued in this vein, but Jay was busy looking around, trying to spot Lee. It didn't take long. The young Brett Lee, looking much as he had in Jay's earlier scenario at Stonewall Jackson High, watched George from a third-row seat, leaning forward eagerly, hanging on every word.

Jay got up and moved to get a better look at Lee.

George droned on: ". . . and did not Plato say, 'No human thing is of serious importance'? How then can the temporary suspension of liberty by a man or even a small group of men compare to the liberty of millions?"

Jay walked to a point where he could see Lee's face.

Hmm. Lee's expression certainly did not seem like that of a young man who scorned what he was hearing. It was more like a believer hearing a sermon by his favorite preacher. Or a young man listening to the words of his beloved. Could these two have been friends who later had a falling out?

This definitely needed more exploration, Jay decided.

But scenario could only do so much. As the speech continued, Jay's attempt to learn more was frustrated by the facts—or lack thereof. Whether in scenario or RW, if it wasn't there, any speculation about an event was just that, speculation. The program would let Jay make anything he wanted to happen in VR happen, but it would not necessarily be what *actually* happened.

Despite Jay's best efforts, he could not put the two boys together at the debate conference outside the presentation done at the quarter-final competition. Sure, it was likely both Lee and George had been at the semifinals and the final team debate. Both the Vermont and Georgia teams had stayed until the conference was over; the records reflected that. They almost certainly would have been in the audience watching, and it was not inconceivable that they had somehow met before or after that.

There were a few records after the quarter-finals on both boys, but nothing that put the two of them in any closer proximity than they were in Jay's scenario.

Maybe wasn't the same as *for sure*.

Even so, Jay felt as if there was something buried here, something he needed to uncover.

The problem was, how?

20

When Toni walked into the kitchen, she saw the microscope. It sat on the table, a red bow stuck to it.

She was stunned. A total surprise.

"Alex! Where are you?"

After a moment, he came into the kitchen, grinning.

"You shouldn't have done this." She waved at the scope.

"Yeah, I should have. I've been slack in my husbandly duties lately."

"I hadn't noticed that."

"Not *those* duties. The, uh, expectant father ones."

"It's a beautiful piece of equipment," she said, touching the scope mount with one hand. "But we can't afford it."

"We can. I had enough left in the car account to get it. You deserve it."

"It was a want, not a need," she said.

"Nah, you *needed* it. I could tell."

She smiled, and realized she hadn't been doing enough of that lately. "Thank you, darling."

"What, you aren't going to make me take it back?"

She laughed, and she knew he'd said it to make her laugh.

"I got two lenses to do whatever it is it is supposed to do so you can work under it," he said. "Supposedly you'll have a foot between the lens and the work object. I hope that's enough."

"It is. My pin vises are only about seven inches long or so."

"Yeah, mine, too," he said, waggling his eyebrows.

Again, she laughed.

"I should buy you one of these every day. Well, go set it up and see how it works."

"Later," she said. "I have something else in mind first."

"What else could be more important?" Butter wouldn't melt in his mouth.

"Come along, and I'll show you."

Now it was his turn to laugh. And even if she was pregnant, they were still newlyweds, right?

Toni headed for the bedroom, and Alex was right behind her. No farther than seven inches, the way she figured it.

Jay was deep in cyberspace, working a scenario that involved hunting something big and mean with a pack of dogs, when a disembodied voice said, "Honey, I'm home!"

He dropped out of VR, blinked, and beheld Saji.

Saji, stark naked.

"Whoa!" he said.

"Sure, now you notice me. I've been here for half an hour. If I were a thief, I could have walked off with everything in the place, including you, and you'd have been oblivious."

"Uh . . ."

"What's the matter, goat-boy? Cat got your tongue?"

"I hope," he said, grinning.

John Howard and his wife Nadine were about to take a shower together, something they hadn't been able to do much in the last ten or twelve years with their son running around the house. But now that he was in Canada, well, it was time to make hay while the sun shone.

"I'm fat and ugly," Nadine said. "I don't know why you want me around."

"Well, you're a pretty good cook," he allowed.

She threw her shoe at him, but he was expecting it, so he managed to dodge it.

"Of course, you also have lousy aim."

She reached for her other shoe.

The phone rang.

"Let the robot answer it," he said.

"This from the master of duty? It could be Tyrone."

Nadine picked up the phone. The extension in the bathroom was a faux antique dial phone that didn't have a caller ID screen. "Hello? Oh, hey, baby!"

Yep. Tyrone.

Howard had mixed feelings about the call. Of course he was happy to hear from his son. He'd have been a little happier if the boy's sense of timing wasn't so lousy. Half an hour earlier or an hour later, those would have been better. People who didn't have children didn't know what happened to their sex lives after the little ones got big enough to pad down the hall and shove the bedroom door open, looking for Mama and Daddy.

"Yeah, sweetie, he's right here. I'll put him on."

Howard took the phone. Unfortunately, he stopped paying attention to Nadine as soon as Tyrone said hello. A mistake.

The second shoe hit him on the butt.

"Hey, ow!"

"Dad?"

"Nothing, son. Your mom is just being cute."

Santa Monica, California

The Hammer was coming on by the time Tad left the movie theater. Like he thought, there hadn't been any surveillance cams set up in the theater proper. There was one installed in the redi-teller in the lobby, but neither he nor Bobby had used the money machine when the Zee-ster had done his private showing. There wasn't any need; everything had been on the tab Zeigler ran.

By the time he got to the gym, the chem was working pretty good in Tad. It had come on faster than usual. Maybe it was because he had tripped such a short time ago and was still wrung out, or maybe it had to do with the other dope he'd been taking to stay ambulatory. Whatever. Thor was on a roll, urging Tad to join him in a night of ass-kicking and taking names, and it was all Tad could do to maintain control.

Steve's Gym was an upscale place just off the PCH that catered to serious jocks. Tad pushed open the door, got a blast of frigid AC in the face, and almost had an orgasm from the cold rush.

Lifting weights had never been Tad's thing. As a kid, his lungs had been too bad to let him do squat physically. Between the bronchitis and asthma that later opened him up for tuberculosis, and his naturally skinny frame, he was never gonna be able to bulk up, so he hadn't ever tried.

With the Hammer working, he could probably go over and grab one of those big barbells and twirl it like a drum majorette's baton if he wanted to, but why bother? Nobody here he wanted to impress.

"Can I help you?" came a deep voice from off to Tad's right.

He looked. There was a woman there who looked like the Incredible Hulk's sister: She was big, heavy, ugly, and looked as if she needed a shave. But she had tits—fake ones—and the red leotard she wore showed an absence of male equipment down south. A definite woman, sort of.

Tad smiled, enjoying a particularly nice rush of something in the chem cocktail. "Steve around?"

According to Bobby, Steve was the owner of the gym. He was a former Mr. America, Mr. Universe, and Mr. Whatever Came After That, past his prime but still as big as a rhino and plated with slabs of steroid-cured muscle. Maybe six two, two sixty, down twenty or thirty pounds from his competition days, Steve was still as wide as a door with arms as big around as most guys' legs. Bobby wasn't in the same class as most of the bodybuilders who came in to move mountains of iron plates, but he was buffed enough so nobody laughed when he took off his shirt, and in better shape than most of the celebrity jocks who made it a point to be seen here. Guys like the Zeester, who had personal trainers the way most people had toothbrushes, would stop by, do a few sets, work up a sweat, and have their pictures taken by their publicity guys as they left, all pumped up and manly.

Anyway, Bobby had told him to talk to Steve, who'd be happy to help out any friend of Bobby's. Bobby dropped a lot of money in this place, doing private sessions, buying T-shirts and vitamins and shit.

The Amazon said, "He's with a client right now. Maybe I can help you?" Her expression at seeing his pipe-stem frame in his black clothes said she didn't really think she could help him, that God Himself would have trouble helping such a pencil-necked geek.

Tad smiled, his mind zipping along quickly, making connections and drawing conclusions that were usually beyond him. The Hammer made you strong as Superman, but it also gave you Lex Luthor's brainpower. That wasn't just subjective on his part, either, he had done some things that convinced him the increase in processing power was real.

He said, "Nah, it's personal biz."

"He's gonna be about an hour," the woman said. "You can wait if you want."

Normally, Tad might have gone for that. An hour was nothing when he was straight—well, more or less straight. But when the Hammer was pounding in your brain, doing nothing for an hour when you were in the gotta-move stage was pretty much impossible.

Another body rush swept over Tad, and as it did, he got an erection, a woody that came up all of a sudden, like a switchblade opening, *boing!*

He looked at the woman bodybuilder. She probably outweighed him by thirty or forty pounds, and no way, no how was she his type, but she was female and she was right here. He said, "You want to screw? I bet I can wear you out in an hour."

The woman laughed, a deep, resonant rumble way down in her belly. "Oh, wow, that's really funny. You and me? Ha!"

Tad smiled pleasantly.

"Even if I was into men, which I'm not, you'd be the last guy I'd choose, fuzz-brain. I'd want somebody who could pick me up and put me down easy, and you don't look like you could pick up an empty beer bottle without help."

Tad continued to smile. Quickly, he stepped up to her,

scooped her up, and held the startled bodybuilder cradled in his arms like a baby. "You mean like this? So, I passed the test, right?"

With that, he used his left arm to support her weight, reached over with his right hand, caught the leotard between her breasts and ripped it down the front, all the way to the crotch. The cloth fell away like tissue, showing the muscular nudity underneath.

The woman was still behind the curve, so startled by what he had done and probably that he had been able to do it, her mouth just gaped.

"Nice hooters," Tad said. "You get a good deal on 'em?"

He stuck his hand between her legs, and whatever surprise she felt faded enough for her to scream and punch him at the same time.

Tad ignored the loose fist she threw as it bounced off his cheekbone, and sought to explore the area his hand had found. She started kicking and screaming, and even with the Hammer, he was having trouble keeping her still.

The cavalry arrived then, three guys who together probably weighed as much as a small car.

"Hey! What the fuck are you doing?!" one of them said. "Put Belinda down, asshole!"

"You got a security cam setup in here?" Tad asked.

"You're damned straight we do, you fucking psycho!"

"Where is it?"

"Charlie, call the cops. And call an ambulance for this moron," the guy said.

"You must be Steve, right?"

"That's right, dickweed, and you're dead. Put her down!"

Tad grinned. As it sometimes did when he got excited, the drugs in the Hammer came up full blast, roaring in like a tornado.

"Here," he said. He threw Belinda at the three. Charlie had stepped away, heading for a phone, but Belinda hit Steve and his Neanderthal buddy hard enough to knock them over. All three of them tumbled to the floor, hard.

Tad leaped at Charlie, grabbed him under the armpits, and lifted him into the air until his feet cleared the floor. Charlie had to go about two fifty, maybe two sixty, a nice hefty lad. "Which way is the security cam control room?"

Charlie, who hung there like a kid's doll, stammered, "Th-th-there!"

He pointed.

Since Steve was almost back on his feet, Tad turned and threw Charlie at him. The collision of beef was pretty hard.

Tad ran for the unmarked door, didn't bother to use the knob, and knocked it open. There was a video monitor and a computer set up, a big hard drive working.

Tad glanced around. No diskettes stacked up anywhere, no removable drives on the shelves. He moved closer and divined that the security device was no more than it appeared to be: a short-time recorder that ran a cycle, recording over and over, using the same storage device.

He grabbed the thing, smashed it against the floor, and shattered it into several pieces. The HD disk popped out, and he picked that up and broke it in half, then stuck the pieces in his back pocket. Never knew but what they could recover stuff even if it was busted.

All done now.

He started for the door.

Steve, too stupid to know when he was outmatched, came at Tad, swinging a steel bar. Even without weights on it, the bar had to go fifteen pounds, and it would have broken something had it hit him.

Tad dodged, ducked, and the bar whistled over his head, slammed into the wall, and punched a long hole in the Sheetrock. The force of Steve's swing buried the steel rod half its length in the wall.

Tad drove his knee into Steve's kidney, and the big man went down as if his legs had suddenly vanished.

Nobody else got in Tad's way as he left the building. He headed for his car.

Nobody came after him. Just as well, too. He had enjoyed wrestling with the folks in the gym, and if they'd come out for him, why, he would just have *had* to oblige 'em.

Now that that was over, he could relax and let the Hammer swing him along.

Gonna be a good night, yessir, he could tell.

Let's move it, Thor!

21

Newport Beach, California

The Newport Beach Community Presbyterian Church (USA) was not as ostentatious as, say, the Crystal Palace, but certainly it was L.A.: in your face enough so it wouldn't pass for a church most other places. Philosophically, God's frozen people tended to have conservative views on politics, conservative views on social issues, and of course, conservative views on religion. They were very liberal on converting the heathen, though, and never let a chance to start up an overseas mission pass by unmolested. An old running joke in the church was, the Presbyterians had offered to completely fund the Red Cross and CARE, provided those organizations would let them pack a dehydrated minister in with each big shipment of blood or food. They were mostly Republicans, Drayne figured out back when he was still going to church, mostly white and old Republicans, at that. His family had been members since Grandpa Drayne, a deacon of his church back home in Atlanta, had moved out here eighty years ago. The synods were different, but California and Georgia weren't that far apart as far as the basics were concerned.

The building itself had a lot of glass, giving it a light and airy look, and the air conditioning unit out back, roaring to keep the assembled cool, was the size of a half-ton pickup truck. Drayne figured the reason the Baptists always preached about hellfire was because in those un–air-conditioned Southern churches, the congregation could relate to the concept. If the AC went out during a mild spring hot spell in a Presbyterian church, services would be canceled for fear the assembly would all die of heat stroke.

The place sure didn't seem somber enough for a funeral, and most of the mourners were wearing anything but black. Looked like a flock of parakeets, all the pastel colors. What could you expect? It was L.A., wasn't it?

Drayne's father had been a deacon at one time, though his FBI travel had cut into that, but last Drayne knew, the old man still attended church every Sunday down in Arizona. If he wasn't a true believer, he sure gave that impression.

Drayne himself had skipped every Sunday when his father hadn't been around to make him go, and hadn't been inside a church except for a couple of weddings since he'd left home for college. Oh, and that once when he made a major chemical sale to somebody who thought a Catholic church in Berkeley would be a safe place to do a dope deal. Turned out the buyer was wrong. He got busted after a fender-bender accident leaving the parking lot.

Drayne had managed to dig up a dark suit, a white shirt, and a plain tie that were all five or six years old, unworn for almost that long, knowing that if he came in a T-shirt and shorts, his father would probably pull his gun and shoot him. And even though he was retired, the old man always carried a piece when he went out, a habit he couldn't let go of. He'd still be protecting the republic when he was in a wheelchair and blind.

Despite the fact he was pushing seventy, the old man still looked pretty healthy. His hair was white, and his fair skin, pale most of his life, was now a ruddy color that was almost a tan, from spending more time out of doors in the Arizona sunshine. Drayne knew he looked just like a younger version of his father. The family resemblance had always been strong, even though he had refused to believe it for a long time. Then one day he'd caught sight of himself in a rest room mirror as he was washing his hands, and lo! there was the face of his father staring out at him. Assuming he lived so long, the old man was what Drayne was gonna look like at his age.

Amazing, that.

His father stood outside the church, looking at his watch, waiting for Drayne. He wore a black suit, probably one of a dozen black or dark gray ones he owned, and since he hadn't gotten fat after he retired, it still fit. A better fit than the suit Drayne himself had on.

"Robert," his father said.

"Dad."

"Let's go inside. We'll sit with Edwina."

People were still filing in. The service wouldn't start for another twenty minutes. Drayne knew that his father would be early, and that he expected everybody in the family to be early, and so it was.

Drayne offered condolences to his aunt and uncle and cousins. Irene, the girl who had showed him hers while he showed her his when they'd been nine, had grown up to be a good-looking woman, though she was married with three kids of her own now, and a little on the hefty side. Sheila, the middle girl, wore dark-rimmed glasses and a black dress with long sleeves, and had also gotten a little chunky. But Maggie, the youngest, who'd been a little geeky-looking girl with thick glasses, was now a beautiful redhead of twenty-five who, he had heard, taught aerobics somewhere in the Valley, and looked as fit and as tight as a violin string.

"Hey, Maggie. I thought you wore glasses. I don't see any contacts. You have the laser surgery?"

"No, I'm on the NightMove system. You wear these hard contact lenses to bed, and when you wake up, you can go without glasses or contacts all day."

"No kidding?"

"Yeah, it's called Ortho-K. Been around for a while, but they finally got it pretty much perfected. You can go sixteen, eighteen hours, and in my case, I have twenty/twenty without glasses."

"Great. Hey, I'm sorry about Creepy."

"Thanks, it's such a shock. Can't believe he's really dead." She leaned over and kissed him on the edge of the mouth.

Definitely a cousin worth kissing, Maggie. If it hadn't been her brother's funeral, he would have thought about hitting on her, though the family would have howled at that. Shoot, he wasn't going to marry her or have kids, what did it matter if they were cousins? He'd seen the way she looked at him, she'd be up for it.

His father said, "How are things at work, Robert?"

He came away from his mild sexual fantasy. "Fine. I'm up for a promotion. They are considering me for head of Polymers. Be worth another ten thousand a year."

"Congratulations."

"How is Arizona? The dog okay?"

"Fine. The dog is fine."

That pretty much exhausted everything Drayne and his father usually said to each other. But sitting here waiting for some preacher, who at best probably had not seen

Creepy in ten years, to talk about what a wonderful boy he had been and God's plans and all, Drayne felt an urge to poke at his father. He said, "You hear about what happened at HQ in L.A.?" There was no need to identify HQ, that was all it had ever been called in their family.

"I heard."

Drayne wanted to grin, but of course, that would have been inappropriate in this place at this time.

"Sounds like something you'd pull," his father continued.

For a second, Drayne felt a cold splash of terror. "What?"

"I haven't forgotten the incident in your English class." His tone was stern, disapproving.

He felt a sense of relief, and at the same time, of irritation. *Jesus Christ! The old man was still pissed off about that?* Drayne hadn't thought about it in years.

It had been nothing. He'd made a little stink bomb, one with a kitchen match and a cheap ballpoint pen, the kind of things kids did. You took the ink cartridge out, put the match inside the body of the pen, and rigged a bobby pin in the spring, then screwed the thing back together. The bobby pin stuck out where the ballpoint tip had been, so when you pulled it back and let it go, it thumped into the head of the match, lighting it. But since the flame didn't have anywhere to go, it flared up and down the pen's barrel and vaporized some of the cheap plastic before it went out. The result was a short blast of godawful smelly smoke; that was it.

Drayne had been fourteen, in the eighth grade, when he'd dropped one of the pen stink bombs into the garbage can next to the English teacher's desk when she hadn't been looking. It had been a hoot, that stinking smoke belching from the trash, but some goody-goody had seen him do it and ratted on him. He'd gotten two days off to consider the heinousness of his crime, and the old man had taken his belt to him when he found out. And never let him forget it.

"I'm not fourteen anymore, Dad. That was a long time ago."

"I didn't say you did it. I said it sounded like the kind of childish prank you used to do."

Drayne didn't say anything, but it pissed him off that the old man was still throwing up ancient history in his face. Even though he *had* done the FBI prank, that shouldn't have been the first thing out of the old man's mouth.

"Nobody got hurt, did they?" Drayne finally said.

His father had been thinking about it. He came back fast: "But they could have been. People unwittingly exposed to drugs are at risk. Somebody could have been injured. What if some of the agents or staff had been allergic to the drug? On medication that it might have interacted with? What if there had been some kind of emergency needing a prompt response? A fire in the building, maybe a bank robbery or a kidnapping, and they had been unable to respond properly? The idiot who thought it was funny to chemically assault an office of federal agents didn't think about those things, you may be sure. It was an irresponsible, criminal act, and he'll be caught and punished for it. I hope they lock him up and lose the key."

Drayne gritted his teeth. It would be a bad idea to say anything. Just let it go. *What did you expect? The old man was gonna express admiration for the cleverness of the stone job? C'mon, Bobby, you know how he is. Now is the time for all good men to shut the fuck up.*

But he couldn't help himself. Drayne said, "Maybe not. From the reports, it didn't sound as if they had any leads. Maybe the guy was too smart for them."

The old man turned to look at Drayne, blinking at him as he might at seeing a dog turd dropped into a church social punch bowl. "If he had been *smart,* he would have known better than to assault agents of the FBI. They'll get him." He paused a second. "Do you *admire* this criminal, Robert? Is that what you are saying? Didn't you learn anything from your upbringing?"

Drayne flushed but finally realized it was time to keep silent. He just shook his head.

Yeah, Dad, I learned plenty. Much more than you will ever know.

But then the minister arrived, a guy who looked to be about a hundred years old, and it was time to get down to the business of burying Creepy.

Malibu, California

Tad was still up, though about to crash, watching the morning bunnies and studs jog along the beach. The early fog had mostly burned off by nine or ten A.M., showing the brilliant blue hiding behind the gray.

Man, he was wasted. As the chemicals of the Hammer faded and lost their grip on him, he felt a bone-deep weariness begin to claim him. This was gonna be a hard one to recover from, he knew. Best thing to do would be to take a shitload of downers and sleep for as long as he could, twenty-four, thirty-six hours, let his body get as much enforced rest as he could. Couple of the long-lasting phenobarb suppositories, some Triavil, maybe some Valium mixed in, to keep the muscles relaxed. Some Butazoladin for the joints, Decadron for the inflammation, Vicodin and little snort of heroin for pain, Zantac for his stomach, maybe even a little Haldol, just for the hell of it.

Bobby, off at his cousin's funeral, wasn't gonna be too happy with him when he found out about Tad busting up the gym. Probably they wouldn't want to be seen hanging together for a while, in case ole Steve the bodybuilder ran into them somewhere and made the connection. Tad didn't think the gym rats knew he was tight with Bobby, he was pretty sure they didn't know, but book it, they weren't gonna forget him after last night.

It would probably be in the papers and on the tube, about the gym, but Bobby wasn't plugged into the news, only what he caught on the radio when he was out driving, so maybe he wouldn't hear about it until Tad had a chance to break it to him, put a little spin on it.

He managed a grin, even though his face was sore from the drug rictus he'd worn for most of the night. Yeah, spin, right. How much spin could you put on trashing a place and beating the crap out of folks because you had suddenly gotten horny?

Well, at least there weren't any public recordings of the Zee-ster and Bobby floating around, Tad knew that. That was the important thing. Maybe Bobby was right. Maybe they should jet over to the islands and mellow out for a few weeks, come back when things settled down. Way he felt right now, the idea of swinging the Hammer again any time soon didn't really appeal. Of course, if he lived through the recovery and got to feeling better, the desire would come back pretty quick. It always did.

Being able to do what he had done last night when he looked like a male version of Olive Oyl? That was a big fucking draw.

Hell, after he'd left the gym, he'd lost interest in sex, but he had driven up to the Hollywood sign, hopped the fence, and climbed up to the top of the big *H*. Sat there watching the city for a while, climbed down, and driven to Griffith Park, where he'd roamed for hours, just enjoying the green. Hadn't gotten home until after Bobby left, which was a good thing, 'cause he'd probably have told him about the gym, being fearless at the time.

No, better he learns about it in a couple, three days, back when I'm straight again and it's all past tense. Bobby could go to World or Gold's or one of the other upscale places to work out, it was no big loss.

"Time to get the doc-in-a-box out, Tad m'man," he said aloud. "And settle down for long nap."

22

Quantico, Virginia

Michaels put a pair of dollar coins into the soft drink machine and pushed the button marked Coke. Change clattered into the return as the plastic bottle hit the bottom slot and rolled into view. He had pretty much given up drinking fizzy sugar water, but now and then he indulged. His father had liked the stuff; he drank three or four a day.

It brought back old, pleasant memories from his childhood to sit and sip one.

He took the Coke out, fed the change back into the machine, added another dollar coin, and looked at Jay Gridley.

"Club soda," Jay said.

Michaels pushed the button. Three bucks for two soft drinks. What a racket.

"So you can't come up with any history on Frick and Frack other than they were at a conference at the same time twenty years ago as teenagers?"

Jay took his bottled drink and popped the cap off, then

swigged from it. "Nope. I know there's something there, but I haven't found it yet."

"Well, don't kill yourself looking. It probably doesn't mean anything anyway. Better you should concentrate on the drug thing. We find what they want, they are off our back. Any leads there?"

"Nothing to speak of. The local cops and the DEA are all over Zeigler's place like white on rice. He had to get the drug from somewhere, and they figure if they back-track him enough, they might find something."

"You don't?" Michaels drank some of the Coke. Okay, so it was bad for you, but sometimes you just had to indulge. He didn't smoke, or drink more than the occasional beer or glass of wine. He ate pretty well; he worked out every day. A bottle of Coke now and then ought not to kill him.

Famous last words.

Jay said, "Maybe, but I wouldn't bet on it. Guy like that, big-time movie star, he probably didn't play golf with his connection. I'd be real surprised if he had a listing in his address book under Dope Dealer."

Michaels shrugged. "So how do we run the dealer? Wait for somebody else to go berserk and backtrack them?"

"Don't have to wait," Jay said. "Apparently some guy walked into a gym in Santa Monica last night and laid waste to the place. Threw some guys bigger 'n Hercules around like rag dolls when they objected to him feeling up the woman working the desk, who apparently was pretty well-built herself. Knocked doors down, punched holes in the walls, like that."

"The police have him?"

"Nope, he got away. We got the description—he sounds like a beatnik from what the witnesses said—and we have the police sketch."

Jay grinned, and Michaels joined him. Police sketches all seemed to look alike, and not very much like any of the guys they were supposed to represent. Plug a saint into an ID kit, he'd come out looking like a thug.

"According to the reports, after he got working, this guy went to the security cam setup, tore up the recording device, and made off with the disk drive medium."

Michaels considered that for a few seconds. "So he was not so stoned he couldn't think about covering his ass."

"Maybe. Or maybe there was something on the disk he wanted, though it probably wasn't him. According to the complaint, all the people involved swear they would have remembered this guy if he'd ever been in their place. Guy was built like a toothpick, bodybuilders notice such things. That he was the proverbial ninety-seven-pound weakling made his rampage all that much more amazing. The bodybuilders couldn't believe it. Got to be our friend Mr. Purple Cap responsible . . . or a major number-busting coincidence."

"So what good does this do us?"

"Well, we know that three of the dealer's customers live in or around L.A. The rich woman, the dead movie star, and the live beatnik. I'm thinking maybe our dealer might like the sunny lifestyle. The shelf life of this mojo drug is pretty short, it rots in a day or so, and for the Zeester to get stuff himself, then to the rich girl, and for her to have time enough to use it? I'm thinking maybe the guy who supplied Zeigler is not halfway around the world. FedEx, or even a paid courier, are limited by the speed of a jet. The farther away he is, the narrower the window when the drug will still work."

Michaels nodded. "Okay. So hypothetically speaking, *maybe* he lives within spitting distance of SoCal. Does that help us much?"

"Narrows down the search. I can start checking chemical companies, drug supply houses, running lists of convicted dealers, like that. And maybe the cops will turn up something on the late Mr. Zeigler's travels."

Michaels said, "Good a direction as any, I suppose."

Jay took another long swallow of the club soda. "Anything new on the drug itself? How'd that cap assay out?"

Michaels frowned. *Crap!* He'd tucked the thing into his pocket and forgotten about it. Those trousers were in a heap on the floor in his closet. He hoped Toni hadn't sent them to the laundry yet.

He smiled at that thought. The only way Toni was going to do his laundry was if he specifically asked her to, and he hadn't done that. The pants would still be there when he got home. She hadn't signed on to be his maid, he'd found that out pretty quickly. Nor had he expected that.

"Boss?"

"Nothing. I mean, nothing on the capsule. I haven't had a chance to get by the lab yet."

It was Jay's turn to shrug. "I got the DEA's breakdown of what ingredients they could find. I'll use those for a starting point. If the guy is smart, he'll buy his chem for cash, and far away from home, but you never know. Sometimes it's the little things that trip you up. Remember Morrison, the HAARP guy?"

Michaels nodded. How could he forget that? "Yeah, I remember."

"He had all the big stuff worked out but slipped up on something as simple as a night watchman. Him and the Watergate guys."

"Well, do what you can do, Jay. Keep me in the loop."

"Sure thing, boss."

Michaels looked at his watch. Getting close to noon. Maybe he'd stroll on down to the gym and do a little workout. That way he could take a break when he got home without Toni making him practice his *silat* first. She'd work him harder than he'd work himself, but if he'd already done his *djurus* for the day, she'd let him slide.

Newport Beach, California

Drayne came away from the funeral experience pretty depressed.

The church service had been fairly saccharine, like he'd expected. The old minister, if he remembered Creepy at all, couldn't speak in anything other than platitudes and generalities, and he put in a pitch to save souls while he did it. Neither Edwina nor Pat could bring themselves to get up and say anything, and Creepy's sisters and ex-wife managed some personal stuff that was touching and surprising. Drayne never knew that Creepy had a collection of Star Wars cards, nor that he coached a boy's soccer team in Utah.

The procession to the graveyard and the internment service at the family plot was no more fun. While he was standing there, a sudden flash of déjà vu hit Drayne. Another funeral he'd gone to when he'd been ten or eleven popped up in his mind, something he had completely forgotten about. A kid a year or so younger than Drayne who lived across the street and down a couple of houses, Rowland, his name was, had been killed in a gruesome freak accident. Rowlie's father had worked at a small private airport somewhere. Rowlie and his two brothers had gone with their father one Saturday to the airport. The boys had been playing chase in and around the hangars. Somehow, Rowlie had run in front of a small plane that was about to taxi out for takeoff. The plane's propeller had hit him. He'd been killed instantly. The coffin had been kept closed because he'd been almost decapitated and chopped up pretty good; at least that was what Drayne had heard.

Jesus. He didn't need another reminder of death, not with Creepy just lowered into the ground.

There wasn't an official wake, though family and friends were welcome to stop by Pat and Edwina's, so of course Drayne had to do that. What did you say at such times? People standing around, drinking coffee or tea, talking about the recently departed as if he'd gone on some kind of trip?

Drayne got out of there as soon as he could. His old man was busy, taking charge, making sure everything was shipshape, and they didn't really have much to say to each other, Drayne and his old man. They never really had. The old man had never thought much of his only son, never seemed interested in what he did, always expected perfection. He brought home a report card with five *A*s and a *B*, the old man didn't say, "Hey, good job! Congratulations!" No, he said, "Why the *B?* You need to apply yourself more."

Once, when he was about twelve, he'd been visiting his grandma, out in the Valley. He found some old photo albums and started digging through them. In the back were a stack of his old man's report cards. The son of a bitch had made straight *A*s through high school. Had been valedictorian of his class before he went off to college and law school, and eventually the FBI. Jesus. Drayne couldn't even bitch about the old bastard holding him to a higher standard than he'd achieved on his own.

Oh, yeah, Drayne had been a whiz in chemistry. It had been his natural element. And he was smart enough to get good grades in his other subjects without having to crack a book most of the time. He just didn't see the point in working his butt off to learn stuff like "Tippicanoe and

Tyler Too!" when it wouldn't ever be any part of his life.
Who gave a rat's ass about gerunds and split infinitives,
or ancient Greek history, or what the current names for
countries in Africa were? Drayne was going to be a chemist, he was going to make his fortune playing with things
he wanted to play with, and to hell with the rest of it.

No, they had not gotten along for as long as he could
remember, his old man and him. And yet he felt some
kind of perverse need to demonstrate to his father that he
was competent. Which was kind of hard to do when what
you were most competent at was mixing and selling illegal drugs, and your old man was a pillar of law enforcement who put people like you away.

The drive back to Malibu was bright and sunny. The
fog had long since burned off, and traffic wasn't too bad.
Neither the weather nor the lack of usual stop-and-go traffic lifted his mood.

He hadn't seen Tad last night or this morning, and he
suspected that was because Tad had taken another Hammer trip, even though Drayne had told him not to. The
Hammer was Tad's reason to get up in the morning. Tad
was a full-time doper, he could mix and match his chems
to suit his needs better than anybody Drayne had ever
known, and for him, Thor was the ultimate party friend,
the guy Tad had been looking for all his life. And Thor
would be the guy who'd kill him, too.

Then again, in his own way, Tad was fairly reliable. If
he had swallowed the cap and gone hyper, it had probably
been after he had done the job Drayne had sent him to
do. It was rare if Tad came home and hadn't done whatever Drayne had sent him to do, and even when that happened, it was due to something Tad couldn't control.

He didn't really know why Tad was so important to
him. They had run into each other doing biz, and something about the reedy guy in black had tickled Drayne.

Nothing sexual, they were into women—though Tad preferred drugs to pussy, mostly—and not as if Tad were some kind of sparkling conversationalist or brilliant intellect. But he was loyal, and he did think Drayne was a genius. And he got the job done. If he wanted to go out in a blaze of Dionysian glory, that was his right. Tad was pretty much the only friend Drayne had. Making and dealing illegal chem didn't open you up to a whole lot of deep relationships with honest people. When Tad croaked, that was going to leave a big hole in the list of people Drayne could relax around.

Of course, he had enough money now that if he invested it right, he could almost live off the interest. Another year or so of thousand-buck-a-hit sales, he'd be set. Then he could retire if he felt like it, maybe move into a better class of people, make some friends who started out thinking he was a dot.com millionaire, or had made a killing in the market or something, who'd take him at face value. Live his life out in the open, perfectly legal, no looking over his shoulder.

That made him grin. Yeah, he could do that. Would he?

Not an ice cube's chance in a supernova he would. Because it wasn't just the money, it was the *game*. The ability to do what he did, to do it better than anybody else, and to get away with it. Hell, if he wanted to, he could take his formulas to the legitimate drug companies, and they'd fall all over themselves to shovel money at him. A lot of what Drayne had discovered and created was what the pharmaceutical giants had been researching for years. Got a patient with muscle wasting who is bedbound and on the way down? What would it be worth to him to enjoy some mobility in his final days? Got a guy who can't get it up, and Viagra doesn't work for him? How much would he spend to get an erection so hard it would hum in a breeze? You about to take the GRE to get into graduate school? What would adding fifteen points to your IQ for a couple hours be worth? Stuff Drayne worked with could do that and more.

Drayne could have gone to work for those guys a long time ago. He could have brought just part of what he knew to the table, and they would have kissed his shoes and given him a blank check to get it. But there wasn't any *challenge* there, not to be straight.

Not to be like his father.

He sighed. He was smart enough to know he was a little fucked up when it came to such things. Had done some reading in psychology, knew all about Oedipus and shit like that. But he was what he was. However he had gotten there, it was his path, and he was going to walk it, and the devil take the reasons.

Jesus, he was tight, wound up like a spring. Maybe he should stop at the gym on the way home, loosen up a little, take it out on the weights. He'd feel better if he did. A good, hard workout was the cure for a whole lot of things, tension, stress, it would mellow you out almost as much as champagne.

Yeah. Maybe he'd do that. It would be relaxing.

23

Malibu, California

Drayne couldn't remember the last time he had been so pissed off. He pounded the steering wheel of the Mercedes hard enough to crack it, and he wished it was fucking Tad's head!

Jesus Christ!

By the time he got home, however, he had calmed down somewhat. He was almost detached, almost fatalistic about it when he pulled into the garage and shut the engine off. He had always known this was a possibility, though he hadn't expected it would ever really happen. He was too smart to be caught by the plodders; he'd been giving them fucking *clues* and they couldn't do it. Only, Tad wasn't. And the boy had stepped in it good this time.

Tad was out cold on the couch, and even the pitcher full of ice water hardly roused him. He mumbled something.

Drayne started slapping his face. Eventually, his hand got sore and tired, but Tad came awake, sort of.

"What?"

"You idiot! You don't have *any* idea what you did, do you?"

"What?"

"The gym! You trashed the gym! I stopped by there to work out, and that was all anybody was talking about! Even if I hadn't sent you, I could recognize you from their descriptions! You moron!"

Groggy, Tad sat up. He rubbed at his face. "I'm all wet," he said.

"You got that right. Christ on a pogo stick, Tad!"

"I don't understand, Bobby. I got the disk from the security drive, the job's done, we're free and clear, nobody has anything to link us to Zeigler. There's no proof of anything."

"You really don't see it, do you?" Drayne sat heavily on the couch next to his partner. Of a moment, he felt sorry for Tad. He kept forgetting most people didn't have his horsepower when it came to cranking up the mental engines. "Obviously, the smart drugs hadn't kicked in when you decided to feel up Atlas's sister. Think about it."

Tad shook his head, still not tracking.

"Look, I know you're tired and stoned, and ordinarily I'd let you sleep it off, but time just got to be a problem. You made a mistake."

"I don't see it. They don't know who I am. No way."

"Okay. Let me explain it to you." He looked at Tad, who made death warmed over seem the picture of health, and realized he had to take it slow for him to keep up with it. He eased off his anger a little. "Let me tell you a story. Just sit back and listen carefully, okay?"

Tad nodded.

"When I was in middle school, they had us in an arts and crafts track. We got three months each of music, art, and speech in one bundle, and three months of drafting, shop, and home arts in another.

"So the first day I show up in music class, and sweet little old Mrs. Greentree, had to be about a hundred and fifty or so, has us all sitting there, and she says, 'What is the universal language?' And of course, none of us have a clue. And she says, 'Music. Music is the universal language. The notes are the same in Germany as they are in France or America.'

"Right, okay, so we got it. Music is the universal language.

"So later that day, we get to to the first section of second bundle, which turns out to be drafting class. This is taught by Coach. Back then, every other male teacher in the school was Coach.

"So we're sitting there, and Coach says, 'Okay, what is the universal language?'

"So anyway, being as how I am newly educated and eager to impress, I shoot my hand up and Coach grins at me. 'Yeah?'

'Music, Coach,' I say. 'Music is the universal language!'

"Coach just about kills himself laughing. 'Music?! Haw! Music ain't the universal language, you dip, *pictures* are the universal language! You in China and you run into some Chinaman and you want to ask him where the toilet is, what are you gonna do, *sing* to him? "Oh, mister Chinaman, please tell me, where is the toilet, la la la . . . ?"

" 'Jesus, get your head out of your butt, son! You draw him a *picture!* Music! Haw!'

"A couple years later, that same question came up in math class, and guess what? I kept my hand down and my mouth shut. Same thing happened when I got to basic computer class. Music, pictures, mathematics, binaries, they are all considered universal languages."

Drayne shut up and looked at Tad, who shook his head.

"Okay, so what's the point?"

"*Context* is my point, Tad. *Context.*" He spoke slowly, as if talking to a retarded child. "Not just what gets said or done, but *where* and *when* it happens is critically important."

Tad frowned, and Drayne could see that he still didn't get it.

"Let me tell you another story."

"Jesus, Bobby, okay, I get it that you're pissed—"

"Shut up, Tad. Once upon a time I knew a guy who was a bouncer at a titty bar. One night, he and some of his friends went to a heavy metal rock concert, you know the kind, head-bangers, primal rock, big crowds standing on the floor screaming to the music, half of them stoned or drunk. So in the middle of the concert, a girl who is sitting on her boyfriend's shoulders decides to pull off her top and flash the crowd, or the band, or whoever."

"I've seen that a few times," Tad said, trying to follow him.

"Right. So'd my bouncer friend, and no big deal. And normally, the way it works is, the girl waves her hooters around, then puts her top back on, a fine time is had by all, and that's that. But this time, while she was unbound and waving in the breeze, her boyfriend reaches up and grabs her breasts, starts rubbing them. Now, she doesn't slap his hands away, she laughs, and next thing you know, she's pulled off her steed and felt up by thirty or forty heavy metal fans. We're talking mob mentality here, and the atmosphere is ripe for trouble. My friend the bouncer is too jammed in to help, and the crowd is so thick that concert security can't get there, either. The girl vanishes.

"Fortunately, aside from getting passed around and fondled against her will, it didn't go any further. They let her go, she gets her clothes back, her nipples are sore, end of event.

"So, whose fault was it she got mauled, Tad?"

"Hers. She should have kept her top on."

"Yes. And people shouldn't get drunk or do drugs and go to rock concerts, and we should always look both ways before crossing the street. No, it's the *boyfriend* who set it off, and the girl, who could have stopped it, made it worse. See, soon as he laid a hand on her boob, she should have slapped the shit out of him. The implied message when somebody flashes in such a situation is 'Look, but don't touch.' When the boyfriend broke the implied rule, the others assumed that a girl who'd do that in public, who was willing to allow touch along with the looking, well, she might be willing to let somebody else play, too, so they helped themselves."

"Not right."

"Nope, it wasn't. But given the circumstances, a bunch of stoned mouthbreathing head-bangers, you can understand how it might progress to that, or worse. There's the way things *should* be, and the way things *are.* You might not like it, but you ignore the way things *are* at your peril."

"And you are saying that I fucked up even though I got rid of the evidence. That it is going to progress to something else?"

"That is exactly what I am saying. See if you can stay with me here: The police and the feds will *know* you were on the Hammer, because nothing else can explain a burned-out matchstick like you kicking major steroid ass like you did. And the bust at Zeigler's was a major deal and on the minds of the cops. And if they dig just a little, they'll come up with the Zee-ster working out at Steve's, and *zap!* A light will flash over their heads and they'll think, 'Hmm. Big movie star shoots it out with the DEA, and they find this superguy drug in his house. Then, within a real short time, somebody trashes a gym where the big movie star works out, obviously on the *same* superguy drug. Say . . . isn't *that* a funny coincidence?' And somebody . . . somebody in the FBI or the local police . . . they are gonna ask themselves the big question: Why? Why'd the guy—that's you—why'd the guy come in and steal the security cam's recording device? Other than coming in to feel up Brunhilda and kicking the crap out of a few bodybuilders, that's all you did. And they are gonna come up with, 'Hey, maybe there is something on that disk the guy doesn't want us to see. What could it be?' And somebody is gonna take it one step further and make an assumption, since they know the Zee-ster worked out there, and that somebody is gonna say, 'Hmm. Maybe because the big movie star was there *with* somebody who really doesn't want to be seen?' "

"But the recording is gone—" Tad began.

Drayne cut him off, but his voice was quiet. "So it is. But the people who work there aren't. I know Steve, the owner, and he might remember that a couple of times when Zeigler was there, he and I came or went together. And if Steve or Tom or Dick or Harry or anybody else in the place remembers that, then my name is gonna come up in a conversation with the feds or cops. And even if Steve *doesn't* remember, the cops *will* get a list of members and go looking for a connection. This is a cop lesson I learned at my daddy's knee: When you don't have anything, you check *every*thing. And sooner or later, they are gonna send somebody out to talk to folks on the list, just routine, and there will be a knock on our door. And I have a nice made-up job that fortunately I didn't mention on my application at the gym, one that's all nice and electronically vouched for, so maybe they can poke at it a little and it might even hold up, but . . . *What is the fucking job, Tad?*"

"Oh, shit."

"Oh, shit, yeah. I'm a *chemist.* Think that'll, you know, raise any red flags or ring any bells? Illicit drugs and a chemist? There are millions of test tube jockeys in the world, but how many of us working out at the same gym as the dead guy they are investigating up the wazoo? Even the stupidest cop alive could run with that one.

"The feds might not be the fastest mill wheels in the world, but they grind exceedingly fine. They are plodders, but that's what they do best, and if they get this far, we are fucked. Even if the house is as clean as a wetware assembly room. If they can't *prove* anything, they'll know who I am, and that will throw a big rock into the gears. I won't be able to go pee from now on without seeing an underwater camera lens in the toilet bowl looking up at me."

Tad shook his head. "I'm sorry, man."

Drayne shook his head in response. "I know, Tad, I know. And it's done. Now, we have to see if we can manage some kind of damage control."

"How?"

Drayne looked at him. "You know the guy in Texas, down in Austin?"

"The programmer who buys two caps every three or four weeks, for him and his girlfriend."

"Yeah, him. I read about him in *Time.* He's supposed to be a genius, supposed to be able to make a computer sit up and bark like a dog, if he wants. Got his start hacking into secure systems just for the fun of it."

"So?"

"So, we make him a deal. He does us a favor, we supply him with whatever rings his bell, for free."

"Dude is richer than Midas, he doesn't need the money."

"But I know how geniuses think," Drayne said. "Especially outlaw geniuses. He'll do it so we'll owe him, and in the doing, he can prove he's still got the chops he started out with. He gets to exercise the old muscles and feel like a badass outlaw again."

"What is he gonna do that'll help?"

"He's going to make us invisible. Get ahold of him."

"Now?"

"Right now."

The more he thought about it, the better he liked the idea. It could work. If they moved fast enough, it definitely could work.

24

Sweat ran down John Howard's face.

In the heat of battle, the SIPEsuit's polypropyl/spider-silk layers didn't get rid of the perspiration nearly fast enough to keep you dry. The weight of the ceramic plates wasn't bad, but it didn't help cool things any. Even during a tepid night, such as it was now, the helmet's sweatband quickly got soaked, and you had to blink away the moisture that oozed down into your eyes. And you couldn't raise the clear face shield to let some air in, because the heads-up display wouldn't work without the shield, and neither would the seventh-gen spookeyes built into the armored plastic.

The good thing was, night was no cover for the bad guys. The latest-release intensifiers in the starlight scopes were powerful enough to let you see with the slightest city glow, and the suit's computer false-colored the images so they didn't have that washed-out, pale green look. The blast shield cutouts had been upgraded so that if some yahoo threw a flare or a flashbang, the filters would pop on-line within a hundredth of a second, saving you from a sudden nova-lume that would sear your eyeballs blind in a heartbeat. Though this was something of a mixed blessing.

"You can run, Abdul, but you can't hide," Howard said.

From the LOSIR headset, Sergeant Pike's voice: "Sir?"

"Disregard that," Howard said. He shifted his grip on the tommy gun. His good-luck piece wore the pistol grip forestock and a fifty round drum, weighed a ton, and it took a little practice to use properly, especially if you were used to the cheek-spot-weld, right-elbow-high, left-hand-under-the-foregrip the Army liked to teach long-arm shooters when Howard had gone through basic all those years ago.

"Sir, I make it nine ceejays coming in through that alley to the left."

Howard's own heads-up display verified that. "Copy, Sergeant. That's two each and one left over. Wake up troops and mind your fields of fire."

The other three men with Howard did not respond. They knew what they were supposed to do.

Howard clicked the selector onto full auto and raised the finned barrel with its Cutts compensator over the top of the rusty oil drum he had chosen for cover. The old drum was full of what looked like brick and concrete fragments, so it was cover and not just concealment. If the enemy spotted him and directed fire his way, he did have some protection.

The first of the nine soldiers appeared at the mouth of the alleyway. They stopped, and the leader held up his hand, signaling for the others to halt. He looked around, didn't see Howard or the rest of his quad, then hand-signaled for the rest to advance.

Howard touched a recessed control on his helmet and shut off the spookeyes. The bright-as-noon scene went immediately dim, but there was still enough ambient light to make out the shadowy forms of the enemy troopers. He slitted his eyelids, to make the scene even darker, forcing his pupil to dilate wider.

When the ninth soldier appeared, one of Howard's quad tossed a five-second photon flare. Bright, actinic white light strobed, casting tall, hard-edged shadows from the startled soldiers.

Howard waited a beat, then opened his eyes wider.

His men let go with their subguns, and the enemy soldiers returned fire, yelling and blasting away.

Howard indexed the two in his assigned field of fire and gave them each a three-round burst.

In the light of the still burning photon flare, the nine went down like pins in a bowling alley. The scene fell quiet. The five-second flare winked out, and it went dark, much darker than before. Even though he had been using hardball .45 auto ammo with low-flash powder, the afterimages of his fire decreased his vision. Howard touched the control, and the spookeyes turned night into day again. The heat sigs on the downed soldiers showed no movement. Good. A perfect ambush.

"End sim," Howard said.

The Baghdad street scene vanished, and John Howard removed the VR headset and leaned back in his office chair. The exercise had been designed to practice with the spookeyes, and it had gone as planned. The ability to see in almost total darkness was a great help, but there were some drawbacks. Because of the automatic filters built into the scopes, any scenario that included random, repeated weapons fire effectively rendered the spookeyes useless, just as it did wolf ear hearing protectors.

With a single bright flash of light, the scopes' filters would kick on long enough to diminish the light to safe levels, then open back up. This worked great for an explosion. However, with multiple flashes of bright orange muzzle blasts going off all around you, the filters would kick on and off, going from light to dark so fast it was extremely disorienting. The effect was rather like being surrounded by strobe lights all timed differently. Early sims showed the accuracy rate of troopers firing in such a scenario dropped dramatically.

So different tactics had been employed to get around the problem.

At first, the scientific types had tried to rig the scopes to drop filters and leave them down for five or ten seconds. Unfortunately, this made the scene too dark to see anything except much-dimmed muzzle flashes, your own or the enemy's. Spray and pray was a sucker's game.

They tried adjusting this, but since firefights sometimes lasted for five seconds, sometimes a lot longer, the results were less than satisfactory.

They also tried raising the gain threshold, so it took more to cause the shields to deploy, but even an amplified kitchen match in the dark would be enough to temporarily blind a soldier.

The scientists and engineers scratched their heads and went back to their CAD programs.

It fell to the men and women in the field to come up with a better way, like it usually did. Using the scopes to find and track an enemy, then reverting to the old-fashioned method seemed to be the best approach. At least it worked in VR scenarios and at the range. How it would work in the real world remained to be seen, at least for his units.

Howard sighed. He had run dozens of war game scenarios over the past few weeks, and there was only so much of that a man could take. In his time as the commander of Net Force's military arm, there had been slack periods, but never as slow as it had been these last few weeks. He knew he was supposed to be happy about that, the idea that peace was better than war, and he was, but—

—sitting around and doing nothing but figurative paper clip counting was boring.

Of course, he wasn't as likely to get shot sitting around and doing nothing, and that had been on his mind lately, too.

Washington, D.C.

Toni tried doing her *djurus* while sitting on the couch, just using her upper body, as Guru had told her. Yeah, she could do it, and yeah, it was better than nothing, but it was like taking a shower with a raincoat on. You couldn't really feel the water.

She stood, moved the coffee table out of the way, and did a little stretching, nothing major, just to limber up her back and hips some. The doctor hadn't said she couldn't stretch, just nothing heavy-duty, right?

The elastic of her stretch pants cut into her belly as she sat and bent over to touch her toes. Damn, she hated this, being fat!

After five minutes or so of loosening up, she felt better. Okay, so she could do a few *djurus* with the footwork, the *langkas,* if she went real slow, right? No sudden moves, no real effort, it wouldn't be any more stressful than walking if she was careful, right?

For about ten minutes, she practiced, moving slowly, no power, just doing the first eight *djurus.* She skipped the forms where she had to drop into a squat, number five and number seven, and she felt fine.

Then, of course, she had to go pee, something that happened five times an hour, it seemed.

When she finished and started to leave the bathroom, she looked into the toilet.

The bowl had blood in it, as did the tissue she had just used.

Fear grabbed her in an icy hand.

She ran to call the doctor.

Austin, Texas

Tad drove the rental car, Bobby riding shotgun and giving him directions.

"Okay, stay on I-35 going south until we cross Lake Whatchamacallit, and look for a sign says Texas State School for the Deaf. We have to find Big Stacy Park— as opposed to Little Stacy Park, which is just up the road a piece—then Sunset Lane, then we turn onto—you piece of Chinese shit!"

This last part was accompanied by Bobby slapping the little GPS unit built into the car's dashboard.

"What?"

"The sucker glitched, the map disappeared!" Bobby hammered the malfunctioning GPS unit again. "Come on!"

"I don't see why we had to come here in person," Tad said. "We could have called or done this by e-mail over the web."

"No, we couldn't have. The feds can monitor phones and e-mail, even encrypted stuff. They were able to do it for years before the public even realized they could and already were. Besides, this guy wants an insurance policy. He wants to see our faces. He'll know the name, and he can use that, but we could change our identities."

"We could change our faces, too."

Bobby hit the GPS again. "Ah, there it is. I got the map again." He looked at Tad. "Yeah, we could, and he'll know that. But the thing is, he wants us to come to him with our hat in our hand and say please. Then he dazzles us with his techno-wizardry, and we owe him big-time and forever. It's an ego thing. Besides, as long as we're in business, he'll have something on us, doesn't matter what our names are or what we look like. We have the market cornered on Thor's Hammer, remember? Whoever is selling it is gonna be us, no matter what we call ourselves."

"Yeah. I have to say, though, this might be out of the frying pan and into the fire, man. Even if it works, we're trading one problem for another one."

"I don't think so," Bobby said.

Tad said, "There's the lake, up ahead."

"Okay, watch for the deaf sign, should be just after we cross over that."

"I'm watching. Back to this *maybe* biz. The guy will have something to trade if he ever gets busted. You think he wouldn't give us up to save his own ass?"

"Don't think that for a second. I'd give him up, if positions were reversed."

"Jeez, Bobby—"

"C'mon, Tad, think a little bit past the end of your nose. The clock is running at the cop shop. This computer dickwad can get into the gym's computer and the police system and make my name go away. He does that before they get to me, we're clear."

"If the cops didn't just get a hardcopy."

"They didn't. Steve told me they downloaded his membership files into their system over the wire. Nobody uses hardcopy for this kind of stuff anymore. I didn't even fill out a treeware registration form when I signed up; I just logged it all into a keyboard at the gym.

"So the *immediate* threat, the law, is taken care of. Mr. Computer Geek is a *potential* problem, but that's down the line. He isn't going to run to the cops and turn us in now, not if he wants help from mighty Thor to keep wearing blisters on his wang with his lady friend. You see what I'm saying?"

"Yeah, but—"

Bobby cut him off. "You know about Occam's Razor?"

"No. You not gonna tell me another fucking story, are you?"

Bobby laughed. "No. It's a way of looking at problems. A rule that basically says, don't get complicated when simple will do the job. The simple thing here is, if the cops don't know about me, they can't come looking for me."

"Okay, I can see that. You buy some time, get out from under the immediate threat. But you still got the potential thing later."

"Well, if you just let it hang out there, yeah. But this computer guy could, you know, have an accident. He could slip in the bathtub and dash his brains out or get hit by a bus crossing the street or maybe an allergic reaction to shellfish, and just up and die. There are certain chemicals that can kill somebody and make it look just like anaphylactic shock. And hey, stuff like that happens all the time, right? Cops would investigate, but if it was an *accident,* that would be the end of it, right?" Bobby grinned, that all-his-shiny-teeth smile that showed he was really amused.

Tad got it, finally. He nodded. "Oh. Oh, yeah. I see what you mean."

"There's hope for you yet, Tad m'boy—there, there's the sign, pull off at that next exit!"

Tad nodded. Bobby was almost always a step ahead of the game, even when things got creaky. Push him out a window, and he would land on his feet every time. He had it under control. It felt good to know that.

25

Washington, D.C.

Jay sat *seiza* and tried, like the old joke about the hot dog vendor and the Zen master, to make himself one with everything.

He was having some problems with it. First, the sitting-on-your-heels position was very uncomfortable. They might do it in Japan, where everybody was used to it, but in America, you didn't normally sit that way, or knotted up in a lotus pose, or even on the floor—not without a cushion or pillow to flop on.

Second, while he was supposed to be concentrating on his breath, just sitting back and watching it come and go without trying to control it or count it or anything, that was almost impossible to pull off. As soon as he became aware of his breathing, he kept trying to slow it and keep it even and all, and that was a no-no. And counting just came naturally for him, it was automatic. So he had to make a conscious effort *not* to count, and that was a no-no. Don't count, and don't think about *not* counting.

Third, you weren't supposed to think of anything at all,

and if a thought came up, you were supposed to gently move it away and get back to nothing but breathing. Thoughts were products of the monkey brain, Saji had told him, and had to be quieted to achieve peace and harmony with one's inner self.

Yeah, well, in his case, the brain was more like a whole *troop* of howler monkeys all hooting and dancing through the trees, and quieting that jabbering bunch was a tall order.

His knee hurt. That last inhalation turned into a sigh at the end. The thoughts about work, dinner, Saji, and how stupid he felt sitting here just *breathing* rolled in like a storm tide, as unstoppable as if he stood on the beach waving his arms at the ocean and telling it to hold it right there.

Get a grip, Jay. Millions of people do this every day!

Who knew that meditating would be so difficult? Sitting here and doing nothing was harder than anything Jay had ever done, or in his case, *not* done.

In the back of his mind, nagging at him, was something about work, some little thing flitting up and around like a moth, something he couldn't quite pin down. Something about the drug thing, and the DEA and NSA agents Lee and George . . .

No. Push it away. Get back to that later. For now, just *be* . . .

Lee and George. Not much to know about them. Close to the same age, both career men, both lived in the District. Both of them married briefly but divorced, no live-in girlfriends at the moment. A lot alike . . .

Don't think, Jay, you're supposed to be meditating!

Oh, yeah. Right. Breathe in. Breathe out. Breathe in . . .

Lee's ex-wife was originally from Florida, now a lawyer in Atlanta who also taught law at a local college. She and Lee had met in law school. Jay had checked her out, and while she was well-regarded as a teacher, she was also considered something of a radical. She was a member of the Lesbian Teacher Association or some such, big on women's rights. A no-fault divorce, no hard feelings, at least not in any official records or interviews. Still, that must have made Lee feel weird. You get a divorce, your ex-wife switches her sexual preferences to the other side of the street. Might tend to make you doubt your masculinity a little.

George's ex was a stockbroker. A law-school graduate who didn't practice but who worked for one of the big trading companies on Wall Street, did well enough that she had a two-million-dollar condo overlooking Central Park, single, no significant boyfriends five years after the divorce, didn't seem to date much, according to what Jay had uncovered about her. Like Lee with his ex-wife, George apparently got along famously with his ex.

We're all very civilized here . . .

Thoughts, Jay, watch it!

Okay, okay! Breathe in, breathe out, breathe in . . .

Kind of made you wonder, though, how a woman who was rich enough to afford a condo that expensive didn't have guys lined up waiting for her favor. Good-looking woman, hair cut short, built like a dancer.

Well, it didn't really matter, did it?

Breathe out, breathe in, breathe out . . .

The next thought that swung down from the monkey tree and chittered at Jay so startled him that his eyes popped open, and he said, "Oh, shit!"

Sitting *seiza* on floor across from him, Saji came out of her own meditation. "What? The place on fire?"

"No, no, I just had a thought—"

"Don't worry, it's part of the process—"

"No, I mean, an idea. About the dope case!"

"Let it wait, it will keep."

"No, it won't. I have to get to my computer *now!*"

"Jay, this is not how to meditate."

"I know, I know, but I have to check this out."

Saji sighed. "Fine. Do what you have to do." She closed her eyes and went back to her sitting. Jay was already up and hurrying from the bedroom to his terminal.

Michaels took the day off to be with Toni. She was still in bed, sleeping hard, and he planned to let her sleep as long as possible. The spotting the day before wasn't a sign of fetal distress, the doctor had told them, but it had caused Michaels more than a little dry mouth and nervousness. By the time he had gotten to the clinic, Toni had already been examined, was getting some blood tests, and the doctor had pulled him aside to talk to him.

The doctor, a tall, very dark, and spindly gray-haired man of sixty or so with the unlikely name of Florid, was blunt: "Listen, Mr. Michaels, if your wife doesn't sit down and prop her feet up and do a lot of nothing for the next four months, there is a chance she is going to have a preterm birth and lose this baby."

"Jesus. Have you told her this?"

"I have. She's still relatively young and healthy, and the baby seems fine, but her blood pressure is up a little. Normally she's one twenty over seventy-four, but today she's at one thirty over eighty-six. That's not technically considered high, but we always watch that, especially in a primagravida . . . that's a first-time pregnancy."

"Why is that?"

"There is a condition called preeclampsia that happens in around five pregnancies out of a hundred. Usually it's mild, and by itself it usually doesn't cause problems, but sometimes it can cause what is known as *abruptio placentae,* which is a spontaneous separation of the placenta from the uterine wall, not a good thing. Usually this is in the third trimester, sometimes at delivery, and we can work around it, but it makes things hairy.

"Worse, sometimes preeclampsia can progress to full eclampsia, which, while very rare, involves seizures, coma, and sometimes, a fatal event."

A fatal event.

Michaels swallowed. Now his mouth was *really* dry.

"Is this what's happening to Toni?"

"Probably not. There isn't any albumen in her urine, and she doesn't have much edema, and usually you get those with the rise in BP, but better safe than sorry."

"Toni is the toughest, strongest, healthiest woman I know."

Dr. Florid smiled. "Yes, I expect she can bend steel in her bare hands. Normally, pregnancy is not a medical problem, women can go about their business and do everything they were doing before they got pregnant. Most women. But interior plumbing isn't the same as voluntary muscles. No matter how strong-willed you might be, you can't toughen up the inside of a uterus. Toni's is fragile; likely she was born that way. Now, she could go on to deliver this baby without any more problems, but I'd be a lot happier and that would be a lot more likely if she took it easy. You need to impress on her how important it is for her to relax. After the baby comes, and assuming she has time, she can go swing on a vine like Sheena, Queen of the Jungle, and kick the crap out of lions and rhinos for all I care, but for now, *no strenuous exercise.* What I think is strenuous and what she thinks that means are probably different. I don't want her doing any heavy lifting, jogging, horseback riding, or deep knee bends, and I don't want her doing those martial art dances she can't seem to live without. She can lie in bed. She can sit in a chair or on a couch, she can walk to the kitchen to take her vitamins, but that's about it."

Michaels nodded. "I understand."

"If we have another epsisode of second-trimester bleeding, I am going to confine her to bed for the duration. I know she won't like that."

Michaels had to grin. "No, sir, that's for sure."

He had another question, started to speak, but decided that maybe it was selfish to ask it.

The doctor read his mind: "Sex is permissible, assuming you don't like to pretend she's a trampoline while you do it."

Michaels flushed, embarrassed.

The doctor laughed. "Listen, I know this all sounds very dramatic and scary, but you need to remember that in medicine, we have to plan for the worst-case scenario. Chances are very good that nothing bad will happen to your wife or your unborn son. But we have to let you know the possibilites, no matter how small. We have to cover all the bases."

"So you don't get sued," Michaels said.

"Hell, son, I could give my patients and their families movies, recordings, documents, a degree in medicine, and get 'em to sign a paper saying they understood them all and would never even talk to a lawyer in church, and we'd *still* wind up in court if anything went wrong. We always get sued when something goes wrong."

"Must be awful."

"Catching babies makes up for it. The look on the new mama's face when she sees her child for the first time is priceless. Pure joy. Long as my malpractice insurance and my hands hold up, I'm going to keep doing it."

He clapped Michaels on the shoulder. "What I personally think is that this pregnancy is going to do fine, if your wife will just kick back and let it roll along."

"Thank you, sir," Michaels said. "I appreciate it."

Now, as Toni slept and Michaels puttered around the

condo, he hoped the doctor had been right in his assessment. Toni wanted the baby, and he did, too. It was going to be the center of their new family and life together, and it would be devastating to lose it.

Him, not it.

In the living room, he came across the box with the two *kerambit* knives. He took them out, put one in each hand, got a feel for how they worked. Odd, to be playing with knives and thinking about a new baby.

Well, maybe not, given the boy's parents.

He moved the knives slowly and carefully. It probably wouldn't do Toni's stress level any good at all for him to accidentally slice his wrist open. Not to mention his own health. Still, the little blades seemed familiar in his grip, comfortable, and the *djuru* moves didn't seem to put him in any danger of cutting himself. At least not this slowly and carefully. One hurried wrong move could put the lie to that quick enough, though.

He put the knives up, and tiptoed back in to check on Toni.

26

On the flight home, Drayne felt pretty good. The computer guy was as good as he'd been cracked up to be. The police in SoCal and Steve's Gym no longer had any reference to one Robert Drayne in their systems. More, the techno-whiz was able to determine that they hadn't gotten around to where his name had been to assign anybody to check it before it had magically vanished. Nor had it been printed out to a hardcopy. The list had been renumbered, and unless you knew somebody had been erased and knew precisely where to look and *how* to look, you wouldn't be able to tell it had been done. And even if you *could* tell that, you wouldn't know who was gone.

Once again, Drayne was golden. And all it had cost was a promise of free dope as long as the guy lived. Cheap beyond measure, even if he had to pay it.

Drayne smiled as the flight attendant walked along the first class rows, asking if anybody wanted complimentary champagne. Probably the stuff was Korbel, or at best one of the California domaines owned by the French. Not bad if you had no experience with the really good stuff, but as far as Drayne was concerned, he wouldn't use it to clean the chrome on his car bumper. Still, the attendant was a babe, not wearing a wedding ring, and the flight from Dallas–Fort Worth to LAX was still hours out from landing. He could strike up a conversation with her, maybe get her number. *Say, have you ever considered acting? You have great bone structure. . . .*

The attendant stopped to talk to a woman Drayne thought he recognized as somebody in L.A. politics, a city council member or maybe a spokesperson for the mayor's office. Drayne glanced at his watch.

About now, Tad would be buying the computer whiz a dinner at a great little out-of-the-way Italian restaurant locally famous for its fresh produce, ostensibly to make arrangements to deliver a dozen caps of the Hammer as a first payment of a lifetime drug supply. The computer geek, a health nut, had raved about the place. The salad that came with the meal featured fresh wild greens, mushrooms, and other local herbs, and was terrific, he'd said.

Drayne had smiled, regretting that he had to be back in L.A. and would have to miss that, but hey, Tad loved salad!

The last time Tad had eaten a salad or anything remotely healthy had probably been twenty years past. Anybody who looked at him could see that. But a guy as full of himself as Mr. Computer Wizard would skate right past that obvious fact without blinking. People saw what they wanted to see, not what was really there.

So the guy had chosen his own exit and made it easy for them to hold the door open.

If everything went as planned, just as the computer geek was about to lay into this garden delight, he was going to get a call on his com. Tad had the number programmed into his own com, and a touch of a button would do the trick. While Mr. Wizard was distracted, Tad was going to add a couple of different kinds of sliced mushrooms to the man's salad that weren't on the menu. These grew wild in places as hot and damp as Austin still was this time of year, easy to find if you knew where to look, and once they were sliced were virtually identical to any other small, white-fleshed mushrooms.

The first variety of these particular 'shrooms contained heavy concentrations of amatoxins and phallotoxins, either of which could be fatal, and both of which would almost certainly destroy liver and kidney functions, leading to death within a week to ten days 80 percent of the time.

The second variety was chock-full of Gyromita toxins, which, while not quite as nasty as the others, also attacked the liver and kidneys, plus the circulatory system, leading to heart failure in extreme cases. Mostly Gyromita poisoning was uncommon in the U.S. because cooking these mushrooms usually mitigated the toxin. Nice, crisp, raw ones in a salad would still pack a nasty punch, however.

Mr. Computer Wizard would enjoy his meal. He and Tad would part company on the best of terms. A day later, maybe two, Mr. Wizard would come down with flulike symptoms: nausea, vomiting, diarrhea, cramps. His doctor would probably miss the diagnosis at first, but even if he didn't, the only way to keep the victim alive would be a liver and maybe a kidney transplant, and even then, the heart was still at risk.

No guarantee, of course, but eight chances out of ten he would croak weren't bad odds. And if he made it, he'd be a long time recovering, on immunosuppressive drugs if they could find him a new liver, and unable to screw with his body chemistry if he wanted to stay alive. And if he made it that far? Well, they could always pay him another visit.

If he died, it would be due to mushroom poisoning, a terrible tragedy, a freak accident. Bad for the restaurant's reputation and insurance carrier, but, hey, that was how life went sometimes. You want an omelette, you gotta break a few eggs.

The flight attendant approached. "Care for champagne, sir?"

"That would be nice. Look, I don't want you to think I'm hitting on you, but I'm a movie producer. Have you ever considered acting?"

He held up his producer business card and smiled.

She took the card, looked at it, and smiled back. "I've thought about it. I was the lead in my high school play."

Life was very good.

Life is crappy, Toni thought. Nobody had told her what might happen when she got pregnant, nobody had said she'd be reduced to the mobility and muscularity of a slug. She hated this.

Alex had hung around to take care of her, but she had made him leave. He was sweet, but she wasn't going to be pleasant company, and she didn't want him thinking of her as a constant bitch. Better he should see her smiling and at least offering some pretense of being happy once in a while.

"You sure?" he'd asked, after three exchanges on the subject.

"I'm positive. Go."

And he had, and that pissed her off, too. Yes, she had said for him to, she had insisted that he do so, but she hadn't really wanted him to leave. Why didn't he know that? How could he just . . . take her at her word that way? Why were men so stupid?

Yes, yes, all right, she knew it was illogical, but that was how she felt.

Now that Alex was gone, she was at a loss for what to do with herself. The doctor had made it crystal clear she was on light duty from now on, and since a big part of her had always been physical, this was proving to be intolerable. She couldn't move, she might as well put down roots and turn into a fucking houseplant. She *really* hated this.

She didn't feel like sitting at the scrimshaw project. She didn't feel like watching television or listening to music or reading. What she felt like doing was going for a five-mile run to clear her mind. Or a half hour of stretching and then *silat* practice. Or anything requiring sweat and sore muscles.

No point in even bothering to think about such things. It would only make her feel worse, if that was possible.

Other women must have gone through this. She could do it if anybody else could, she kept telling herself. But that didn't help.

The house was clean. She had spent way too much time doing that lately, wiping counters, sweeping floors, rearranging shelves. You could eat off the floor—if you were allowed to bend over and take the risk.

She wandered into the bedroom. The bed was made. The bathroom was clean. Nothing.

The floor in Alex's closet by his shoe rack had some clothes piled up to be dry-cleaned. Well, she could do that. Surprise Alex, given as how she didn't usually fool with his chores.

She picked up a suit, a sports jacket, a couple of good silk shirts, a few ties. The laundry-to-go basket was in the garage, where Alex would usually notice it when it got full, toss the dirty clothes into his car, and drop it off at the Martinizing place run by a family of Koreans on the way to work.

As she started dropping the clothes into the hamper,

she automatically went through the pockets. Being raised in a family full of brothers had taught her that when doing the wash. Boys left all kinds of crap in their pockets, and a handful of coins clattering in the washer or dryer would drive you nuts, not to mention chipping the inside of the machines. Ink pens could ruin a load of whites, and it was no fun picking lint from a washed, shredded, and dried paper napkin from a load of dark shirts, either.

In the suit trousers, Toni found a paper clip box, and inside that, the capsule.

She knew what it was from Alex's description, it being big and purple and all, and it puzzled her as to why it was in his pocket. But maybe it was important. She seemed to recall the stuff had some kind of timing chemical in it, and it would be inert after a day or so. Alex hadn't worn this suit yesterday, had he?

She reached for the phone on the workbench, looking at the capsule. She put it down next to the scrimshaw piece she'd been working on as Alex's com bleeped.

"Hey, babe, what's up? You okay?"

"Yeah, I'm fine. I was taking your dry cleaning out to the hamper—"

"You were what?"

"Don't sound so amazed."

"Sorry. Go on."

"Anyway, I found this purple capsule in your pocket."

"Ah, damn. I keep forgetting about that. I was going to take it by the FBI lab and have somebody look at it. That's the one John got on the raid I told you about."

"I can do that for you, run it by the lab."

"No, you can't. You aren't supposed to be driving, re-member? Hang on to it for me, I'll do it tomorrow."

"Fine."

"Uh, thanks for calling me about it."

"You at work yet?"

"Almost there."

"I'll see you later," she said.

After she broke the connection, Toni stared into space. She sure hoped this baby was worth all this crap. He'd better be.

She wandered back into the house. All of a sudden, she was tired. Maybe she would lie down and take a short nap. Might as well. She couldn't do anything else.

Jay shook his head, feeling stupid. It had been right there in front of him all along, and he had just skipped over it. He had narrowed his focus too much and missed the connection.

Maybe all this navel-gazing was good in the long run, learning how to clear your thoughts, to relax your mind, but the old Jay Gridley wouldn't have let this slide past unseen.

Maybe it wasn't a good idea to be too relaxed mentally in his business.

He ran it down. The most important piece took a while, but finally, he got it. Wasn't proof of anything, of course, but certainly it was a circumstantial lump that would choke an elephant.

Jesus.

He needed to fly it past the boss, to get his hit on it, but he was pretty sure it meant something important. He reached for the com to call, then decided maybe it would be better to avoid using the phone or net. Net Force's coms, especially the virgils, were scrambled, the signals turned into complex binary ciphers that were supposedly unbreakable by ordinary mortals. That little episode in the U.K. with the quantum computer had cured Jay of his faith in unbreakable binary codes, however. And given the people with whom they were dealing, maybe face-to-face was better.

"I have to go into HQ," Jay said to Saji on his way to the door.

"This late?" She opened her eyes and stared at him, still seated in her meditation pose.

"It's important. I love you. See you later."

"Drive safe," she said.

He thought about his discovery all the way to Net Force HQ. Boy, wasn't the boss going to be surprised at this twist!

27

Tad sat at the gate, slouched in a chair, waiting for his connecting flight back to LAX. Even full of painkillers, speed, and steroids to the eyeballs, it was all he could do to hold himself up. Every muscle, every joint, every part of him he could feel ached, a bone-deep, grinding throb that resonated through him with every heartbeat. The best dope he could get only dulled the pain, it didn't come close to stopping it. He was so tired he could hardly see straight, and the way he felt, if he sneezed, his head would fall off. But his fuck-up was fixed, and, yeah, okay, he'd had to ice some poor sucker to wrap it. At least Bobby wasn't pissed at him anymore. He hated to disappoint Bobby, who put up with a lot of his crap without kicking him out. Only friend he'd ever had, Tad knew, and the only person on earth who had ever given a shit about him. You just didn't let people like that down.

A goth girl of eighteen or nineteen walked by and slouched into the bank of chairs across from Tad, eyeing him. She wore a torn black T-shirt under a distressed

black leather jacket with the sleeves cut off, black sweatpants, and pink tennis shoes. She had short hair dyed purple, a nose ring, lip ring, eyebrow ring, and nine ear studs
showing. Tad would be real surprised if she wasn't wearing more gold and steel in her belly button, nipples, and
labia. She gave him a twist of a smile—yep, there was
the tongue stud—and he managed a lifted lip in return.
Probably saw him as a kindred spirit, and what the hell,
probably he was. Some of the kids who dressed the part
were wanna-be's, some of them were nihilists, some of
them true anarchists. You could usually tell after thirty
seconds of conversation which they were, but right now,
he couldn't summon the energy needed even to wave her
over and see. Not that it much mattered if she did come
over; he wasn't in any condition to slip off to the john to
snort some coke, smoke a joint, or screw, if any of those
were her pleasure. Truth was, he liked Bobby's kind of
woman anyhow, the pneumatic bunnies who pumped dick
as well as they did iron. Not that he'd had much interest
in that area lately. Well, except for that royal fuck-up in
the gym with Wonder Woman.

The announcer came on and garbled something out.
Tad didn't have any idea what she'd said, but people
started to get up and shoulder their carry-on bags or tow
them behind them on little leashes, like Samsonite dogs
who didn't want to go for a walk and had to be dragged.
Tad didn't have any luggage. If he needed clean clothes,
he bought them and threw the old stuff away, shirts, pants,
underwear, socks, whatever. It was a trick he'd learned as
a street kid in Phoenix a thousand years ago. If you have
to travel, better to travel light. If you don't have nothin',
nobody can steal nothin' from you. You don't have to
remember anything, and if you have to split, you can do
so without looking back. He had his e-ticket printout, a
wallet, five hundred or so bucks in it, a couple of credit

cards, and his ID. That was his luggage, and it was zipped into a back pocket. Unless somebody came up and did a butt slash and rob, he wasn't gonna lose that. And if he did? Fuck it. It didn't really matter, did it? You could get another wallet, more cards, more money. None of that was important.

The goth girl got up and sidled in behind Tad as he moved toward the woman taking tickets. She said, "I got some coke. You wanna do some, head to the bathroom when you see me go there."

Tad lifted his lip in his half-assed grin. "Cool," he said.

But he doubted he'd see her when she went. He was in first class, and he'd bet she was in tourist, unless she was slumming, and he didn't think she was. Besides, he had his own coke, and he knew how pure it was. Street drugs were always risky. Maybe if he felt better in a little while, he'd share that with her. Find out what she could do with that tongue stud.

He planned to crash when he got back to Malibu, and sleep for a week. Maybe by then, he would have recovered enough to pick up the Hammer again. Now that everything was copacetic with Bobby, there was no need to fly to Hawaii or even slow down biz. Life was normal again, such as normal was, and he could get back on the road to Hell as soon as he was able.

Quantico, Virginia

Jay was almost hopping up and down he was so full of whatever it was that he had to say.

Michaels smiled and waved at the seat. Jay headed in that direction, but he didn't sit.

"Okay, tell me. You caught our dope dealer?"

Jay frowned, as if that thought was the last thing on his mind. "What? Oh, no. If we were doing a movie, that would be the A story. What I did is figure out the B story. Well, at least part of it."

"You want to run that past me again?"

"Okay, okay, look, I was all over the DEA guy Lee and the NSA agent George. Nothing, no connection. But I expanded the search, and I came up with Lynn Davis Lee and Jackie McNally George."

"Who are—?"

"The ex-wives. Lee and George met their wives in law school, got hitched, went their separate ways a couple years later. Both are divorced."

"So am I, Jay. So is roughly fifty percent of everybody who got married in the last twenty years."

The younger man grinned. "Yeah, but Lynn Davis and Jackie McNally were roommates in law school."

"Really? That is an odd coincidence"

"It gets better, boss. Lynn Davis—she dropped her married name after the split—is a lawyer and part-time teacher in Atlanta. From what I was able to determine, she . . . ah . . . prefers the company of women to men."

"How shocking. So?"

"Same deal with Jackie McNally. She is very low-profile about it, but apparently she is also a lesbian."

Michaels thought about that a second. "Hmm."

"Yeah, you see where I'm going here? Doesn't that seem, well, *queer,* that two guys married and then divorced college roommates, both of whom are lesbians?"

"Doesn't speak highly of the boys' lovemaking skills, but it also doesn't prove anything, does it?"

"Nope. But what if Ms. Davis and Ms. McNally had the same sexual preferences *before* they got married? From what I can tell, that was the case."

Michaels chewed on that for a moment. "Ah," he said, beginning to understand.

"It makes sense," Jay said. "There are a lot of places where—laws notwithstanding—being gay is still a problem. Federal agencies aren't allowed to discriminate about such things, but you know how it is. Come out as gay, you put a glass ceiling over your own head."

Michaels nodded. That was true, like it or not, especially in security agencies. The theory was, an openly gay operative wouldn't be a problem, but somebody in the closet might be a candidate for blackmail, if he or she didn't want to be outed. And he had a pretty good idea of where Jay was going with the rest of it, but he didn't say anything, just waved for him to keep rolling.

"So, consider this scenario. Lee and George are . . . well, let's say, men's men. They know that being that way is likely to top them out at a low level in a lot of agencies. And lesbians have the same problems."

"So you think we have a case of two gay men marrying two lesbian women to provide each other with solid heterosexual backgrounds?"

"It wouldn't be the first time," Jay said. "Having an ex-wife or husband on paper would forestall some tongue-wagging, especially if you were discreet from then on. Only now, Lee and George, who maybe aren't so close anymore, really don't like each other. Might explain some things."

Michaels nodded again. "That could be. You did good, Jay. Thanks."

After Jay was gone, Michaels thought about it some, then reached for the com. He wanted to talk to John Howard. An ugly idea had just entered his mind, and while he hoped things wouldn't go down that road, he had to check it out.

• • •

Howard nodded at Michaels. He'd been figuratively shuffling paper clips when the commander called, and any excuse to get up and move was good.

"No doubt in your mind?" Michaels said.

"No, sir. Lee flat assassinated the man. Zeigler was clearly about to drop his knife. He had started to step back from his hostage, and when Lee fired, he was no more than twenty-five feet away. Plus, my radio mike was still on. Lee heard Zeigler say he was surrendering. No, sir. This guy was a DEA field agent for years, he went on scores of raids, some of which had gunplay on both sides, I checked his record. When he pulled the trigger, he had to know the situation was under control."

"Okay, let's assume for a moment that he didn't panic and do it by accident, he iced the man on purpose. That brings up a big question, doesn't it?"

"Yes, sir. Why would he do that?"

"Any theories you want to share?"

"I have been thinking about it. Assuming there was no personal hatred of the man, the only thing I can come up with is that he didn't want Zeigler giving up his dealer."

Michaels said, "That doesn't make any sense, because the whole purpose of the raid was to bust the guy hard enough so we could find that out."

"Yes, sir. Thing is, Zeigler was in a panic, and he was about to spill his guts when Lee double-tapped him."

Give the commander credit, he picked up on it right away. "Where somebody other than Lee could hear him. You."

"Yes, sir, me. And the maid."

Michaels shook his head. "I don't like this worth a damn, John. Something stinks here."

"I do believe so myself."

The commander steepled his fingers and leaned back in

his chair. "If it had just been Lee there, he could claim he shot Zeigler to save the maid."

"Who speaks about five words of English and was so terrified she didn't know which way was up," Howard added. "Not a great witness either way."

"So come the shooting review or whatever it is DEA does, anything you have to say is going to make Lee look real bad. He had to know what he did was going to cost him big time."

"I'd assume so, yes, sir. If they believe me, it ought to be worth his job. If he was one of mine, I'd kick him out and tell the local DA to burn him, manslaughter at the very least, maybe murder two."

"Which he has to know, and even so, he's willing to horizontal somebody in front of a witness."

"Maybe he thinks he can blow enough smoke to get past it."

"I wouldn't underrate yourself, John. You are the military commander of Net Force, a general. You can shine a lot of light on him."

"Yes, sir. So we're back to the big question. Why'd he do it? What did he have to gain that was so important he'd risk his job?"

"I don't know. But I certainly think we need to find out."

"Yes, sir, I believe that's true."

"There's one other thing we need to think about here, too, John."

"Sir?"

"Maybe Lee loves his job and is willing to do anything to keep it." He raised an eyebrow.

Well, Mama Howard didn't raise any stupid children, either. Howard said, "Bit of a stretch, isn't it?"

"He killed a world-famous movie star in front of a witness who, at the very least, can get him fired and maybe charged with a nasty felony. Maybe if something happened to the witness, he might not be so worried."

Howard nodded. "I take your point. I'll make sure my brakes are working before I go for a drive."

"And make sure nothing is attached to the ignition switch, too, John. I'd hate to have to break in a new military commander."

"Yes, sir, I'd hate to put you to the trouble."

They smiled at each other.

But when Howard left, he considered what Michaels had said. Lee did seem to be something of a loose cannon. He didn't want to be in front of him if he went off.

28

Drayne was not a man to make the same mistake twice, especially on something that, in theory, could cost him his freedom. As soon as he was back on the ground in L.A., still in the car on the way home, he made a call to a real estate agent he'd never met. He got her name out of the phone directory and picked it because he liked the sound of it.

"Silverman Realty," the woman said, "this is Shawanda speaking."

Shawanda Silverman. What kind of intermarriage produced such a great name? He loved it.

"Yes, ma'am, my name is Lazlo Mead, and I'm going to be living here in the Los Angeles area for about a year or so for a project I'm just starting to work on."

"Yes, Mr. Mead?"

"What I want is to lease a three- or four-bedroom furnished house not too far from things, but in a nice area, you know, maybe out a little ways, in one of the canyons?"

"Certainly I can help you with that. What . . . ah . . . price range are we talking about?"

"Well, the company is paying for it—I'm in aircraft supply and maintenance—so maybe you could find one where the rent was somewhere around eight to ten thousand dollars a month?"

He could hear the cash register in her voice: "No problem with that," she said too quickly. "I can make a list of a few places, and we can get together and view them."

"Well, here's the thing. I'm kind of in a hurry, but I'm up to my eyeballs in work. Somebody gave me your name as having done this kind of thing for people before, so maybe you could just, you know, pick a place that would work for me and my wife and just go ahead and lease it for us. I'll e-mail you a transfer, you know, first month, last month, cleaning and security fees, whatever—say forty thousand?—and e-sign any paperwork to get the ball rolling. We can get together later. Sooner I get out of the hotel and into a real place, the happier I'll be."

"I understand that, Mr. Mead. I'm sure I can find a house that will work for you. Any preferences as to furniture or schools or such?"

"Well, my wife likes modern stuff, so we want to keep her happy. No early American or like that. No kids, so schools don't matter."

"I'll see what I can do. I'll e-mail you pictures, if you want."

"That would be good." He gave her one of the remailing addresses he used. She probably already had caller-IDed the number of the clean phone he kept for just such transactions, the one made out in the name of Projects, Inc. Now there was a term that could be stretched to fit virtually anything. What did it mean? Nothing. He gave her the number. Soon as she found something, she said, she would call. He got her e-mail address and promised to send a fund transfer first thing in the morning.

After he broke the connection, he felt a lot better. In a day or two, he'd have a hideout, so if he had to leave the Malibu house in a hurry, there would be a place he could run to where he could sort things out. He had a big, fat, five-hundred-pound gun safe bolted to the concrete floor in a U-Store-It place way out Ventura Boulevard; he'd drive over the hill and move most of the cash from the beach house to that tonight, as a matter of fact. Maybe some of the better champagne. The locker, which was eight by ten feet, was air conditioned, he'd made sure of that. With his money safe and a place to hide if it came to that, he would be halfway ready.

Lazlo Mead was about to come into full existence, too. Drayne had a wonderful, illegal software program and card stocks for making phony IDs. A couple of hours and a good color laser printer, a few watermarks and holograms, and presto! Mr. Lazlo Mead would have a driver's license from, oh, say, Iowa; a social security card, maybe a library card, and a couple of credit cards that looked perfect, even if they weren't valid. The program would also print out pictures of a mythical wife and parents, if he wanted.

That would take care of the basics. When Tad got home, he could do the other part, the hired muscle. A few armed bodyguards could buy them enough time to haul ass if somebody came calling, especially if Drayne gave them the right story. *"Somebody yells 'Police!' they are lying,"* he'd tell the shooters. *"It's guys trying to rip us off."* Tad knew people who wouldn't care if whoever hired them were dope dealers or gunrunners, long as they got paid. Guys who'd shoot it out with cops anyhow, if the pay was rich enough.

Maybe he ought to get a gun, too. He'd never had much use for those, but after the Zee-ster bought it, the thought

had popped up. He didn't have any training, but you
didn't have to be a rocket scientist, now did you? Any
fuzz-brained gangbanger in East L.A. could use a gun,
how hard could it be? Point it and pull the trigger, it went
bang. Wave it, and it was like a magic wand; people sat
up and paid attention. Something that looked cool, one of
those stainless steel movie guns the action adventure guys
used, pearl handles or something.

Of course, all this would tap into his money pretty
good, forty grand for the house, probably fifty or sixty
more for five bodyguards, just to get started. But it had
to be done. He'd been lax before, but not anymore. All
this had been a wake-up call, and he didn't want to be
caught by surprise. It had been a big game, really, but
when customers started getting cooked by feds, the seriousness factor went way up. He hadn't really believed
he'd ever be caught, not really, and the idea of spending
years in a federal prison somewhere fending off some big
horny con named Bubba did not appeal at all. So it would
cost, big deal. Money was the easiest part. If he put the
word out, he could move fifty or sixty hits of the Hammer
a week, easy. Couple, three months of doing that every
week or two, he'd make expenses and a whole lot more.
Clear, say, half a million in the next few months, then
take a break?

Cross that bridge when he got to it. It had been a close
call, that business with the Zee-ster. He would not get that
involved with the customers again. He was smarter than
most people, he knew that, and he knew he could see
things better, but when you were moving in a hurry, you
had to watch your step. All kinds of things out there that
could trip you up.

The "office" com number went off. He frowned at it.
Saw there was no caller ID sig lit. He knew who it had
to be.

"Polymers, Drayne."

"Robert. This is your father."

Jesus. Didn't the old man think he could recognize his fucking *voice* after all these years? "Hey, Dad. What's up?"

"I'm leaving your aunt's to go back to Arizona tomorrow. I thought we might get together for breakfast before I go."

Drayne felt a cold finger along his spine. His father wanted to see him? That was very strange. "Sure. I know a couple of places near Edwina's that are pretty good."

"Give me the name, and I'll get directions from Edwina."

"Sure."

"We'll meet at seven A.M.," his father said. It was not a question.

"Seven sharp," Drayne said. Which, when speaking to his father, was redundant. He gave him the name of a good breakfast place just off the Coast Highway.

Drayne frowned again as he severed the connection. Well. His father was leaving town, and it might be a year or two before they saw each other again. Breakfast was not such a big deal. Except that his old man had not invited him to such an event in what, ten years?

Maybe he just wants me to help Edwina out, Drayne reasoned. *Or maybe he felt the clammy hand of death touch him while he sat in the church and wants to tell me about his will.*

Drayne laughed aloud at that thought. *That would be the fucking day.*

Washington, D.C.

Toni, feeling better after an afternoon mostly spent sleeping, listened to Alex's day. At least he thought her brain was working well enough to ask her advice about work. Of course, she had been his assistant for a long time, she knew the game.

"So that's what we've got on our friends at the DEA and NSA," he finished. "What do you think?"

She considered what he'd said. "Well, you know the classic motives for crime: passion, thrills, revenge, psychosis, personal gain. On the face of it, Lee wouldn't have any particular reason to want Zeigler dead for any kind of personal vendetta, unless maybe he *really* hated his movies. I don't think he was that bad an actor. From what you've said, he doesn't seem like a thrill-seeker or a psycho. So what's the personal gain?"

"I don't see any right off," he admitted. "Killing a big movie star doesn't win you friends or money."

She said, "You remember those calls you got offering you work with the pharmaceutical companies?"

He chuckled. "Yeah."

"Well. From what you've said, there seems to be a lot of interest in this drug. We're talking about big money. Maybe somebody convinced Mr. Lee he could cash in big time if he got the dealer and delivered him—or his formula—to the right party. He wouldn't want Net Force getting to the guy first, so he wouldn't want John to know the dealer's name, right?"

He stared at her. "Wow."

"Don't you *dare* sound so surprised, Alex Michaels," she said. "My mind does still work from time to time, when my hormones aren't blowing my head apart."

"You said that, not me." He grinned.

She pretended to glare but couldn't hold onto it. She smiled in return.

"Anyway, it's a good theory. Maybe Jay can make a connection, some record of contact or something."

"These guys would be pretty good at covering their tracks," she said, "if they've had years to practice it like Jay thinks."

"Still, it's a place to look. Even though it is all moot if we can't run the dealer down."

"You'll find him," she said. "I have great faith in you."

"You'd be the only one."

"How many do you need?"

He smiled again. "Why, ma'am, I do believe one will be just exactly enough."

29

Howard was tired of running scenarios, more tired of sitting around. He was itchy to do something, and he was considering running some real-world field exercises just to clear the cobwebs from his brain. Get the troops sharpened up; even though there was nothing to get sharp about now, there would be, eventually. He hoped.

"Love to see a man hard at work."

Howard looked up and saw Julio standing in the doorway of his office. "Lieutenant Fernandez. What brings you here?"

"I believe that would be my size-eleven combat boots, sir."

"And is there a purpose for this visit?"

"Why, good news, General Howard, sir."

"Come on in, then. I can use some news. Any news, good or bad, would be a change."

"I think you're gonna like this."

Howard looked at the flat-black hard case Julio held. It was about three feet long, half that wide. "You have my attention, Lieutenant."

"Sir. You might recall the Thousand-Meter Special Teams Match for United States Military Services held at Camp Perry every November?"

"Oh, I recall it, all right. That would be the match where Net Force's sharpshooters always come in last place . . . behind the Marines, the Army, and even the *Navy?*"

"Only because you won't order Gunny to enter. He'd beat 'em. And we did beat the Navy that one year," Julio allowed.

"Because their shooter lost his hearing protection in a freak accident and blew out an eardrum is why."

"Still beat 'cm. Take it any way you can."

Howard nodded at the case. "This a secret weapon?"

"Well, a weapon, yes, but not so secret. Just new. Take a look."

Julio set the case down on the old map table across from Howard's desk, popped the latches on the case, and clamshelled it open.

Howard walked over and looked at the components inside the case.

"Why, it is a gun. It appears to be a bolt-action five-oh BMG rifle," Howard said.

"Yes, sir, but not just *any* five-oh. This is a prototype, one of only two built, of the upcoming EMD Arms Model XM-109A Wind Runner, designed by Bill Ritchie himself. Third generation."

Julio reached into the case and pulled out the stock and receiver assembly. "This here receiver is made of 17-4 PH stainless and, with improved heat-treating, now Rockwells out at forty-five-plus. Sixteen pounds, wire-cut, tolerances you wouldn't believe, and with the fully adjustable stock here retracted, a mere twenty inches long. Stock is equipped with a carbon-fiber polysorb monopod recoil pad and nice cheek piece incorporating no-tear bio-gel."

"You have to go looking for your shoulder after you fire it?"

"No, sir, it kicks about as hard as a stout twelve-gauge. Of course, it will shove you back about a foot if you shoot it prone, and you will want to be lying down behind it and not firing offhand."

"I bet."

"Speaking from experience, sir. You'll notice the M-14 bipod and mounted scope, the latter of which is a U.S. Optics adjustable, 3.8X–22X, very nice optical gear, sighted in for a thousand meters. And here is a nifty little red dot switch, automatically adjusted for parallax, that gives you short-range capabilities. Short range in this case being three to four hundred meters. Put the dot on the target, that's where the bullet goes, plus or minus a few inches.

"Might as well throw it as shoot that close, though.

"The new model Son of Wind Runner here uses a five-round magazine like the older models, and has a Remington-style adjustable trigger, set to three pounds. Uses your standard MK211 caliber .50 multipurpose cartridge as the primary tactical round, though match-grade handloads are the ticket at Camp Perry, of course." Julio held up a box of ammo. "Like these."

He opened the bipod and set the receiver and stock up on the table. He reached back into the case and came out with the barrel.

"Your barrel here is a twenty-eight-inch fluted match-grade graphite from K&P Gun, with an eighty-port screw-on muzzle brake, the holes set at thirty degrees. You secure the barrel to the receiver like so, using an Uzi-style nut and a self-locking ratchet, right here."

Julio put the barrel into the receiver and tightened it. It didn't take long.

"Total weight, thirty-four pounds. Insert a loaded magazine, and there she is, ready to rock 'n' roll."

"Very nice," Howard allowed.

"The original XM 107 was designed for use by the Army, particularly the Joint Special Operations Forces, and the Explosive Ordnance Disposal teams. And, theoretically, the Infantry, though the groundpounders didn't get too many copies. SOF uses 'em against soft or semi-hard targets out to seventeen hundred meters, and EOD uses 'em to blow up unexploded ordnance from a long way outside proximity fuse range."

"Like I said, a nice toy. How much?"

"These things are like hen's teeth, sir. The waiting list is a mile long, and how can you put a price on this kind of quality?" He stroked the barrel with one hand. "There are only two of them exactly like this in all the world."

"Let's try, shall we? How much?"

"Well, with our discount, a hair over five thousand dollars each."

"That actually sounds pretty reasonable." Then, knowing Julio for all the years he'd known him, he said, "A 'hair over' you said. How thick a hair we talking about?"

"Call it three thousand and change," Julio said. He grinned.

"What? For eight thousand dollars, this beast had better dance and whistle 'Dixie,' Lieutenant!"

"Well, I wouldn't know about that, sir. But EDM Arms guarantees one-minute-of-angle accuracy at a thousand meters right out of the box."

Howard raised his eyebrows at that. "One MOA? Guaranteed?"

"Just as you see it. I thought that would get your attention. But that's only to keep the lawyers happy. EDM

Arms has got *verified* five-round groups at a thousand meters of *one-half MOA*. They say they got a couple groups that good at seventeen hundred meters, even a little longer."

Howard looked at the weapon again. "Good Lord. That's a tack-driver."

"Yes, sir. And Bowens, our newly recruited ex-Army shooter, has been doing just that with this very piece, starting yesterday. Talking about a pie-plate-sized group from a mile away. He didn't want to let me take it long enough to show it to you."

Howard grinned.

"So, come next month, Net Force's little piece of the National Guard is going to shoot the living asses off the Navy, the Marines, *and* the Army."

"If one of them doesn't get his hands on the other one," Howard said.

Julio grinned real big.

Howard stared at him. "You didn't."

"Well, sir, yes, sir, I did. If something broke on this here weapon—highly unlikely, I know, given the fine, fine quality, but if something *did* break—we'd want proper backup, wouldn't we?"

Howard shook his head. "I'll have to beat the budget to cover this."

"Not the way I figure it. We do it right, we can make our costs on side bets. I can get three to one against us, easy. I wouldn't be surprised to even make a small profit."

They both grinned at that.

"Anyway, I thought you might like to take it to the outdoor range and put a few through it. That is, if you aren't too busy here." He looked around.

"You missed your calling, Lieutenant. You should have been a comedian."

"Yes, sir, I believe I could have sparkled in such a profession."

Howard looked at the weapon. Why not? He didn't have anything better to do.

"You coming along?"

"No, sir, I have diaper duty, starting in—" he looked at his watch "—forty-six minutes. Best I not be late."

Howard chuckled. "No, I understand. It has been a while since I had such duty myself, but one cannot stress the importance of it enough."

"If one's wife is Lieutenant Joanna Winthrop Fernandez, one can sure as hell stress it high, wide, and repeatedly," Julio said. "You want me to show you how to break it down? Where the cartridges go?"

"I believe I can manage on my own, thank you."

"Have fun."

"Oh, you, too."

"Yeah, right."

Howard looked at the rifle after Julio was gone. Well, why not? He was the commander of Net Force's military, he ought to know how the hardware worked, right? It was training. He could justify that.

Besides, blowing holes in a target three-quarters of a mile away sure beat sitting here doing zip.

The Texas Panhandle, North of Amarillo

Jay Gridley walked along the trail, cutting sign. This was an exercise Saji had taught him when he'd been recovering from his electronically induced stroke, how to track somebody. A bent twig here, a blade of grass lying there, the signs were there if you knew how to look.

In the real world, he was backtracking e-sig, net and

phone and globeSat connections, but here, he was after a bad man on foot, Hans, a notorious drug seller.

It was hot, and Jay paused to take a swig of tepid water from his canteen, the fabric of which was wet to allow some small cooling from evaporation. He thought that was a nice touch, even though he wasn't sharing the scenario with anybody. Those little things counted. Anybody could plug off-the-shelf view- or feelware into their computer and walk through VR; a pro had higher standards.

He took off his broad-brimmed planter's hat, wiped his sweaty forehead with a red bandanna, replaced the hat, and stuck the handkerchief back into his pocket.

There, just ahead, he saw something. Or rather, he *didn't* see something. He bent and looked at the hot ground from only a few inches above it. There weren't any real tracks, but the dry ground was too smooth. Carpet-walker, turned and headed that way.

Jay kept walking. Ahead and in a little declivity was a stand of cottonwood trees and what looked like willow. Water, a pond, or an underground stream come up to the surface, he figured. He could almost smell the moisture.

Sure enough, there was a small stream, maybe as wide as Jay was tall, clear water bubbling over a rocky bottom. The stream wound away, and Jay stepped into the water and started to follow it. A man looking to hide his tracks would use such cover, probably staying with it until he found a rocky enough spot to exit where he wouldn't leave footprints.

Jay enjoyed the feel of the water around his ankles as he moved slowly along. Half a mile ahead, he paused. There, to the right, were six or eight big rocks leading to a patch of gravel. That's where he'd leave the water, if he wanted to get back on his previous heading.

It took him more than a hundred yards before he spotted something. Another flat patch of dirt, too smooth.

There were no wind riffle marks, no raindrop patterns, none of the natural weathering signs that ought to be there. Jay grinned. Bad man Hans had been here; he was sure of it.

In the distance, Jay saw a small village. That it had a Germanic look to it didn't really fit the Texas panhandle, but it was okay to mix scenario now and then. It kept you from getting into a rut.

He'd bet diamonds against dog doo that Hans was in that village, smug in his belief that nobody could track him there.

Why didn't these fools ever learn they couldn't screw with Lonesome Jay Gridley? Must be some kind of genetic defect that ran in bad guys.

He picked up his pace a little. He didn't need to worry about the signs now, he knew where Hans was. All he had to do was go and identify him. Once he was sure of that, the game would be over.

30

Washington, D.C.

Toni felt terrific. She and Alex had a great night together, and when she awakened this morning, she'd been rested and much refreshed. Being able to help him with the case he was working on, that had been something, too. For a few moments there, she hadn't felt totally useless. She hadn't lost all her chops. Maybe that was a good sign.

After Alex left for work, she felt creative. She decided to go and work on her scrimshaw for a while.

At the bench, she turned on the gooseneck lamp, gathered her tools, and was about to get started when she saw the purple capsule lying there where she'd put it and forgotten all about it.

She reached for the cap, looked at it, and decided what the hell, as long as she had it in hand . . .

She put the cap on the table in her work field and adjusted the lamp to shine on it. Focused the stereoscope on it . . .

Ah. Here was a major discovery. It was a purple gelatin capsule with some kind of pale powder inside it. *Oh, boy. Way to go, Sherlock.*

Maybe something inside was more interesting. If she opened it very carefully . . .

"Shit!" she said, as the powder, which was a kind of bubble gum pink, spilled all over the table. She dropped the halves of the cap and grabbed a little paint brush she used for dusting the ivory. She swept the pink powder into a little pile, then onto a sheet of paper. There it was.

As she picked up the larger of the now mostly empty capsule segments to reload the powder, she noticed an odd strip of coloration on one end, just inside the edge. Hmm. What was that?

She held the cap under the scope, couldn't quite make it out. It looked almost like some kind of pattern. Well, we'll see about that. She put the cap down, removed the auxiliary lens, and brought the scope's magnification to 10X. Let's have another look, shall we?

Jesus! What was that? She fiddled with the light, turned the cap this way, then that, and got the shadows just right so she could make it out.

Etched into the material of the cap were tiny words. "Hi, Feebs! Want to find me? Ask Frankie and Annette's grandkids, they know where! Sincerely Yours, Thor."

Hello!

She reached for the phone on the end of the bench. She had to get Alex. He was going to want to hear about this.

Newport Beach, California

The restaurant, Claudia's Grill, was half a block off the highway and slightly up the hill, so it had a nice view of the water. Drayne pulled his Mercedes into the parking lot, gave the key to the attendant and got a parking stub, then went inside. It was three minutes to seven, and the place was pretty full. They served a good breakfast here, and it was a great location.

His father sat alone in a booth, staring out through a wall of glass at the Pacific, the waters already changing from gray to blue as the sun began to burn off the morning fog.

"Hello, Dad."

"Robert."

Drayne slid into the booth. "What's up?"

"Let's order first."

The waitress came by. Drayne ordered poached eggs, chicken apple sausage, and whole-grain pancakes. His father asked for white toast, corn flakes, and decaf coffee.

When she was gone to put their order in, his father cleared his throat. He said, "I'm glad your mother isn't alive to see what you've become."

Drayne stared at him as if his father had just sprouted fangs and fur and might start baying like a werewolf. "What?"

"How stupid do you think I am, Robert? Did it never occur to you that thirty years with the Bureau might have taught me something?"

"What are you *talking* about?"

"PolyChem Products," his father said.

Drayne felt his belly spasm, as if he had just gone over the big drop on a roller coaster. "What about it?"

His father looked disgusted. "There is no 'it.' It's a paper corporation, a phantom. The bank records, the history, none of it is any deeper than a postage stamp. You thought I might look at it, but not too closely, didn't you? *You* are PolyChem Products."

Drayne couldn't think of anything to say. He was cold, as if he had suddenly found himself shoved headfirst into a refrigerator. He'd never expected this.

The old man looked away from him, out at the ocean

again. He said, "I have friends, boy, people who owe me favors. I know where you live, and I know you live well, but I also know that you don't have any visible way of earning money. So that means you are into something illegal or immoral. Probably both. From the way you talked about admiring that criminal who assaulted the agents and staff at HQ recently, I surmise it probably has something to do with drugs."

"Dad—"

His old man turned back to face him, held up his hand to silence him, and in that moment, he was Special Agent in Charge Rickover Drayne of old, steely-eyed and fierce, one of the most stalwart protectors of the republic. "Don't say anything. I don't want to hear about it, I don't want to *know* about it. You're an adult; you can make your own choices. I expected better of you, that's all."

Drayne lost it: "You expected me to turn into a fucking robot without feelings who would grow up to be just like you." He was amazed at the sudden venom in his voice. "You wanted a carbon copy of yourself to send forth, a grown-up Boy Scout who was trustworthy, loyal, friendly, obedient, who would cog his way into the system and stay there smiling until he wore out, just like you. You never once asked me what I wanted to be when I grew up or cared what I thought about anything."

The old man blinked at him. "I wanted the best for you—"

"*Your* best! What *you* thought I should be! Face it, Dad, you were always too busy saving the country from the forces of evil to give a shit what I did, as long as I kept my grades up, my room clean, and I didn't bother you."

"Robert—"

"Jesus fucking Christ, listen to yourself! Everybody in the world calls me Bobby except for you! I asked you to do that a hundred times! You didn't listen. You *never* listened."

Nobody said anything for a long time. Finally, Drayne said, "So, what are you going to do? Give my name to your friends who owe you favors? Have them investigate me?"

The old man shook his head. "No."

"No? Why? Because I'm your son and you love me? Or because you wouldn't want your old FBI chums to know *your* son was anything less than the soul of respectability?"

The old man was spared whatever answer he might have made as the waitress returned with their breakfast. Drayne had never felt less like eating in his life, but both he and the old man smiled at her.

When she was gone, the old man said, "You can think whatever you want. You . . . You're a brilliant man, son. Smarter than I ever was. I always knew that. You could have gone into legitimate business and made a fortune. You could have been somebody important."

"What makes you think I can't do that now?"

"Oh, you could. I don't think you want to. You were always more interested in pulling my chain than anything else, weren't you?"

And I still am, Drayne was smart enough to realize. But he didn't want the old man to walk away with any kind of victory, no way, so he said, "No. All I wanted was to get your attention. Any attention, good or bad, was better than indifference. That's what you gave me, Dad. Indifference. So now you finally notice me, enough to bust my balls. Thank you so fucking much. You want to turn me in for being a criminal, go ahead. I don't care." *And if you do turn me in, I win,* he thought.

Drayne stood, dropped a fifty on the table, and said, "I'm not hungry, but you enjoy your breakfast. It's a long drive back to Arizona. Give my regards to the dog."

Drayne turned and stalked off. Dramatic, but he'd made worse exits. Let the old bastard chew on that for a while.

Once he was in his car, he realized how shaken he was. Even after all the years of layering scar tissue and callus over it, on some level, he still cared what the old man thought of him. Amazing to realize that.

Tad couldn't sleep. He was topped off with enough drugs to put a stadium full of rabid football fans into a trance, but his mind wouldn't go down.

He had taken a hot shower. He had tried to blank his mind. He had gotten up and eaten another phenobarb, and while he was so stoned he could hardly move, he was no way about to sleep, and he needed that, bad.

Bobby had told him about the new operations plan, the safe house, moving the money, and wanting to hire some armed muscle to ride shotgun. Tad had shrugged that off. Whatever Bobby wanted was fine. Tad had made some calls. Some guys were coming by to see Bobby later, shooters who didn't care who they cooked, long as the money was good. It wouldn't cramp things here, they had five bedrooms, plenty of space. Bobby was thinking he could post one as a lookout, have him watching the road, scanning police radios, shit like that. Somebody came calling, they'd hit the beach before the visitors got to the door, jog a ways down to the parking lot where his car was already parked, ready to roll. Could maybe leave another ride in the opposite direction, at the bed-and-breakfast place, slip the owner a few bucks for parking. Maybe even have a jet ski or something, take to the ocean. Maybe rig a bomb to the front gate or something.

Bobby got into the details of stuff like this, and once he did, he covered it pretty fine.

Tad didn't think it was gonna come to that, but that

last biz had put the fear of God into Bobby a little, so that was cool, whatever.

Tad went out on the deck, sprawled in the padded lounge chair, lit a cigarette, and blew smoke at the ocean. The wind blew it back in his face, and he smiled at that. Bunnies in thong bikinis jogged past, guys with tans dark as walnuts, all going about their boring lives. Tad waved at them, some of them waved back. Jesus.

A helicopter zipped by a few hundred feet up, probably looking for people caught in the rip and pulled out beyond the surf. Welcome to the Promised Land, folks. Sun, water, beautiful people, even airborne lifeguards to make sure you don't venture too far away from paradise by accident.

Tad finished the cigarette, ground the butt out on the arm of the chair, then snapped it out toward the water using his thumb and middle finger. This was what his life had come to: There was the Hammer, and then there was waiting for a chance to grab the Hammer; that was it.

Except for the waiting part, it was okay.

He leaned back and watched the seagulls wheel and work the uncertain air currents over the beach, diving and rolling, sometimes hovering almost still against the force of the wind. Some real intricate patterns there, those flights.

The aerobatic dance of the gulls was what finally lulled him to sleep.

31

Michaels said, "Mean anything to you?"

Jay shook his head. "Nope, not right off, but I've turned the searchbots loose on it. I should be getting a first-hit list any moment."

Howard came into the conference room. "Sorry I'm late. I had to park in the secured lot. There's some, ah, hardware I was checking out locked in the trunk of my agency car I didn't have time to return yet. I wouldn't want to lose it."

"No problem. Do you recognize the names Frankie and Annette?"

"No, sir."

Michaels slid a hardcopy printout across the conference room table to Howard, who picked it up and looked at it.

Howard shook his head. "And this came from where?"

Michaels explained how Toni had discovered the hidden message inside the capsule. He was feeling a certain sense of pride when he told them.

Jay said, "Tell Toni that's nice work. Nothing in the

DEA reports about this. Somebody there is maybe sitting on this information?"

"That's what I thought," Michaels said. "I asked the director to pull some strings, and she's gotten the original lab reports from DEA. They went over the caps they've recovered with a fine tooth comb. None of those have this little grandkids riddle inscribed in them."

"We think the DEA might be hiding things from us?" Howard said.

Michaels nodded and brought him up to speed on what Jay had discovered.

"And there's one more little tidbit," Jay said when Michaels had finished. "I have a record of a telecon between Hans Brocken and our Mr. Brett Lee, of the DEA, from three months back. Herr Brocken is the chief security officer for Brocken Pharmaceuticals, of Berlin, Germany."

"Careless," Michaels said.

"I did have to look for it. It wasn't something you'd stumble across accidentally. They made a pretty good effort to hide it."

Howard said, "You really think Lee is in bed with a drug company? Looking to sell the formula for this stuff?"

"It makes a certain kind of sense," Michaels said. "We talked about reasons for him shooting the movie star before, remember."

"And you think Lee is in league with the NSA?"

"Only with one particular person there. No point in casting aspersions on the entire agency," Michaels said. "It seems that Mr. Lee and Mr. George have history about which they have not been entirely forthcoming, though this is still circumstantial evidence."

"I'll get harder stuff eventually," Jay said. "Oops, speaking of which—" He tapped keys on his flatscreen. "Okay, here's what the Sherlock searchbot has to say about my query . . ."

Jay frowned at the flatscreen.

"You want to let us in on it, Jay?"

"Huh? Oh, sorry." Jay tapped a key.

The flatscreen's vox began reading aloud in a smoky, sexy woman's voice:

"Frankie Avalon and Annette Funicello, teen singing and television idols from the late 1950s and early 1960s, first appeared together in the low-budget movie *Beach Party*, from American International Pictures, 1963, co-starring Robert Cummings, Dorothy Malone, and Harvey Lembeck, and featuring musical roles by Dick Dale and the Del-Tones, and Brian Wilson and the Beach Boys. The movie was the first of several in the chaste surf-and-sand genre, which was to remain viable and popular for the next two years.

"Avalon and Funicello were paired in several additional surf movies, including a distant sequel, *Back to the Beach*, Paramount Pictures, 1987, also starring Lori Loughlin, Tommy Hinkley, and Connie Stevens."

The computer's voice went silent, and the three men looked at each other.

Michaels said, "The stars of fifty-year-old teenybopper movies? Fine. Who are their grandchildren?"

Jay shook his head. "I'm cross-checking here, but it does not appear that the two had any off-screen relationship that would have resulted in children together. They were both married to other people."

"Not having children would make it hard to have grandchildren, wouldn't it?" Howard observed.

Michaels said, "Maybe we aren't talking about literal grandchildren. Maybe movie grandchildren?"

Jay tapped away at the keyboard. A moment passed. "Nope, nothing that fits. Nobody ever did another beach movie with the actors who played their children in the '87 picture."

"Maybe the message is speaking metaphorically?" Howard said.

Jay looked at him.

Howard said, "Anybody make any similar kind of pictures recently? Celluloid grandchildren, so to speak, of the originals?"

Jay smiled. "Well, film isn't made out of celluloid anymore, but that's pretty good, General. Let me see . . . Okay, here we are, under Beach Movies, there are several, hmm . . . ah. I think I found it!"

A few seconds passed while Jay read to himself.

"Jay?"

"Sorry, boss."

The flatscreen's vox said, "*Surf Daze*, an homage to the surf movies of the early 1960s, Fox Pictures, 2004, starring Larry Wright, Mae Jean Kent, and George Harris Zeigler. Set in Malibu in 1965, *Surf Daze* chronicles the adventures of—"

"Stop," Michaels said.

Jay paused the recitation. "What?"

Howard beat him to it. He said, "George Harris Zeigler."

Jay nodded. "Oh, yeah. The Zee-ster."

"The recently departed Zee-ster," Michaels said.

Jay said, "This was, um, seven years ago. Before he hit it big. He'd have been about, what? Twenty-four or -five then. Thing is, where he's gone, I don't think he'd be telling us anything useful."

"This is too much of a coincidence. This dope dealer is pulling our chain. We need to talk to the other actors."

"You gonna turn it over to the regular feebs?"

Michaels took a deep breath and let it out. "No. I think maybe we ought to go check this out ourselves."

"Not in our charter," Howard said.

"The current waters are very murky," Michaels said.

"Given the capabilities of the DEA and NSA, I'm not altogether sure just who we can trust. Sure, the FBI are our guys, and they love us—in theory, anyway—but we can't cover any leaks on their part. We don't want to be behind the eight ball on this, do we?"

"No need to convince me, Commander," Howard said, smiling. "I'm going senile from boredom in my office. The drug raid was the most interesting thing that's happened in three months. I'm game."

"Me, too," Jay said.

"I thought after your last adventure in the field you'd want to avoid it," Michaels said.

"I was alone then," Jay said, "and dealing with a militant gun dealer. With the general here and you, I'd feel secure enough to interview a drop-dead gorgeous movie star. Did you see Mae Jean in *Scream, Baby, Scream?*"

"I must have missed that one," Michaels said.

"Me, too," Howard said.

"I'm telling you, she's got lungs could raise the dead, aurally and, um, visually. One of the great on-screen screamers of all time, right up there with Jamie Lee. And did I mention she was drop-dead gorgeous?"

"I thought you had a pretty intense relationship going, Jay?"

"That's true, boss, but that doesn't mean I'm gonna do anything. I can look, can't I?"

Howard and Michaels grinned at each other.

Howard went back and collected his staff car, then headed for home. He didn't want to take the time to return the rifle right now, but it would be safe enough at his home; safer, in fact, than in the general access parking lot at Quantico. Since they weren't going to drop everything and rush over to La-La Land in the next few minutes, he'd have time to pack a bag and tell Nadine good-bye.

They'd be flying commercial—Commander Michaels did not want to attract any attention by cranking up one of the Net Force jets—and they'd be flying incognito, on open-ended agency tickets, so they wouldn't have to put any names on a passenger list until just before boarding, and those would be cover noms anyhow.

Given that he'd just been out to the left coast, it might not be as big a thrill for him as it was for Jay Gridley; still, it would get him out and moving, and at this point, anything was better than spending another day doing make-work.

He headed out toward the freeway and the drive back to the city.

Normally, the drive was a straight run up I-95 and into the District, loop around the belt and to the north end of town where he lived.

But after a couple of miles, he spotted what he thought was a tail.

A lot of people drove this stretch of road, and there were scores of cars and trucks heading in the same direction, so there was no way to be sure, but he first saw the car as he changed lanes to pass. A little way farther, when he pulled back over into the right lane, the car did likewise.

Big deal. This was hardly conclusive evidence. But he had been through the standard Net Force surveillance course as part of his in-processing, and something one of the sub-rosa guys from the FBI who'd taught the class had said always stuck with him: *"If you think you're being followed, it is easy to check, and very cheap insurance. If you're wrong, you might feel a little silly. But if you are right, you might keep yourself from winding up in deep shit."*

Maybe he was overly cautious, but as a professional military man, Howard had learned long ago that being prepared was not the same as being paranoid. And like the instructor had said, checking it out was easy enough.

There was a little state road running northeast to Manassas not far ahead, and Howard eased over into the exit lane. If the car behind him—looked like a white Neon—kept going, he'd catch the next on-ramp and head on home.

Six cars back, the Neon reached the off-ramp and exited a couple hundred yards behind him.

Well, well.

That didn't prove anything for certain. Two or three times, he remembered the FBI guy saying, it could still easily be a coincidence. *"Think about it. What would happen if one of your neighbors heading home happened to get behind you on the freeway? They'd make every turn you would, right? Could be perfectly innocent. Don't jump to to a conclusion until you are sure."*

And there were several simple ways, Howard remembered, to be sure.

He tooled along on the state road, which was narrow but scenic, heading away from the suburbs toward the more rural country. There was an intersection ahead, and apparently the Occoquan Reservoir was to the left. *Fine, left it is.*

He went maybe a quarter of a mile, didn't see the white Neon turn behind him.

So, okay, he was paranoid. He'd find a place to turn around and go home. He was relieved.

There was a little gas station minimart a half mile or so ahead, and Howard pulled in there, stopped, and went inside. He used the bathroom, bought a pack of Corn Nuts and a can of root beer, and headed back to his car. If anybody had been following him, he'd had an excuse to stop. The idea was, the surveillance guy had told them, not to let the people following you know you knew they were there. Better the tail you know than one you don't.

He kept going the way he'd been going, figuring to loop back around to a main road or the freeway eventually.

Five hundred yards out of the minimart, he caught sight of the white Neon in his rearview mirror. The car was a ways back, maybe half a mile, but he was pretty sure it was the same vehicle.

Hmm. He was pretty convinced, but a few more tests should make it interesting.

Howard made a series of turns as he came to little branching streets, right, left, right, right, driving several miles until he was on a nice little country road—and thoroughly lost. He was going to need to use the GPS to find his way out of here. He had no idea where he was.

Eventually he found himself on another road that led, so the sign said, to the Civil War battlefield of Manassas. The two big battles there had been originally named, he recalled, for the little river that went through the area, Bull Run.

Several times, the Neon disappeared from sight, sometimes for as long as two or three minutes, and it seemed to Howard that the guy tailing him had an uncanny ability to guess the right way to turn.

Then it dawned on him that there might be some kind of bug on his vehicle, and all the guy had to do was follow the signal.

Damn, he should have thought of that sooner.

But after half a dozen random turns, there was no doubt in his mind that the Neon was shadowing him. Now, the questions were, who was it, and why were they following him?

He could have called the highway patrol, had a few beefy state troopers pull the Neon over and politely ask those questions. Of course, if the shadower turned out to be Lee, he'd just as soon not air that laundry in front of Virginia authorities; best to keep that in house. Or he could have scrambled a Net Force military team and had them brace the driver, but the truth was, he could take care of his own business. He had his side arm right here, and as yet there was no reason to call out the troops, especially if this turned out to be a huge coincidence. Somebody lost trying to find their way out by following him.

Yeah, right.

He was mindful of what Michaels had said about the DEA agent Brett Lee. After that shooting in L.A., Howard could cost the agent his job, maybe even cause him to face a criminal prosecution. And since the man seemed to be involved in something illegal besides that, he might not be too unhappy if Howard were to run his car into a tree somewhere and not survive the accident.

Of course, it was a long way from following somebody around in your car to premeditated murder, and maybe that wasn't what this was all about. Maybe it was somebody else altogether. Somebody Howard had run afoul of and didn't recall, out stalking for other reasons entirely.

So, the thing was, he needed to box up whoever it was tailing him, stroll on over, and have a few words with him and find out.

Out here in the country, among all the trees and fields and pastures, he ought to be able to find a place to do that.

He started looking.

32

Drayne was not surprised when Shawanda Silverman got back to him within a day. She had a nice place all lined up, and any time he wanted to come by and take a look, she would make herself available.

Times must be hard in the real estate biz, he figured.

He got the address and information and said he'd be by to pick up the keys soon. All the legal stuff had been handled over the net, e-sigs and the money transfer from one of the blind-alley addys. It was a done deal.

He wouldn't go himself, of course, he didn't want his face to stick in her mind. Normally, he would have sent Tad, but Tad was still zoned out on the deck. Drayne had tossed a blanket over him when it got dark and cool, then put a beach umbrella up to shade him when the sun came up. Old Tad might not move for another day or two, if ever he moved again at all.

Fortunately, the bodyguards had shown up, and while two of the four he hired weren't the sharpest knives in the drawer, the other two were fairly bright. All were

armed with handguns, they had a couple of pump shot-
guns in a big case, and all claimed fighting expertise in
some Oriental martial art or another. The biggest of the
bunch was six two and two fifty, easy, and had a face that
had stopped a few punches. One of the smarter ones was
Adam, a tall and muscular dishwater-blond in his late
twenties who looked as if he might have done some surf-
ing at one time.

Drayne decided to send Adam to meet with Ms. Silverman, to collect the key for the new place.

"Your name is Lazlo Mead, M-e-a-d, and you work for
Projects, Inc.," he told Adam. "If she says anything about
your voice sounding different, tell her you had a cold
when you talked on the phone."

"Won't be a problem," Adam said. He took a breath,
blew half of it out, then said, "Hello there, Miz Silverman.
I'm Lazlo Mead."

Drayne had heard his own voice on recordings enough
to recognize that Adam's impersonation was dead-on.
"Jeez, that's good."

"I do a little stand-up now and then," Adam said. "Unfortunately, it doesn't pay real well. Not yet, anyhow."

After Adam was gone, Drayne pondered the bodyguard
situation a little. He wasn't planning on telling any of
them the location of the safe house, just in case push came
to shove and they got left behind when he took off. Adam
was smart enough to figure it out, and if he wanted to
bother, he could con it out of Silverman easily enough.
After all, he would be Lazlo, wouldn't he? That might be
a problem, so if things went into the toilet, he'd have to
make sure Adam either got clear with him or wasn't going
to be able to tell anybody what he knew about the hidey
hole.

Maybe it was time to get that gun, Drayne figured.

But at least things were on the move, his insurance was in place, and he felt a lot better.

He had put the word out to his customers that the Hammer was going to be available with the timer starting in forty-eight hours. Within a matter of a few minutes, he had twenty orders, and an hour after that, twenty-five more. That was forty-five hits of the drug, plus one for Tad, if he was awake by then. And since Tad was out cold, Drayne would have to do the deals himself, but that wasn't a problem, he'd use net cutouts and FedEx Same Day only, no Zee-ster face-to-face to worry about. Now all he needed was some chem.

With the guards, he didn't want to start out too wild, so he decided to go to the RV to do his mixing when it came time. He wouldn't need them to go with him, they were mainly to protect his castle and his retreat if he needed to run. Nobody would know him from, well, Adam out in the desert where the RV would meet him.

He grinned. Yep, things were back on track. Except for that crap with his old man. Well. He could sort all that out later. Come up with some story that would make the old man feel bad, like maybe he was a spy or an undercover cop or something. Yeah. Wouldn't that be poetic justice? Having his father think he was serving his country while being accused of doing something illegal and immoral. That would be a hoot.

For now, maybe it was time to pop a cork and have some bubbly. And maybe get one of the new bodyguards to show him about guns, too.

Washington, D.C.

"You are leaving me here and going *where?*" Toni said.

"Hey, you discovered the clue," Alex said. "We need to follow it up."

"*We* need to do that? Net Force doesn't do that kind of field work, that's for the regular FBI."

"Yeah, well, I don't know how secure that would be now. If Jay's suspicion is right, we have two guys who are capable of getting information not normally available. NSA has ears everywhere."

"Come on, you couldn't figure a way around that? Couldn't you hand-carry this info to somebody in the shop and have them check into it without exposing it to outside ears?"

Alex continued packing his overnight bag, tucking his bathroom travel kit into the case. "If I knew who to trust, sure. The director is on our case about this. If it goes wonky, even if it's not our fault, you know who will get the blame. Much easier to shove it off on Net Force than to admit problems in her house. Or worse, making accusations against a brother agency without ironclad proof. You've been around long enough to know which way that wind blows."

"It sounds like rationalization to me," she said. "An excuse to get out of the office. And out of here."

He stopped packing and looked at her.

"I'm fat, hormonal, pale, and pregnant," she said. "And I'm driving you crazy."

He came over and caught her shoulders. "No. You are carrying our child, and I love you. You are the most beautiful woman in the world, more so now than ever."

"You're just saying that to make me feel better."

"Well, yeah," he said. But he grinned.

She grinned back at him. "You're a bastard."

"Take that up with Mom. She never told me, and I'm sure my father would have been surprised to know that."

"A smart-ass bastard at that."

But she grinned, too.

"I'm meeting Jay and John Howard at the airport in about three hours. We have time for a shower and a proper good-bye, don't we?"

"A smart-ass goat-boy bastard."

He laughed, and she did, too.

The area around Manassas was, like much of northern Virginia, rolling hills, suburbs and mini-malls, and roads that gridlocked during rush hour. Still, there were areas where the pine and oak trees still held their own, and there were a few stone fences and old houses standing against the weather.

Howard had driven for about thirty minutes, until he found an empty, tree-lined rural road narrow enough for his purpose. He drove along until he was a half mile or so ahead of the Neon, then turned right into a narrow tractor path leading to a cattle-guard gate in a barbed wire fence. He shut off the engine. There were no houses nearby, just some brown and white cows grazing in the pasture.

What he planned to do was get out, head through the cow pasture and into the little patch of woods opposite it, and then circle behind the Neon, which he figured would stop and wait to see what he was up to. Once he was behind the shadower, he'd creep up on him with his revolver in hand, and find out exactly who he was and what he wanted. A simple plan, but one that should work.

Behind him, the Neon pulled off the road about four hundred meters away, turned sideways with the passenger side facing Howard, and stopped.

Howard waited a few seconds, then got out of his car.

He was still on the driver's side closing the door when there came a *chink! chink!* as the passenger's and driver's side windows shattered, followed by the sound of a rifle shot. The bullet, traveling faster than the sound, missed him by maybe two inches.

Shit!

Howard took two steps to the front tire and dropped into a crouch behind it. He pulled his revolver. The engine was the best protection, and the heavy steel wheel would probably deflect a sniper's bullet aimed lower.

Another shot, another round pierced the car's doors, through and through, and if he'd been there, it would have gutted him.

This was bad.

There was no other cover nearby. It was fifty meters through an open pasture to the tree line, and trying to cross the road the other way would be equally stupid, he'd be exposed. A decent shooter could nail him. And his handgun, while a fine weapon, was not going to do the job at four hundred meters unless God intervened in his favor.

He risked a quick look.

Another shot echoed over the pasture land, and the round smashed into the car's side above the front tire but stopped when it hit the engine. Made a terrific clang.

If the guy came toward him, he'd still have the advantage for another three hundred, three hundred fifty meters, and if he circled around, Howard was really in deep shit.

He could call for help, but it would never get here in time. What the hell was he going to do?

Memory was a funny thing. Up until that moment, he had forgotten what he had in the car's trunk. He felt a sudden surge of hope and possibility flow over him when he remembered.

Howard scooted toward the rear of the car.

Another shot hit the car amidships and must have struck a frame support or something in the door; it didn't go all the way through to his side.

He reached the back tire. He had his keys, and the trunk release was on the electronic alarm and opener. He took a deep breath, put his revolver over the car's trunk, pointed it at the Neon, and triggered off three shots as fast as he could.

At the same time, he popped the trunk control, lunged under the still-rising lid, and grabbed the hard-shell case inside. He jerked it out and fell back behind the tire.

The sniper's next shot was great; it hit the passenger-side tire, lanced through the steel-belted radial, hit the driver's side tire and penetrated that, then punched a hole in the corner of the hard-shell carrying case, almost jerking it from Howard's grip.

The car dropped to its rims, and he wasn't going to be driving it anywhere any time soon.

Howard popped the latches and dumped the parts of the .50 BMG rifle onto the ground. The bullet had missed anything important. He put his handgun down and, with a speed aided by adrenaline, assembled the rifle in what had to be record time. He loaded the magazine with five cartridges of the match-grade ammo, chambered a round, and lit the red-dot attachment on the scope. It was sighted in at three hundred meters, he recalled, so he'd have to adjust his aim a bit. Or maybe not. This thing shot pretty flat for a long way.

Time to make an assumption here. The shooter was probably using a scoped deer or sniper rifle, 30-6, maybe .308, something like that, and if it was, it would likely be a bolt action. So he was going to have to manually chamber a round after each shot, which meant that Howard would have half, maybe three-quarters of a second between shots.

Not much time to get set up. And if it was a semiauto, that would be really bad. But it was what he had.

Howard took a grip on the heavy rifle. He stuck his head up, held it there for an agonizingly long time, maybe half a second, then ducked.

The shot came, hit the trunk, zipped through, but missed by a good six inches.

Then Howard leaped up, dropped the .50's bipod on the trunk's lid, slamming it shut, and put the red dot on the middle of the Neon. He squeezed the trigger, a shade too quickly, and the recoil from the weapon knocked him back and almost off his feet. The blast of sound was like a bomb; it deafened him. Even as he fought to regain his position, he chambered another cartridge, the empty extracted and smoking to his right.

That would give the son of a bitch something to think about! *Not so much fun when the victim can shoot back, is it?*

Howard looked through the scope. On high magnification, he could see the bullet hole where the side of the Neon had buckled in around it; it had blown paint off in a hand-sized crater, but there was no sign of the shooter. If the guy had any brains, now *he* would be behind the front tire with the engine block protecting him. When the .50 went off, it sounded like the wrath of God, and the assassin would know that the odds had just shifted dramatically into Howard's favor.

Howard's ears were ringing and he couldn't hear anything over that. He looked down, saw the earplugs that came with the rifle, and risked the second it took to scoop them up. He shoved them into his ears.

No sign of the shooter.

Fine. Let's see how *you* like being dinner, asshole.

He put the red dot on the top of the front tire and squeezed a shot off, more careful now.

The bullet hit a few inches high and must have shattered and sprayed the engine compartment. Vapor came out from under the hood, maybe from the radiator, maybe coolant for the AC. He'd bet that car wasn't going anywhere, either.

Now it was time to get the troops out here. He pulled his virgil and hit the emergency sig control in a rapid sequence.

"Sir?" came a voice.

Howard smiled. *Gotcha now, sucker.*

"Hold on a second." Howard shot the Neon again. Hit the front tire this time. The car sagged.

"I want a helicopter with a squad of troops ready to shoot landing twenty meters east of the GPS location of my virgil in fifteen minutes maximum. This is not a drill."

"Yes, sir!"

"Here is the situation. . . ."

But when the chopper from Quantico arrived and a dozen of Net Force's finest hit the ground, fanned out, and surrounded the mortally wounded Neon, the shooter was nowhere to be found. The car was much closer to the tree line than Howard's car was, and somehow, the would-be assassin had managed to slip away without Howard spotting him.

Damn!

33

Jay looked up from his flatscreen at the boss and the general. "The shooter's car was stolen," he said.

They were in the airport, in one of the VIP lounges that the boss had access to, waiting for the flight to L.A. If John Howard was rattled about somebody trying to shoot him out in the boondocks where Stonewall Jackson had earned his fighting nickname, you couldn't tell it by looking at him.

As a licensed federal agent, however, Howard would be carrying a gun with him onto the plane, this at the boss's insistence. Both Michaels and Jay had their air tasers with them, too, though Jay had only fired his in the required semiannual qualification sessions, and the last of those had been four months past. He didn't try to kid himself that he was any kind of gunfighter, even with the nonlethal shock 'em and drop 'em tasers most Net Force personnel outside the military arm were issued.

"A stolen car. Not a major surprise there," Howard said. "It would have been too much to hope for that he'd use his own vehicle. I don't suppose the lab rats managed to get any fingerprints or DNA for a match?"

"Not yet, sir," Jay said.

"That isn't a surprise, either," Michaels said. "Not if it was who we think it was in that car. How about Lee's whereabouts?"

"That's a little trickier," Jay said. "We couldn't just have the FBI hunt him down and grab his ass, not without tipping our hand. According to a sub-rosa contact we managed with the DEA, Mr. Lee was today taking some personal time. He was in Maryland, visiting his paternal grandmother, who is in a nursing home just outside Baltimore. Accessible on-line records at the Sisters of Saint Mary's Home for the Aged indicate that Mr. Lee did sign in about an hour before the attack on General Howard, and he signed out ten minutes after the attack. Nobody has gone in and done a face-to-face with the staff to check that yet, however."

"How easy would it be to fake the in and out signatures and records?" Howard asked.

"I could do it with both hands tied behind me and a cold so bad the voxax could only pick up every thirteenth word," Jay said. "While blindfolded and in my sleep."

"That hard, huh?"

"Shoot, boss, *you* could do it."

"All right, so we get an investigator out there to see if Lee actually did go visit his old granny."

"If he was there, that would make it impossible for him to have been the shooter," Jay said.

"Let's just see before we try to cross that bridge."

"I'd be very surprised if we can find a nurse or ward clerk who remembers seeing Lee there today," Howard said.

"Anything on other forensics at the scene?" Michaels asked.

"Nothing to write home about," Jay said. "No empty shells lying on the ground, no blood, no hair, no dropped bar matchbooks or IDs or maps showing how to get to the perp's house. Shoe prints are a popular brand of cheap sneaker. Fibers from where the shooter kneeled appear to be lightweight gray cotton, probably sweatpants."

"And the clothes and shoes and no doubt gloves are probably in a trash bin or burned to ash by now," Michaels said.

"This was a pro," Howard said. "If I hadn't had that portable cannon, I think he might well have taken me out."

"You tell your wife about it?" Michaels asked.

Howard looked at him. "Would you have told yours?"

The boss looked uncomfortable. "Maybe. Toni was a Net Force op, she knows how things go sometimes. Of course, she's pregnant, and I wouldn't have wanted to upset her once everything was over with."

"The local cops weren't called in, the media doesn't have it, we're keeping it in house," Howard said. "I didn't want to worry my wife, either. I'll mention it to her later. After we catch the son of a bitch who did it."

Jay didn't say anything. He'd have told Saji, but she was a Buddhist, they were into the real world and all. He looked around. Technically, they weren't supposed to be doing this, since it wasn't really part of their mission statement. Plus they weren't supposed to be flying on the same jet. If the flight went down, it would take out the commander, the military chief, and the head of Computer Operations, which would be bad for Net Force. The director would be royally pissed; then again, Jay wouldn't much care about that, being dead and all. What the hell.

Jay wasn't worried about flying, that had never bothered him. A plane went down now and then, that was awful, but it was like being struck by lightning. If it happened, it happened. What were you gonna do, stay home all your life?

He was looking forward to visiting Hollywood. Outside virtual visits, he had only been there once in real time, on a trip when he'd been in high school, part of a computer team entered into a national contest. They'd come in second and should have won, except that one of the twits on his team had flubbed an easy program a third-grader could have managed. As much time as Jay did creating scenario in VR, he felt as if he'd be right at home among the moviemakers. It would be the middle of the night before they got there, and they'd head straight for the hotel, but tomorrow would no doubt be sunny and delightful.

He spun up the flatscreen's power, hit the wireless air-net key, and logged via an encoded sig into the Net Force mainframe again. He had VR gear in his bag, but he didn't like to do VR work in a public place, too many people, no telling who might decide to come up and swipe your luggage while you were sensory deprived and deep in scenario. Probably they'd be okay here in the VIP lounge, but no sense in developing bad habits. He'd just have to do it the old-fashioned and boring way, using the vox controls and hand-jives, a pain, but there it was.

Banning, California

Drayne had the air conditioner going full blast in the RV, and Ma and Pa Yeehaw had unshipped the little car they towed behind the RV and gone into town to do a little bar hopping or whatever, while Drayne mixed up a new batch of the Hammer. He'd hold off on adding the final catalyst until he got back to town. Now was a good time to check out the new safe house, and nobody would be looking over his shoulder there while he did the final mix. Once the clock started running, he'd send one of the body-guards to FedEx with the packages, and that would be that, another forty-five thousand into the secure e-account, and wasn't life beautiful?

He grinned. *I wonder what the poor folks are doing now?*

Beverly Hills, California

Mae Jean Kent was an impressive-looking woman, Michaels noted, oozing sexuality, and however powerful her lungs might be, they were certainly augmented with a major pair of headlights, double-D, at least. Toni had been quick to tell him these weren't real, but nonetheless . . .

She was beautiful, blond, tanned, fit, and wore a halter top and hip-hugger pants and sandals. She also wore big sunglasses. She agreed to meet them at some local restaurant that was apparently *the* place to meet locally, and she was constantly waving at people who passed the outdoor table at which she, Michaels, Jay, and John had been situated.

"Hi, Muffy! Hey, Brad! I'm sorry, Alex, what was that again?"

"Ms. Kent—"

"Oh, please, call me MJ, everybody does!"

Michaels guessed her age at thirty, judging from her hands, but she was acting more like eighteen. Part of the youth culture out here, where you might be over the hill at twenty-five.

"MJ. So tell me about this beach picture."

"Oh, it was a terrible shoot! First thing was, Todd— that's Todd Atchinson, the director?—was having a major crisis and he ran out of Paxil and was a bear to work with. He just kept *yelling* at everybody. Then Larry—that's Larry Wright—had a major fight with his boyfriend, he's gay, such a waste of a perfect bod, you know? Anyway, Larry was so depressed he just moped around like an old hound dog. And George—I was so sorry to hear that he died, so sorry, but he was a major doper, major—kept getting a, you know, a *woody* every time we shot a scene together, and they had to shoot around it because his bathing suit was, you know, bulging all the time!" She giggled and took a deep breath, showing off the results of what must have been expensive plastic surgery.

Michaels wished Toni were here, so she could see just how vapid and unattractive this woman was, despite her looks and attempt at what she thought passed for sophisticated animation.

Michaels glanced at Howard, who kept a straight face but offered no help. Jay seemed entranced by the rise and fall of MJ's hooters under the barely-able-to-hold-them halter top.

"Is there anything you can think of that might have a connection to something called Thor's Hammer?"

She turned and waved at somebody passing the tables. "Hey, Tom, baby! How *are* you!" She made a kissy face at Tom baby.

Michaels caught the hint of a grin on Howard's face, but when he looked closer, the grin vanished.

"MJ?"

"What? Oh, no, I don't remember anything about a sore hammer."

"Where was the movie shot?" Jay asked. Apparently his breast-induced trance was not as deep as Michaels thought.

"Where?"

"Yes. The location."

She glanced upward, as if expecting the answer to be written on the underside of the big umbrella sheltering their table. Then she looked at Jay and gave him her full-wattage smile: "Malibu," she said. "On the beach."

Michaels got the gist of Jay's question and followed it up. "Anything unusual about the location?"

"Unusual? No, I don't think so. It was kind of like a private beach, Todd knew some of the owners who had houses right next to it, so they roped it off for the shoot. A lot of tourists came by every day and asked for autographs between setups. I have a lot of fans."

"I heard a critic say your performance in *Scream, Baby, Scream* was first-rate," Howard put in. He smiled.

Michaels looked at Howard. Butter wouldn't melt in his mouth.

"Really? I tried hard to get some subtext into that, but the script was, you know, just full of major problems. Writers just don't understand what a proper vehicle should be like for actors. They are all hacks out here."

Probably used too many big words, Michaels thought. *Those two- and three-syllable ones must be killers.*

That was unkind, Alex. This is Hollywood, remember, it's all about what looks good. It's not her fault how it works.

"Well, we thank you for your time, MJ," he said. "You've been a great help to us."

"Hey, no problem. I'm glad to cooperate with the government any way I can. If you get a chance to talk to the IRS, tell them to quit auditing me, okay?" She flashed the smile, inhaled deeply, and then turned to wave again. "Barry! How are you!"

Waiting for the parking lot attendant to fetch the rental car, Howard said, "Well, that was helpful in a major way, you know?"

Michaels said, "And when did you see *Scream, Baby,*

Scream, John? Dial it up on your room cable last night?"

"Just my bit to keep the conversation moving," he said. "Besides, I didn't say I'd *seen* it, I said 'a critic said.' That would be our staff critic here. I was just taking Gridley's word for it."

"Well, I suppose we should go try Larry," Michaels said. "And hope that he and his boyfriend have patched things up since *Surf Daze.*"

"Or Todd," Howard said. "Maybe he's gotten his Paxil refilled."

"Maybe we don't need to," Jay said.

Michaels and Howard looked at him.

"The inscription in the capsule said the grandchildren would know where to find him. I think MJ might have told us."

"The beach at Malibu," Michaels and Howard said together.

"Big-time drug dealer could afford to live there."

"It's a long stretch of coastline," Howard said. "Hundreds of homes."

Jay said, "But movie shoots in cities have to have all kinds of permits. I can access the records for the surfer pic and find out exactly where the location was. That would narrow it down to a handful of houses. We could check ownership records on those, eliminate some of them."

Michaels said, "That's good thinking, Jay."

"I didn't think you were paying full attention to your work back there," Howard said.

"Silicone doesn't do it for me," Jay said. "Besides, she's much smarter in her movies, which ain't saying much."

"Okay, get on-line and find out what you can."

"One other thing," Jay said. "I got a blip during the interview." He waved the flatscreen, looked at Howard.

"Several witnesses, a couple of them nuns, attest that Brett Lee was in the nursing home yesterday when you were being shot at. It couldn't have been him."

"Damn," Howard said. "Then who?"

"Maybe your dog crapped on somebody's lawn," Jay offered.

"I don't think so," Howard said. "We don't have a dog."

"Maybe you should get one. One with big teeth."

The car hop arrived and pulled the rental car to a stop. Michaels took a five from his wallet and gave it to the man, who looked at it as if it were a piece of used toilet paper. Lord, what kind of tips was he used to getting?

Inside, Michaels said, "Find us a place to go, Jay."

"I'm on the case, boss."

34

Malibu, California

When Tad woke up, he noticed a couple things: First, he was on the deck, with the beach umbrella doing its best to keep him in the shade, but starting to lose that battle.

Second, there were some men with guns wandering around in the house.

Fortunately, he recognized one of the gunslingers, so he realized the bodyguards had showed up, and Bobby must have decided to hire them.

Shit happened when you went into hibernation. You got used to it.

He looked at his watch, and the date showed he'd been out for a couple of days. Not too bad.

His head felt as if somebody had opened it with a dull shovel and poured half the beach into it. He was way beyond grainy. All the rest of him just hurt. Bad.

He managed to get to his feet, using the umbrella for support, and headed toward the bathroom. Once, after sleeping for a couple of days, he had stood over the toilet peeing for more than a minute, on and on, must have pissed half a gallon. For some reason, his bladder never let go while he was out, and he counted that as a blessing.

The guy with the gun that Tad recognized nodded at him. "Hey, Tad."

Tad nodded in return. The name came to him, slow, but there. "Adam. How's it going?"

"Good. Bobby's out. He's supposed to be back in a while."

"Cool."

He shambled into the bathroom, cranked the shower up, then stripped. He waited a few seconds for the water to heat up, then stepped into the shower. He stank, and he could pee just as well in the shower.

He needed to get to his stash. He wasn't gonna be able to function real well for a couple of days yet, no matter what, but certainly not straight.

He opened his mouth, let the needle spray rinse the taste of tar and mold out, spat three or four times, then swallowed a couple of mouthfuls of the hot water. He knew he was dehydrated, and if that got bad enough, his electrolytes could get wacky enough to stop his heart. He'd known guys on speed who hadn't eaten or drunk anything for a couple of days who'd died that way. Heart just stopped beating.

He stayed in the shower for ten minutes, letting the spray pound him. He felt a little better when he stepped out onto the cool tile floor and started drying himself with the big fluffy beach towel. A little better wasn't going to cut it.

His stash was in the wheel well of his car's trunk, and the car was parked in the lot of the sandwich place two down from them. When Bobby was running in paranoid mode, which was most of the time, he wouldn't let Tad keep anything in the house that might get them busted. Not even in the car, if Tad wanted to park it in the driveway or garage or anywhere inside the security gate. Nothing more than you can swallow, Bobby told him, and close enough so you can do that if somebody crashes the gate.

Tad mostly tried to do it that way. For a while, he buried his drugs on the beach. He had kept his stuff in a mason jar with a plastic lid so no coin-hunter or narc would find it with a metal detector. He would sneak out late at night and bury the jar in the sand. But he'd lost one that way, completely spaced out on where he'd hidden it. And another time, somebody's dog had dug up one of the jars, so he'd stopped that. The walk to the car wasn't that far, half a block, but of course, it felt like a thousand miles after a session with the Hammer.

Well, there was no help for it. He wasn't going to send Adam or one of his hard-ass friends to collect his dope. He didn't trust anybody that much except Bobby, and Bobby wouldn't do it anyway.

Tad slipped on a pair of raggy black sweatpants, a black T-shirt, and a pair of black zorrie sandals. Might as well get to it. It was gonna take a while.

"I'm walking over to where I parked my car," he told Adam. "Don't fucking shoot me when I come back."

"Why waste a bullet?" Adam said. "You look like somebody could kill you with a hard look. Hell, you look dead already."

"You need to work on your material, Adam. I heard that one already."

"Lots of times, I bet."

Tad thought about his route for a minute. Out the front gate and along the road was longer. But walking along the beach through the sand would be harder. The road would be noisier, all the traffic. The beach would be hot. He'd have to walk around cars parked on the highway. He didn't need any more obstacles at the moment. Until he got his medicine mixed and working, just breathing was an effort.

Okay, the beach. He headed for the deck stairs.

Michaels said, "One of those three or four houses?"

Howard drove, Michaels rode shotgun, Jay sat in the back. As they idled slowly along the highway, looking toward the beach, Jay said, "Got to be. Permit specifies this part of the beach. That sandwich shop over there is in the movie. I pulled it up and scanned location shots. That house to the far left was built two years ago, so it wasn't there then."

"Do we have owners on these?"

"Yes. The pinkish one is owned by the actress Lorrie DeVivio. She got it in the divorce settlement with her fifth ex-husband Jessel Tammens, the movie producer."

"DeVivio is what . . . sixty and rich? Hard to image her making and peddling dope," Howard said.

"Ah, you know the old movie stars, eh, General?"

"She won an Oscar," Howard said. "And not for her looks."

"What about the other houses?"

"Second one belongs to the chairman of the board of the Yokohama-USA Bank. He's also sixty-something and also richer than God.

"Third one, the pale blue and white one, is owned by a corporation called Projects, Inc. Some kind of corporate retreat, maybe. I'm running down the incorporation stuff now. They are out of Delaware.

"Fourth one belongs to one Saul Horowitz. Don't know who Solly is, and the searchbots haven't been more forthcoming so far."

"That sounds promising. Pull over there, into that restaurant lot, and let's think about this for a minute," Michaels said.

All four of the houses had security gates and fences, at least to the road side. As Howard parked the car, a Mercedes convertible arrived in front of the third house and pulled up to the gate. The car's top was down, and a sun-bleached blond, deeply tanned young man in a Hawaiian shirt who looked like a surfer held up an electronic remote and pointed it at the heavy steel gate, which slowly swung open to admit his car. He pulled into the drive, and the gate started to close behind him.

"Yo, kahuna dude!" Jay said, in a valley-boy voice, "Surf's up!" Jay held up his hand, the middle fingers closed, his thumb and little finger extended. He waggled his hand back and forth. "Mahalo!"

"Thank you, Brian Wilson. You get the license plate number?" Michaels said.

"Crap! I'm sorry, boss—"

"It's a vanity," Howard said. "P-R-O-J-E-C-T-S."

"Run it," Michaels ordered.

Jay, chagrined at his failure to catch the number, dialed up the California DMV and logged in, using his Net Force access code.

A few seconds later, he said, "Car is owned by Projects, Inc.," he said. "Big surprise there, huh? Looks like you get wheels to go with the house. Nice perks."

"So, what do you think?" Michaels said.

"Either it's that one or the Horowitz place," Howard said. "Rich bankers and rich movie stars might use dope, but they don't need to sell it."

"Just FYI, General, they found a bug on your car. That's how the shooter kept from losing you." Jay pointed at the flatscreen. "Also, Mr. Lee, who as we all know couldn't have been said shooter, called in sick today."

"Something fatal, I hope," Howard said.

"And to keep things interesting, Mr. Zachary George is on vacation this week and next," Jay said.

Michaels said, "Anything on the searchbots for Mr. Horowitz here yet?"

"Nope," Jay said. "But I don't think we need it."

"And why would that be?"

"Take a look at the death-warmed-over stick in black walking along the road there, coming from the sandwich place," Jay said.

"So?"

"Look again, boss."

Michaels did. He frowned.

"Yeah," Jay said. "Kind of hard to picture him beating the crap out of a room full of bodybuilders and trashing a gym, isn't it?"

Michaels nodded. "But that's the guy."

"Never thought I'd see an actual match to a police ID composite," Jay said. "All we have to do is watch and see if he chooses door A or door B. Whichever one he picks, I'd bet my next month's salary against a bent quarter that's our dealer's house."

The three watched the man, who looked as if he might fall down any second, as he shambled along. It took him a while to get there, but he finally did.

"And we have a winner," Jay said. "It's the surfer dude's pad. Net Force rules!" He looked at Michaels. "Now what, boss? We gonna go kick ass and take names?" He held up his air taser and waggled it.

Both Howard and Michaels laughed.

Michaels said, "I see your experience in the field didn't teach you anything. We're not going anywhere. We're calling the FBI. They'll go in."

Drayne parked the car and went in. He saw one of the bodyguards skulking behind the banana and short palm trees nod and wave at him. Good to know they were watching the place like they should.

Inside, Drayne walked out to the deck. Adam was there, looking at the ocean. "Where's Tad?"

"He stepped out, said he was going to his car," Adam said. "Said he'd be back in a few minutes."

Drayne nodded. Tad would be self-medicating as soon as he was ambulatory again, and his pharmacy would be in his car, parked away from the house. It better be.

The front door opened, and speak of the devil.

"Hey, Bobby."

"Tad. You all right?"

"Will be in about half an hour." He headed for the kitchen.

Drayne followed Tad into the kitchen, watched as Tad counted out ten or twelve pills, caps, caplets, and tablets, filled a glass with water from the tap filter line, and washed the drugs down in one big swallow.

"While you were napping, I set up some things," Bobby said. "I was gonna send one of the bodyguards, but now that you're awake, you can make the FedEx run."

"Okay."

"We're moving forty-five hits of the Hammer."

Tad raised an eyebrow.

"Might as well make hay while the sun shines," Drayne said.

"You mixed it already?"

"Yep. Did the final at the new house, so the stuff is just under an hour old."

"Got mine?"

"It's too soon, Tad, you ought to sit this batch out. I'll be doing another bunch next week."

Tad didn't say anything, and Drayne shook his head. "It's your ass."

"Such that it is, yeah," Tad said. "Give me thirty minutes for the stack to kick in, I'll be ready to roll."

Drayne shook his head again. "Your funeral."

• • •

"Geez, Boss, you don't think the three of us could take one surfer dude and a zombie?"

Michaels had already put in the call to the director, and she in turn had called the local FBI shop and started the ball rolling. He said, "Isn't this the zombie who wiped up the floor with a gym full of guys strong enough to pick up tractor trailers? Didn't you just bring that up?"

"Yeah, but—"

"And don't you recall the recordings of a white-haired old man who shrugged off a cloud of pepper gas and air tasers like they were mosquitoes and tossed guards and cops around a casino like a kid throwing toy soldiers? Or a woman who ripped an ATM machine out of a wall with her bare hands?"

"Yeah, but he can barely move now. He can't be on the drug."

Howard said, "There are too many things we don't know here, Jay. Think about it. What is the lay of the house? Can they sneak out the back while we're climbing the front gate? Are they armed? Who else is in there with them? I'm the only one with a gun here, so do you and the commander run around back and make sure they don't escape with your tasers while I try to kick in what might be an armored front door? Not to disparage your shooting ability, but even if you hit something, you've only got one shot before you have to reload, and the fastest AT reload I've ever seen took almost two seconds. I'd guess you couldn't do it in five or six. In two seconds, a man can run twenty, twenty-five feet, knock you down, and take off. In six seconds, he could be down the road having a beer, figuratively speaking. And that's unarmed. If the surfer or the zombie have weapons, what do you think they'll be doing with them if you miss? Or if you yell 'Stop!' and they shoot first? They could have a submachine gun in there, and they could take out twenty civilians out there on the beach. That would be after they cut you down."

"Mm," Jay said. "That would be bad for public relations, not to mention my personal love life. So why didn't we call in Net Force troops? We can trust them."

"That would have been my choice," Howard said, "but the commander is right. We found them, but it isn't our operation, we aren't supposed to even be here, we're outside our job description. If we had a dozen Net Force military troops kick in the door of a Malibu beach house, we'd all be looking for jobs. Assuming we could even get our people here in the next couple of hours, which we could not."

Michaels said, "By rights, this belongs to the DEA. Even if the director decides to let FBI agents make the arrests, it's still a hot political potato. The director can risk pissing off a brother agency, we can't. We can't even get warrants, so even if we were willing to get fired, the capture wouldn't be legal. Even an ambulance-chaser lawyer with a lobotomy could get them off. The arrests would be completely illegal."

"Yeah, okay, I can see all that," Jay said. His voice was reluctant.

Michaels looked at his watch. "We should have agents showing up within thirty or forty minutes, if we're lucky. We do it by the numbers, get part of the credit, and most importantly, the drug dealer is off the street. The end result is the same, no matter who hauls them off."

"For how long is he off the street?" Jay asked.

"Excuse me?"

"This guy is carrying around a secret that is worth millions, maybe tens of millions, you said so yourself. Won't the drug companies be falling all over themselves to be first in line to hire him the best legal team in the world? How high can his bail be?"

Michaels nodded. He knew what Jay said was true. "Probably. But that's not our worry. We were supposed to find him. We found him. We did our part. What happens to him after they catch him isn't our problem, we don't have any control over that. We're just a cog in the big machine, Jay. We do our job, we have to hope the rest of the system does its job. Can't be everywhere."

"That sucks," Jay said.

"Welcome to the real world, son," Howard said.

35

Drayne gave Tad the minipackets with the Hammer caps, the list of addresses, and pointed him at the door. By now, most of the payments would have already been transferred electronically into the safe accounts. Before Tad stuck a packet into the FedEx clerk's hands, he'd check again to make sure the payment for it had cleared.

As the door closed behind Tad, the phone rang. It was the business line.

"Polymers, Drayne—"

"If you have a lawyer, call him," came his father's voice. "You'll need him soon."

His father hung up without identifying himself, and Drayne felt a rush as cold as liquid nitrogen envelop him.

"You!" he said, pointing at the nearest bodyguard. "Go get Tad! Don't let him outside the gate!"

The bodyguard hurried away.

Drayne's fear, cold at first, now flushed into an uncomfortable warmth that suffused his whole body.

The old man had turned him in!

No. If his father had done that, he wouldn't have had

any second thoughts. The old man never apologized for anything once he decided it was the right thing to do. And though he hadn't said anything specific, it didn't take a rocket scientist to read the volumes between those lines.

Drayne was about to be busted. The old man had found out about it, and he'd called to warn him.

Son of a bitch.

Almost more important than getting arrested was that his father had gone against thirty years of duty to tell his son he was in trouble. Couldn't bring himself to give it all away, of course, but even this much, knowing how smart Drayne was, and that he would figure it out, was nothing short of a miracle.

Son of a bitch.

Drayne went to the security console in the kitchen and looked at the camera focused on the front gate. Nothing there. He touched the controls. The cam was mounted on a gimbal, could look pretty much in any direction. He put the cam into a slow 360-degree pan.

Across the street at the Blue Gull, a car was backed into a parking slot, and a man sat in the passenger seat, the window down, looking in the direction of Drayne's house.

Drayne stopped the pan and focused the cam on the car.

Okay, that could be somebody waiting for his wife to come out of the bathroom or something.

He hit the zoom. The glare on the windshield wouldn't let him see inside, but the security folks knew about glass glare, and a dial let him polarize the lens. The windshield cleared to show a second man in the driver's seat and a third man in the back.

Shit! They were already in place!

Tad came back into the kitchen. "What's up?"

"Company," he said. "Look."

Tad looked at the screen. "So? Some guys in a car. Don't mean nothing."

"Yeah, except that my father just called and told me to call my lawyer."

"Your father? Oh, shit."

"Exactly." Drayne took a deep breath. He said to Adam, "Go see if anybody is hanging around out back."

Adam returned in thirty seconds. "Nope. Couple of girls with their tops off lying facedown on beach towels next door, that's it."

"Okay, they haven't covered the rear of the house yet. Tad, Adam, we're going for a walk. The rest of you stay here. If anybody comes to call in the next five minutes, don't let them in. After that, it doesn't matter. You don't know anything. Not who I am, not where I've gone. You got that?"

There was a murmur from the guards. They pulled their pistols out.

To Adam, Drayne said, "You have an extra one of those?" He pointed at the gun in Adam's holster.

"Sure."

"Give it to me."

Adam did so. The gun was kind of squarish, black, and made out of some sort of polymer. Drayne said, "What do I do?"

"It's a Glock .40," Adam said. "Point it like you would your finger and pull the trigger. It's ready to go. You have eleven shots."

Drayne hefted the black plastic gun, then tucked it into his pants in the back, under the tails of the Hawaiian shirt.

"Let's go," he said.

"Here comes the cavalry," Howard said.

Three unmarked late-model sedans cruised slowly up

the highway from the south. The cars turned into their parking lot and pulled to a halt.

"More behind us," Jay said.

Howard looked around and saw three more cars and a van convoy into the lot.

A tall man in a gray sweatsuit got out of the lead vehicle and walked to the passenger side of their car. "Commander Michaels? I'm Special Agent in Charge Delorme."

Michaels waved at Howard and Gridley. "SAC. General John Howard and Jay Gridley."

"No offense, sir, but isn't Net Force supposed to be a computer-based operation?"

"It is."

"With all due respect, sir, once you located the suspects, you should have called the proper agency in right away, not come out here on your own."

Gridley leaned forward and said, "Yeah, well, last time we found a suspect, the proper agency rolled in like gangbusters and shot him dead. We were kinda hoping to avoid that this time."

Howard grinned a little. He was a mouthy kid, but he did put his finger right on the problem from time to time.

"Thank you, Jay," Michaels said. To Delorme, he said, "Don't worry. We'll sit right here out of your way while you do your job."

"Sir," Delorme said. He stood and waved his hand in a circle, index finger pointing up at the sky. Three of the cars pulled out of the lot and across the highway, skidding to stops on either side of the target house. Doors opened, and agents in body armor with FBI lettered in big Day-Glo yellow on their backs, armed with assault rifles and wearing goggles and LOSIR headsets, boiled out of the cars. Delorme pulled a headset on, caught a vest somebody tossed at him, and moved toward the highway.

Other agents alighted from the cars still in the lot and ran across the road.

Two cars rolled toward places where the beach was accessible from the road, and more agents leaped out and hut-hut-hutted toward the ocean, to circle around behind the house.

"Not bad deployment," Howard said, after watching them move into position outside the gate. "A little slow, kind of sloppy, but not bad for civilians." All the high-tech gear in the world, and when it came right down to it, it was still going be the ground troops who had to gain the territory.

"Might as well sit back and enjoy the show," Michaels said. Then he said, "Shit!"

"What?" Howard and Jay said together.

Michaels pointed. A big Dodge rolled out of the sandwich shop parking lot and roared away, heading north.

"Sir?" Howard said.

"The zombie is driving that car!"

Howard didn't hesitate. He started the rental car's engine and pulled out onto the highway.

Jay said, "Why don't you get closer, General? We might lose them!"

Howard said, "If they see us behind them, we'll sure as hell lose them. We're going up a hill here. This gutless piece of crap rental can't begin to keep up with that hot rod they are in. So far, they are obeying the speed limit, but if they see us and decide to run, we can't keep up with them."

Michaels was on his virgil, trying to call the SAC running the bust.

The man wasn't answering.

"Come on, come on!"

"He'll have his com shut off, tactical channels on LO-

SIR only," Howard said. "You don't want to have to answer the phone in middle of a firefight."

The boss swore.

"Try FBI HQ," Jay offered.

Michaels shook his head. "Probably half their guys are on this raid already, and it's gonna take anybody else as long to get here as it did to get to the beach. Maybe longer."

"What about the local police?" Howard said.

"Who *are* the local police? Where are we? Who has jurisdiction?"

"Call CHP," Howard said. "Probably they can get here fastest. Put up a roadblock. Better than nothing."

Michaels nodded. He tapped a button on the virgil, waited a few seconds, then started talking. The woman's voice coming from the virgil was calm enough, but her news was bad:

"Sorry, sir, but we have a major traffic accident on the Ventura, ten cars and a semi full of hazardous chemical that's on fire, all available officers are there or on the way there. I can put you through to the county sheriff's patrol."

"Damnit!" Michaels said. He shut the virgil off.

"We're okay," Howard said. "We stay with them, they'll stop sooner or later. When they do, we'll get whatever police agency that covers the area to roll."

"If we don't lose them," Michaels said.

"If we don't lose them," Howard agreed.

"Close," Adam said. "FBI assault team, looked like. What did you guys do?"

"Don't worry about that," Bobby said from the backseat. "Close only counts in horseshoes and hand grenades. They didn't follow us, right, Tad?"

Tad looked into the rearview mirror, but anything more than a few feet back was a blur. He hadn't gotten his stack just right; he was having a little trouble focusing his vision. But nobody was within a block of them, and if the feds were there, they'd have already zoomed up and tried to run them off the road by now, right? Out here on a road over the hill with nobody around, that was the way to do it. There was a curve maybe a quarter mile back, and if he squinted hard, Tad could see that the road was empty at least that far.

Tad said, "No. Nobody followed us."

Adam, in the front, turned around and looked. "Looks clear." He rolled the window down and stuck his head out, glanced around, then pulled his head back inside. "No helicopters. Where are we going? The safe house?"

"Yeah. For now. After that, I think maybe we need to take a nice long trip somewhere out of the country."

"All of us?"

"No reason for you to go," Bobby said. "Nobody knows who you are. We'll give you a nice bonus, you can get back to your life."

Fuzzed as his brain was, Tad didn't think that was a very good idea, but he didn't say anything. Bobby knew what he was doing. Bobby always knew what he was doing.

"Fine by me," Adam said. He turned around to watch the road in front of them again.

Bobby said, "Loud noise, Tad."

Tad didn't have time to think about that when two bombs went off—*Boom! Boom!*—that fast, and the windshield spiderwebbed on the passenger side.

"Fuck!" Tad screamed. The car slewed onto the shoulder, hit a couple of rocks, and jounced hard. He fought the wheel, managed to get it back on the asphalt.

Tad looked into the mirror, saw Bobby just leaning back into the seat, that black gun in his hand. He glanced over at Adam. There was a bloody splotch on his chest and more blood oozing from a hole right over his heart. His left eye and part of his nose was also gone, shredded, gore running down his face. He was slack, only the seatbelt keeping him upright.

It took a second for Tad to get it.

Bobby had just shot Adam. Twice. In the back and in the back of the head. One of the bullets had gone right through him and through the windshield, which was now whistling with the breeze coming through it—what he could hear with his ears ringing from the noise.

"Jesus fucking Christ, Bobby!"

"He was a liability," Bobby said. "He knew where the safe house was. He knew you personally. We have to make a clean break here, no loose ends."

Tad nodded. "Yeah, okay. Whatever you say."

"What was that?" Jay said. "Sounded like some kind firecracker—look at the car!"

Howard eased up on the gas pedal and the rental car slowed dramatically. The little four-cylinder gas-alkie engine with battery backup was barely able to move them uphill.

The Dodge ran off the road, hit something and bounced, then scraped and skidded back onto the tarmac.

"Gunshots," Howard said. "Two of them. Pistol caliber."

"They shooting at us?"

Michaels said, "No, not us. Somebody in the car."

"Why?"

Michaels looked at Jay over the back of the seat. "Did I get here before you? What can I see that you can't? I don't know."

The three men stared at the car, which rounded another curve in the wavy road and disappeared.

Howard shoved the accelerator pedal down. The little

car moaned, and not much else. Their speed picked up slowly. He pounded the steering wheel. "Piece of Japanese crap! Go!"

Michaels reached for the in-dash GPS, thought better of it, and pulled his virgil. Its GPS would be more accurate. Better find out where they were. Maybe they could get a helicopter from somewhere.

Los Angeles DEA had those, didn't they? All the drug raids they went out on, they'd have to have air cover.

Could he risk calling the DEA in?

Well, why not? Lee wasn't the guy who shot at Howard, he had witnesses saying he was elsewhere. And he didn't have to call Lee back in D.C., just the local HQ.

He didn't want to do it. But what was more important here? Letting the DEA get the credit? Or maybe losing the drug dealer altogether?

Crap—

The decision was interrupted by his virgil beeping. Michaels pulled it from his belt. The ID showed it was the director. He tapped the link-on, and the vid control, held the virgil up so the cam could see his face.

"Yes, ma'am?"

"My SAC tells me that the drug dealer was not in the house they raided, nor was the other man. What is the situation there, Commander?"

"Three men managed to escape by car just as the raid went down, ma'am. The agents didn't see them. General Howard, Jay Gridley, and I are in pursuit. We are heading east over the mountains at the moment. We have been unable to contact SAC Delorme's team."

"I'll have them spot on your GPS signal," she said.

"I was thinking we might call in the DEA," he said. "They'll have air support."

"Already done, Commander. They should have a helicopter in the air by now, and they are also tracking your virgil's GPS, have been all along."

Howard nodded. "I see."

"We have to let them in, Commander. There is no choice in the matter, you understand?"

He understood, all right. "Yes, ma'am."

"Try to maintain your surveillance. I expect you'll be seeing the DEA forces show up soon. Call me when you have something to report."

"Yes, ma'am."

Michaels discommed. Howard glanced over at him.

"You heard the director. Try to stay with them. DEA is in the air."

But that wasn't quite true, Michaels realized a few seconds later. The DEA had a helicopter, all right, he saw it not more than a block ahead as they rounded the next curve.

The copter was parked across the middle of the road.

36

Drayne saw the helicopter blocking the road a good two seconds before Tad's drugged reaction time finally kicked in and he slammed on the brakes. The big Dodge's wheels locked and the car skidded to a rubber-burning stop.

Adam's body twisted out of the seat belt's shoulder strap and he thudded against the dashboard, then slid sideways into the door, smearing blood all over the window and door post.

"Shit!" Tad said.

"Turn around, turn around!"

But as he said it, Drayne looked over his shoulder in time to see a car a hundred feet behind slew to a stop and turn so it blocked the road.

Tad saw it, too. He hit the brakes again.

To their left was a rocky slope, the wall of the mountain. To the right, a fairly steep drop down the hillside into a valley of rock, dried brown bushes, and eucalyptus.

A half-dozen men with guns were crouched around the copter, pointing their weapons at the Dodge. Drayne looked back in time to see three men pile out of the other side of the car behind them. They came up behind the hood and trunk, and pointed weapons, too.

Well, *shit.*

"Fuck! What do we do?"

Drayne thought fast. There was a dead body in the front seat of their car. Tad had enough drugs to stone a parade, not even counting the scores of Hammer caps. This was bad.

Drayne leaned forward and gave Tad the pistol he had. "Here, take this."

"We'll get slaughtered," Tad said.

Drayne reached around the seat and took Adam's pistol from the dead man's holster. "Maybe not, I've got an idea. Stick the gun out the window and shoot it into the air."

"Why?"

"Just do it."

Tad did, the sound loud in the quiet afternoon.

The men behind the copter ducked, but they didn't return fire.

Drayne almost smiled. Good, that was good. They wanted him alive. Alive, he was valuable. Dead, he was worthless.

And now Tad, bless him, had powder residue on his hand showing he had fired a gun.

"Okay, okay, let's think about this. We got their attention, but we're boxed, so we're gonna have to do this with lawyers. We have money, and we have power. The pharmaceutical companies want what I have. So we get out with our hands up, and surrender."

"You sure?"

"Trust me, I know what I'm doing. One phone call, we'll have some very heavyweight people lined up to help us."

"Okay, man."

Of course, Tad would have to take the fall for killing

Adam. And since Tad would get shot resisting arrest or trying to escape, he wouldn't say otherwise. Drayne could pull that off. If he yelled, "Hey, don't shoot, Tad! Put the gun down!" at the right moment, the feds would hose Tad. DEA rules of engagement wouldn't be that different from the FBI rules when facing an armed perp. Too bad, but Tad had one foot in the grave anyhow. He liked him, but his death might as well count for something. No point in Tad being dead *and* Drayne being in jail, was there?

Drayne climbed over the seat.

"What are you doing?"

"I want to be right behind you when we get out, we don't want them to think you're reaching for something when you move the seat to let me out."

"Oh, yeah."

"Tuck that gun into your belt and keep your hands in the air when you get out."

"Okay."

"Let's do it. Just stay cool. We'll walk away from this, believe me. Once we're out on bail, we can take off and stay gone forever." Not that they would get bail with a corpse in the front seat of their car. Judges frowned on that.

Tad nodded. "Okay."

Howard had braked and turned the car to block the road, and the three of them jumped out on the driver's side, away from the stopped Dodge.

"Get those tasers out, for all the good they'll do," Howard said. He pulled his gun from under his jacket, crouched behind the front wheel, and pointed the gun over the hood. "See if you can get the DEA there on your virgil's emergency band and tell them not to shoot us."

Michaels nodded. He was the commander of Net Force, but he was willing to defer to the general in this kind of situation. He wasn't going to to let his ego get them killed.

He hit the emergency call button, got the Net Force operator, and told him to patch them through to the DEA team. The FBI Director should have their number.

Crouched behind the trunk, his taser clutched in both hands and pointed at the Dodge, Jay nervously said, "I think . . . I think I'm gonna throw up. And I gotta pee, real bad."

"It's okay," Howard said, "we all feel like that."

Oddly enough, Michaels didn't. He felt relatively calm, almost as if he were watching and not participating. His mouth was awful dry, though.

Behind them, a car approached. Howard turned and waved at it frantically. "Stop!"

The car, a dark minivan, did stop. The passenger door opened and a man jumped out and ran toward them.

He had a *gun* in his hand.

Howard swung his revolver around and almost shot the guy—then they all recognized him.

Brett Lee, of the DEA

Lee crouched into a duckwalk the last few steps. "What's the situation?" he asked.

"What the hell are you doing here?" Michaels responded.

"I was following you," Lee said.

They all stared at him.

He said, "Look, okay, I screwed up on the bust at the movie star's house, okay? My job is going away, at the least. I need to help catch this guy so I don't leave in total disgrace. I need a little victory."

That made sense. Before anybody could speak, Michael's virgil started its musical sting. No ID sig. That damned thing was practically useless. He thumbed the connect button. His camera was still on, but the incoming screen was blank, no visual transmission.

"Commander Michaels? Riley Clark, DEA. Is that you in the car behind the suspects?"

"Yes. And I have Brett Lee here with me."

"Hold your positions, and please don't shoot unless you are fired upon—"

As if his words were a signal, a gun went off. Michaels ducked instinctively.

From the virgil, Clark's excited voice came: "Negative, negative, do *not* return fire, the gun was pointed into the air, repeat, hold your fire!"

Michaels raised from his squat and looked. The driver's side door opened, and two men stepped out, their hands in the air. The zombie and the surfer. What an odd-looking pair they were together.

"Which one is the chemist?" Lee asked.

Jay said, "Gotta be the surfer."

Drayne felt tight, knowing all those guns were pointed at him, but he also knew he was the golden goose, and while the DEA field guys might want to burn his ass, the higher-ups would know which way the political winds blew. Sure, he might have to do some time at one of those country-club honor farms somewhere, working on his tan and Ping-Pong game, but in the end, he was going to cut a deal, and he was going to walk away rich. Guys worth tens of millions of dollars didn't go to jail very often, almost never, and he'd be very cooperative. The feds would bargain with him, because he had something everybody wanted. He could turn people into superhumans. Hell, the Army would be first in line, if the Navy and Marines didn't beat them to it.

He was smarter than the guys they sent against him, always had been, always would be. He could think circles around them. This was a temporary setback, that was all.

He was a genius, and he'd show them just how smart he was.

He smiled. "Don't shoot!" Drayne yelled. "We give up!"

Something was wrong, Howard felt, but he couldn't put his finger on it. Lee was right here next to him; Howard didn't trust him, and if Lee raised that pistol, he was going to bat it down, but that wasn't it, it was something else.

Then he knew. It hit him like a lightning bolt.

Lee had gotten out on the passenger side!

He twisted around, looked at the van, said, "Shit!"

The driver's door was open, and a man was behind it, a rifle resting on the windowsill, but not aimed at Howard or Michaels or Jay or Lee.

Howard swung his revolver around.

The rifle went off.

Tad was looking right at him when Bobby's head exploded. The skull deformed in front, like it was plastic, and Bobby's whole forehead spewed into the air, blood and bones and brain in a greasy fluid like a water balloon bursting, spraying every which way.

Fuck. They shot Bobby.

Tad didn't even think about it, he bolted, ran straight for the only way not full of guns, right over the side of the hill. He hit five or six yards down, his legs collapsed, and he rolled himself into as much of a ball as he could, bouncing and smashing into creosote bushes and rocks and dirt, until he hit something so hard it took his consciousness.

Michaels watched in slow motion as John Howard shoved his handgun forward and started pulling the trigger. There were orange flashes from the muzzle and smaller flashes from the cylinder, but the sound was oddly quiet, like a cap pistol.

Brett Lee screamed—Michaels saw his mouth open—and he tried to point his pistol at Howard.

He's going to shoot John, Michaels realized.

Michaels lunged, slamming into Lee. They both sprawled on the road. Lee dropped his gun to break his fall, hit, rolled up, and kicked at Michaels.

Without thinking or pausing, Michaels swept his right hand down and up again in an arc, caught Lee's ankle and, at the same time, dropped into a low position and shoved with his left hand at Lee's chest.

Lee fell backward, hit the road flat on his back, and his head thumped the asphalt and bounced. He was stunned enough so he didn't move.

Michaels blinked and realized he had just done an *ang-kat*, a throw against an unweighted leg. Huh.

Jay, who probably didn't have any more of an idea of what was going on than Michaels did, stepped up and shot Lee with his taser. Lee juddered and jittered on the dusty road as the electrical charge spasmed his muscles.

Michaels turned to look at Howard, who was up and moving toward the minivan, gun still extended in front of him. Michaels didn't see his taser, he must have dropped it, but he hurried to join Howard.

Behind the still-open driver's door, which had several holes in it, a man lay on the ground, bleeding, a rifle next to him. His chest was a ruin, dark with arterial blood, and Michaels knew the man had been shot in the heart. He'd be dead soon, if he wasn't already.

He couldn't see the man's face until Howard kicked the door shut, and when he did, it was not really all that much of a surprise:

The heart-shot man was Zachary George of the NSA.

37

When Tad woke up, he didn't know where he was. Outside, somewhere, and buried in some kind of sweet-
smelling brush. He had cuts and bruises he didn't
remember, and felt like crap, but that wasn't anything
new, it had happened before. Lots of times.

He tried to sit up, couldn't make it, then fell back and
gulped for air.

This might be it, Tad, old son. The last roundup.

Damn. How'd he get here? Where *was* here, anyway?

The sight of Bobby's head blowing apart filled his
memory.

Aw, *shit! Shit, shit, shit!*

It all came back to him in a jumbled rush of pain and
emotion. Killing Adam, the helicopter in the road, the leap
he'd taken to get away—

Bobby's head exploding. In slo mo and Technicolor.
Jesus!

He looked at his watch to see how long he'd been out,
but the crystal was shattered, the minute hand bent to the
face and stopped, the hour hand gone completely. The

feds would be coming for him, they might be almost here, and he had to get up, he had to get moving, or they'd catch him. Probably none of them would have just jumped off the fucking cliff like he had, but they'd figure a way down soon enough to grab his ass. He didn't know how long ago it had been. It felt like it was still afternoon going into evening, so maybe he'd only been out for a few minutes.

He wasn't going to get far in his condition, he knew.

He reached into his pocket and came out with one of the Hammer packets. A couple of them fell on the ground, but it was too much trouble to bother picking them up. Well, he sure wasn't going to be making any deliveries anytime soon, and the clock was running on this batch. He had until tomorrow around noon before the stuff would all go sour. Use it or lose it, and he couldn't take them all.

He tore open the packet and dry-swallowed the Hammer cap. Thought about it for a few seconds, then ripped open another packet and took that cap, too. It would be a while before the stuff would kick in, and he couldn't sit here waiting for it, no matter how much he hurt.

The gun he'd had tucked in his belt was gone. His car was God knew how far up the hill, surrounded by feds. He was screwed.

And Bobby was dead. That hadn't really sunk in, it didn't seem real. They'd killed him, they'd fucking *executed* him, he'd had his hands up, and they had blown his head off!

Tad felt a surge of anger well up, filling him with murderous rage. He wanted to run back up that hill and tear them apart with his bare hands, rip their arms and legs off, stomp on the bloody torsos.

The anger was good, but it was barely strong enough to get him to his feet and moving. If he could stay clear long enough for the Hammer to kick in, he'd be okay. Once the drug took hold, he'd be able to travel at speed.

And go where?

The safe house. They didn't know about that. Bobby had the place stocked, there was some running-away money stashed there, more in the safe at the storage space.

Bobby was dead.

Tad couldn't believe it. Bobby was smart, good-looking, rich, he had everything going for him. And they cooked him, *blam!* Just like that.

Tad stumbled, fell, and managed to get back to his feet. Oh, they were gonna pay for killing Bobby.

He was fucking going to *make* them pay.

"No sign of the zombie?" Jay said.

"The DEA people haven't found him yet. Local deputies will be joining the search soon," Michaels said. "General Howard went down with them and found this." He held up a purple capsule. "There were several of them under a bush down there. DEA got the rest, but it doesn't look as if they have turned sour yet. So this is still an active capsule."

"No great loss. We got the chemist."

"We have his body," Howard said.

Jay nodded and blew out a sigh. What a fuck-up this had been.

"I bet forensics will match that rifle George had to the bullets they found in my agency car at Manassas," Howard said. "George was the shooter. That's why Lee had such a great alibi."

"So they were in it together all along. But why shoot this guy Drayne?"

"I don't know," Michaels said.

Lee had recovered from the fall and taser shock and was handcuffed and sitting in the back of one of the DEA vehicles that had finally arrived. He was more than a little distraught when he saw the body of George covered up and waiting for the coroner.

He'd sobbed and begun crying. Not really the kind of reaction an op from one agency usually had for an op from another agency, certainly not the same sex. Something there, all right.

"Bastard," Lee had said to Howard. "You *killed* him!"

"Damn straight," Howard had replied. "I only wish I'd shot him two seconds sooner."

"Bastard. You're a dead man."

"Not by your hand, pal. You're an accessory to murder and attempted murder, probably seven kinds of conspiracy, and God knows what else. You're going away for a long, long time."

"Maybe not. Maybe I have something to trade."

"Better be damned good, whatever it is," Howard said. "And between you and me and my colleagues here, if I see you on the street anywhere close to me or mine, I'll drop you and worry about the consequences later."

"You threatening me, General Howard?"

Michaels said, "You must be mistaken, Mr. Lee. I didn't hear any threats. Jay?"

"Nope, I didn't hear anything at all."

Howard nodded at Michaels and Jay.

Jay smiled. Well, what the hell, they were a team, right?

On the drive down the hill, Michaels called Toni.

"Hey," she said. "How's the glamour there in Tinseltown?"

"Great, if you like chase scenes and shoot-outs."

"What?"

"We tracked down the dope dealer. He's no longer with us, however."

"What happened?"

Michaels filled her in on the operation.

When he was done, she said, "That's good work, Alex. Nobody got hurt except the bad guy, and Net Force gets the credit. How are they going to play it with the media?"

"Straight, I hope," he said. "But I wouldn't bet on that. Camera teams were all over us ten minutes after it happened, news choppers circling like mechanical vultures. I let Jay talk for us and he kept it vague, but I don't know what the DEA and FBI guys had to say. Rogue operatives are never a good spin for any agency. You can say, 'Yeah, we had a problem but we cleaned it out,' but the first question from the reporters will be, 'How'd you get a problem like that in the first place?' It's a no-win situation."

"Not for Net Force."

He grinned at the small image of her on the virgil. "Well, yes, that's true. We get off smelling like roses."

"So, when are you coming home?"

"Probably tomorrow morning. We need to file reports with the local FBI and DEA offices, talk to their supervisors, like that."

"Couldn't you file those reports on-line from here?"

"You know how that is, they want to see us when we tell it. Won't take long, but by the time we get done, it'll be late, and we're flying into a three-hour time difference. Might as well wait until the morning."

"At least it's all wrapped up."

"Not completely. The zombie—that's Thaddeus Bershaw, we got that from his car registration—got away."

"That's not major, is it?'

"Not that we can tell. We don't know for sure what his part was in things, but he wasn't the brightest bulb on the string. Jay dug up his background, and he was an uneducated street kid. Probably no more than an errand boy. The dealer was Robert Drayne; he had a degree in chemistry. Also had a father who was with the Bureau for thirty years, retired to Arizona."

"Interesting."

"DEA and FBI put out an APB net and street on Bershaw. They'll find him eventually. Anyway, he's not our problem anymore."

"I miss you," she said.

"Yeah, I miss you, too. See you tomorrow. I'm thinking maybe I'll take a couple personal days and we can do something."

"I'd like that."

Michaels discommed and leaned back in the seat. It had been a long day, and he wasn't looking forward to the double debriefing. It would be nice if they could do it once, with ops from both the DEA and FBI listening together, but that wasn't how it was going to go, of course. That way would make too much sense.

They were way too slow coming down the hill to find him. By the time he heard them yelling at each other, Tad was six hundred yards away, and the double-hit of magic purple was coming on *strong*. Ten minutes after that, he was feeling good enough to jog, and ten minutes after *that,* he was able to run like the wind, hopping over rocks and bushes in his path, covering ground much faster than any normal man would be able to do on foot in the gathering darkness. He could run faster, see better, and make quicker decisions, and no way were they going to catch him from behind, if they even had a clue which way he had gone. Probably still looking for his body under the bushes back there.

Three miles or so away, he angled back up toward the road, then paralleled it for half a mile until he came to a tiny shopping center. He found a motorcycle chained to a light pole, and it took all of thirty seconds to find a rock big enough to smash the lock. The owner had trusted the lock and chain, and so he'd left a spare ignition key under the seat, tucked in the cushion springs, where Tad and ten other guys he knew always kept their spare bike keys, and the sucker, a midsized Honda, cranked right up.

They'd probably have roadblocks set up on both sides of the hill looking for him, but he could dance that or maybe go off road and around it. Now that it was fully dark, he would have an advantage: He didn't need to use the headlight; there was enough city glow for him to see the road. Time they spotted him coming, it would be too late.

The double dose of Hammer was something. He had never felt so strong, so fast, or so quick-witted. They didn't have a chance. If they did stop him? Well, he would just kill them all.

Tad sailed eastward down the hill in the dark, hitting speeds of eighty, ninety miles per hour with the lights off, whipping past startled drivers who heard him but couldn't see him him until he appeared in their headlights. Must have scared the crap out of them.

If the fed had roadblocks, they must have been closer to the place where the copter had been, which made sense, sort of. They weren't figuring on a guy who could run three miles in the dark before he got back to the road. They didn't have the Hammer and he did.

Once he was down and in the flats around Woodland Hills, he flicked the headlight on. He didn't have far to go now.

He made it to the safe house without incident. Inside, he flipped on the television and tuned it to CNN *Headline News*. He didn't feel like eating, but he knew he needed fuel and liquid, so he grabbed a big can of ham slices and a six-pack of Evian water. He peeled ham slices off two at a time and washed them down with water as he watched the news. He needed information as much as he needed fuel.

The info wasn't long in coming. A local camera crew had gotten to the site of the shooting, and while most of what the reporter had was probably total bullshit, there were a couple of things that stood out: The drug dealer who had been slain had been located through the efforts of the FBI's computer arm, Net Force; the leader of that organization, Commander Alexander Michaels, had come all the way from Washington, D.C., to be in on the raid. The newscam had footage of Michaels, right out there on the road, looking down at the body of some agent who had been killed by the drug dealers during the raid.

Yeah, well, if one of theirs was dead, the feds had done it themselves. Bobby hadn't done it, and except for that one shot Tad put into the sky, he hadn't fired, either. Lying fuckers.

There were interviews with local DEA and FBI agents, as well as some computer geek for Net Force. It had been a coordinated operation among the three agencies, so it seemed, but Net Force got the big pat on the back for coming up with the information that led to the suspected drug dealers. One of said drug dealers had escaped, was still at large, and considered armed and dangerous. They flashed a picture of Tad, along with his name. Driver's license photo. So they had IDed him, no big deal.

The news moved on, and he shut it off.

When he looked down at the ham can, it was empty. He had eaten two pounds of ham and downed six bottles of water, and he didn't even feel full. Probably his last meal.

Tad thought about it for a few seconds. Commander Alexander Michaels. Net Force. Washington, D.C. A long way to travel for somebody in his shoes. And nothing he did would bring Bobby back, dead was dead. Why bother?

Yeah, well, fuck it. He'd almost reached the end of his string anyhow.

He went into the bathroom. Bobby had stocked the place with all kinds of shit they might need if they had to run. He found scissors and an electric razor with a trim attachment and cut his already-short black hair into a flat-top. The Hammer made him want to jump up and down, but he held himself steady by force of will so that the do wasn't too ragged. He used half a bottle of hair coloring on his new cut. He shaved off his lip-hanger goatee. Pulled out his earrings and tossed them.

After the hair color was done, bleached to an ugly yellow, he showered. Got out, and rubbed himself down with bronzing gel, applying it carefully with the little sponge thing.

Okay, so he wasn't gonna pass for a surfer, but he wasn't the same fish-belly white beatnik in the picture, he was blond and tanned. He found some slacks, a dress shirt, socks, and running shoes, all in pale gray or white, not his look at all. There was a pair of wire-rimmed glasses with plain glass lenses, and he put them on. He could almost pass for normal.

There was about fifty thousand in cash in frozen food packages in the freezer. He took about ten grand. He didn't expect he'd need that much, and if he somehow got back here—unlikely—he could get the rest then.

There were some fake photo IDs in a desk drawer, three or four sets each for him and Bobby. Tad picked up a set, looked to see that the driver's license was from Texas, and that the name was Raymond Selling. Bobby's little joke: Selling was the winner of last year's Los Angeles Marathon race. He'd done one for Richard Kimball, too, from the old TV series, *The Fugitive*. The last one was for Meia Rasgada, which was Portuguese for "torn stocking," yet another kind of runner.

Bobby was a riot.

Had been a riot.

He needed to move, he really *needed* to move, but he had one more thing he had to do before he could. He took one of the clean digital phones in the kitchen and punched in a number from memory. His memory at the moment was excellent; he could draw on anything he had ever seen, smelled, tasted, heard, felt, or done if he needed it, and he knew it would be there.

"Yo," came the deep voice.

"Halley, it's Tad. I need something."

"Yeah, me, too. Your money in my pocket. Go."

"I want an address for Commander Alexander Michaels, M-i-c-h-a-e-l-s. He's the head of Net Force."

"I can give you that without having to burn an electron, dude. Net Force HQ is in Quantico, Virginia, part of the new FBI complex next to the Yew-Nite-Ted States *Muh*-rines—"

"No, I want his *home* address."

"Ah. That'll take a little more. They'd keep that buried pretty good."

"How long?"

"Ah, forty, forty-five minutes."

"Call me back on this number when you get it."

"Cost you five hundred."

"Not a problem."

"I'm on it, dude."

Tad took his new self outside. There were two cars in the garage. A year-old tan minivan with a Baby on Board sticker on the back window, and a three- or four-year-old Dodge Dakota. Both had keys in the ignitions. He paused long enough to grab the rear bumper of the truck, to squat and lift the tires clear of the pavement a few times, to burn off some of his excess energy. Then he climbed in and cranked the engine.

He pulled out of the driveway and headed for the airport. On the way, he called and booked a first-class seat on the next nonstop flight to Washington, D.C. The plane wouldn't leave for three hours. Another five or so hours to fly there, figure on maybe two more to find the place. Call it ten hours all totaled, be there by eight or nine A.M. at the absolute latest. He'd be riding the Hammer for that long, and when he started to come down, he had a whole shitload of caps that would be good until noon, and another twelve hours of Hammer to ride after he took it. Midnight tomorrow, easy.

That should be more than enough time to have a long chat with Commander Alexander Michaels of Net Force, and to teach the fucker what a bad mistake he had made in helping get Bobby Drayne killed.

Plenty of time.

38

Los Angeles, California

Michaels had just finished shaving and was getting dressed when there came a knock on the hotel room's door.

It was Jay. He said, "FBI got a lead on Bershaw."

Michaels waved Jay in as he continued to button his shirt. "Yes?"

Jay held up the flatscreen so Michaels could see the image thereon. A blond-haired man with glasses, dressed in casual sports clothes.

"They sure this is him?"

"Check the side-by-side."

A magnified image of the blond appeared next to an identical-sized head shot of Tad Bershaw. Overlay grids appeared, numbers scrolled, and yellow highlight outlines pulsed over the features.

"The feeb surveillance matchware doesn't worry overmuch about hair, eye, and skin coloring, it compares ear size and lobe shape, nose length and nares spacing, eye spacing and brow angle. Plus somatotypes, though those can be altered by shoe lifts and padding. This is him."

"Where was this taken?"

"LAX, last night. The matchcam sent a sig to FBI HQ, but the priority tag imprint apparently was malfunctioning; instead of an A-1 stamp, the file was batched with a bunch of routine no-hurry PPOIs . . . that's possible persons of interest. So they should have seen it last night, but nobody got around to scanning the file until a few minutes ago."

"So much for infallible technology," Michaels said. He sat on the bed, pulled on his socks. "So where did he go?"

"According to the gatecam at CrossCon Air, he took a nonstop red-eye to Washington, D.C. Plane landed around two A.M. this morning, eastern time. Dulles matchware showed him getting off the jet, but that's the only image they got. FBI checked the rental agencies, he didn't get a car, and they are talking to bus and limo drivers and cabbies. No hits yet. From the passenger list, they know he's using the name Raymond Selling."

"Like the marathon runner?"

"Who?"

"Selling is the fastest long-distance man in the country, probably the world."

"I don't follow the sport. Running for twenty-six miles hurts me just to think about it."

"Why Washington?"

Jay shrugged. "Why not? Maybe he's got an old girlfriend there, somebody he used to run with. Easier to disappear in a big city than a small one."

"Well, maybe we'll bump into him when we get home."

"I hope not," Jay said. "If he's got any of that dope left, he's not somebody I want to meet face-to-face."

Michaels tied his shoes, stood, and reached for his sport coat, which hung on the bathroom door. "What time does our flight leave?"

"Couple hours. Be back in Washington about seven P.M. Five-hour flight, add three for the time zones."

"Well, let's go have breakfast and enjoy the L.A. sunshine. It'll probably be raining when we get back to the East Coast."

Jay closed the flatscreen, and they started for the door. He still had a worried look.

Michaels said, "Something else?"

"Yeah, a major problem. In-house Security says somebody got past the Net Force firewalls and into the mainframe last night."

"I thought that wasn't possible."

"It's not, for most people. I could do it. And if I could, some others could. A handful."

"Was anything damaged or stolen?"

"Fortunately not. The file protection programs make that real hard without the encryption keys. Even I might have trouble wrecking any big part of the system from outside. Security says the probe rode in on a GAO line and managed to get into the personnel files. It didn't damage them, they are read-only for the GAO auditor, who, by law, we have to let in. Somebody had to know about that to use it."

"Who would know?"

"Ex-programmer, maybe ex-ops, FBI, GAO. Maybe even Net Force."

"Really?"

"We've had people quit. Fired a few, too. Programmers always leave themselves a back door when they are building secure systems. We vetted ours, and I had our people checking, but the guy who builds it can hide a few things when you are talking millions of lines of code."

"So what now?"

"We'll run down all ex-employees with enough skill to pull it off. My hope is that it'll turn out to be some kid hacker counting coup. But that wouldn't be the way smart money bets."

"Mm. Stay on it, Jay. In the meantime, let's don't keep General Howard waiting."

On the way to the elevator, something about what Jay said bothered him. He couldn't quite nail it down as they stepped into the lift. Jay pushed the button for the lobby; they were on the sixteenth floor.

As the elevator descended, pinging as it passed each floor, Michaels said, "That intrusion last night. Do we know where it came from?"

"Not really," Jay said. "It bounced off a couple of satellites. We were able to track it as far as the West Coast, that's it."

Michaels thought about that for a second. "Why would anybody capable of breaking into a secure system like Net Force's mainframe want to look at our personnel records?"

"If that's what they planned to do, boss, rather than just stumbling into those records by accident."

"Just for the sake of argument, let's assume they meant to go there."

Jay shrugged. "Who, where, what, when, why," he said. "Find out if somebody works there, what they do exactly, how long. Maybe how much somebody gets paid."

"You skipped one," Michaels said. "Find out where somebody lives."

"Yeah, that could be."

Michaels felt a sudden chill frost him.

Jay said, "I see where you're going here, but it's probably just a coincidence."

"What if it isn't? What if it's Bershaw? What if he is looking to even the score for the death of his friend?"

"That's a reach, boss. Guy who pulled the trigger on Drayne is dead."

"Bershaw wouldn't know that. He went over the side of the hill as soon as the shooting started."

The elevator reached the ground floor and opened. The two men stepped out and walked toward the hotel's coffee shop.

"He could have heard or watched news reports about it," Jay offered.

"You were on CNN's coverage. The FBI and DEA weren't saying much. Nobody said who shot Drayne, only that he was killed. And who was getting most of the credit for finding the drug dealers?"

"Uh, that'd be us," Jay said.

"Yes. And there were only three of us there: you, me, and General Howard."

"Still a reach," Jay said. "It doesn't necessarily follow."

"Bershaw escapes. Somebody on the West Coast gets into Net Force's personnel files within a few hours. Bershaw disappears, then shows up on a flight to Washington. I don't like it. If you were him and you were pissed off because somebody had murdered your friend, blasted him while he stood there with his hands up, and you wanted to do something about it, who would you go after?"

Jay didn't say anything.

"Yeah. That's what I thought. The man in charge, who was right there on the scene. You could be waiting for him when he got home. Only thing is, Toni is already there."

He pulled his virgil, hit the voxax, and said, "Call home."

The virgil made the call.

After five rings, the message recorder came on. "Hello. You've reached area code two-oh-two, three-five-seven . . ."

"Toni, if you are there, pick up or call me back ASAP."

Michaels felt a sense of panic threaten to take him as

he ended the call. He tapped the resend button and selected five-minute intervals, to repeat until a connection was made or he shut it off.

"She's not answering."

"She could be asleep. Outside watering the plants. A dozen things," Jay said.

John Howard stood in the short line of people waiting to get into the coffee shop. He saw Jay and Michaels approaching, smiled at them. Michaels didn't feel like smiling back.

Howard caught it. "What's the matter, Commander?"

Michaels ran through it, feeling more and more nervous as he laid it out.

Howard said, "Jay's probably right, it's probably nothing. But just to be on the safe side, how about I have a couple of my people drop by and check."

"I would appreciate that." Being all the way across the country made him feel helpless. Once he knew Toni was okay, he'd feel a lot better.

Howard looked at Michaels a moment longer. "One more thing, Commander," he said. "Jay's the one who got all the attention on TV. It might not be a bad idea for him to get hold of Saji and tell her to get somewhere safe."

Michaels nodded, but Jay was already pulling out his virgil. A few seconds later, Saji answered, and everyone relaxed a little.

Howard pulled his own virgil and spoke quietly into it, muted the sound so he had to hold it to his ear like a mobile phone to hear the reply. When he was done, he turned to Michaels and said, "Somebody will be there in twenty minutes. They'll call you back or have Toni call you."

Michaels nodded. "Thank you. Call home yourself, John, just to be sure, then we might as well go have breakfast." But until he heard from Toni, he wasn't the least bit interested in eating.

Washington, D.C.

It was almost noon, and Toni was in the kitchen and about to fix herself some lunch when there came a terrific crash, as if a truck had slammed into the house.

She knew who the intruder was as soon as he came through the side door—a door he opened by kicking it, smashing the lock, and almost tearing it from its hinges. Splinters of shattered wood flew everywhere, and the door slammed against the wall hard enough for the knob to break the spring stop and punch a hole in the Sheetrock.

She didn't recognize him, but it had to be the drug guy who had escaped. His hair and eyebrows were bleached and his skin color was dark, but it was him.

As she stood there in her nightgown and ratty bathrobe, she knew she had only one advantage: What he saw was a small, pregnant woman who couldn't possibly be a threat to him.

And in truth, she wasn't much of a threat. Any strenuous activity could cause her to lose the baby. A full-out hand-to-hand fight would certainly do it. Even if her skill at *silat* was enough to overcome his drug-induced strength, she couldn't risk applying it. She had to fall back on one of the first principles of her art: deception.

So she played it as he would expect: "Who are you? What do you want?"

"Alexander Michaels," he said.

"He's not here."

"I figured that. He's still in Los Angeles, isn't he?"

She didn't say anything. She couldn't make it too easy.

He grinned, a maniacal, over-the-edge expression. There was a wooden coat tree by the door. He grabbed it, turned it sideways, brought his knee up and the rack down, and snapped it over his thigh as if it were a twig. He dropped the broken halves. "Don't fuck with me, lady, I'm not in the mood, okay?"

It wasn't hard to act afraid. She had never seen anybody do anything like that before. The man was a scarecrow missing half his stuffing, and no way should he be able to do what he had just done.

"He . . . he won't be home until tonight. His flight gets here around s-s-seven o'clock."

Bershaw—that was the name Alex had told her—grinned his mad smile again.

"Ah. Good. That will give us plenty of time to get acquainted. What's your name?"

"Toni," she said.

"Wife or girlfriend?"

"W-w-wife."

"Well, don't worry, Toni, I'm not gonna hurt you." He looked at her. "Got a bun in the oven. How far along are you?"

"Five months."

"Congratulations. You do what I tell you, you and the kid will live to get to know each other. You can call me Tad. Why don't you take me on a tour of the place, since we have some hours to kill?"

"Okay."

The com chirped.

"Don't answer it," he said.

Toni's thoughts ran at top speed, banging into each other as she tried to keep them straight. She had to get word to Alex somehow. This man had come here to kill him, she was certain of that, and he might or might not kill her and the baby. She had to go along with whatever he wanted until she could figure out a way to stop him.

Tad followed Michaels's wife as she led him through the condo, where he made sure there weren't any surprises waiting for him. It was an okay enough place, nothing special, and there were some pictures of her and her husband here and there, other images of their families, easy to see the resemblance in those.

Every five minutes or so, the phone would ring, and he'd just shake his head at her. He didn't want her talking to anybody, especially her husband, and maybe giving him some secret code kind of clue.

In the garage was an old Chevrolet convertible, the hood up, and parts of the engine laid out on a workbench.

"Very nice," he said. He walked over and put one hand on the car's fender, rubbed it lightly. "Your old man is into cars."

"Yes. He rebuilds them. It's his hobby."

Tad needed to work off some of the Hammer's bubbling and insistent energy, and while he was horny again, a pregnant woman didn't do it for him. He looked around for a pry bar or a hammer. A little drum work on the Chevy would do fine. He'd be sure to let Mr. Michaels see his project car was gonna need a lot more effort to bring back to cherry condition before he did the same deconstruction on *him*.

He saw a ball peen hammer hung on pegs over the workbench and went to get it. The Hammer working a hammer, he liked the symmetry in that.

But when he got to the bench, he noticed something else. Little pieces of ivory, needles, a microscope. Scrimshaw.

"Your husband has a lot of time on his hands," he said.

He nodded at the bench. "Cars and art. That's when he's not having guys murdered."

"My husband doesn't have people murdered," she said. She glared at him.

He smiled. She had balls, this pregnant woman did. She'd seen what he could do, and she knew he could kill her with a backhand, but here she was defending her old man anyway. Tad had never heard his mother ever say a kind word about his father. "That fucking asshole," was about as good as it ever got. Give Toni here a point for loyalty.

"Tell that to my friend Bobby," he said. "He was standing in the middle of the road with his hands in the air, and the feds gave him an instant craniotomy. *Blam!* Blew his head apart."

"My husband didn't order that. Net Force does computer investigation, they aren't field operatives on drug busts. And they'd never shoot a prisoner, anyway."

"Yeah, well, he was there, I saw him on the evening news. He should have stayed at his desk on this one."

He twirled the hammer in his fingers, was about to go do the car, when he saw the capsule. He looked at it, saw that it was open under the microscope, and the powder emptied out. He put the ball peen hammer down and moved to look.

He shook his head. "That fucking Bobby. He was too smart for his own good sometimes." He turned to look at her. "You know about this? Your old man talk to you about his work?"

"Yes. Sometimes."

"Bobby was a genius, you know. Certifiable, high MENSA grade, smarter than almost everybody. Even when I'm Hammering and all my edges are sharp, Bobby could still think circles around me. He had contempt for the feds, 'cause of his father. You don't know about that part, but his father was with the FBI for like a hundred years. He and Bobby didn't get along. So Bobby left clues in every fifth cap: little riddles, each one different." He waved at the cap. "That's how they found him, isn't it? Some geek at your husband's computer farm turned the machines loose on this and figured it out, didn't he?"

She didn't say anything.

"C'mon, you might as well tell me. I can't kill him any deader than dead, can I?"

"Please don't kill him."

"Bobby might have fucked up and gotten caught because he underestimated his opposition—you tend to do that when you are always smarter than them—but he should be alive. Somebody has got to pay for that."

He was really ready to pound the car now, and he reached for the tool to do it with, when the doorbell rang.

"Don't answer it," Bershaw said. "They'll go away." He considered it for a second. "No, maybe we ought to see who it is."

The security cam Alex had installed showed two men in uniform, with holstered pistols. Net Force troopers.

"Cops?"

"Net Force Security."

"I thought your husband was a desk jockey."

"He is, but they have some special teams for certain situations."

"Yeah, like executing drug dealers."

The two at the door rang the bell again. And again. They weren't going away, and she wondered why they were here. The missed phone calls, maybe.

Toni felt a surge of hope, but she quickly quelled the feeling. The two men at her door were in immediate danger. Bershaw was a killer, and he had a drug-driven rage that couldn't be easily stopped. A wrong word, and he might go off like a bomb.

"Get rid of them, some good reason to go away, and you better not give them a fucking hint," Bershaw said. "You do, they die, you and the kid die, and I might get bored waiting here alone for hubby to come home, but that's how it will go down."

"I understand."

Bershaw stood behind her and to one side, out of sight, as Toni opened the door. He didn't have a weapon that she could see, but he didn't really need one.

"Yes?"

"Mrs. Michaels. We're sorry to bother you, but Commander Michaels has been trying to contact you."

"Oh. Oh, yes, I'm sorry about that. I was working out, doing my aerobics, and then I took a long hot bath to relax." She was in her bathrobe. "I turned off the ringer and let the computer take messages."

"Yes, ma'am. If you would call Commander Michaels at your convenience, that would be very helpful."

"I will. I'm going to go take a nap, and I'll call him when I wake up. Sorry to have caused you any trouble."

"No trouble at all, ma'am. Have a good day."

When they were gone, Bershaw said, "That was all right, except for the part about calling your husband. Now you'll have to do that. But I'm gonna write a script for you. You will make the call, and you will say exactly what I tell you to say, not one word more or less, you understand?"

"I understand."

"Good. We have a little time to work on it, since you are going to take a nap and all. Tell me about your family, brothers, sisters, like that. I've seen some of the pictures, so don't lie to me. If I think you're lying, I'll just kill you, okay?"

Toni felt her heart pounding harder than usual. He was being very cautious, and she might not get another chance to warn Alex. She had to hope he would get the message she had been able to send.

Los Angeles, California

They had almost finished breakfast when Michaels's virgil announced an incoming call. He had it off his belt and thumbed to receive in two seconds. "Yes?"

"Sir, this is Chris Carol, military ops. We just spoke to your wife at your house. She seems fine, sir."

Michaels blew out a sigh. Thank God!

"Did she say why she wasn't answering the phone?"

"Yes, sir. She was taking a bath, sir, and had the ringer turned off."

He shook his head. Of course. It had to be some piddly thing like that.

"We'll remain in the area on surveillance, sir, as per General Howard's orders."

"Thanks," he said. "Ask Toni to call me as soon as she can, will you?"

"She says she will call you, sir, after she has a nap. She must be tired from her workout."

"What? What did you say?"

"Sir?"

"About her being tired?"

"Sir, I just assumed she might be. She said she had been doing her aerobics, before her bath, sir."

Michaels felt a shard of icy steel stab deep into his bowels. He looked at John Howard. "He's there," he said. "He's got Toni."

39

The general had pulled strings in a hurry and gotten them
fast rides. The National Guard fighters had zipped from
Los Angeles to the East Coast at speeds more than twice
supersonic most of the way. By the time they were on the
ground again, the trip had only been a little over two
hours. It was almost two-thirty in the afternoon when the
escort picked Michaels, Howard, and Jay up at the air base
and took off with lights flashing and sirens screaming.
They'd shut those off before they got to his neighborhood.
Howard had set up a command post a half mile away from
the house, and there were more Net Force people on the
scene, far enough back to stay hidden but close enough
to see if anybody left.

An hour into the flight, Toni had called, and it had
twisted his stomach to hear her speak the words that Bershaw must have made her say:

They exchanged greetings, he'd asked how she was doing, and she'd said she was fine, then she said, "I'm sorry
I missed your call earlier, I didn't mean to make you

worry. Listen, I can't talk now, I've got my mother on the other line, some crisis with my sister-in-law she has to settle. Call me when you get to the airport tonight, okay? Bye."

He put in a call to Toni's mother in the Bronx. She was surprised to hear from him, and he pretended he was calling to check on Toni's *silat* teacher. Guru was doing okay, his mother-in-law told him. Say hello to Toni when he saw her, tell her to call and visit.

If he needed any confirmation, that did it. Toni wasn't talking to her mother. And she was being held hostage by some psychotic drug fiend who almost certainly blamed Michaels for his buddy's death. It was a nightmare.

"How do you want to play it?" Howard asked, as the Net Force car careened toward the city. "You want to call in the FBI kidnap teams?"

"Would you call them in if it was your wife?"

"No, sir."

"We have snipers, don't we?"

"Yes, sir. A couple of very good ones."

"Have them meet us at the staging point. I'll try to get him in front of a window. If they have a shot, tell them to take it. It will have to be in the spine or the head to be sure to drop him."

"Yes, sir." Howard didn't say anything about job description or rules of engagement. He pulled his virgil and made a call.

"You're not going in there alone are you, boss?"

"Toni's my wife. It's my house. I know them both better than anybody else. Damned right I'm going in."

"Jesus, you've seen what this guy is capable of. Even if you shoot him, you can't be sure of stopping him."

"I know that. What choice do I have? I'll have surprise on my side. Maybe that will be enough."

"We could storm the place, hit it with fifty guys—"

"And he could break Toni's neck before they got through the door. No. It's me he wants, so if he spots me alone, he'll have what he came for. If he's in my face, Toni can get clear."

"And you might get dead."

"Yeah, well, that's how it is. Better me than her."

What he didn't say was that he still had the capsule Howard had found at the shooting site in his pocket. And that if he took it before he went in, he'd be more than a match for the zombie. He was in better shape, he had some training as a fighter, and he was motivated. The drug would cancel Bershaw's advantage.

But there was a big problem. It was risky. He didn't mind the jeopardy to himself, but what if the drug didn't do exactly for him what it did for Bershaw? What if he went crazy like some of the other druggies who used it? Saw snakes coming out of the walls or thought he was being chased by demons or whatever those people who had gone mad and committed suicide had seen?

Could he risk Toni's life and the baby's life like that?

Six of one, half a dozen of the other, his little inner voice said. *If the zombie goes through you like Sherman through Georgia, he'll probably kill Toni anyway, don't you think?*

Michaels stuck his hand into his pocket and fingered the capsule.

Devil or the deep blue sea, Alex. And you better decide soon. You don't know how long it'll take before the stuff kicks in if you decide to go that way. It might not help in time, even if you do eat it.

Shit.

"Ten minutes to the staging point," Howard said. "My snipers will be there. If they can see him, they can casket him."

Michaels nodded. He fingered the capsule.

• • •

Toni was sure Alex had gotten her warning. She could hear
it in his voice when she called, and she was fairly certain
the rumbling noises in the background had been a jet engine and wind noise. That meant he was on his way home,
and he'd be here sooner than Bershaw expected him.

What was he going to do when he got here? Would he
bring in the regular FBI hostage negotiators? She tried to
put herself in his position, and that answer came up a solid
no. He would know Bershaw was desperate, probably
know he was on the mind-altering drug that made him
fast, smart, and strong. Alex wouldn't take the risk that
Bershaw would hurt her or the baby.

What would he do?

And her greatest fear was that he would try to sneak
into the house and take on Bershaw alone. It wasn't a
macho thing but just how Alex was. He would see her as
his responsibility, and his coming in alone as the best
chance of drawing the killer's attention away from her.

If she had not been pregnant, she would have already
tried to take Bershaw down herself. He was fast and
strong, but she had more than fifteen years of *pentjak silat*
training and practice, and she would risk that her skill
could offset his drug-powered strength.

Silat was a weapons-based art. Toni was comfortable
with a knife, a stick, a sword, whatever came to hand. A
knife from the butcher block rack wouldn't take a second
to pull. No matter how resistant to pain, no matter how
strong a man might be, he couldn't walk if he had no
blood circulating or if the tendons controlling his feet or
legs were cut or if his spine was severed.

But in her condition, the slightest mistake would cost
her. She wouldn't risk the baby unless there was no other
way. If it came down to it, she would not let this psychotic
kill Alex, even if it meant she and the baby didn't make

it. You didn't stand by and allow the man you loved to die if you could prevent it, no matter what it cost you.

She had already rehearsed grabbing the knife in her mind a dozen times, never looking at it so as to give it away, but planning how to step, what to throw to distract him, what her targets might be.

She had to expect Alex to show up hours before he was supposed to show up. She had to be ready.

Right now, she had to pee. And she didn't much want to do that with Bershaw watching her, but better that than to wet herself.

"Tad?"

"What?"

"I need to go to the bathroom."

"Let's go."

He followed her down the hall. "Go ahead."

"Can I close the door?"

"No. Just pee. I'll look the other way."

"Thank you."

She thought she might be able to use that, somehow, if she could think of a way.

While the woman was on the john, Tad turned away and dry-swallowed two more of the Hammer caps. He could feel the first ones start to wane, and a few seconds later, he took a third. He had built up a tolerance to the stuff by now, but it didn't matter; the remaining caps were all going to be deactivated soon, anyhow, and any way you looked at it, this was going to be his last Hammer ride. When Ma and Pa at the portable lab heard about Bobby getting killed, they would get rid of the RV and hit the road for parts elsewhere. The plan he'd had of getting to the lab and mixing his own caps wouldn't happen now. He could mix the stuff, but some of the chem was just beyond his ability to create from scratch. Bobby had never written his formulas down anywhere, figuring if the cops ever grabbed him, those would be his best bargaining chip.

He heard the toilet flush, turned and saw the wife stand up, her robe falling to cover the short nightgown. She had good legs under that rounded, pregnant belly, and he caught a quick glimpse of her bush. Maybe that was worth exploring, even though it wouldn't be his first choice. Any port in a storm.

But there was something else he wanted to do first. That car was still in the garage. The wife could watch him trash her husband's toy.

"Come on," he said. "We have stuff to do in the garage."

He led her down the hall.

"Sir, the snipers are set. We've got three, two in front, one in back. They know what our man looks like. If they see him, he's history."

"Thank you, John."

Howard handed Michaels his revolver. "Point it at his head just like you would point your finger at his nose and pull the trigger. It will kick some and buck, so hold it two-handed if you can. A head shot is the only way to be sure to stop him."

Michaels took the heavy black handgun and hefted it.

"Is your ring updated?"

"Yes."

"You have six shots. If he's still coming after that, reloading won't help. Aim for the head. Don't say a word, don't hesitate, if you get a shot, take it. If you don't, he'll kill you."

"I got it."

"Leave your virgil on and sending. We won't try to call, but we'll monitor you. As soon as we see Toni, or you indicate that she is clear, we'll come in."

Michaels nodded. His mouth was dry, and his stomach fluttered.

"Whatever happens, he won't be walking away from this."

Michaels looked at Howard, realizing what he was saying. "Thank you."

"Good luck, Alex."

Michaels nodded. He took a couple of deep breaths and let them out, rubbed his eyes, and started toward his home to save his wife.

He was half a block away from where Howard and Jay were when he realized he had made his choice about taking the Hammer cap. No. His mind was his best tool, and he did not want to risk Toni's life on his mind being fuzzed, even if it gave him the strength of Hercules to do so.

He would have to do it the hard way.

Toni watched, feeling detached, as Bershaw swung the pry bar and punched a bar-shaped hole through the safety glass windshield. Little squarish chips of glass flew like jewels under the garage lights as he pulled the bar back and struck with the ball peen hammer he held in his other hand. It took four or five hits, and the windshield was gone.

He had already done the headlights and taillights.

After the windshield, he walked around the car and shattered all the remaining glass, the sides, the rear, scattering glittering shards in all directions.

Then he started on the front fender, alternating the hammer and pry bar like some kind of mad drummer following a tune only he could hear.

It wasn't until he started on the metal that Toni got an idea of just how much power he had. The heavy gauge steel of the car's fender and hood not only buckled like aluminum foil, several times he actually punched holes right through, trapping his tools so that he had to yank them free. The impacts were loud, the *grinch!* of a pry bar pulled from a car's hood sounding like Toni imagined the unlubricated gates of hell might sound when opening.

The destruction was terrible to watch. More terrible was Bershaw's expression. He was laughing, having the time of his life.

The effort had to be burning him up, tearing muscles and tendons, doing major damage to his very bone structure, but he kept laughing and pounding, hitting with such force that the fiberglass handle of the hammer finally splintered and broke, leaving the rounded nose of the hammer buried in the passenger door, and the pry bar's loop bent almost closed.

Toni realized that attacking this man physically would be suicide if she made even the tiniest mistake. Even with a knife.

After what seemed like a long time, he dropped the bent pry bar, rolled his shoulders, then turned to look at her. He stared at her for a few seconds, unblinking.

He looked like a raptor about to swoop down on prey.

"What would you do to save your husband's life?" He finally said.

"Anything."

He grinned. "Good. I have something in mind. Let's go to the bedroom."

Toni felt a small surge of hope. If he wanted sex, he would have to put himself into a more vulnerable position. He would have to allow her to get close. *Silat* was an in-your-face art. If he let her get close, she would have a chance. A small chance, maybe.

If she had the shot, she might be able to take him.

Michaels tucked the gun into his back pocket as he slid open the garage window. He had heard the noise half a block away, and by the time he got to the garage, he had a pretty good idea of what he would see.

He was wrong. What he saw was much worse than he'd expected. Jesus Christ, how could a man built like Bershaw do this much damage with a hammer and pry bar? The Chevy looked as if it had rolled off a cliff.

He saw that the door into the house was open, and he climbed through the window, pulled the revolver out, and made his way across the floor, trying to avoid stepping on all the shattered bits of glass. A head shot. Point the gun like your finger, and pull the trigger. Hit him in the head with a bullet, and it was all over.

Michaels edged into the doorway and into the house.

In the bedroom, Tad said, "Get on your hands and knees."

The woman climbed onto the bed and did what he said. He moved to stand behind her. "Back up a little."

He reached out with both hands, caught the middle of her robe, and ripped it apart, exposing her bare bottom. He reached for his zipper.

Toni gathered herself as she heard the sound of his zipper going down. A twist, a hard fist to the testicles, grab and rip them off, roll to the side and onto the floor—

Michaels stepped into the bedroom, saw Bershaw's back to him, Toni beyond him on the bed. The years of law and order training tried to assert themselves. Maybe he should give the guy a chance to surrender.

Hell with that. The bastard was about to rape his wife, he was tanked on drugs that made him the most dangerous person Michaels had ever seen. He pointed the gun at the back of Bershaw's head and started to squeeze the trigger.

•   •   •

Tad heard something, or maybe he felt the air pressure in the room change. Suddenly, he knew they weren't alone. He spun. There was the husband, with a gun.

Good! Tad lunged.

Michaels saw Bershaw spin, his speed was incredible, and leap at him. He was halfway though squeezing the trigger. Fast as Bershaw was, Michaels was ahead of him. The gun went off.

Bershaw tried to duck, but the bullet hit him. Michaels saw it plow a furrow into his skull, just under the hairline, but then the mirror on Toni's closet door shattered.

Bershaw kept coming, but the bullet's impact changed his angle a little, so he veered to the left slightly. Michaels dodged to his right, and Bershaw almost missed him.

Almost. His flailing hand smashed into the revolver and tore it from Michaels's grasp. The gun flew, and Bershaw slammed into the dresser and landed on his hands and knees. But he looked up at Michaels and smiled—smiled!—with blood oozing from the head wound.

The bullet hit at an angle and glanced off, Michaels realized.

He had to get this maniac away from Toni, who was on the floor next to the bed.

Michaels grabbed the small television set on the stand next to the door and threw it at Bershaw, who reached up and batted it aside like it was a pillow. The TV set hit the floor and ruptured into three pieces.

He had to lead him out of here! Away from Toni!

Michaels backpedaled through the door.

Bershaw came to his feet, wiped the blood from his eyes, stuck one finger into the gory groove on his forehead, and looked at his finger. "Close, but no cigar."

Michaels turned and ran for the living room. "Come and get me, asshole!"

Michaels risked a glance at his virgil. As soon as Bershaw came after him, Toni would be safe. The general's men would be ready to hit the door when they heard Michaels yell for them.

Oh, shit! It was gone! The virgil was gone! Where had he lost it? The window?

He didn't have time to worry about that now.

He made it to the living room, and he looked around frantically for a weapon, something to throw, anything!

He saw the little wooden case with the two *kerambit* knives in it. He grabbed it and jerked the lid off just as Bershaw came into the room. The man was moving a little slower, he was a little unsteady on his feet. The bullet glancing off his head must have had some effect.

Bershaw grabbed the end of the couch as Michaels ran around behind it, trying to slip the rings of the little curved knives onto his index fingers. Bershaw heaved, and the couch came off the floor and twisted, flew five feet, and landed upside down with a crash.

"You can run, but you can't hide. Joe Lewis said that, did you know?"

Stall him! "What do you want?"

"You killed Bobby. I kill you. Even trade."

"I didn't kill him. He was shot by a rogue NSA agent working for the drug companies! That man is dead, too!"

"Doesn't matter. You pointed the shooter at him. You get to pay."

Bershaw moved in, his hands held out to grab.

Michaels had the little curved-bladed knives gripped solidly now, hidden behind his forearms and closed hands, only the forefinger rings showing. If Bershaw saw that, or cared, he didn't give any indication, he just kept coming, moving like some Frankenstein's monster that couldn't be stopped.

Michaels took a deep breath and held it.

It might be his last.

40

Toni hurried down the hall. In her hand, she held the *kris* that Guru had given her, the wavy-bladed Javanese dagger that had been in the old lady's family for years. Such daggers had been more ceremonial than used for a long time, but it was still a knife, when stick came to stab, and it was the only weapon in the bedroom.

She heard a loud noise, felt the floor shake as she reached the living room and saw the two men there.

Bershaw advanced on Alex.

Alex stood in a *djuru* stance, and Toni immediately realized he had the *kerambits* in his hands, even though they were all but hidden.

Even with a head wound, the man was supernaturally fast. He lashed out with one hand, and before Alex could move, he caught him with a slap that knocked him backward into the bookcase, showering him with hardbacks.

"Hey!" Toni yelled.

Bershaw turned, smiled at her. "I'll take care of you later. Better put that down before you cut yourself, honey."

The distraction was enough for Alex to recover a little. He grabbed several books from the shelf behind him and threw them at Bershaw.

Tad turned back to finish Michaels. He saw three books coming at him in slow motion: a red one, one with a dark dust cover, and one that opened so that the pages were flapping in the air. He dodged the dark dust covered one, backhanded the red book, and let the flapping one hit him on the chest; it was nothing.

Michaels was right behind the books, though, and just quick enough to get a punch in on him before Tad could block it. No big deal, he would absorb that and crush the fucker.

His vision went out on the left side, just flashed red and . . . went away.

Tad frowned and backhanded Michaels, knocking him sprawling over the overturned couch. He put his hand to his face, and it came away covered with blood and some kind of clear gel. His mind made the connection.

The son of a bitch had ripped his eye out!

How?

Michaels came up, and Tad saw how he'd done it. He had a little knife in his hand. Looked like a claw.

Tricky shit, hiding that.

Well, fine. He'd just step in, break that fucking arm, and shove that little sticker up the man's ass, that's what—

Tad moved in.

Something hit him in the back, and he felt a stab of minor pain.

He reached around, realized the wife had thrown that fucking curvy blade and stuck it up in the middle of his back. He grabbed the thing by the blade, pulled it out, and brought it around in front of himself. The blade was black with funny little patterns in the steel. He waved it at the woman. "Thanks. Just what I needed."

He turned in time to see Michaels come over the couch, that little knife leading.

Tad grinned. He still held the wavy knife by the blade, only a few inches of it sticking out, but he jammed the somewhat dull point at Michaels's forearm, drove it into the muscle, felt it grate on bone, to stop only when his hand hit Michaels's arm.

Michaels's hand spasmed open. So much for his little claw.

But the knife didn't fall, it was as if it was glued to his fucking hand.

Fine, fine. You want to play? Tad jerked his own weapon free, shifted his grip, and figured he'd just get a good swing and take the whole arm off. *That* would get rid of the little knife damned quick. After that, he'd just carve the bastard up in little chunks.

Michaels felt the *kris* go into his right forearm, felt the tip hit his radius and then slip past and saw it come all the way through, just an inch or so of the point sticking out.

His hand opened on its own.

Bershaw jerked the *kris* free and lifted it past his ear like an ax, and he knew the man was going to chop down. Knew with his maniacal strength, the man might cleave right though the muscle and bone and slice Michaels's hand completely off.

But he had the other *kerambit*. And now he was close, inside, right where a *silat serak* player wanted to be when it all came down. He had one chance, maybe, and he took it. He lashed out in a punch at Bershaw's neck, a short left hook, twisting his fist as he threw it.

The tiny blade of the *kerambit* bit into the right side Bershaw's neck a couple of inches below the jaw and ripped a channel all the way to his Adam's apple.

The man frowned and paused in his downstroke.

Michaels collapsed, just let his legs go limp. It was the fastest way to get clear, and as he fell, he punched with the knife again, scoring a nasty slash across Bershaw's thigh, just below his groin.

Bershaw drew back his unwounded leg and kicked. His foot took Michaels in the side, just under the armpit, and he felt and heard ribs crack, a wet *snap-snap* that stole his breath.

Blood fountained from Bershaw's neck, jetting out with each pulse, spewing with his trip-hammer–fast beat like a torn garden hose spraying water under pressure.

Bershaw kicked him again, but not as hard. Michaels managed to turn a little, so he caught it on the shoulder. Muscle tore, but he didn't think the arm broke, even though the force of the kick turned him a hundred and eighty degrees around.

Michaels hooked his right foot behind Bershaw's right ankle, then drove his left heel into the bloody cut on Bershaw's thigh.

Bershaw lost his balance and fell backward, slamming into the couch.

Michaels rolled away and up. He held the *kerambit* in his left hand up point-first at Bershaw.

The right side of Bershaw's body was soaked in blood from the carotid artery Michaels had sliced open. The blood still pulsed out, but much slower and with less force now.

Bershaw came up, grinned, and took two steps toward Michaels. But now it was his turn to move in slow motion.

Michaels stabbed at him. Bershaw put up an arm, and the blade scored a line from the wrist to the elbow, but it hardly bled at all.

• • • •

Tad suddenly felt tired, so very tired. Yeah, he had to kill this guy, for Bobby, but as soon as he did that, he was gonna have to go sit down. The Hammer was slowing, he could feel it, and it wasn't time yet. Not yet. Just this one thing left to do first, then he could take a break. Go see Bobby.

Bobby?

Something about Bobby . . .

Fuck it. Kill the guy, then worry about it.

Bershaw grabbed Michaels's knife arm with both hands and squeezed.

Michaels felt his wrist crack, and in desperation he snapped his other elbow out in a horizontal shot, right out of *djuru* one, out in front of him like Dracula behind his cape, only with all his weight behind it. He hit Bershaw square on the temple.

Man! Who would have thought this guy could hit so hard? He'd have to tell Bobby about this.

But he felt so tired. So weak. It was so much trouble just to stand here, and why should he even bother?

The Hammer left him then, all by himself here with this stranger who hit him. The gray closed in on Tad.

Bobby? Is that you, man?

The light in Bershaw's remaining eye flickered as he let go of Michaels's arm and stumbled back a step.

Then the light went out, and Bershaw fell, a puppet with his strings cut.

Michaels turned and saw Toni, a book gripped in her hands, advancing toward them. In that odd interplay that sometimes happened in scary situations, he noticed the title of the book, and he started to laugh.

Toni stopped. "Alex? Are you all right?"

He waved at the book. "You were going to hit him with that?"

Toni looked at it.

It was *How to Win Friends and Influence People.*

EPILOGUE

Washington, D.C.

Michaels's arm itched, and he wanted to tear off the plastic flesh bandage and scratch the cut. The surgical glue was holding the wound closed just fine, and he had pain medicine if he needed it, for the broken wrist that ached dully and the cracked ribs that hurt every time he breathed, but nothing seemed to help with the itching.

He sat in the kitchen nook at the table, looking at Toni as she came back from the fridge with a beer for him.

"Thanks," he said. "You should have let me get that."

"I'm in better shape than you, pregnancy notwithstanding."

He took a sip, put the bottle down on the table.

"So what's the latest from the office?"

"Well. It turned out that Lee and George were working for the drug company, like we thought. Lee is trying to cut a deal, but I don't think he has enough leverage."

"So why'd they kill the chemist?"

"That's the twist. The pharmaceutical house they were in cahoots with—"

"Did you just say, 'in cahoots with'?"

"You want me to tell this story or not?" But he grinned.

"Go ahead."

"It turned out the drug company already had a similar line of research going, upon which they had spent a lot of money, and in which they had a lot of confidence. Not as extensive as Drayne's, but going in the same general direction. They were far enough along that they had already started some testing protocols, gotten some government approvals, and they didn't want somebody stealing their thunder."

"They were trying to *suppress* Drayne's stuff?"

"Yeah. George and Lee had been given big blocks of stock to make sure Drayne's formulas didn't wind up on anybody else's table. If their company reached the market first, they'd be millionaires."

She shook her head. "Huh. Didn't see that one."

"Nobody else did, either."

"What about John Howard?"

Michaels took another sip of his beer. "He says he is gonna retire. Says life is too short, and he wants to be around when his son graduates from school and goes out into the world on his own."

"I don't blame him for that."

"Me neither."

"Jay Gridley still a Buddhist?"

"Mostly lapsed, if there is such a thing. He can't sit and contemplate his navel and stay sharp enough to run with the bad boys on-line, he says. He'll have to work all that out. But he and his girl are going to get married."

"That's great."

"Going to honeymoon in Bali, so he says."

"And what about us?"

"Us? We're fine. I guess I won't be spending much time in the garage until the Chevy gets back from the body shop. Incredible what damage he did."

"Yes, it was. I can see why so many people wanted to get their hands on this drug. If he had been a jock on the stuff, he could have taken the entire house down to the foundations."

He nodded. "Tell you what. If I ever complain about things being slow at work again? I want you to slap me upside the head."

"My pleasure," she said.

They smiled at each other, and despite his aches and itches, Michaels was very happy to be able to do that.

It sure beat the other options.